The Wilderness Bird

by

Elizabeth Webster

Dales Large Print Books
Long Preston, North Yorkshire,
BD23 4ND, England.

British Library Cataloguing in Publication Data.

Webster, Elizabeth
    The wilderness bird.

    A catalogue record of this book is
    available from the British Library

    ISBN   978-1-84262-498-2 pbk

First published in Great Britain in 2005
by Publish and be Damned

Published in Large Print 2007 by arrangement with
Elizabeth Webster, care of David Pearson Associates Ltd.

Dales Large Print is an imprint of Library Magna Books Ltd.

Printed and bound in Great Britain by
T.J. (International) Ltd., Cornwall, PL28 8RW

'There is no lonelier wilderness than the big city; and nowhere that gives greater solace than the untouched secret heart of the wild world.'

Duncan MacNab

1. THE ECHOING SILENCE

The silence was never absolute. There were always sounds in the night. It was never completely dark, either. There was always a faint glow over the heart of the city, reflected in the clouds from the sodium glare of the streetlamps far below. The light comforted her, but the night sounds made her ache. They spoke of a world that went on out there, filled with its own preoccupations in the living, breathing entity of a city that never sleeps.

She could not sleep either, and the voices of the night caught at her with slow pain. The sound of a tug hooting down river – a snatch of music, a burst of laughter from an open door – footsteps going down the street towards home. *Towards home...* A plane droning overhead, shattering the stillness with its terrible throbbing, thrusting on through the hazy sky to far distant places... A couple of alley cats serenading the moonless dark... And the taxis, oh, the London taxis, cruising slowly down the road looking for house numbers, pausing, engines ticking over while descending passengers laughed and fumbled for change, the slamming of doors, voices calling 'Goodnight,' feet stumbling up steps, and wavering hands searching for elusive keyholes... Was it one reveller going home, the other going on in the taxi to yet another solitary bed-sit? Or was it a couple, opening the door amid more stifled laughter, tripping over the hall rug, blundering into the kitchen for a late-night hot drink, and at last struggling up the stairs – more laughter, the warmth of close companionship like a cloak around them, and finally falling into bed together...? *Together?*

She turned restlessly in her narrow single bed, and sighed. The taxis below revved their engines in the empty echoing streets and cruised off, looking for more late revellers to be ferried home.

No, she thought, there is nothing more lonely in the world than the sound of a London taxi driving away. But then she admitted, with despairing honesty: Yes, there is. The sound of my own voice saying in helpless incredulity: *'Why didn't you tell me?'*

And then the whole tide of memory and loss that she had been staving off for so long swept over her, and she could not escape it any more.

She had been so happy that day. The sky was blue as a starling's egg, and the old Vicarage – her childhood home – bloomed in golden warmth under the summer sun. Her life was serene and full of promise – plans laid, pledges given – a whole rosy future before her. Only a few minor details to arrange now – a lick of paint here, and a bit of last-minute dressmaking there, before the whole thing swung into its final crescendo of excitement. Really, she almost wished it hadn't got quite as out of hand, but her mother was a great organiser and a great believer in ceremony, and in 'making everything as beautiful as possible' as she often told her.

She came down into the kitchen, alight with flying energy, and said: 'I'm going down to the cottage to do a spot of painting. Is that all right?'

Her mother was cheerfully engaged in making late-plum jam, and looked up at her daughter, smiling. 'Why not? Will Tim be there?'

'No. He said he might be late. There's an audit on at the office, or something. But in any case, I can get on better on my own!'

Mary Somerford laughed. 'I can imagine!' She glanced at her daughter's incandescent face and felt, not for the first time, a faint flicker of disquiet. It was so perilous, that flaring happiness – so vulnerable... And she knew – oh, how well she knew, being the busy and virtuous vicar's wife that she was – how the bright dreams and aspirations of youth can get quenched in the endless struggles and compromises of everyday living... But she said nothing of these misgivings – how could she cast any shadow on that searing brightness? So she merely repressed a sigh, and spooned a little golden-red liquid jam on to a saucer.

'Do you think it's ready yet?' she asked, tilting the saucer sideways so that the liquid ran in a slowly-congealing stream towards the side. 'Is it going to set?'

Abbie reached out a long brown finger and touched it. 'Yes. It's almost jelling now. Can I try some on a bit of bread?'

Mary grinned. 'I never know how you can put away so much stodge and stay so slim!' She smoothed down her rather shapeless T-shirt over her non-too-slender hips in their elderly working jeans, and added forlornly: 'I wish I could!'

Abbie flung an arm round her and hugged her. 'You look smashing, Mum. You always do!' She turned to look at her mother's round, compassionate face in its halo of wildly-curling silver-grey hair, and thought soberly: And it's true. She does always look smashing. Trim and unfussy and competent, and somehow immensely reassuring behind that unruffled calm. There is a curious beauty in tranquillity.

'What is it?' said her mother, meeting Abbie's glance in faint surprise. 'You were looking at me as if I was a stranger.'

Abbie's grey eyes were as honest as her

10

mother's, and suddenly serious. 'I was just thinking how lucky I was...' and then she laughed to cover her sudden lapse, and reached out to spread a little of the cooling jam on a thick slice of bread. 'By the way, talking of slim hips – did Linda come for her fitting?'

Mary frowned a little, and gave the jam a final stir. 'No, she didn't. But she's already had one fitting, and she looks very nice in that dark green velvet, like a sort of latter-day Maid Marian!'

Abbie grinned. 'I'll remind her to come back. There's not long to go now.' She was still looking at her mother rather thoughtfully, and suddenly broke into abrupt speech. 'Mum – are you sure you can afford all this?'

Her mother gazed at her in astonishment. 'Abbie! What's got into you?'

'Oh, I don't know... It's all snowballing somehow, isn't it? I could have – Tim and I could have done with something simpler–?'

Mary shook her head at her in mock reproof. 'Now she tells me!' Then she drew a sharp breath and spoke sternly. 'Listen to me, Abbie. You are my only daughter – and the Vicar's daughter at that. Your father is performing the ceremony in his own church, remember. How could we possibly not make it all as glorious and beautiful as possible!'

Abbie nodded and sighed, and gave her mother another fierce hug. 'I know ... I know ... I do appreciate it. It's just that – I wanted you to know that a tin of baked beans in the kitchen would have done, so long as you and Dad were there!'

They giggled happily together over that, and then Mary said; 'You'd better get going then, if you're going to get back for supper. Your father will expect more than baked beans I can tell you!'

Smiling, Abbie picked up her tin of paint and her overalls. 'I won't be all that long,' she promised. 'There's only one wall left to do.'

She swung out, whistling, down the lane, her hair as wildly-curling and unruly as her mother's, but glintingly dark, not grey, and her face still alight with the same untroubled joy – but not in the least tranquil like her mother's.

It was a gold-and-green day, sunlight on the hedgerows, cow parsley tall in the ditches, and a flutter of wings in every bush. Not much birdsong though. It was too late in the summer for territorial rites of passage. *The time of the singing of birds is past...*' said her mind, unexpectedly misquoting the familiar lyrical ecstasy of the Song of Solomon. But as if to contradict her, a spruce young robin perched itself on a laden blackberry twig and burst into a sudden little ripple of song.

'I'm glad to hear it!' said Abbie, smiling up at the bright bird with its knowing eyes and pulsing throat. 'Your singing time is never

12

past, is it?'

She strode on down the dappled lane, through sunshine and shadow, till she reached the field gate leading to the cottage.

There, she paused for a moment to look approvingly at the small, unpretentious house standing foursquare in front of its sheltering belt of trees. It was plain enough, but built of good, solid local stone. Thick walls – cool in summer but warm in winter. A slate roof – no frills – but quite wide windows, aglow now with reflected sunlight. And a solid oak front door, newly oiled and brushed down by Abbie herself.

It looks welcoming enough, she thought. It may not be very big, but it'll do us very nicely for the time being – until we have a family... What with Tim's accountancy job and mine with the travel agents, we'll manage very well... And it's not far from Mum and Dad... She paused then, frowning a little as she pursued a glancing thought in her mind. It had occurred to her recently that her father was getting increasingly vague and dreamy, wrapped up in mystical visions that seemed to take him a long way from his wife and daughter – and his parishioners... Maybe, she thought, her mother would not be too unhappy to have Abbie near by – in case of emergencies...?

But she shook these vague misgivings from her mind, opened the field gate, and went up the path to the door. It was not locked, which surprised her rather, though she supposed Tim had forgotten to lock up when he was down there last. They each had a key, and now she put her own unwanted one back into her pocket.

It was cool and dim in the little hall, and she stood for a moment looking round at the freshly painted white walls. They had stained the narrow staircase black, since the wood was not particularly good or suitable for scraping down, and now she went up the neat dark steps towards the two small rooms on the landing. It was the larger of the two – the master bedroom – that still needed to have one wall repainted. Vaguely, she thought she heard a faint scuffling from somewhere as she climbed the stairs, and hoped there were not any mice in the house.

She reached the bedroom door and flung it open, the paint tin swinging in her other hand, and stood on the threshold, half-dazzled, while her eyes adjusted to the flood of sunlight streaming in from the west-facing window.

And there they were – the two of them. Tim, the man she loved and trusted above all others – and Linda, the friend from her childhood who had always been her most staunch companion and confidante.

They sat there, in the big double-bed, shocked and frightened – their faces blanched with the awfulness of her discovery – the shamed admission of their betrayal. Linda's blonde hair was tousled, her creamy face suffused with a painful flush of embarrassment, her mouth a round O of dismay, the tears already gathering in her blue, childish eyes. Tim looked like a guilty small boy caught stealing apples – stricken, bewildered, and slightly at bay.

It was such a classic, absurd situation that it was almost funny – like a scene out of a corny film – and Abbie had a sudden hysterical desire to laugh. But she couldn't laugh – not in the face of all that shame and grief.

For there was grief – on all sides – she could see that. They were not just shocked at being found out. They were sorry. Sorry for her. Sorry for themselves. Bitterly sorry for the whole tangled mess.

'*Why didn't you tell me?*' she cried, for this, to her mind, was the worst betrayal of all. People did fall in love, after all, and they usually said they couldn't help themselves. But to go on and on, and let it come to this – ten days before the wedding – and say no word, give no hint of trouble...? What did they think was going to happen? How was it going to end? Or wasn't it supposed to end at all?

Sickened, she turned away. There was nothing left to say – nothing to do now. All she could think of was to get away. Get away. Fast.

She left the cottage at a run, pursued by furies, and plunged away across the fields, unaware of anything except the need to escape.

Sometime later she thought she remembered being sick into the hedge, and later still she began to feel very cold. And finally she found herself walking through deep twilit woods. There were no birds singing now, not even a robin. *'The time of the singing of birds is past,'* said her treacherous mind again, and she began to realise that it was true. Childhood was over. Tim, her one-time hero and perfect knight, had very ordinary feet of clay. Trust and reliance were gone, like the vanishing sunlight, along with friendship and the innocent belief that everyone was good.

A sudden enormous sadness came over her as she stood there, staring into the green shade of the darkening wood. It was worse than outrage, worse than anger or shock – this sudden sense of terrible loss. Gone – all those years of love and companionship, of growing up together in a world that had flowered and glowed with promise...

Growing up, she thought. Yes, I have grown up today. I was a child, with a child's blind faith in goodness. I suppose it was all too easy – too perfect to last... I suppose I expected too much... *But why didn't they tell me?*

Sighing, she turned to look at her surroundings more closely, and realised that it was really growing quite dark. It must be late, she thought. I'd better get back. They'll be getting anxious. And it came over her then, with a dreadful sense of reluctance, that she would have to tell her trusting, other-worldly father the truth about Tim and Linda. Her mother, she thought grimly, would probably take it in her stride, though the shock and disappointment would be great. But her father – her saintly father who still believed (as she had) that everyone was good?

She shivered, feeling colder than ever, and began to walk very fast back the way she had come.

'You're very late,' said her mother indulgently. 'I take it Tim was there after all?'

'Yes. Tim was there,' said Abbie, in a voice that was very small and cold.

Mary Somerford looked sharply at her daughter's face, and went swiftly towards her. 'Abbie? What is it? What on earth has happened?'

'You'd better sit down,' said Abbie, very quietly and clearly. 'I've got something to tell you.'

So Mary sat down, and Abbie told her.

After she had finished, there was a long silence, and then Mary simply got up and folded Abbie in her arms. But Abbie remained stiff and unyielding in her embrace,

17

and could not even cry.

'What you need is a drink,' said Mary practically, though her heart ached for the stony-faced stranger in her arms. 'And I kept you some supper.'

'I couldn't eat,' said Abbie, and shivered again. Then she added in a stifled voice: 'I suppose I shall have to tell father.'

Mary nodded, glancing again at her daughter with troubled eyes. 'He's getting rather ... withdrawn lately, Abbie. You may have difficulty getting through to him. Maybe you'd better leave it till the morning?'

'No,' said Abbie. 'I've had enough of deception. He's got to know the truth.'

'I suppose so,' agreed Mary sadly, though she didn't sound wholly sure.

But when Abbie tackled her father, alone in his cluttered study, he listened quietly, eyes very intent and alert, and did not seem vague or withdrawn at all. At last he sighed, and put out a gentle hand to pat Abbie's clenched one. 'Betrayal,' he said slowly, 'is the ultimate wound. Even Christ found it hard to bear.'

He looked at Abbie, and she looked back at him in helpless acknowledgement of the truth. But in some strange way, his simple acceptance of the facts comforted her. He understood. He neither condemned nor forgave, nor made excuses for anyone. It was something that had happened, and the consequences had to be lived through – that

18

was all.

'It will be all right,' he said gently. 'In the end, you will see that it is all right. In the meantime, it just has to be endured. But we're with you, Abbie. You're not alone.'

She thought he might be going to pray over her then, and she could not bear that tonight. So she fled from him rather too fast, and left him staring after her with a gaze that was neither distant nor remote. But he did not try to follow her.

The next day, of course, there were plans to unmake, letters to write, cancellations, explanations, and all the painful rearrangements of a life that had to be rebuilt overnight.

As Abbie had expected, her mother was her usual tower of strength and made no fuss about the changed situation, or about the time and money involved. But at last she said to Abbie, with a hint of extra firmness: 'You'll have to see them, you know.'

Abbie's steel-hard competence seemed to freeze even harder. 'Must I?'

'Yes. Tim keeps on asking. So does Linda. They've been ringing me all morning. And now–' She looked at Abbie's white face with compassion. 'Best to get it over, Abbie. It'll haunt you otherwise.'

Abbie sighed. 'I suppose so.' She paused, considering the matter, and then added with sudden decision: 'All right. But I want you to be there.'

Mary Somerford looked troubled. 'Oh, but–'

'No. Not without you. They'll get sentimental and try to apologise. I can't stand that.'

Her mother nodded understanding.

'Very well.' She got up and went to the door. 'I'll tell them.'

'Are they *here?*'

'Oh yes. They've been here a long time. Waiting in your father's study.'

Abbie looked confused by this. 'Is – is Dad with them?'

'No. He had to go out early today. They've been there alone.'

'How long for?'

'Ever since lunch. About four hours.'

Abbie laughed. 'It won't do them any harm to cool off.'

'Abbie!'

'Oh, I know.' She sounded only faintly contrite. 'But you should've seen them–! And in my brand-new double bed too! They might at least have spared me that!'

My marriage-bed, she thought, and brushed it hastily aside. No good thinking along those lines. All that is over now.

'What do you want to do with the cottage?' asked her mother, trying to ignore the bitterness in Abbie's young voice.

'Get my deposit back,' said Abbie shortly. 'For the rest, they can do what they like with it. Maybe they'll want to keep it – they've tried it out enough.'

Once again, Mary was on the point of protesting at Abbie's brittle, sardonic tone, but instead she went away and fetched Tim and Linda – the hopelessly guilty pair.

Tim, by this time was in a state of utter confusion – a man beset by too many emotions that he could not handle. His fair good looks were over-shadowed with the conflicting strains of guilt and genuine grief – the blue eyes already dilated and shiny with unshed tears, the tawny-gold hair flopping limply across his forehead, and the wide, laughter-loving mouth clamped tight with bewildered pain. He simply did not know what to do, what to say.

Linda, who had been unwilling to come anyway but had been persuaded by Tim against her better judgement to face up to Abbie, looked even more confused than he did, and somewhat sullen as well. Like Tim, her blonde, usually sunny countenance was overcast with the unwanted stress of tangled loyalties – honey-gold hair drooping, wide, tear-dark eyes and trembling mouth filled with mute appeal.

They were, somehow, pathetic in their abject surrender, and Abbie was suddenly enormously sorry for them. For a moment she was almost tempted to go forward and embrace them both and say: 'Oh, for God's sake, don't look like that!' But she didn't. She was made of sterner stuff than that, and she had things to say to them that must be said. And besides, Linda's appealing waif stuff cut no ice with her.

'Oh, *Abbie*–' began Tim, taking an uncertain step towards her.

But Abbie held up her hand to ward him off. 'Don't say anything, Tim. It's too late for any of that. We've got things to sort out now. There's only one question I have to ask. *Why didn't you tell me?*'

Tim blinked, and looked uncertainly from her to Linda. 'I – we didn't know how,' he said, quite simply.

'We didn't want to hurt you,' added Linda helpfully.

Abbie just looked at her. 'Don't you think finding out like this has hurt me?' she said.

They were silent, abashed by her strange, cold voice.

'Now, I want you to listen carefully,' Abbie said. 'There are things I want you to do. First of all, Tim, I want you to repay me the deposit on the cottage. I don't care how you do it, but I shall need my savings when I go to London.'

'To – to London?' He sounded totally at sea.

'Yes. I've been busy today. I've made

arrangements with the Travel Agency in Ilchester to be transferred to one of their London branches. They found a vacancy for me. As a matter of fact, they asked me before, but I refused – *then*. Now it suits me very well. It will be promotion of a sort, but I shall need something to live on to start with.'

'Of – of course,' stammered Tim.

'Then – the wedding invitations. They will all have to be cancelled, of course, but I want the reception to go ahead as planned.'

'You *what?*'

She glanced at him impatiently. 'Tim, I am not going to run away to London like a frightened rabbit. We are going to say that we have cancelled the wedding by mutual consent – and we are going to hold the reception for all our friends as a sending-off party for me as I am starting out on my new venture. It's not much of one, I know, but it will do for the time being. Understand?'

There was a stunned silence from both of them.

'My mother will see to the letters – but Linda, I think you'd better help her with those. There will be a lot to write, and of course all the wedding presents will have to be returned. You can see to that.' There was a glint in her eye as she witnessed Linda's utter confusion at this, and she added sweetly: 'After all, you were supposed to be my chief bridesmaid and helper.'

Linda just stared, swallowing hard.

'My father was meant to be officiating at this ceremony,' Abbie went on, still in the same cold voice of reason. 'I don't want him disappointed and plagued with gossip. I shall ask him to make a small speech wishing me well – wishing us *all* well. And shall expect you both to be there and to put as calm and brave a face on it as you can. We may as well part friends. After that, you can do what you like.'

She stopped there, the steel almost gone from her wavering will as she saw their distress and confusion mount. But she was nearly done now. She took a step backwards, and reached out for her mother's hand and held on to it, clutching it rather more convulsively than she meant. 'And as to the expense, Tim – my mother will have borne the brunt of all this, not to mention the extra work involved... I shall expect you and your family to contribute a fair share.'

She felt her mother begin to protest at this, but shook her head at them decisively. 'No, I insist on this. It's only right. You shall *not* have to cope with it all on your own.'

'I – oh, very well,' said her mother meekly, astonished at this new, coldly decisive daughter she did not know.

Abbie looked at Tim with cool enquiry. 'Well?'

Tim stared helplessly back at her – also

seeing a girl he no longer knew. 'I – er – of course. I'll do anything you say.'

'Linda?'

'Yes,' said Linda, and then added desperately: 'Abbie – can't we–?'

'No,' said Abbie. 'We can't. I'm sorry.'

'I'm sorry, too,' whispered Linda and began to cry.

But that was too much for Abbie. She cast one appealing glance at her mother and said: 'For God's sake, get them out of here – before I throw up again.'

Mary gave her daughter one fiercely disapproving look and began to usher Tim and Linda out of the room.

'Abbie, please–' began Tim again, driven to desperation. But she would not let him continue.

'Go away, Tim,' she said wearily. 'Words don't mean anything any more.' And she turned her back on the two of them and did not watch them go.

During the next ten days, Abbie's world seemed to tilt on its axis and take on a strange, unreal dimension. Faces looked sharpened and unfamiliar, voices sounded distorted and distant, as though her ears were playing tricks. At one moment everything looked very far away and dream-like, and at the next it was all too near and too loud, sharply in focus like a drug-ridden hallucin-

ation. Not that she had ever taken drugs –
except in hospital once when they gave her
too much of something which made the neat
friendly ward take on the quality of a child's
nightmare... In fact, it was a bit like a child's
nightmare now, and Abbie walked doggedly
through it with a face of stone, doing everything required of her, and just willing the
time to pass till she could make her escape.

Mary Somerford watched her daughter
with aching compassion, but she did not
attempt to break that icy calm. Better let the
child get through it as best she could, and
send her off to her new, independent life
with a smile and a wave and positively no
regrets. It would never do, she told herself,
to let Abbie know how much she would be
missed – how much of a gap there would be
in her mother's life when she had gone...
But, in truth, Mary had come to depend a
great deal on her daughter's company lately
– especially now that James was becoming so
vague and disorientated. She was worried
about James. He was coming up to sixty
now, and seemed to be finding it increasingly
difficult to concentrate on the needs and
problems of his church and his parishioners.
Most of the time he seemed to have his head
buried in his favourite books – the medieval
mystics and the metaphysical poets. She
sometimes thought he scarcely saw the real
world at all these days. (Though he had been

good about Abbie, so her daughter had told her.) But was the time coming, she wondered, when he ought to give up his parish to a younger man, and retire gracefully into his happy dream-world of the saints and martyrs...? She did not know. But the future troubled her a little – and not only for her shocked and injured daughter. There were many changes coming, she thought, and the golden days in this beautiful old Vicarage might well be coming to an end...

'What do you think?' said Abbie's voice beside her.

Mary jumped. 'What do I think about what?'

Abbie was almost laughing. 'Flowers, mother. You didn't hear a word I said, did you? The question is, do you have flowers at a wake?'

'Abbie!'

The laughter was nearer the surface now. 'Well, let's face it – a wake is what we are having, aren't we?' Then she softened a little, seeing her mother's outraged face. 'It's all right – I'm not complaining.'

No, you're not, thought Mary sadly. I almost wish you would. 'There are some roses left–' she began.

'They'll do. The villagers always love your roses.' She smiled at her mother, almost naturally. 'And you can put them in the church afterwards!'

For some absurd reason this made them both laugh, and Abbie put an affectionate arm round her mother's shoulders. 'You were worrying about something when I came in. Is it father?'

Mary looked startled. Abbie had always had this unexpected capacity to read her thoughts – but lately, with all this crisis to occupy her, she had seemed too immersed in her own troubles to notice other people's anxieties. And yet, here she was, clearly well aware of this different and equally upsetting problem. 'You're very on the spot today,' she said.

Abbie gave her a little shake. 'I'm not blind – even if I am knee-deep in self-pity!' She felt her mother begin to protest and went on swiftly: 'I could tell it was worrying you before – before all this fuss. He's not really ill, is he?'

Mary hesitated. 'N-no, I don't think so. Just ... increasingly shut in on himself... His books have always been a bit of an escape for him, as you well know – but now they seem almost to be taking over...'

'Ought we to do anything about it?'

'I don't think we can. But I daresay the Bishop may.'

It was Abbie's turn to look startled. 'Is he *neglecting* the parish?' She sounded almost shocked.

Mary sighed. 'Not deliberately, no... But

he's getting very forgetful, and – and somehow *detached* from it all.' From us all, she meant, though she did not say so.

Abbie was working it out in her mind. 'Do you mean he might have to retire? You might have to *leave* here?'

Her mother shook her head slowly. 'I don't know... It hasn't come to that yet... We'll just have to see ... and face up to things when we have to, like you!' She returned Abbie's hug, and firmly closed the subject. 'Let's go and get some tea.'

But Abbie was looking at her mother rather anxiously, and now she took her by the shoulders and turned her round to face her. 'Are you going to be all right without me? I hadn't thought–'

'Of course I am.' Mary spoke more firmly than ever. 'Don't let that worry you on top of everything else.' She grinned at Abbie's troubled face. 'It was time you got away from home anyway,' she said, all at once sounding clear-sighted and serious. 'I will confess to you now that I was a little concerned that maybe it was all too easy and cosy – especially for me: Your life was being fixed into a pattern before you'd had time to find out what you really wanted...' She looked straight at Abbie and said gently: 'This way may be better ... in the long run.'

Abbie nodded, half-smiling. 'That's what father said. 'It'll be all right in the end.' At least he wasn't vague about that! I hope to God he's right!'

'Tea!' said Mary, tucking her arm through Abbie's. 'No more dark doubts about the future! Tea solves everything.'

She led her away, talking cheerful nonsense, and kept the shadows at bay with consummate skill.

So the last day came. Abbie put on her 'going away' suit. (After all, she *was* going away.) It was a soft and elegant rose colour – which was just as well because Abbie herself was very pale indeed. But she smiled and smiled until her face ached, and listened politely to everyone's good wishes. It began to dawn on her, as she dutifully moved around the room from one well-wisher to another, that in spite of her attempt to keep the reasons for her change of plans quiet, all friends in the village really knew, and were going out of their way to be exceptionally kind and affectionate. Nothing was said, of course. Everyone accepted the pretence and went along with it, determined not to cause Abbie any embarrassment. But there was an extra warmth about them all as they saw Abbie through that perilous day and tried – as she did – to make it as cheerful an occasion as possible.

At first she had been a bit annoyed by their obvious kindness. She didn't want their pity. But then she reflected that it was churlish and ungrateful – not to say arrogant – to refuse their sympathy. They were all old friends. She was fond of them all. How could she reject them? Especially as she was going away, and who knew when she would see any of them again?

So she relaxed a little and her smile got less stiff, and finally, when her father had made his little speech (prompted by Mary) and she had said goodbye to almost everyone, she found herself standing beside Tim and Linda, and knew she could not leave without a single word of reconciliation. She had known them so long. They had been part of her life for all those golden years of childhood and adolescence – the slow, gentle years of growing up in this enchanted place. She could not ignore them. So she turned to them quietly and dared to meet their anxious, grief-filled eyes.

'Well, goodbye,' she said. 'I hope things work out for you.'

There didn't seem much more to say, but Tim lurched forward and took her hand in his, murmuring with desperate sincerity: 'We – we still love you, Abbie. Both of us.'

'I know,' Abbie said. 'I still love you, too. Isn't it sad?' Then she turned away and went to collect her coat in the hall.

'The car's here,' said her mother. 'Are you quite sure you don't want us to come and see you off?'

'*Quite* sure,' Abbie confirmed. Then, aware that she sounded much too stern, she softened it by adding: 'I'd much rather remember you and Dad where you belong, with all your friends round you.'

Her father smiled then and said obscurely: 'Launch out into the deep.' And her mother just flung her arms round her and said nothing at all, except to whisper very softly into her hair: 'Well done!'

It's all over, thought Abbie. I've done it. I've got through. Now I can stop pretending. Soon I shall be quite alone.

She climbed into the car. The little crowd of friends waved and called 'Goodbye – Good luck – God speed' – and anything else they could think of to send her on her way. She couldn't see Tim or Linda anymore – the flutter of hands shut them out.

The last thing she saw, looking back was her father gently putting an arm round her mother and standing with her, smiling into the sun.

Then the car turned a corner, and they were gone.

Grey morning light – the faint rumble of traffic beginning to grow – feet already hurrying to work along the echoing pavements – and Abbie, waking out of a fitful doze, trying to summon up some enthusiasm for the day ahead.

Really, she thought, looking round at the featureless box-like room with its awful dingy paint and threadbare beige curtains, I must start looking for a room of my own – *today!* – and stop living in this soulless grotty hotel that is eating up all my savings. I'll go after work and look for something. I can't stand this another day...!

'You want the Evening Standard,' said Sandra, her colleague in the Travel Agency. 'But you'll have to ring right away. Things get snatched up. And you could try the news agent on the corner. He has ads on the door. Can't say how respectable they are though. Might be a bit dodgy.' She grinned at Abbie, and tossed a mane of bright yellow hair out of her eyes. 'Can't be too careful, can you?'

Sandra was, Abbie had discovered, friendliness itself, enormously swift and competent at her job, especially getting 'availability data' out of the computer, and extremely helpful and decisive with dithering customers. She seemed to be able to produce flight tickets, hotel bookings, villas, apartments, car hire firms and ferry crossings at the drop of a hat – and if she did rather dazzle people with her persuasive smile and unstoppable flow of cheerful reassurance, together with a stream of irrefutable reasons why her travel plans for them were absolutely unmatchable, most of her clients went away satisfied, if a bit dazed.

Abbie, on the other hand, was a little

slower, but more painstakingly sympathetic about their clients' specific demands.

Maurice Chargrove, the manager and their immediate boss, was well-pleased with the contrast in styles, and congratulated himself on having got two girls who were such perfect foils for each other. Sandra, he judged, was rather better-looking in a brash sort of way, with that bright yellow hair and those well-mascara'd velvet-brown eyes and that infectious smile; but Abbie, with her cooler, more reserved approach and those extraordinarily beautiful grey eyes, was somehow the one he knew his more anxious and indecisive customers would trust. Maurice himself was smallish and sharp, and very, very alert to his clients' needs. He was a good manager, if a bit too full of his own driving force to make allowances for weakness or mistakes, but on the whole he didn't push his staff too hard.

'Abbie,' he said now, sounding brisk and efficient, 'You'd better put those new Morocco posters in the window – and the Greek ones. Very eye-catching colours.'

Abbie nodded, reaching for the roll of publicity material that had just come in that morning.

'And while you're at it, you can nip out and buy a paper from the kiosk. Might help to have an early look.'

Abbie smiled at him gratefully. She hadn't

realised he had overheard her conversation with Sandra. But Maurice never missed a trick. 'Thanks,' she murmured.

'You can ring from here, if we're not too busy,' Maurice added magnanimously. 'Save time. But only this once, mind! Can't make a habit of it.' He went swiftly off into his inner office before Abbie could answer.

'Well,' grinned Sandra, 'you *have* melted his granite heart!'

Abbie grinned back and went to buy an Evening Standard. But though she dared to make one or two quick phone-calls, the rooms had all gone before she even began to ask.

'Never mind,' said Sandra, always the optimist. 'Try the papershop. Or Tubby's round the corner.'

'What is Tubby's?' asked Abbie.

Sandra laughed. 'If you don't know Tubby's, you haven't lived...! It's a café – not very groovy, but the food's OK. And Tubby has feelers out everywhere, like the octopus he doesn't know how to cook! He might know of somewhere.'

'Sounds interesting,' said Abbie, admitting to herself that almost everyone and every-thing sounded interesting at this hollow stage when she knew no-one and nothing about her surroundings. 'I'll go there tonight.'

'You do that,' counselled Sandra approvingly. 'Time you got a place of your own. Hotels are pretty soulless places!'

'As a travel agent,' said Maurice's crisp voice over her shoulder, 'You have no business saying that! But I know what you mean.'

The girls both looked at him and laughed. They were beginning to know when Maurice was approachable or not. But Abbie thought uneasily: they are both being extra kind to me, and I know I ought to be grateful. Does it show so much that I am trying to put the pieces of my life together again?

She gave them both a fleeting grin, and went off into the grey tide of home-goers in the street to look for Tubby's. It was an unpretentious place – a red-brick corner site next to the news-agents'. A bright red sign with white lettering over the door said: 'TUBBY'S PLACE' and the wide windows on both sides of the corner were half-curtained in red gingham check, like the tablecloths glimpsed inside. There was a long wooden bar counter with a red plastic top, and tea-urns and coffee machines hissing behind. A chalked blackboard proclaimed dish-of-the-day delicacies – 'Steak-and-kidney Pie, Faggots and Peas, Sausage and Mash, Southern-fried Chicken...' and another, smaller board said: 'Tubby's Apple Pie and Custard...' Clearly, Abbie thought, it was a place for simple, homely fare – and curiously enough the atmosphere of the

36

place seemed simple and homely, too.

There were one or two customers already eating at the neat-checked tables, and there was one man – presumably Tubby himself – behind the bar, frying bacon and eggs. Tubby was, not to put too fine a point on it, exactly like his name. Or nickname rather. His face was round and rosy, with lugubrious spaniel-brown eyes and a smiling mouth, and his body was round, too, rather like one of those Russian dolls that were hollow inside. But there was nothing hollow about Tubby. He was solid flesh all through – and he was solid worth all through as well, though it would never have occurred to him to think so. He served his customers cheerfully, he cooked for them as well as he knew how, (and his steak-and-kidney pie was a knock-out, though he said it himself), and he listened with attentive sympathy to all their woes, fancied or real. He knew a lot about human nature, did Tubby, and though he was sometimes surprised (even amazed) at people's loves and hates and insoluble knotty problems, he never judged anyone. He just shrugged his plump shoulders philosophically and said: 'Oh well. It takes all sorts...' and smiled his seraphic smile and went off to get someone another coffee.

'Can I help you?' he said to Abbie, and noted to himself that here was someone who really did need helping. That wide-eyed look of stress, and the telltale shadows under those eloquent eyes told an unmistakable story.

'Oh – er – a cup of coffee, please,' said Abbie.

'Sit down over there by the radiator,' said Tubby. 'You look kinda cold. It's chilly tonight. I'll bring your coffee over.'

'Thanks,' said Abbie, and wandered vaguely over to the chair he had been pointing at. She sank gratefully on to it, admitting she was tired. She was always tired these days, but she supposed it was the effect of all those sleepless nights – and the shock. They said it took time to get over shock. But really it was quite time that she pulled herself together... Mooning about like this did nobody any good.

'Here you are,' said Tubby's warm, comfortable voice. 'Nice and hot. Can't abide lukewarm coffee myself.' He stood beside Abbie's chair, looking down at her with a friendly, enquiring gaze. 'Anything else?'

'Er – no,' began Abbie, and then, somehow heartened by that easy, uncritical glance, added awkwardly: 'At least – that is, a friend recommended your café and said you might know of a room somewhere round about–'

Tubby continued to look at her gravely and quietly, and then he said in a careful voice: 'I might.'

Abbie looked up at him hopefully. 'It – it

really is rather urgent.'

He nodded, and laid a hand on the other chair at her table. 'Mind if I sit down?'

'No. No, of course not.'

'Hard on the feet, cafés are, you know,' he said, grinning. 'And it's easier to talk sitting down.' He lowered his bulk comfortably on to the chair. 'Now. What kind of a room? Where?'

'Almost anywhere,' said Abbie desperately. 'I'm in the Bancroft Hotel at the moment.'

'That dump!' snorted Tubby. 'Mud-coloured paint and antimacassars! Enough to make a cat cry.'

I'm not a cat, thought Abbie ruefully, but it certainly makes me want to cry. 'It certainly isn't very – er – cheerful,' she admitted. 'And it's eating up my savings fast.'

Tubby nodded. 'Got a job?'

'Oh yes. Thank God.'

'Permanent?'

'Yes – I hope so. With a travel agent's.'

'Whose?'

'Mossfords. I got them to move me up from the country.'

He looked at her quizzically, but forebore to ask why. It did occur to him, though, that Abbie must have been quite good at her job if they had agreed to move her up to one of their London branches. 'They're quite solid,' he said approvingly. 'You should be all right there.'

Abbie sighed. 'They're pretty competitive. The other girl there is much brighter than me.'

Tubby regarded her with the same quizzical half smile. 'I doubt that. More pushy, perhaps?'

Abbie laughed. 'Could be.'

There was a moment's silence while Tubby still watched her. Some deep trouble there, he thought. She needs somewhere friendly. No good burying herself in some miserable little bed-sitter... I've seen that bleak sort of look before. You can be as lonely as hell in this God-forsaken city if you don't watch out. 'I think I'd better introduce you to the Duchess,' he said.

Abbie stared. 'Who?'

'The Duchess. Well, she's not really a Duchess, you know. But everyone calls her that. She was on the stage once – gold lamé and fake diamonds, you know the style. But a heart of real gold – not fake at all. You'll like her.'

'Will I?' Abbie sounded distinctly bewildered.

'Lets rooms,' explained Tubby. 'Flatlets, really. Good landlady. And the place is clean – and cheerful. No mud-coloured paint.'

Abbie grinned. 'Sounds wonderful.'

Tubby looked over his shoulder as the door to the street opened and a tired-looking platinum-blonde woman came in, with a small, red-haired freckled boy in tow. 'Pauline – come over here a minute, will you?'

The woman dumped her bag on the counter, shooed the small boy round the back, and came strolling over. 'Yeah?'

'Mind the place for five minutes, will you? We're not busy. Want to take this young lady over to see the Duchess.'

The blonde woman's weary, rather scraped-looking face relaxed into a grin, and she nodded at Abbie. 'Got you under his wing already, has he? Better watch out with the Duchess. Some folks say she's a witch!'

'Pauline!' protested Tubby, laughing. 'Don't go putting her off before she's started.' He got to his feet and laid a plump hand on Abbie's arm. 'You coming, then...? I promise you she's OK – whatever Pauline says!'

'Why not?' said Abbie recklessly. 'What have I got to lose?'

'Your money,' said Pauline flatly. 'Mind you beat her down, Tubby! She's pretty fly, that one!'

'So am I,' said Tubby, chuckling hugely, and led Abbie out of the cafe and across the street.

The Duchess was at home. That is to say, she was sitting in her big front room, playing solitaire. She had the round board on a small table in front of her and was pondering over the polished glass marbles, trying to find a way to beat herself at her own game.

She was wearing one of her best outfits – she had been quite a hit in it once, and even now it suited her pretty well, she thought. There was a flamboyant lilac silk turban with a diamanté clasp holding a small froth of white osprey feathers – like a rajah's plume. Then there was that special grey silk suit with the full, swirling skirt that had always looked spectacular, especially when she danced, with a floaty lilac silk scarf to set it off, and to add the final perfect touch, a pair of high-heeled shoes made of finest leather, the exact shade of her lilac turban. She had put on her amethyst earrings and the big amethyst ring that made her fingers look small and fragile, and she had found her favourite lipstick in her old crocodile-skin handbag, and one way and another she felt well-heeled and at her elegant best. Not that there was anyone to see it, but still, you never knew who might turn up.

The Duchess's house was the end one of a terraced row of well-proportioned houses that had seen better days. They all had white-pillared porticos above neat white steps, and all had fairly wide windows and lofty ceilings in the downstairs rooms. They each had a basement and area steps, but only the Duchess's had a tree on the corner by her boundary wall. It was a solid old city plane tree with spreading branches and a lofty crest close to her rooftop. In summer it spread a pleasant shade on the pavement below, and it somehow made her house look the most inviting of the row.

Tubby and Abbie stood looking at it for a moment, and then crossed the road together and went up the steps to the front door, Tubby pressed the intercom button and announced his presence – the door clicked open, and he and Abbie went through the hall to the Duchess's open door, and knocked discreetly.

'Come in, Tubby,' she said, and sat there, looking queenly and composed, while Tubby and a strange, pale girl came into the room.

'This is Abbie,' said Tubby, smiling at the Duchess with a mixture of affection and mischief. 'She wants to escape from the Bancroft.'

'I should think so, too,' agreed the Duchess in her most bell-like, authoritative tones. 'That place ought to be closed down!' She looked at Abbie with commiseration, and – like Tubby – did not miss the signs of strain in the pale face. 'Whatever made you go there?'

'It was the first place I came to,' said Abbie simply, and something in the bleak young voice made the two older people look at one another.

'Well,' said the Duchess, after exchanging

that brief and meaningful glance with Tubby, 'there's the top flat – if you don't mind the stairs.'

'I don't mind anything,' said Abbie humbly, 'if I can be quiet on my own.'

'Oh, you can be that all right,' boomed the Duchess. 'Up there, you've got no-one but the housetops – and the pigeons.'

'Pigeons?' Abbie was a trifle confused.

'There's a flat roof,' explained the Duchess, waving the amethyst hand so that the stone flashed bravely in the light. 'You'd better come and see.' She got up and turned to Tubby with regal grace. 'Will you join us?'

'If you're not too long,' he said, playing up to her and tucking her arm through his. 'Pauline's on her own over there. But I should hate to miss a personally conducted tour!'

The Duchess giggled musically, and together they went upstairs with Abbie following behind.

On the first floor there were two closed doors, and the Duchess gestured grandly at each in turn. 'Olive Ashridge – a librarian – very polite and tidy.' Her smile was indulgent, not malicious. 'And this side is Synco.'

'Who the hell is Synco?' asked Tubby, also smiling.

'He's an arranger of pop music,' the Duchess explained. 'Fortunately, he shares a studio somewhere else where he – ah – synchronises or syncopates or – er – synthesises, I believe!

He looks a fright, but he's harmless.'

Abbie didn't see how she could make any comment, so they went on up the stairs. On the second floor there were also two doors, and again the Duchess gestured widely, with theatrical grace.

'Number Three – Henry Grey, civil servant, very quiet, goes home to Mother at weekends.' She winked at Tubby. 'No trouble at all. But Number Four might bother you a bit.'

'Why?' asked Abbie.

'Music students – Nicky and Sammy. Mostly they practice at college – but there are times–' she made a face at Abbie. 'There are times when César Franck gets quite a bashing.' She looked for signs of disapproval in Abbie's face, and finding none, added consolingly: 'But I don't let them go on after ten.'

Abbie grinned. 'That's all right then, isn't it? And I rather like César Franck.'

Tubby made a curious noise between a snort and a laugh, and they went on up the stairs to the attic rooms at the top of the house.

'As a matter of fact,' said the Duchess, waving a hand yet again, 'you'd have more room up here than anywhere else in the house. I only made one flatlet up here, so you've got two rooms, with a kitchenette at one end of the bigger room, and a shower unit with a loo next to the smaller room.

You'd have to share the bathroom down-stairs for a real bath. Would that bother you?'

'No,' said Abbie, who was already looking round her with increasing enthusiasm.

'So long as she didn't meet Henry Grey in his dressing-gown,' put in Tubby, grinning.

The Duchess looked scandalised. 'He'd have a fit!' Then she laughed and added, with a distinctly roguish glance at Tubby: 'But it might do him good!'

Abbie vaguely joined in their laughter, but she was much too interested in the flatlet to pay much attention. The attic walls were all painted white, and the two rooms the Duchess led her into were airy and light, with windows looking out – as she had said – over a small expanse of flat roof to the housetops and the hazy city sky beyond. There was even an attempt at a windowbox on one side.

'The last girl tried to grow flowers,' explained the Duchess. 'Only she forgot to water them.'

'Could I?'

'Water them?'

'Grow them?' suggested Abbie.

Somehow, it was as simple as that. Abbie had decided with one look that this airy space was the place for her. And the Duchess seemed to know already that Abbie belonged there. As for Tubby, he smiled a secret smile, and began to argue with the Duchess about the rent.

'You're not to overcharge her – d'you hear?'

'When did I ever overcharge anyone?' protested the Duchess, in deep outrage. 'I'm always fair.'

'Fair as a lily, and twice as pure,' said Tubby, grinning, as they all began to go downstairs again. 'All right. If Abbie is satisfied, so am I. Are you satisfied, Abbie?'

'Absolutely,' said Abbie, amazed at how easy it had all been, and wondering vaguely where the catch was. 'When can I come?'

'This weekend,' decreed the Duchess. 'You are not to stay in that decrepit old pile of decaying death-watch beetles a day longer than necessary! Have you got a lot of stuff?'

'None,' said Abbie bleakly. 'I came with – with just a suitcase.'

'Good,' pronounced the Duchess. 'No clutter. You can buy a few bits as you go along. The basics are there, anyway.' Her remarkable eyes – almost black in some lights, especially on the stage – were fixed on Abbie's face with knowing amusement. 'No catch, Abbie. We aren't all crooks in this damn crooked city.'

Abbie blushed.

'Besides,' added the Duchess softly, 'no-one can be down on their luck for ever – can they, Tubby?'

'Absolutely not,' agreed Tubby, and went on laughing all the way down the stairs.

'You'd better come back in and have some supper,' said Tubby, 'Before you go back to that Bancroft place.' He glanced at Abbie's slightly dazed face. 'It'll warm you up.'

Abbie agreed meekly. Events seemed to be taking her over and she did not seem to have the will to resist. 'She didn't even ask for a reference,' she said, still mildly amazed.

Tubby laughed. 'She's a good judge of character, the Duchess... Besides, you've got a steady job – you told me.' He did not add that he was a good judge of character, too, and if ever a girl was in need of sanctuary and protection, Abbie clearly was.

'My father's a vicar,' admitted Abbie, half-smiling. 'Though I don't know if that automatically makes me respectable?'

'Shouldn't think so,' grinned Tubby. 'I've know some pretty wild vicar's daughters in my time!'

He led Abbie back inside the steamy warmth of his café and settled her at the same table by the radiator. She still looked pinched and cold.

'Try the steak-and-kidney pie,' he suggested. 'Very warming, that is.'

'All right.' Abbie's smile was dim and tired, but she was gamely trying to accept his friendly concern without getting prickly. And Tubby's easy way of dealing with things somehow made her lower her defences without even trying.

'Pauline will bring it over. I'd better get back to the kitchen. Will you be all right now?'

'Of course. And Tubby–'

'Yes?'

'Thanks.'

He grinned comfortably at her. 'You're welcome,' he said and there was something in his voice that really meant it.

Abbie sat back and relaxed in the fuggy heat of the little café. It was good not to have to think, just to sit here and let the warmth wash over her ... and know that there was someone here to talk to – who seemed to understand her needs without being asked.

'Hallo?' said a bright, small voice beside her. 'I'm Bobby. Who are you?'

She looked up and found herself staring into the face of the freckled small boy who had come in with Pauline. He was carrying a knife and fork, a side plate and a paper napkin, which he proceeded to lay out in front of her with expert precision.

'I'm Abbie,' she answered, smiling at him. 'You're a very good waiter.'

The boy's cheeky face screwed up with pleasure. 'Tubby lets me help out a bit after school – while Mum's working the tables.'

Abbie nodded.

'Saves her feet a bit,' Bobby added, straightening a fork with meticulous fingers. 'And Tubby gives us a free meal if I make myself

49

useful.' He sounded curiously adult and old-fashioned, as if he was quoting the grown-ups' words in his cheerful young voice.

'Does he, indeed?' Abbie said, matching the child's infectious grin. This was another side to Tubby's kindly good nature that she had not expected.

'Food won't be long,' said the boy blithely, and scampered off.

The next one to come up to her was Pauline, bringing a steaming plateful of 'steak-and-kidney with veg.' 'Is he pestering you?' she asked, looking round for Bobby with a suspicious glare. 'Bobby, don't bother the lady, d'you hear?'

'He's not bothering me,' protested Abbie mildly. 'I like children.'

We were going to have two – Tim and I – she thought, with instant painful clarity. Two – a boy and a girl, we hoped ... and perhaps another one, if it happened like that... She was suddenly assailed by an unstoppable procession of agonised questions. In this grey wilderness of a world she walked in now, where were the bright dreams and promises of childhood? How could all those plans of theirs, so lovingly thought out together over all those happy years of close companionship, be utterly overthrown – shrugged off and forgotten – in one short moment of truth? Did they count for nothing? Had Tim abandoned them and their whole future together without a moment's thought? Was it so easy to forget everything they had been to each other? To allow all that affection and reliance – that love, why not name it? – to be totally swamped and annihilated by a whole new range of emotions with someone else? How could it happen so swiftly and so remorselessly that everything else was cancelled out? Where had all that early joy and loving-kindness gone?

'Are you all right?' said Pauline's voice at her side. 'You're very pale. You're not going to pass out, are you? Bobby – fetch the lady a glass of water pronto – and put some ice in it.'

'I'm – I'm all right,' whispered Abbie, trying to focus on a wavering world. 'Very – very hot in here...'

Pauline stood looking at her, concern in her tired face, and waited till Bobby had returned – very pronto indeed – skidding up to the table with the glass of iced water in his hand.

'Drink some of this,' said Pauline, an arm round her shoulders now. 'That's it... Soon put the world to rights...' She waited to see a little colour return to Abbie's face, and then added shrewdly: 'And I should eat a bit of this food, if I were you. Been going a bit light on meals, have you?'

'A bit,' admitted Abbie, who couldn't really remember when she had last eaten anything solid.

'Try some,' coaxed Pauline. 'Tubby's food is worth eating...! You'll feel better with a bit of that inside you.' She set the plateful a little closer, and waited patiently to see Abbie pick up a fork. Then she tactfully went away and left her to recover on her own.

Presently, young Bobby returned with a plateful of apple pie and custard and an extra cup of coffee, and said seriously: 'Tubby sent these. He says to sit there till you feel better, and he wants a word with you before you go.'

'Oh,' said Abbie vaguely. 'Thanks.' But she was in truth beginning to feel better, and Tubby's food was very comforting.

'Now, see here, Abbie,' said Tubby, coming over to her table at last, and sitting down beside her again for a moment, 'seems to me, you need a bit of a talking to! Can't have you fainting all over my café, can I? Give the place a bad name!'

Abbie began to laugh, which was what he had intended anyway. 'It's none of my business, really, I know,' he went on, 'but you don't cure grief by starving yourself to death, you know.'

Abbie stared at him, unable to say a word.

'Now, I suggest,' Tubby continued, sounding brisk and practical, 'that you come in here to supper every night – at least until you move into the Duchess's house. That way we can keep an eye on you! It's warm in here, and the food's not bad, though I say it myself, and the company is friendly... What do you say?'

'I–'

'And we usually give a discount to our regulars,' he added slyly.

Abbie had been about to protest that she was perfectly all right, thank you, and she could manage very well on her own – but at this latest attempt at persuasion she suddenly burst out laughing.

'Oh Tubby – you are absurd! A *discount!*'

'Well, will you come?'

'Of course I'll come. How could I refuse?'

'That's all right then,' said Tubby, grinning, and got to his feet again. 'See you tomorrow. *Without fail?*'

'Without fail,' promised Abbie, smiling, and also got to her feet to face the no-longer-weaving world. It was still a wilderness out there, she knew, but it no longer seemed quite so grey and lonely. 'Goodnight, Abbie!' called Bobby, happily waving from behind the counter.

'Mind how you go,' called Pauline.

'Pork and beans tomorrow,' called Tubby.

The warmth of their concern and kindness followed her down the street, wrapping her in an unexpected cloak of comfort. She decided she wasn't afraid of the dark lonely night after all. Not at all.

It came in the darkest part of the night when senses were dulled with sleep and there was no expectation of danger – some kind of call that was not an animal's, the sound of padding feet, and then the sudden crack of an axe on splintering wood, and the smell of smoke.

Perry was awake, listening vaguely to the usual night sounds of the forest, but this was not a jungle sound, and it was not usual.

He started up, crawling out of his mosquito net, and emerged from his hut in time to see dim figures on the wooden verandah of the lab hut, apparently hacking at the poles that supported the roof.

Appalled, he began to run, but another figure was before him, and Duncan's voice called out, sharp and clear: 'Who's there? What the hell's going on?'

And then there was the sound of a blow – a grunt from Duncan, and several more heavy thumping blows before Perry charged into the affray, brandishing the first hefty bit of wood that came to hand.

After that it was chaos. Perry hit out wildly at whatever dark body he could reach, and one particularly tall one swung round and caught him a fierce blow across the ribs, knocking the breath out of him for a moment. Another dark shape loomed up in front of him, aiming at his head with some kind of club, but Perry ducked sideways and almost tripped over Duncan's body as he lay prone on the ground.

Then Jonty stumbled out of his hut and fired his gun in the air. He fired several times, and roared some sort of furious warning at the marauders, and Perry, taking his cue, began to shout as well. The uproar had the desired effect almost at once, and the unknown assailants turned and fled.

By this time, the others had arrived as well, and Judy gave a cry of alarm as she saw the smoke pouring out of her cherished lab hut. Paul had followed her, and they both rushed over to the little wooden hut, regardless of any attackers that might still be lurking about, and started beating at the smouldering timbers with anything they could lay their hands on in the dark.

Perry, seeing the last of those dark, menacing shapes slip away through the shadows among the tall forest trees, turned swiftly back to Duncan and knelt down beside him.

'How bad is it?' he asked. 'Where did they get you?'

'Never mind that,' rasped Duncan, his breath coming in curious gasps. 'See to the fire! For God's sake, put out the fire! Everything's tinder dry. The whole forest will go up if it spreads!'

Perry hesitated, not wanting to leave Duncan until he had found out what his injuries were, and whether they needed urgent attention.

'Go on,' Duncan urged. *Put it out! ... I'll keep...*' He did not manage to say any more, but Perry was used to obeying him, and went quickly over to help the others with the fire. There wasn't much water in the camp in the dry season – it all had to be brought up from the stream and that had almost run dry, though Paul had prudently rigged up a makeshift tank to collect some of the deluge that fell from the skies in the rainy season. Now, they squandered what supplies they had, pouring meagre bucketsful on the tongues of flame that kept on leaping out of the hissing timbers and the dangerously dry palm-leaf thatch of the hut roof.

In the end, they put the fire out, and Paul and Judy went to inspect how much wanton destruction had been done inside the hut to the precious laboratory equipment and plant specimens.

Jonty, having satisfied himself that no other attacker was still hanging about, came over to join Perry who was once again kneeling beside Duncan's untidy, sprawling form.

'He's passed out,' said Perry, in a worried voice.

'Better get him inside,' suggested Jonty, his deep, velvet voice sounding deeper than ever with suppressed anger. Like Perry – indeed like all the team – he was devoted to Duncan, and to see his chief lying unconscious, felled like an ox by those marauding thugs, whoever they were, filled him with rage.

Judy appeared then, carrying a storm lantern, and Paul came just behind her with a hammock slung between two short poles which he thought they could use as an improvised stretcher. Together, they rolled Duncan on to it, and began to carry him back to his own small hut.

But on the way, Duncan suddenly came round and said sharply: 'No! The lab. I want to see the damage.'

'But the smoke–' protested Judy.

'Is the fire out?' Duncan's voice still rasped, but it was fainter now.

'Yes, but–'

'Well, then. Take me there.' They all looked at one another, but they knew better than to disobey him.

The little procession turned round and proceeded to carry their domineering chief into the wrecked laboratory hut.

'There isn't even a bed,' muttered Perry mutinously.

'I'll get mine,' volunteered Paul, 'If you can keep him steady in the hammock for a minute...'

And at that moment, a deeper, darker voice spoke from the shadows behind them. 'I heard the shots... I came as quick as I could. How much is he hurt?'

It was Nguni Xavier – their chief guide and helper in this little encampment, and also their main link with the friendly villagers in the valley below. Perry was glad to see him. Problems had a way of diminishing when he was around, and his powerful strength was a great asset. Besides, he had been educated and sent to Luanda university by Duncan himself, and he was devoted to his benefactor.

The big black man came into the little laboratory, instantly making it look overcrowded, and stooped to make a swift assessment of the state of his boss in the fitful light of the storm lantern swinging in Judy's hand. Duncan's craggy face was pale, the bush of white hair over his high forehead tangled and dishevelled, with one ominous sticky patch where the blood from a jagged head wound was already beginning to congeal. And his breathing was still ragged and uneven, as if there were other, hidden injuries somewhere that had not yet been discovered.

But even as Perry and Nguni stooped over him anxiously, the famous, startlingly blue eyes opened suddenly, and the long, stern mouth began to smile. 'Nothing to worry about,' he said to Perry, signalling instant reassurance.

But Perry was not fooled. He was too fond of Duncan not to know when he was in pain – a lot of pain. And out here in the wilds of nowhere, it was not easy to get help.

Paul had returned with his camp bed by this time, and now they set about making the injured man as comfortable as possible, and Judy got more light on to the scene so that they could examine Duncan more thoroughly.

He protested only once, and then passed out again, which made it easier to have a look, but was also more worrying. There was a deep, ragged gash on his left leg, probably the work of a machete. It looked nasty, but it had almost stopped bleeding. There was a lot of bruising, and the dull red mark of a heavy stick across his back and on his right side over his rib cage. Perry thought there must be several broken ribs there, but he could not tell what other internal damage might have been done. And he didn't like that shallow, uneven breathing. Duncan was not a young man – well into his sixties – and his many expeditions had led to various accidents and attacks of various fevers, culminating in a heart condition which they all knew about but which he refused to take seriously.

Perry looked now from the tired face of his old friend and mentor the concerned ones around him, and wondered which of them was the wisest and would know best what to do. The soft light of the circle of lamps round them threw each face into sharp focus – Jonty, dark-haired and bearded, with eyes as velvet-brown as his voice, and a steadiness in adversity that was unshakeable; Paul, long and thin and precise, (known to them all as 'Sticks' because of the stick insects he was obsessed by) and with a cool, assessing brain and a fanatical attention to detail; Judy, brisk and competent but oddly attractive in her no-nonsense way, and feminine enough to have a teasing affection for Duncan which he rather enjoyed... And Nguni who knew the forest and all its ways better than any of them, dark-eyed and serious and always willing to help... But which of them would be able to tell Perry what to do?

No one, he thought. They will all look to me. Even Duncan. I am supposed to be his second in command – the one to take decisions when he cannot... So what am I to do?

'We can dress his leg – but it ought to be stitched, I think,' he said slowly. 'And the head wound, too. But it's the blow over the ribcage I don't like... God knows what damage may have been done.' He looked at Jonty, whose steady gaze offered unquestioning support, but no decision. 'I think we ought to get him to hospital. Is the radio working?'

Jonty nodded, and got swiftly to his feet. 'See if I can raise them,' he said and hurried off to his own hut where the unpredictable bush radio was kept.

Judy and Nguni, meanwhile, had brought water and disinfectant and bandages, and

Paul had brought more light and a brazier in case Duncan got chilled, for the nights up on the heights could be cold. And Perry hovered over them anxiously to make sure that Duncan got the best treatment they could offer – though he knew very well that it wasn't enough.

At last they had done everything they could, and Judy had produced hot tea for everyone – including Duncan who woke fitfully from his concussion and then lapsed into half-conscious drowsiness again. Jonty came back to report that the local plane was out somewhere, but they would try and contact it and a message would be sent as soon as possible.

Perry sighed, and ordered everyone back to bed to get some sleep, while he kept an eye on Duncan and big Nguni said he would keep watch outside, in case any of those brigands decided to come back. Tomorrow, he said, he would bring some help up from the village to repair the damage. Perry agreed somewhat wearily, and smiled round at his colleagues with as much reassurance as he could muster.

'Go and get some sleep,' he said. 'There's nothing more we can do tonight. All we can do is wait.'

And he settled down beside Duncan to wait and watch till the pale dawn crept up between the trees.

Abbie watched the thin grey light of dawn filter into the room behind the beige curtains for the last time, and heaved a sigh of enormous relief. She was leaving this place at last, and the clean, airy spaces of the Duchess's flat were waiting for her. Things would be bound to improve once she got there, she felt sure. Already there were friendly faces, friendly voices beginning to penetrate the cold, wilderness world.

She arrived at the Duchess's house with her suitcase as soon after breakfast as she dared, and found the Duchess herself standing in the hall (clad all in pink today), talking to a tall old man in dungarees and a dumpy woman in overalls who was polishing the floor.

'This is Mackintosh,' said the Duchess grandly, making a large and stately gesture with her hand. 'He does the boiler and the garden – such as it is. And this is Mrs. Mac who does the cleaning. They have the basement flat.' She beamed at them both. 'And if you want anything, they can probably get it for you!'

The woman – Mrs. Mac – turned round on her hands and knees and began to laugh. 'You make us sound like the black market!'

'So you are,' boomed the Duchess in her famous bell-like tones. 'You always could get hold of impossible things when no-one else could.' She turned to Abbie, smiling benignly. 'Iris used to be my dresser long ago, before she became Mrs. Mac. Didn't you, Iris dear?'

'I did,' agreed Iris, spreading more liquid polish on the floor and rubbing at it furiously. 'And a fine old dance you led me and all! Never knew what was coming next.'

The Duchess laughed roguishly, and gave a fine theatrical sigh. 'Ah, but it was <u>fun</u>, Iris, wasn't it? We had a high old time, didn't we – one way and another.'

'Speak for yourself!' said Iris tartly, but she looked up and grinned at the Duchess, sharing some private joke, and Abbie perceived that the two of them were old and trusted friends.

'I'll take your suitcase up for you,' said Mackintosh suddenly, as if compelled to take some part in the action.

Abbie looked surprised. 'I can manage it, thanks.'

'Nonsense!' pronounced the Duchess. 'You don't look strong enough to carry a thistledown. Always let a man help you if he offers, that's my motto. Isn't it, Mackintosh?'

The old man's serious face was suddenly lit with mischief. 'I rather think it is,' he replied, and picked up Abbie's case and started up the stairs, with the Duchess's laughter following them.

Mackintosh did not speak again till he got

to the top, and then he opened the door of the flat, took the suitcase inside, and handed the key to Abbie. 'All yours now,' he said, and managed a creaky smile. 'And the Duchess is right – anything you want, just let us know.'

'I will,' said Abbie, rather bemused at all this unexpected goodwill.

The old man turned to go then, and said over his shoulder: 'They pigeons will come for crumbs. But don't you go feeding them too much, or you'll never get rid of them!' He laid his hand on the door, and added as an afterthought: 'Still – they're company. And can't answer back!' Then he shut the door behind him and went away down the stairs.

Abbie stood looking at her new home, still smiling a little at the old man's final thrust, and saw her surroundings in a great deal more detail than she had managed to take in on her first visit with Tubby.

The main room was L-shaped, with the kitchen unit and a small breakfast bar in the short end. She saw with approval that there was a neat little sink, a microwave oven, a small electric boiling ring, a toaster and an electric kettle. Everything for basic living, she thought. All I could possibly need... There were cupboards above the worktop, and these, she discovered, had a minimum supply of plain white china, some glasses and a couple of saucepans. A drawer in the break- fast bar yielded cutlery, a corkscrew and a tin-opener. She's thought of everything, our friend the Duchess, Abbie told herself, and turned then to look at the rest of the room. There were two armchairs and one long, practical-looking sofa-bed, all covered in a plain, creamy material with a roughish texture like knobbly unbleached linen. There was a plain oak table on one side of the window, with two matching chairs, and a bookcase on the other side, and nothing much else at all, except for one large, floppy beanbag covered in the same creamy material. The floor was bare polished boards – probably oak, Abbie thought, since this was quite an old house – and there was one warm-looking brown rug in front of the electric fire. The curtains were of the same cream-coloured material, and the whole room, with its white walls and wide window, had an air of calm, uncluttered space and light.

I think I'm going to like it here said Abbie to herself and went across to look out of the window. Yes, there was the windowbox with its bedraggled flowers – and there were the many-coloured rooftops and chimney-pots silhouetted against the morning sky, and beyond them the sky itself, lots of it, alight now with hazy city sunshine, and as she gazed at it, in relief and gladness, a couple of inquisitive pigeons came down to the little flat roof to have a look at their new neighbour.

'I haven't got anything for you,' she said aloud. 'I haven't been shopping yet.'

But they looked at her so reproachfully out of their beady eyes that she went to rummage in the cupboards, and finally found two stale biscuits in one of the tins. 'Here you are,' she said, opening the window to throw out the crumbled biscuit. 'It's the best I can do for now.'

The pigeons put their heads on one side to listen to her voice, decided she was harmless, and then strutted forward on their neat pink feet and began to peck at the crumbs.

'Company!' said Abbie, echoing Mackintosh's remark.

She left the window open a crack, and went out of the door and past the tiny shower unit and went to look at the other room, admitting to herself that she had put it off as long as possible. She was still afraid of lying awake in the dark – still afraid of all the thoughts and memories and regrets that she tried so hard to keep at bay... She had hoped that getting away from all the familiar places of home which reminded her at every turn of what she had known and lost, would free her from the tyranny of remembered grief. But during those first long nights in the hot little hotel bedroom, she had found no escape, no respite from all that haunted her. Would it be any better here?

She stood on the threshold of the smaller

room and willed herself to relax and not look at it with dread. And to her surprise she found herself accepting it with a curious sense of rest. For it was quiet and unobtrusive, offering her nothing except the same airy lightness as the living-room, and an unemphatic atmosphere of neutral peace.

A broad divan rather than a bed, with a white coverlet, a neat hanging space (no wardrobe) with a white curtain in front, a long white-painted table with a mirror on it, and one soft white armchair. There was no colour in the room at all, except on the floor where there was one deep blue rug. The rest was emptiness and space, and room to breathe.

She went over to the window, and there was the same view of rooftops, but from a different angle, and no small flat roof outside this time. But there is sky, she thought, there are clouds... There may even be a moon... I shall not mind lying awake if I can look out at the sky, and who knows? I might even sleep.

She gave the little room one more approving look, and then went back into the main room and picked up her handbag. I am going to be all right here, she said. I *am*. I'm going to get over it, and get on with living. I must. It's absurd to go on moping over a finished dream. Yes, *finished*. Over. Done with. Now is the time to begin again.

She went down the stairs, meaning to go

shopping, and then suddenly caught sight of the pay-phone in the hall. I must ring them at home, she thought. They will be wondering... Surely I'm not too uptight even to bear to hear their voices? How selfish can you get?

So she picked up the receiver and punched out the familiar number, and tried to ignore her own awful reluctance to get caught up again in anything to do with home.

But Mary Somerford was well aware of Abbie's reasons for wanting to get as far away as possible from all that had hurt her, and she was very careful to sound cool and undemanding, however much she might secretly long to have her staunch and loyal daughter back.

'Abbie! How nice! What's new with you?'

'I've found a flat,' said Abbie, breathing a sigh of relief that her mother didn't immediately ask how she was. She gave Mary her new address and phone number, and added: 'But don't give them to anyone else.'

'Of course not!' Mary assured her, sounding suitably indignant. 'What's it like?'

'It's at the top of a house, and I can see over the rooftops. Lots of sky.'

'Sounds good,' said Mary, also breathing a sigh of relief, and carefully refraining from asking what she most wanted to know. 'How about the job?'

'It's all right. Tougher than Ilchester. The pace is faster! And Sandra – the other girl –

is frightfully efficient. But I'm learning to hold my own!'

'Good,' said her mother. 'That's what I wanted to hear!'

Abbie laughed. 'I've met a very nice man called Tubby, who runs a café. He's been amazingly kind... And the Duchess – who owns these flats – has been very kind, too. Aren't people wonderful?'

Mary, at the other end of the line, smiled to herself. For it was clear to her that Abbie was beginning to recover, and – it seemed – was being well looked after. 'Your father always said you rode your pony best when you let go,' she murmured, wondering whether she was allowing herself to say too much.

Abbie sighed. 'Yes. I know. Free rein... No shackles... I'm trying.'

'Bless you,' said Mary, 'You'll be flying over the jumps soon. Ring again when you can,' and she rang off before the two of them got embroiled in too much family feeling... Better to keep it light.

Then she went off to tell James that Abbie was all right, and tried not to feel frustrated that she could not put her arms round Abbie as any good mother should and hug all her hurt away as she used to do. Abbie put down the phone and was just going out of the front door when a long, lean boy in leathers, with long thin hair and a pretence of a beard, came bounding up the steps.

'Hi,' he said. 'You must be Abbie. The old girl told me about you.'

Abbie grinned. 'Nothing bad, I hope?'

He grinned back. 'Nope. Refugee. Fleeing from the Bancroft, decay, despair and disillusion. Join the club.' He held out a long, rather grubby hand. 'I'm Synco. Spend my time trying to get things together. Fond hope.'

'Hi, Synco,' said Abbie, rather liking his lopsided smile.

'Grotty old world, isn't it?' said Synco. 'Any time you want a moan, come and bang on my door. I'm good at moans. I specialise in 'em. I even record them. OK?'

'OK,' agreed Abbie, and went on down the steps, strangely heartened by Synco's laid-back growl of a voice. One more glimpse of light in the grey, she thought. I'm getting on.

2. THE SAME SKY

On Sunday, Abbie followed the custom of many space-starved Londoners and went for a walk in the park.

There was something about London on a Sunday morning that intrigued her. It felt so different – as if the relentless, churning turmoil of the week had been suddenly overwhelmed with a vague and dreaming languor. People strolled instead of rushing, idled in the sunshine arm-in-arm, wandered hand-in-hand along the paths, dawdled, pushing prams, walking dogs, flying kites, feeding the ducks, chasing children on the baked summer grass, or dozed lying in amorous heaps under the trees... There was a lightness and brightness in the air – even the colours seemed more vivid, and the sky was almost blue and free from city haze...

It's like a spell, she thought, a Sunday-special spell, transforming the known grey world into something unknown and full of promise. There was a glimmer – a sparkle of expectation – about the day. Even the couples wandering by, discussing earnestly the latest hit, seemed enchanted with themselves, oblivious of everything round them, except the sun on their faces and the warmth of their close companionship... *Couples*, thought Abbie, armoured against loneliness... How lucky they are... But then she dismissed it from her mind, fiercely determined to find other things to distract her.

There was an old man with a white dog walking along in front of her. At, least, the old man was walking, yanking at the lead, and the dog was trying to cock his leg on every tree, every bench, every deck chair and every trouser-leg he could find. The old man shouted and swore at the dog in a continuous snarl of rage and frustration, and the dog snarled back, when it had time between lifted legs and smell investigations. Their progress was slow and erratic, especially as every so often the lead got entangled round the old man's feet, or wound round the nearest lamppost, and the two of them came to a furious halt, swearing at each other louder than ever.

'You miserable bag of bones,' yelled the old man, adding a few choice epithets to make himself clear. 'I'll cut your tail off right up to your ears, you cantankerous cur!'

The white dog merely looked up at him with a malevolent eye and growled back. But Abbie, smiling at their absurd antagonism, could not help reflecting that the whole little war was really just a game – and the curious bond between these two unlikely protagonists was probably much stronger than they knew.

As if to confirm this, the old man finally sat down on a convenient bench, yanking the dog to a standstill at his feet, took out a crumpled sandwich from the pocket of his deplorable coat, and proceeded to share it with his grumpy companion. The stream of mild abuse did not stop, however, except while he was chewing bread and ham, and the dog also continued a *sotto voce* grumbling between mouthfuls, as if to say: I'm not a bit grateful, so don't go getting any ideas. I hate you as much as you hate me – so there!

The Sandwich Duet, thought Abbie, and went past them, still smiling a little, to look for a sandwich of her own at the cafeteria in the park. She was surprised, when she came to think of it, how small the distances were. (She was so used to walking the long sweet miles of countryside at home.) The Duchess's house on the fringe of Paddington was within easy reach of these pleasant open spaces. So was the Travel Agency, come to that, being not far along into the respectable reaches of Notting Hill Gate... I could come here in the lunch-hour, she thought. Better than one of those stuffy little sandwich bars... I wouldn't feel nearly so shut in then... She looked up into the almost clear sky and smiled. It did not have the infinite distance of the translucent skies of home – but it was better than nothing.

She spent a long time that day just wandering, looking at people, admiring the ducks on the Serpentine, listening to a rather frightful band playing snatches of out-of-tune Gilbert and Sullivan interspersed with bumpy marches embellished with tuba solos, and fled from that down quiet Sunday streets to the embankment and the placid old Thames flowing by in a sluggish, sunflecked tide. There were ducks here too, and already a few geese coming in after the long hot summer to their winter quarters. I know where you're going, she told them. For this, she knew, was just their stopping-off point, their resting place, before they flew on to the welcoming wetlands of the Severn estuary, below the water meadows of home...

I can't escape it, she thought. Everywhere I look I am reminded of it. How does one get over the loss of a whole countryside, as well as everything else?

But a curious thought came to her as she stood staring down at the slow, mud stained waters of the Thames below the bridge. I haven't really lost them, she told herself – all those sunlit fields and shadowy woods. They are still there. Why should I let one happening take them from me? I can still see them – why should I shy from memory? They were not to blame, my lovely fields – they did me no harm. Why should it hurt me to remember them? *I won't let it.*

'Water under the bridge,' said a voice beside her dreamily. 'Nothing left ... only reflections...'

She turned in slow astonishment to see a tall, shaggy man in an ancient army greatcoat, leaning on the parapet of the bridge. He was gazing down at the water in a ruminative stare, but now he looked up and smiled at Abbie with extraordinary sweetness. 'Comforting, isn't it?' he said, and turned back to his rapt contemplation of the river, taking no further notice of Abbie.

Comforting? she wondered. Yes, I suppose

it is. And she wandered away then, and left the shaggy man to his own quiet thoughts.

It was late when she got back to the Duchess's house, and she was just beginning to climb the stairs when the breathless figure of little Miss Olive Ashridge came up behind her, struggling to carry an unwieldy cardboard box of spindly geranium plants.

'Can I help?' asked Abbie, putting out a hand to steady the toppling flower pots.

'Oh, would you...? It's Abbie, isn't it?' She beamed shortsightedly up at Abbie. 'I seem to have got more than I bargained for here!'

Abbie took the box from her while the anxious little librarian fumbled for her key and went on talking at the same time.

'It's always the same with me – about plants, I mean. I can't resist – especially the feeble ones. They look so pathetic – I just have to try to revive them somehow, and I usually succeed.' She finally got her key into the lock, and gave Abbie another transparent smile. 'Oh – just put them down there on the table. Thank you so much.' She paused, and then added shyly: 'I suppose... you wouldn't like to stay for a cup of tea? Or coffee?' And then, when she saw Abbie hesitate, she added swiftly: 'But no, of course, you must be dying to get back to your own bit of peace and quiet...'

Abbie had been on the point of a polite refusal with just that object in mind, but she suddenly recognised the look of resigned acceptance of an inevitable rebuff on the timid librarian's expressive face. It was a look she understood – so she changed her mind and smiled into Olive Ashridge's faded blue eyes, saying gently: 'I'd love a cup of tea.'

The pale blue eyes seemed to flood with surprise and gratitude, and the slight figure in its sensible Sunday suit went bustling off to put the kettle on.

'Where did they come from?' asked Abbie, fingering a crimson geranium leaf on a thin, leggy stalk.

'The Horticultural Society,' said Olive, plugging in the kettle. 'Leftovers. Not worth taking home.' She glared at the kettle as if it was its fault. 'They meet once a month in one of the Library rooms. I – er – I don't *have* to supervise at weekends – just make sure they have the key – but I usually go in to see that they've tidied up properly.' She looked at Abbie, round-eyed with indignation. 'You've no idea! Bits of twig and compost all over the floors and wilted cuttings that nobody wanted. These were just sitting there in their box, forgotten – looking so *forlorn!*' She laughed apologetically. 'Silly of me to mind!'

Abbie shook her head. 'I don't think it's silly at all. My mother is a keen gardener. She couldn't bear to let anything go to waste, either!'

The two of them looked at each other and

grinned. Alliance had been established.

'As a matter of fact,' said Olive, sounding shy again, 'I thought of you. The Duchess said you wanted to brighten up the window box... There are far more here than I could use...'

Abbie looked interested. 'Are there? Are you sure?'

For answer, Olive led her across to the window, where she had managed to fix up one rather narrow wooden box, just outside the sill. It already had some straggling lobelia, and a few late summer pansies doing their best to keep alive.

'You see? I can only get in about four... But they'll last till the late frosts with any luck.' She glanced at Abbie hopefully. 'You could have the rest ... and you'd better have some of this compost stuff, too. The soil in that window-box of yours is probably a bit exhausted... Like most of us!' she grinned, and waved vaguely at a half-full bag of brownish compost lying propped against the skirting board below the window. 'I've laced it with some extra growmore or something,' she added cheerfully, 'So it ought to help!'

Abbie agreed to that. 'I'm sure it would!'

Olive's round, gentle face looked quite rosy with relief. 'Oh, I'm so glad you like the idea. I was so afraid you'd be offended!'

Abbie laughed. 'Who could be offended

by an offer of free plants and gingered-up compost!'

The librarian joined happily in the laughter, and went to make the tea. She also found some chocolate digestive biscuits (her favourites) in the biscuit tin, and put them tidily on a plate.

'There!' she said. 'Quite cosy. Come and sit down.' She gestured to a chair by the window, and sat down herself with the small teatray in front of her on a nearby table. Her eyes, bright and observant like a bird's, looked from Abbie to the window and became fixed on the glimpse of the old city plane tree outside. She sighed a little. 'The light goes from here towards evening. The houses are so high... But you must get the sunset upstairs where you are?'

'I – yes, I suppose I must,' said Abbie, and then admitted slowly:

'I haven't been up there much yet!'

Olive poured out some tea, and passed the biscuits. 'It takes time to get used to a place,' she said. 'But if you're going to live there permanently – like me, I mean – you want to be aware of its advantages as well as its disadvantages!' And then, fearing she had sounded rather ponderous, she added with a hint of mischief: 'I mean, sunsets are important – especially in London!'

Abbie nodded, absently stirring her tea with one of Olive's best silver Apostle spoons, though she didn't take sugar. 'There's more light than you'd think...' she murmured, almost as if reassuring herself.

Olive Ashridge smiled. 'You're used to the country, aren't you...? All that space... It must be hard to adjust.'

'I'm beginning to get the hang of it,' said Abbie cautiously. 'The Park is really rather fun on a Sunday.'

Olive nodded with enthusiasm. 'And there's Hampstead Heath ... and Kenwood House where they have open-air concerts ... and the river boats... Lots of places with room to breathe – if you know where to look.' She offered Abbie another biscuit.

'I don't mind if I can see the sky,' said Abbie, with her mouth full.

The bird-bright eyes regarded her knowingly, full of a quiet but unspoken sympathy. 'The same sky – everywhere?' she suggested, a faint question in her voice. 'Is that a comfort or a threat, I wonder?'

'A comfort,' stated Abbie, and lifted her cup in silent tribute to the evening sky.

And when she finally got upstairs to her attic flat, she found that Olive Ashridge was right, and the whole of her front room was flooded with golden sunset light, streaming in through a gap in the dark frieze of chimney-pots, and laying a patina of red-gold glory on the whole of her rooftop world.

Even the inevitable plane droning overhead was touched with magical light – a silver bird flying high in the sky to all those far-off distant places she was busy sending other people to all day long. The sunset changed even that throbbing pilgrimage to the stuff of dreams...

A comfort? thought Abbie. It's odd, but two complete strangers have talked to me of comfort today... Is it so obvious that I need it? Or are they, perhaps, in need of it, too?

She did not know. But the sunset sky was so incandescent – so filled with distant beauty – that all the perplexing questions still haunting her faded from her mind.

It was enough to be here – up here on her own – with all the limitless golden sky above her. Nothing had any power to hurt her here.

The silver bird came down in the forest clearing, skimming the trees and just managing to stop before the end of the tiny runway.

Perry watched it come with a mixture of relief and dread. He didn't want to leave this place and all the careful work he had been doing here – or his hard-pressed colleagues on the research team. But they had talked it all over while they were waiting for the plane to come, and two imperative reasons for Perry to desert them had topped their painful list of priorities. They had to get Duncan MacNab to hospital before it was too late to help him, and Perry was the one he trusted most and might possibly accept as 'nurse' on the difficult journey. And also, Perry was the one who ought to go home and set about raising some more money for the conservation project. This would mean lecture tours and social events and lobbying influential people – all tasks that he disliked profoundly – but it would have to be done if the work was to continue. And since Duncan could not do it himself, it would have to be Perry. Somehow, he would have to turn his back on this lovely unspoilt corner of forest – the tall trees of the canopy and the green tangle of undergrowth beneath them – and face the fierce, thrusting world outside in a different kind of jungle mostly made up of concrete and poisoned air.

'Hallo?' said the pilot of the small plane, jumping down and striding towards him. 'Farquhar?'

'Yes,' said Perry relieved that the man spoke in English, though by now Perry's Portuguese was pretty good. 'Glad to see you.'

'How's the patient?'

'Not very good.' Perry's lean brown face looked a little grim. 'And very unwilling to leave!'

The pilot grinned. 'Been out here a long time, hasn't he? On the original famine relief food programme, wasn't he? Looks on the whole thing as his baby?'

Perry smiled back. 'Just about. He can't

imagine the place surviving without him.'

'Could it?' The question was serious. The pilot knew very well that Duncan MacNab was a name to conjure with out here. The authorities allowed him to stay – even approved of his work up to a point. But they might not be so co-operative without his benign presence at the head of the project.

Perry sighed. Could it survive? It was a question he had been asking himself many times lately. The rest of the team were very good at their work, and very loyal – Judy, the botanist, precise and delicate like her flowers but tough as old boots underneath; Paul, the lepidopterist, clever and meticulous and almost as self-effacing as one of his own stick insects; and Jonty, the zoologist, with his gentle hands and unflagging patience. They all loved their work – and they all loved Duncan. So, in fact, did the villagers in the valley whom Duncan had begun to educate in conservation awareness, and big, friendly Nguni who already knew so much about the project through Duncan's educating influence. Yes, they all loved and revered Duncan. So, too, did Perry, who had known him longest and shared most of his dreams of the preservation of the forest's bio-diversity and the hope that this battle-scarred country might be opened up to eco-tourism one day... Perry, who was not only an ornithologist who had learnt to climb trees like the natives and wait with his camera and his notepad almost as patiently as Jonty stalking a rare primate – but was also the most knowledgeable and ardent conservationist of them all. But could they manage without Duncan? He was the driving force behind the whole research programme. *What would happen if he didn't come back?*

'I don't know,' he said slowly to the pilot's serious question, unaware that he had taken a very long time to answer. Then he seemed to pull himself together with a conscious effort, and make up his mind to get on with the task in hand. 'Come on. You'd better see him before we move him. He may take some persuading.'

The two men crossed the clearing to where several wooden huts stood grouped round one central slightly larger one, also thatched with palm leaves in the local tradition. One end of it had been seared by fire, the pilot noticed, and a couple of the supporting log pillars had been damaged and were held together by extra splices of new-cut wood.

'What happened here?' asked the pilot, glancing round to see whether there were any other signs of damage.

Perry shrugged. 'A band of marauders – rebels – deserting soldiers from the last bit of fighting...? Who knows? They came by night. They had machetes and clubs, but no guns, thank God. Or at least, they didn't use them.'

He shook his head, trying to make light of it. 'Duncan came out first, and they felled him to the ground. Then we all tumbled out, making a lot of noise. I hit someone and someone hit me. Jonty fired his gun into the air, and. they all fled. They tried to fire the lab hut, but we managed to put it out... And when we examined Duncan, we found he had got this nasty gash on his leg, a crack on the head, and a lot of heavy bruising over his ribs which seemed to be affecting his breathing... That's why I sent for you.'

The pilot nodded soberly. 'Sensible. What about the local police?'

Perry laughed. 'Out here?' Then he, too, grew serious. 'It's still a very lawless country, especially in remote areas like this, isn't it...? We're trying to set up wardens among the local people and get the whole district declared a nature reserve – as you know. But it takes time. And the wheels of officialdom grind very slow... As for the police – where they exist – they are apt to be almost as unpredictable and fierce as the villains they are supposed to be catching. The law of the jungle certainly applies out here!'

His companion grunted agreement, and they went up the steps of the central hut together.

'He insisted on being taken in here so he could assess the damage,' explained Perry. 'I think he had ideas about picking up all our slides and samples and re-cataloguing them instantly on the spot, but of course he couldn't.'

'Is there much damage?'

Perry sighed again. 'Quite enough... It puts our work back a few months... But I daresay we'll catch up.'

As he spoke, Judy, the botanist, rose from her place by the camp bed where she had been sitting and said very firmly: 'I've got him ready. But you'll have to persuade him to go.'

She was a pretty young woman, Jack the pilot thought. Pleasant, in a tough, no-frills way. Straight brown hair with reddish lights in it – a straight nose and a straight mouth to match, but very alert brown eyes, and a sort of calm, smiling assurance that was reassuring to see.

Duncan MacNab, on the other hand, looked dishevelled and cross, white hair standing up like a cockatiel's crest, brown face seamed with angry frown-lines, and eyes as blue as cornflowers out snapping with inner rage.

'This is all nonsense!' he barked. 'I can manage perfectly well here. No need to go <u>anywhere</u>!'

Perry went over to him and laid a restraining hand on his arm. 'You know that isn't true,' he said gently. 'Just as we know you are much too valuable to take risks with...' He smiled at Duncan's mutinous face, and after a moment the sick man smiled rather fiercely back.

'Fuss about nothing–'

'Duncan,' said Perry crisply: 'you have a high fever. That gash on your leg isn't healing. I suspect you've got at least a couple of broken ribs in there – and you're certainly not right in the head!'

Duncan began to laugh, but it clearly hurt him to do so, and he stopped short with a faint gasp of frustration. He and Perry looked at one another, old friends and sparring partners, but there was a deep affection there behind their warring glances.

By this time, the rest of the team had come in through the doorway and were mustering forces to persuade their chief, or even to move him by force if necessary.

'It's true, Duncan,' said Jonty, in his deep, rich velvet voice that was almost as gentle as his hands when handling one of his frightened creatures.

'Expert help is clearly needed,' added Paul, in the precise, dry tones of a scholar who could deal with technical data better than human emotions.

'You see?' Judy supported roundly. 'Carried unanimously.'

Duncan glared round at them all, and gave a cautious sigh. (It hurt to sigh as well). 'Oh well, in that case–'

'I don't want to hurry you,' put in Jack the pilot briskly, 'but I have to get you back in daylight. Can't fly these little planes in jungle country after dark.'

'But how will you manage?' Duncan began, stalling yet again.

Jonty spoke for them all then. 'Very well. We'll make good the bits of data we've lost, tidy up, and just tick over quietly till you get back... And Perry will go on home and raise some more cash. We've lost quite a bit of equipment here – we'll need to replace it.'

Duncan had to admit to himself that this was true. And Perry was very good at raising money. He had done it before, several times, to good effect.

'It makes sense,' urged Judy. 'Come on, Duncan.'

'You'd be the first to admit that a wounded animal needs treating,' pointed out Jonty, in his dark brown voice.

For some reason, this final argument defeated Duncan. He gave in, ungraciously, and struggled to sit up. 'Oh – have it your own way!'

But he couldn't sit up unaided, and between them they got him on to a makeshift stretcher and carried him out to the plane.

'Can you manage the two of us?' asked Perry anxiously. The little winged bird looked such a flimsy machine.

'Yes, if you're not too heavy!' grinned Jack,

assessing the two men who were neither very big-boned nor in the least overweight. 'Hope the runway's long enough!'

Perry said goodbye to the others rather swiftly, grasping Jonty's arm and adding under his breath: 'Take care of 'em!' and tried to answer their cheerful send-off smiles with one of his own. He didn't know quite why he was so full of foreboding, but he was.

Duncan didn't try to smile at all. The transfer to the plane had obviously shaken him, and he lay with his eyes closed, looking very pale.

'OK?' said Jack. 'Here we go!' And the little plane raced along the narrow open space, pointed its nose at the sky, and took off over the trees.

During the next few days, Abbie followed up her Sunday experiment and took her lunch-time sandwich into the park. The summer weather had remained fine and warm enough to sit out, and a great many more office workers than Abbie took advantage of it.

Several times she saw the old man and his white dog, jerking and swearing along together as usual, and several times she watched them settle down together (still growling) to share whatever scraps of lunch they had. She got quite intrigued by the two of them, and even began to look for them each day, and to be in some strange way relieved to see them lurching towards her over the brown summer grass. But she did not try to speak to them – either the old man or his dog. What could she say? 'A nice day?' He'd be sure to snarl that it wasn't... And if she tried to make friends with the dog, it would surely bite. So she contented herself with watching their struggling progress, and settling down to eat her own lunch when she saw the two of them settle for theirs. It was a simple enough distraction, she had to admit, yet it somehow began to make a pattern in her day.

But one morning, the pattern was rudely interrupted. She came back from the park to her office door, to find Tim – her ex-fiancé – waiting on the pavement. For a moment she was tempted to turn and run, but then something about the wretchedness and desperation of his expression made her pause.

'Tim? What on earth are you doing here?'

He gulped and took a hesitant step forward, holding out a pleading hand. 'I'm sorry, Abbie – I wouldn't – I wouldn't have bothered you – but I'm desperate, and I don't know what to do...' He took a swift, nervous breath, and blurted out: 'Is – is Linda with you?'

'Linda? With me? You must be joking.' Her voice was cold.

'No. No, I'm not joking, Abbie. I thought she might've come to you...?'

'I should think I'd be the last person she would come to,' Abbie told him flatly.

But he would not be put off. 'You're wrong, Abbie. She – she respected you. That was the trouble – she couldn't bear what she had done to you.'

'And you could, I suppose?'

He shook his head. 'Neither of us could... But she was the one who ran away from it – and I've got to find her.' His voice shook with a curious mixture of shame and fear. 'I don't know what to do...' he repeated, and looked helplessly at Abbie for some kind of response.

But Abbie was suddenly so angry that she felt hot all over. 'Let me get this straight,' she said. 'You and Linda have a long-running fling behind my back, leaping happily in and out of my new double bed when I'm not looking – you break up our marriage plans and our whole future – and now Linda runs off somewhere, and *you want me to help you get her back?*'

Tim groaned, but he did not back away. 'I know. I know it's awful... There's nothing you can say that I haven't said to myself already but – but I don't know where she is, or what she might do. I think she may be in danger – she's such an innocent.'

'Not that much of an innocent, Tim, surely?' Abbie's voice was even colder.

'You don't understand,' he said. 'She's not

90

– not strong, like you... She might do any-thing–' He rubbed a wild hand through his hair, and added in the same, bewildered, helpless tone: 'You are the one person I could trust – who would know what to do.'

Abbie was silent, looking at him in dis-belief and wonder. For she saw now that the man she had loved so much was just a rather overgrown child – caught out by his own desires, and confused and frightened by their consequences...

'What made you think she might be in London?' she asked, trying to put a calm face on things.

'She bought a one-way ticket to Padding-ton,' he said. 'The booking-clerk told me – he knows her quite well. It's the only clue I have.'

Abbie was thinking hard now, and reso-lutely trying to be fair to Tim. Anger was no use. It didn't solve anything. At last she said carefully: 'I can't talk now, Tim. I have to get back to work. But there is a café called Tubby's just down the road. I'll meet you there after work – if you think it will help.'

He looked pathetically grateful. 'Of course it'll help. I – I'll be there.' He was about to take her hand and press it, but thought better of it. 'I'm so grateful, Abbie,' he said, and stood back humbly to let her go inside.

It was this unlikely gesture of humility that nearly threw Abbie. How could her erstwhile fair-haired hero have come to this – this abject, wretched creature? 'Half past five,' she said crisply, and turned away to the door and went inside before she could put her arms round the idiotic fool and say: 'Oh Tim! How could you be so silly?'

'Are you all right?' asked Sandra, who was so on the ball she never missed a trick.

'Yes,' said Abbie. 'Family problems. Sorry.'

'Gotta spot of brandy in the cupboard.' Sandra shot her an encouraging grin. 'Better swallow it down before Maurice sees you. Might send for an ambulance!'

'Strait jacket, more like,' muttered Abbie, but she obediently swallowed Sandra's small tot of brandy (purely medicinal, of course) and tried not to cough. Or was it cry? Or laugh?

She decided, on consideration, that it was laugh. And laugh she did – so much that Sandra got quite worried.

'Oh Sandra!' she gasped, wiping her eyes on a convenient leaflet about Tunisia, 'you should have seen his face!'

When she got to Tubby's that evening, Abbie cast one swift assessing glance round the room to confirm that Tim was there, and then walked resolutely up to the counter and ordered a coffee.

'You OK?' asked Tubby, eying that telltale pallor with some misgiving.

'Yes. Tubby, I may need your help. If I – if things begin to look fraught, could you come over and interrupt?'

'Sure,' said Tubby, wiping down his countertop with unnecessary vigour. 'Good at interrupting.' He winked at Abbie. 'Do I wait for your hair to stand on end, or what?'

'It is already,' said Abbie, grinning. 'I'll … wave.'

Tubby snorted. 'As long as it's waving, not drowning,' he said, and watched her go over to the table where the nervous, fair-haired young man was waiting.

Abbie sat down opposite Tim, put her elbows on the table, holding her coffee cup in both hands, and said firmly: 'You'd better tell me what's happened so far.'

'Yes,' agreed Tim wretchedly. He looked at Abbie in mute appeal, but he found that she was not looking at him, merely frowning down into her coffee cup.

'Well,' he began, sounding almost afraid to put the frantic happenings of the past few days into words, 'she and I – since you went, things haven't been easy between us… I knew she was upset, and feeling guilty – we both were. But I – I didn't realise how upset…' He stalled there, and Abbie had to prompt him, rather brusquely.

'Well?'

'She was supposed to be meeting me that day–'

'Which day?'

'Last – last Wednesday – after work. But she didn't turn up. I waited and waited, and then in the end I rang her mother. She said Linda had gone out early – to work, she supposed, and hadn't been back all day.' He paused then, trying to sound rational and collected instead of panic-stricken, which he was.

'And then?' Abbie's voice was still very crisp.

'I left it that night. But in the morning her mother rang me and said Linda hadn't been home all night. She was–' he gulped a bit, 'she sounded very frightened, so I went round there...We checked Linda's room. Her handbag was missing, but no suitcase or clothes or anything... So then I thought of asking Bowles, the taxi-man, and he said he'd driven her to the station quite early in the morning the day before. So I got hold of the booking-clerk – as I said – and he confirmed she'd gone on the London train...' He stopped there, looking tired and worried, and more like a bewildered small boy than ever.

Abbie hardened her heart. 'No note or anything?'

'Yes. There was. But I didn't find it till the next day. She'd pushed it through the letter-box in the cottage, and I – I hadn't been down there since...' He didn't specify since when, but Abbie guessed and watched his embarrassment rise as he fished in his pocket and brought out a crumpled piece of paper. 'I – I brought it with me – in case it helped.'

Abbie smoothed out the untidy note and looked at it under the light. It said simply: 'Sorry, Tim. I can't bear it. L.'

She sighed, and looked up then into Tim's stricken face. She thought there were tears in his eyes. 'Did she have any particular friends in London?'

He shook his head distractedly. 'I thought you might know that better than I would...?'

'No,' said Abbie. 'If there were any, she didn't tell me.'

'But where could she go?' Tim burst out. 'What would she do? If she knew no-one, who would she turn to?' It was a question he had already asked himself many times over, and the answering possibilities were too frightful to contemplate... He already had a countryman's natural distrust of London – the wicked city that he was sure offered all manner of awful temptations and was full of unprincipled rogues and vice... The thought of Linda – childlike, trusting Linda – alone in this predatory jungle filled him with terror.

Abbie did not have the same view of Linda. She thought, privately, that the girl had managed very well so far in getting what she wanted, and would probably be well able to look after herself, wherever she had got to... And maybe having a frantic Tim running after her was all part of the game? But she was a little ashamed of this thought. (Maybe I ought to try saying: 'I can't bear it!' and batting a few eyelids and uttering a sob or two she thought).

'Let's just get one thing straight, Tim,' she said, fixing him with as fierce and demanding a stare as she could muster. 'What do you want Linda back for?'

He looked astounded. 'I – what do you mean?'

'I mean – what sort of future were you planning? Do you want to marry her? Make an honest woman of her is the phrase, I believe. Or just go on romping in the hay – I mean, my double bed?'

Tim was so shocked by her flippant tone that he failed to answer at all. But Abbie softened then, having almost found out already what she wanted to know. 'I mean, Tim, do you really love her?'

'Oh yes,' he said, sighing with sudden enormous weariness. 'Oh yes, I love her all right... But you know that, really, don't you?'

Abbie nodded slowly. 'Do you remember "The Once and Future King?"'

He looked at her, uncomprehending. 'What?'

'We read it together – you and I – when we were children... Arthur and Lancelot and Guinevere... Don't you remember?'

(If I can put the whole thing on a more romantic footing, she thought desperately –

less silly and sordid and obvious – maybe we'll both feel better about it.)

He began to understand her then. 'Oh yes ... that last, final meeting...?'

'It was so sad,' said Abbie, spelling it out. 'I remember thinking it was the saddest parting in the world... Those three – they all loved each other – they were all friends – all bound up in it together ... and there was nothing they could do to put it right.'

Tim was silent.

But Abbie had more to say. 'And I remember thinking it was such a waste,' she went on. 'Those perfect heroes of mine – two brave, noble men facing inescapable battle and death – and one lovely woman shutting herself up forever in a convent...'

The young man before her who was not a hero suddenly looked terrified again. 'You don't think–?'

'No, of course I don't.' Abbie almost laughed. '*But* I do think all this is a waste.' She looked at Tim quite calmly then, as if he ought to understand her reasoning without further explanation. 'You love her. She loves you. So we've got to find her. We may as well salvage *something*.'

He looked back at her with a mixture of profound relief and unresolved anxiety, 'How?'

Abbie turned then, and waved a hand at Tubby, who was unashamedly watching them from behind his counter and waiting for a signal.

He wasted no time. He poured himself out a coffee, and came over to their table. 'Mind if I join you?'

'Please do, Tubby. We'd be so grateful.' She smiled up at him, aware suddenly how perilously near the edge her own emotions were, and how very glad she was to have his solid, comforting bulk beside her. 'We have a problem here,' she said, glancing from him to the troubled young man across the table, 'and we wondered if you could help us?'

Tubby sat down, and Abbie told him the whole sorry story. Tim said nothing to excuse himself, only reiterating towards the end that he had got to find Linda, and at least know that she was safe, even if he couldn't put things right between them. He seemed to be past having any pride or regard for himself, his whole mind concentrated on Linda's safety – and Abbie liked him the better for it.

'I think you'd better talk to Raine Medwin,' Tubby said, after Abbie had told him all she could. 'I'll go and ring her now.' And he got up from his chair.

Abbie looked up at him incredulously. 'The *dating agency*?'

Tubby smiled. 'Yes. But you needn't look so disapproving. There's more to Raine's work than meets the eye, believe me.' He went away then for a few moments, and Abbie saw him talking quietly on the telephone in the corner behind the bar.

Tim sat there, silent and exhausted – seeming unable to think of anything more to say.

'It's all right,' Abbie said, trying to sound kind and reassuring. 'Tubby is wonderful at fixing things...' She did not say any more. In truth, she was feeling almost as exhausted as Tim, though she was careful not to show it. Emotional see-saws were very tiring.

'She'll see you now,' said Tubby, coming back to them cheerfully. 'It's after hours, but she'll stretch a point for me... I can take you round there and introduce you, but I'll have to get back. We get busy here in the evening. All right?'

Abbie nodded, and got up to follow him, with Tim close behind.

'Can't promise anything,' said Tubby, as they went out into the street. 'But Raine will help, if anyone can.'

Raine Medwin, they found, was a quiet, elegant woman of forty-five or perhaps a little older, with smooth, well-cut dark hair, wide, watchful eyes and a compassionate smile.

Tubby introduced them briefly, and hurried away again, saying to Abbie as he left: 'Come back to me, Abbie, and report. And if there's anything else I can do – ask!' Then he left them to tell their story all over again to that tried and trusted listener, Raine Medwin.

She listened carefully, asked a few questions, and then went over to the second computer ranged behind her desk against the wall.

'I'd better explain the set-up here,' she said to them both. 'That computer over there is set up to deal with the dating agency.' She waved a graceful hand in the direction of the other computer and screen by the wall. 'I don't suppose you know much about dating agencies. But we make each client fill in quite an extensive questionnaire. You know – likes and dislikes – temperament – education – intellectual pursuits – sport – preferred looks, and so on...'

Abbie nodded comprehension. Tim seemed a bit fazed by the whole idea.

'And we feed all that data into the computer so that we can do cross-referencing and matching. That's how Medwin Meetings works. Understand?'

'Yes,' Abbie said.

'We also see every client personally and listen to their history – as much as they like to tell us – and sometimes, you know, it's a whole lot...! And that's where the other computer comes in. It was Tubby's idea, really – Medwin Findings.' She smiled and added softly: 'He's a good man, our Tubby!'

'Yes, I know,' agreed Abbie warmly.

'Well – we set up a list of useful rooms – bedsits, B & B, small hotels, hostels ... where people could stay safely – particularly girls on their own.' She turned to Tim then, seriously: 'You are probably right to worry. All sorts of people approach young girls at the railway stations, you know – offering all the wrong things – including drugs and prostitution. It's none too safe, unless you know the ropes... The charities have special people up there, watching out for anyone who looks lost or troubled ... and so do we... There's quite a network now. And if they get a name, or better still a home address, they feed it into the general register where people can be traced... Sometimes, of course, they don't want to be traced, and we have to respect that. But we can usually manage to persuade them to ring home – or let us ring their home and at least tell their parents that they are safe...' She looked at Tim hard. 'D'you see the set-up?'

'Yes.' He still seemed a trifle shaken. 'I'd no idea. It sounds a wonderful idea.'

She sighed. 'It's not foolproof. A lot of them slip through the net, of course... And there are the homeless ones on the streets. They are even harder to trace... At least in rooms and hostels they expect the visitors to register – though they may give false names, of course.' She was still looking at Tim with enquiry. 'Would Linda give her own name, do you think? What is it, by the way?'

'Fielding, Linda Fielding...' He pondered. 'She might... It might not occur to her to disguise it.'

'Especially if she was acting on impulse, in a state of emotional turmoil,' added Abbie fairly.

Raine glanced at Abbie with approval. She liked this clear-headed girl who was trying so hard to put her own feelings aside. 'Well, we can quite easily check whether anyone of that name was registered in any of our "safe" houses,' she said cheerfully. 'And if that doesn't turn up anything, I can give you a few other addresses to try who may not have come back to us with new information.' She was looking at Tim again now. 'It would mean a bit of hard foot-slogging... They aren't all good at answering the phone – especially if it's a communal one in the hall.'

Tim said steadily: 'I don't mind that. *Anything* to help find her...'

Raine nodded. 'Well, wait a bit. We'll try.' She sat down at the computer and went through a number of complicated lists and addresses. But no Linda Fielding turned up on the screen.

Then she rang a couple of 'friends in the business' – including a Salvation Army officer who was concerned with the Missing Persons Register, and after him, an equally co-operative ally in the police force who was also concerned with the same heartbreaking register. But there was still no Linda Fielding.

Tim looked more desperate by the minute, but Raine turned to him kindly as she finished the last fruitless phone-call and said: 'Don't despair. It often takes several days to find someone, you know – or even several weeks... But we usually succeed in the end.'

'Several weeks?' muttered Tim, as if it was the end of the world.

Raine did not add 'several years' to her cautious prediction. But it had often taken many, many months of fruitless searching by anxious relatives before the elusive missing person was found... Better not make the poor, wretched boy more despondent than he was already, though. Give him a modicum of hope.

She turned suddenly to Abbie, as if already aware that she would get more practical support from her. 'You and Linda were close friends, you say... Did you ever come up to London together to go shopping – or to a concert or a gallery, or something?'

'Yes,' said Abbie 'now and then ... especially before Christmas.'

Raine nodded. 'Well, was there anywhere special you used to go? A favourite café or bar...? Somewhere that meant a lot to you? Or somewhere that was a sort of ritual for the day?'

Abbie thought back slowly to the golden,

carefree days of adolescence and first essays in grown-up independence... And a far-off recollection of Linda's young, solemn voice saying 'I love this place... If anything bad ever happened to me, I'd always come here...' came into her reluctant mind.

'St. Martin's-in-the-Fields,' she said. 'We used to go there for a few moments quiet. Linda was – was fairly religious in those days – and I was brought up to be...' She paused, almost smiling at the memory of her father's strict regime. 'And then we'd go to the National Gallery to look at the Rembrandts.'

Raine looked pleased. 'That's a real lead, you know. People often go back places where they have been happy.'

'Or at peace,' muttered Tim suddenly.

And Abbie then realised that this confused, muddled man beside her really was suffering – and would go on doing so for a very long time unless she could put it right.

'I suggest,' said Raine, sensibly, 'that you, Tim, follow up the addresses I gave you – tomorrow. It's a bit late now, though you might get one or two in before people lock up for the night... And you, Abbie–' she turned back to Abbie with an unexpectedly warm and friendly smile, 'go back to your old haunts – the same sort of time you went there before. Would that have been lunch time?'

'Yes,' agreed Abbie, wildly juggling with

her own working day, and then remembering that it was Saturday tomorrow, and it was her turn to have the weekend off. 'Yes. At lunch time. We used to end up in the National Gallery Cafeteria...'

Raine nodded understanding. 'Then – if neither of you have any luck, come back to me tomorrow evening. I might have something else to offer by then. All right?'

'All right,' confirmed Abbie.

'It's very good of you–' began Tim.

But Raine interrupted him. 'Wait till we have a few results before you begin thanking me,' she said. 'Go on home now – and get some sleep if you can. You may need a lot of stamina to see this through.'

You can say that again, thought Abbie, and then observed the shadows under his blue eyes with a kind of odd, detached compassion.

They went out into the street, and Tim turned to walk along beside Abbie, not quite knowing what to do next.

But Abbie knew. 'Go on home, Tim, like Raine said – to where it is you're staying. Or follow up a couple of those addresses on the way... I'm going back to my own place now.'

'But – how shall I know where to find you?'

'At Tubby's,' she said firmly. 'And you've got Raine's phone number, too. We'll meet at Tubby's...'

'When?'

'As near six as you can make it. Will that do?'

'I – I suppose so,' he said, still sounding bewildered and confused. But then, realising that he was probably asking too much of Abbie already, he added awkwardly. 'Yes, all right. About six... Thanks, Abbie ... for all your help.'

'Goodnight, Tim,' said Abbie, more firmly than ever. 'Let's hope we have better news tomorrow.' And she turned and went rather swiftly away down the darkening evening street, without looking back.

St. Martin's-in-the-Fields was much the same as ever – dim and cool and rather empty. There were people sitting on the steps outside, as usual, and someone selling copies of The Big Issue, but inside there were few heads – bowed or otherwise – visible among the pews. And none of them was Linda's.

Abbie sighed, and wandered round for a while along the quiet aisles before settling down herself in a nearby wooden pew. I can wait for a while, she thought. It won't do me any harm to sit here and think things out in peace and quiet... And maybe I'll be able to stop minding so much about the whole sorry mess... I can't spend the rest of my life feeling hard-done-by and resentful. It won't get me anywhere – or do those two any good, either...

She sat on, letting the undemanding silence wash over her, and presently found herself almost nodding off in the filtered twilight of the familiar building – for in spite of lecturing herself severely and plying herself with hot drinks and aspirin, she had not slept much last night.

This won't do, she said, sitting up with a start. I won't find Linda or anyone else with my eyes shut! She looked at her watch and decided that she had been sitting still long enough.

Would it be a good idea, she wondered, to go across to the National Gallery and take a quick look in the Rembrandt room...? There was always a chance that Linda might have been in here earlier – or she might have done things the other way round...? Or, of course, she might not have come anywhere near here at all...?

Well, I'd better do *something*, she told herself crossly. Sitting here in a trance will get me nowhere... So she got up and left the echoing aisles of the great church, and crossed the busy street to the National Gallery steps.

There were plenty of people looking at the Rembrandts, but none of them was Linda. Abbie stopped by one of her favourites – the old man as St. Paul – and fell to admiring the quietude and patience of that lit, contemplative face and the folded hands...

There is true humility, she thought wistfully – true submission to the will of God. I wish I had it...! But, when I come to think of it, I'm not sure that Paul had it either! Maybe Rembrandt's model was a gentler man than that fiery saint!

She turned away, unable to bear that luminous resignation, and did not stop to look at all the other blooms and gleams of light in the Rembrandt portraits. I'd better get back to my vigil, she thought, with a sudden sense of urgency. I might miss her altogether, mooning here... Maybe if I go back and sit down to wait again, I'll develop some of that old man's unshaken patience!

She hurried out of the room, out of the building, down the steps, back across the stream of traffic, dodging the buses and taxis, and up the shallow steps of St. Martin's again, and into the quiet gloom within its tall stone walls.

And there she was – the fair head bowed, the slight shoulders stooped in tired despondency, the young, childish arms spread out in front of her on the wooden pew back as a prop for her weary head to lie on ... the picture of a remorseful, grief-stricken girl who knew no way out of her insoluble dilemma. How Rembrandt would have loved to paint her, thought Abbie, watching the gleams of light touch that weary head in the shadows... How he would have revelled in all that dimness and sudden flecks of bright gold... Then she moved quietly across and went to sit beside Linda, taking care not to do anything too sudden, but at the same time blocking her escape.

'I thought I might find you here,' she said.

The blonde head went rigid with shock, and then lifted so that the dilated eyes could stare into Abbie's face. 'You! But how–?'

'You always said you'd come here if anything bad happened,' said Abbie gently. 'Don't you remember?'

But it was clear that Linda *did* remember – why else was she here? And somehow the reminder of those old days of childhood innocence recalled in Abbie's gentle voice utterly overthrew her. 'Oh – *Abbie*–!' she whispered, and put her head down again on her arms and wept.

Abbie let her weep for a while. Maybe it would resolve some of the tension, anyway – and it could do no harm to either of them. But at last she thought it was time to get a few things sorted out before she took the weeping girl back to her frantic Tim – if she would go back.

'Why did you run away?' she asked. 'Was it so bad?'

'Yes, it was,' gulped Linda. 'You *know* it was...' She lifted a swollen, tearstained face to look helplessly at Abbie. 'I just couldn't bear it... I – I told Tim.'

'I know you did. But had you any idea how that little note of yours might be interpreted?'

She looked totally uncomprehending. 'Wh – what?'

'"*I can't bear it!*"' quoted Abbie. 'Don't you see? He thought you might be about to jump off a bridge or something!'

Linda looked appalled. 'I didn't think... I only meant I – I wanted some space ... some time... I didn't see how we could – just ... carry on as if nothing had happened...'

Carry on is right, thought Abbie grimly. But she did not say so. Instead, she went straight into the attack. 'But that's just what I want you to do.'

Linda stared, looking pale and dishevelled, and heart-breakingly young. 'What?'

Abbie tried doggedly to spell it out. 'Linda – Tim is in a wretched state – you are in a wretched state – and it doesn't make me any happier to see you like this. For God's sake, go back and pick the pieces up, and make a go of it together. Otherwise, what was all this upheaval for?'

Linda was struck dumb by Abbie's logic. She had expected all kinds of recriminations and condemnations – but not this cool, fair-minded reason.

'I – do you mean it?'

'Of course I mean it. You and Tim fell in love. It's not the end of the world. People do it all the time!' There was a smile in her voice now, which somehow made Linda's eyes open wider than ever.

'I thought–'

'I know what you thought,' countered Abbie, smiling openly now. 'And you were wrong... As things are, there's only one sensible way out. At least let two of us be happy, even if all three can't.'

Linda shook her head in slow disbelief. 'But you–'

Abbie met her tearful gaze quite calmly and honestly. 'It would never have worked, Linda. I know that now...' She did not add that she now saw Tim in a very different light, and had somehow outgrown him altogether in these last few weeks of soul-searching and growing self-awareness. 'Came the dawn...' she muttered, half aloud, and suddenly wanted to laugh. 'And to tell you the truth,' she admitted, rather more cheerfully than she had expected of herself, 'I wouldn't want him back now if you offered him to me on a plate!' She grinned at Linda's shocked face. 'But don't tell Tim that!' She watched Linda try to take in this latest bit of news, and then went on practically: 'It's just as well we all found out when we did. Imagine my father, if I asked for a divorce!'

At this absurd and frightful picture, even Linda began to laugh.

'That's better,' said Abbie. 'You see? It all makes sense in the end. *But you mustn't spoil*

it, Linda. Grief and guilt are all very well –
but you can't build a future on them.'

Linda looked at her uncertainly. She did
not really know this new, fiercely positive
Abbie – or how to live up to what she was
asking. 'You make me feel ... ashamed,' she
said.

'No.' Abbie was quite definite. 'You've got
to go *past* all that. Be happy. Make Tim
happy. Is that so difficult?'

But this brought a new thought into
Linda's confused mind. 'Where is Tim...?
How did you know about it?'

Abbie sighed with exasperation. Just when
she was getting the child to see reason, she
was off on another tack. 'He came to see me
– at the Travel Agency. He thought you
might have come to me–'

To her surprise, Linda did not look astonished at this. 'I – I probably would have, if I'd
known where to find you,' she whispered.

Abbie nodded, accepting it, but more
touched than she cared to admit. 'He's
pretty desperate, Linda... I think it's time
you put things right between you.'

'*Can we?*' She stared at Abbie, desperately
seeking reassurance, not quite daring to
believe that happiness was something they
either deserved or dared to hope for.

'For heaven's sake' said Abbie, suddenly
losing her temper. 'That's what I've been
trying to tell you – you half-wit! Of course

you can. You *must!*'

And then the two of them looked at each other and began to laugh, and somehow Abbie's arm came round Linda's shoulders and gave her a hard, reassuring hug. 'Come on,' she said, 'Let's go and look at the Rembrandts. And have some lunch. It'll be like old times.'

But she knew, sadly and clearly, that those old times were gone, and would never come again.

Once inside the National Gallery, Abbie managed to telephone Raine Medwin and tell her that Linda had been found safe and well, and to ask her to pass the message on to Tim if he should ring through. She also got hold of Tubby and repeated the same news, adding that if Tim got there first, would Tubby please warn him not to rush things... She was still a little afraid that Linda would take off again if she felt too pressurised.

After that, there was nothing to do but have a very long, slow lunch, a long, slow look at the Rembrandts, and a long slow walk through St. James's Park, before they finally took a taxi down to Tubby's.

They walked into the warm, friendly little café together, and Abbie said urgently in Linda's ear as she saw Tim waiting there: *'Put it together again, somehow. Remember!'*

Then she took Linda over to the table and

113

almost literally handed her to Tim. 'All safe and sound,' she said. 'I'll get us all a coffee.' She turned round then and went back to Tubby's counter, but not before she had seen the relief and gladness in both their faces.

'You OK?' asked Tubby, not for the first time.

'Fazed,' admitted Abbie, grinning. 'But I'll live.'

She gave the other two a few minutes, and then carefully carried the tray of coffee over to them. 'Now, just you listen to me a minute, you two,' she said severely. 'No more cantrips. As my mother would say, you've made your bed – now you must lie on it!' She looked at Linda and began to giggle rather more than she meant to, and Linda, after a moment's confusion, began to giggle too.

'It's hopeless!' said Abbie, wiping her eyes on one of Tubby's serviettes. 'I can't lecture you. For pity's sake, let it all go, and make peace as best you can!'

Tim, understanding that she wanted to make it easy for all of them, lifted his coffee cup in a gesture of hopeful reconciliation, first to Abbie and then to Linda.

'Peace?' he asked.

'Peace,' agreed Linda.

'Peace at any price!' grinned Abbie, lifting her eyes to heaven. 'And now, for God's sake, *go home!*'

And, to his eternal credit, Tim took Linda

114

by the hand and did just that.

Abbie watched them go with an extra-ordinary sense of exhausted relief. Then she put down her cup rather suddenly, and passed out cold on the floor.

During the bumpy plane ride to the hospital on the coast, that veteran traveller Duncan MacNab passed out altogether, and Perry began to get very worried.

He had a long wait at the hospital while the doctors assessed the damage, and then the Senior Registrar came to see him, looking grave but not funereal. Eduardo da Silva was Portuguese – like several of his skilled colleagues who had all stayed on under the new regime, determined to continue their useful work in the big Luandan hospital – but he also spoke excellent English, and he and Perry were old friends who had dealt with several crises before this one in the turbulent history of Duncan MacNab's adventurous life. Now he spoke to Perry in a straight-forward way and did not hide his anxiety.

'His age is against him,' he said. 'And the fact that I suspect he never lets up at all, does he?'

'No,' agreed Perry heavily. 'We all try to take some of the responsibility off his shoulders, but he won't let us.'

Da Silva nodded, smiling. 'So I supposed.' He paused, and then went on to offer a

cautious assessment of his patient's condition and prospects of recovery. His tone
was not sanguine. 'Three fractured ribs, and
one of them dangerously close to punctur-
ing a lung. We may have to operate to repair
that before the lung collapses, but we need
to get the fever down first... The leg
lacerations should heal with antibiotics...
There is a hairline fracture of the skull, but
that will mend in time, given rest and quiet.'
He looked at Perry and sighed. 'But his
general condition isn't all that good, as you
know. He's had a heart condition for some
time – we've treated it before. And it is
always on the cards that an incident like this
could trigger off another heart attack.'

Perry agreed. 'I know – that's what I was
afraid of, really... He's had one or two goes
already, out in the field... He makes light of
it, of course, and says his pills will do the
trick. But–' he sighed and looked at
Eduardo da Silva with a mixture of
resignation and despair, 'I'm afraid we all
know he's living on a knife-edge.'

Eduardo was a kind man, well used to
dealing with the anxieties of the friends and
relatives of his patients. But with Perry, he
knew, soft promises of hope would not do.

'We'll do our best for him,' he said, 'you
know that. For the rest – we must wait and
see.'

Perry accepted this quietly. It was all

anyone could say at present. 'Can I see him?' he asked. 'Is he conscious now?'

'Oh yes.' A faint smile twitched at the corners of the doctor's firm mouth. 'Very much so. He keeps telling us what to do.' He laid a consoling hand on Perry's arm. 'I'll take you along to see him. But don't stay too long, he's very tired.'

Perry found his old friend propped up on pillows, with an oxygen mask to help his breathing, but as soon as he saw Perry, he discarded this, out-of-breath or not, and started scolding.

'Ridiculous – lying here – waste of time – so much to do. Perry, did you leave enough instructions for Jonty and the others?'

'Of course I did,' Perry assured him, making his voice sound as calm and certain as he could. 'Minute detail – for all of them! I sat up all night doing it!' He grinned at Duncan's troubled face. 'Not that they needed it. They've got brains of their own, you know!'

Duncan sighed (though it was more of a gasp) and tried a tired smile. 'You're a good fellow, Perry...' He pulled himself up a little straighter in the bed. 'Something I want to say...' He began, but immediately started to cough. He tried to draw a couple of rasping breaths, and reached out for the oxygen mask again, but after a few minutes' respite, he pushed it aside. 'About the project–'

'Yes?'

'Finish it – whatever happens?'

Whatever happens to you, you mean, thought Perry, riven by his old friend's laboured breathing and evident distress. 'Of course,' he said again, summoning a smile. And when Perry Farquhar smiled, his whole saturnine face lit up with extraordinary sweetness, and his friends usually blinked in astonishment.

But Duncan did not blink. He knew Perry through and through, and he knew his smile. 'That's all right then,' he said, and retreated behind the oxygen mask again.

Perry sat for a while watching him, aware with a sinking heart that his old friend had virtually laid the responsibility of the whole research project on his reluctant shoulders and said an oblique farewell.

He had known Duncan MacNab for twenty years – ever since he was a green young undergraduate studying natural sciences, and Duncan had been his tutor. And his mentor. He had looked up to him then, as had most of Duncan's students, with an admiration bordering on idolatry. That rapturous acknowledgement of the great naturalist's gifts and ability to inspire his young protégés with his own enthusiasm had sobered down over the years into a steadier and more stable regard. But Perry had never lost his admiration for him, and had worked for him tirelessly in pursuing the various conservation projects Duncan had promoted over the years. That he had also come to love him deeply – more-or-less as an all-wise, all-knowing father figure – he had scarcely known or acknowledged even to himself until lately when that long and fruitful relationship had become threatened. Now, he did not know what to say to his old friend, or how to say goodbye – for he felt in his bones that this was probably their last meeting.

'Perry–' said the husky, breathless voice.

'Yes?'

'Thanks–'

'What for?'

'Oh ... *things.*' There was silence between them, and then Perry answered him slowly.

'Reciprocated!'

They smiled at one another.

'Don't ... wait,' said Duncan, rousing himself to one more effort. 'Go home, Perry... Raise the flag... Get that extra cash... Important.'

More important than staying with you? wondered Perry. But Duncan saw that thought in his eyes, and answered it.

'Get your priorities right.'

'Yes,' said Perry, obeying him as usual. He bent his head in a gesture of painful submission, and did not see the flash of something equivalent to tears in Duncan's fierce old eyes.

A hot, feverish hand came out and grasped

Perry's briefly. 'God bless,' murmured the tired voice, with a smile behind it now.

'And you,' answered Perry, and knew that he was dismissed.

He looked back at Duncan once, as he left his bedside, but the weary eyes were closed now, no longer looking at him with fierce, unspoken demands. But the smile still lingered round his mouth and made him look curiously triumphant.

Perry carried that look of secret triumph with him all the way home in the plane, and did not dare to question its significance.

It was several evenings after Tim and Linda had finally gone home before Abbie could summon up the courage to go back to Tubby's and thank him for his help. In truth, she was a little ashamed of her collapse – though he had neither reproached her nor lectured her at the time. He had merely picked her up off the floor, administered brandy and coffee until she was fit to move, and then sent her home with Pauline to escort her safely to her door. Pauline had been unsurprised by anything, and entirely practical. She had steered Abbie up the stairs, put the kettle on and made some tea. Filled a hot bottle (for Abbie was shaking by this time) and ordered her brusquely to bed. And she had even stayed to see that Abbie obeyed her, only clattering away down the stairs when she had actually seen her under the covers.

'Sleep it all off,' she commanded. 'Forget it. Tomorrow is another day.'

Yes, thought Abbie gratefully, tomorrow was another day – and today she felt sufficiently poised and confident to face Tubby's observant gaze and give him the thanks he deserved. She meant to tell him that she had settled into the flat, she was feeling much better, and she would be all right now, thank you. But it didn't turn out quite like that.

'I came in to thank you for all your help,' she began. 'And the flat is very nice – I'm going to be fine up there.'

'That's good news,' said Tubby, and stood for a moment looking down at her, as if making up his mind about something. Then he added suddenly: 'Can I ask you a favour?'

Abbie's eyes went wide with surprise. 'Of course. I owe you more than one, anyway!'

He grinned vaguely at that and waved a dismissive hand. 'No. This is something important.' He hesitated, and then sat down beside her, signalling to Pauline to bring over two cups of coffee. When they arrived, and Tubby had laced his liberally with sugar (which he knew was bad for his figure) he spoke slowly and carefully, as if feeling his way.

'Has it ever occurred to you how many lost and lonely people there are out there?' He waved a hand again, this time at the darkening street outside his door.

'I – er – no,' admitted Abbie, suddenly aware of her own colossal arrogance in thinking she was the only one in the world with such problems. A slow flush of shame touched her pale face, and Tubby did not miss it.

'People come in here...' he said dreamily, 'on the chance... Somewhere warm that looks cheerful – or welcoming...' His voice was curiously soft and spellbinding. 'They sit at a table alone ... they are probably dying for company – someone to talk to – *anyone* – but they are much too shy to speak ... you know?'

'Yes,' Abbie nodded. 'I know.'

'I talk to them sometimes,' he went on, still in that odd, rapt voice. 'If there's time... And young Bobby's quite good at it. Nothing shy about him!'

Abbie smiled. 'So I've noticed!'

'The thing is,' said Tubby, coming to the crux of the matter, 'I – er – have links with a couple of charities...'

'What kind of charities?'

'Oh, people who try to help newcomers to the city–'

'How?'

'Find them somewhere to stay – find them jobs, if they can – *listen* to them. Didn't Raine tell you?'

Abbie looked surprised. 'The same links as Raine Medwin?'

'Yes.' He looked slightly confused.

'Is that what you did for me?' she asked, beginning to bristle.

'No,' said Tubby roundly. 'You *asked* me about a room, remember?'

'So I did,' admitted Abbie, feeling instantly contrite for being so prickly. 'Go on, Tubby.'

He sighed, and tried to explain. 'Well – there's the Missing Persons Bureau – Raine told you about that, I'm sure... The Sally Army are very good with that, and work in with the police when they can – especially in persuading kids to ring home. I expect Raine told you about that, too – she's rather good at it... Parents worry, you know.'

'Yes, they do,' agreed Abbie, ashamed when she thought of the careful restraint in her own mother's voice which could not quite hide the relief and gladness at hearing Abbie on the line... And she began to understand the purpose of Tubby's curious set-up. 'So where exactly do you come in?' she asked.

'Why, right here, don't you see?' Once again he swept a plump hand round at the warm little room. 'All I do is cast an eye over my customers ... find out if they need any help and so on... Sometimes, as I said, they only want someone to talk to...' He looked at Abbie hard. 'And a woman is often easier to talk to than a man...?'

Abbie looked at him in horror. 'What are you suggesting?'

'Think of it,' said Tubby persuasively, 'if you came in here, alone and rather desperate – wouldn't you rather sit at a table with a woman?'

Abbie began to laugh. 'I'd probably rather sit by myself.'

'No, you wouldn't,' Tubby contradicted. 'You'd tell yourself you did. But you'd be longing to make contact with someone – *anyone* who was a fellow human being on this lonely planet!'

Abbie was silent, considering the matter. Hadn't she been lonely enough herself, these last few weeks? And hadn't she been extraordinarily lucky to have been directed here by the brisk and competent Sandra, and to have found Tubby who had solved nearly all her problems in one short evening? Wasn't she even now 'making contact' with a number of fellow human beings...? The Duchess – Synco – Mackintosh and cheerful, cocky Mrs Mac, and shy little Olive Ashridge – not to mention Pauline and Bobby right here...?

'I – I see what you mean,' she said humbly.

'I thought you would.'

She began to think it out. Hadn't Tubby helped Linda and Tim, too?

'What happens if they really do need help in dealing with their problems...? Like Tim and Linda?'

Tubby smiled. 'Raine is a counsellor, you know.'

124

'Is she? How did that come about?'

'I – er – persuaded her that it would be a good idea. She gets a lot of experience from the dating agency, you know – trying to link Mr. Right to Miss Perfect Match.'

Abbie was looking at him curiously. 'How did you get mixed up with all that in the first place?'

Tubby just looked at her and went rather red.

'Tubby – you *didn't?*'

'Of course I did,' he said crossly. 'What you think? Look at me! What chance have I got of finding Love's Young Dream?'

Abbie was relieved to see he was laughing and not at all offended. 'So what happened?'

Tubby's round rosy face suddenly looked immensely sad. 'Nothing!' he said, and shrugged fluid shoulders.

'It didn't work out?'

'She didn't show up.' His voice was flat. 'Or, if she did, she took one look at me and fled.' He grinned sadly at Abbie, like a forlorn clown. 'You know that fat little bloke in the ad, waiting by the clock? That's me!'

'Oh Tubby, no!' said Abbie stoutly defending him (even if he was stout). 'You're much more personable than that!'

'Personable!' crowed Tubby, still laughing. 'I like it!'

'So didn't you try again?' asked Abbie, knowing his resilient, optimistic nature.

'No fear,' said Tubby. 'Once bitten, twice shy! And I mean *shy!*' His grin was entirely without self-pity, and without rancour. 'But I did stay friends with Raine – and between us we set up this – this sort of "contact" network...'

'I see,' said Abbie, as a lot of things that had puzzled her began to fall into place. 'Tell me a bit more about it.'

'Well – Raine did a course in counselling, and I – er – just learnt to keep an eye out for lonely customers! ...The Duchess helps, too.' He glanced at Abbie, hoping she was not going to be prickly again. 'She's lonely, too, you know, Abbie... She misses the theatre, and all her friends in "the profession"... So she goes out of her way to fit people into that house of hers. It's usually crammed to bursting point. You were lucky.'

'I *was*,' agreed Abbie fervently.

'She has Soirées, you know,' Tubby said, grinning even more widely.

'*Soirées?* I thought they went out with Queen Victoria!'

'Oh no,' Tubby informed her gleefully. 'Not in the Duchess's circle! You wait! She asks her old friends to come and sing – or play – or even dance – and asks all of you in the house as well. It's her way of "getting people together," she says. And she'll be mortally offended if you refuse!'

'I wouldn't dare,' said Abbie, laughing.

Tubby glanced at her approvingly. She was really very pretty when she laughed – though she was still a bit too pale and thin for comfort. (His view of comfort!)

'So – will you join us?' he asked, coming back to the point.

Abbie was instantly terrified. 'But I wouldn't be any good! I'm much too shy!'

Tubby shook his head at her. 'Don't under-estimate yourself! Raine was very impressed with the way you handled those two mixed-up friends of yours... So was I, come to that.'

Abbie sighed. 'But I knew them, Tubby. I – I knew what made them tick... It would be different with total strangers.'

'Not very,' said Tubby. 'Most people are alike underneath – when they're up against life's little problems. Just lonely and shy, and desperately wanting someone to tell them what to do!' He grinned hopefully at Abbie. 'Not very unlike your Tim and Linda, is it?'

Abbie had to admit he was right. 'I suppose not... What – what would I have to do?'

'Just *listen*,' said Tubby. 'And remember that they are probably dying to talk to someone, and they are much shyer than you are!' He saw her still hesitating, and added suddenly: 'Abbie – one way to lay one's own ghosts is to tackle other people's.'

Abbie sighed again, and looked at Tubby ruefully. 'You know too much!'

'Sorry,' he said, still with a faint fleck of mischief in his smile. 'But I do speak from experience!'

Abbie stared at him in astonishment. For Tubby was deliberately offering her a confidence. 'Tubby?' She wondered if it would be impertinent to follow it up. 'Were you ever married?'

'Yes,' he said cheerfully. 'Long ago.' He did not sound unduly disturbed at the thought.

'What happened?'

'She went off with a sailor.' He laughed at Abbie's expression. 'Well, what could you expect? Young, slim and handsome in his sailor's blues – romantic shore leave – no more washing up in a grotty café with a fat, dull little man who couldn't dance!'

'*Tubby!*'

'Well, it was true,' he said, fairly.

'Did it last?'

He shrugged. 'No. I don't think so. But she didn't come back.' He sighed – only vaguely sorry about it by now. 'I waited a good while – eventually there was a divorce, for desertion, I think...' He laughed again, 'She was living with a butcher by then. Couldn't keep away from food, could she?' He paused, and then added with serious intent: 'So that was when I tried the dating agency – and met Raine. And that is why I do what I can to stop the rot now!'

'I see,' said Abbie again. And truly she did

see, and looked at Tubby's kind, cheerful face with new eyes.

'Well?' he asked again, his eyes bright with challenge.

'I – if you think I'd be any use...' she began.

But before she could go on, Tubby let out a whoop of approval. 'That's my girl! New recruit! Pauline, what about some of my Special with the chicken casserole?' He beamed happily at Abbie, and did not add that he had also skilfully devised a way to make sure Abbie ate a good hot meal from time to time. (It was Tubby's best way of offering comfort.) 'Not every day,' he allowed, smiling. 'But come when you can. OK?'

'OK,' agreed Abbie, knowing very well that she had allowed one more chink to creep into her armour of lonely pride.

But Tubby knew that too, and he just patted her arm and gave an enormous wink. 'Warriors!' he said. 'It's all the same war!'

And Bobby skidded speedily over to their table with a bottle of Tubby's Special and two glasses, beaming all over his freckled face.

It was the kind of late summer golden weather that made Abbie ache for the harvest fields of home – but at least it meant she could still sit out in the park during her lunch hour and pretend the baked and trodden grass was the burnished stubble of cut corn.

She saw the old man and his white dog several times, and once he came and sat on the next bench, swearing at the dog as usual, and actually gave her a cracked and crooked smile.

'Cantankerous old devil,' he remarked, aiming a half-hearted kick at the luckless dog, who dutifully snarled back. The old man waited to see if Abbie would agree with him, and when she remained silent, added with a malicious grin: 'Like his master.'

Abbie grinned back. 'He probably can't help it,' she said.

The dog's owner let out a dry cackle of laughter. 'Nor can I,' he said, and took out his usual squashed sandwich and began to eat.

'Would you like some of mine?' asked Abbie, holding out her (less squashed) package.

The old man looked at it suspiciously. 'What is it?'

Abbie inspected the sandwiches carefully. 'That one's ham and pineapple, and that's cream cheese and chives.'

'Ho – fancy!' he grunted. But he took a ham one, somewhat grudgingly.

The white dog showed a passing interest in the ham, so Abbie dared to slip him an extra bit of his own. Tubby said *'Listen'* she thought, smiling to herself – not *feed* them! But I'm sure he'd approve. And anyway, he often feeds them himself, doesn't he?

She wondered whether to break into some bright conversation about the weather, and decided not to. The crabbed old man didn't seem the kind of person to suffer fools gladly.

'Silence of the lambs,' he said obscurely, munching his sandwich.

Abbie looked surprised. 'Meaning what?'

'Meaning I like a silent woman,' he said, shooting her a sharp, faintly mischievous glance. 'Even if it is – *threatening*.'

'Threatening? Me? Why?'

His grin was even more malicious than before. 'Girls who pick up old men in the park *are* threatening!'

Abbie laughed. 'You spoke first.'

'So I did,' he admitted. 'More fool me!' But he was still grinning.

'I promise I'm harmless,' said Abbie, and offered the dog her last piece of sandwich.

'That remains to be seen,' growled the old man, and got creakily to his feet. 'Come on, you decrepit old tyke!' and he gave the dog a fierce tug on the lead.

The dog growled vaguely in return, but got to his feet too. He stood there looking up at Abbie with a puzzled stare, and then unexpectedly began to wag his tail.

'What's your dog called?' she asked, at last thinking of what she hoped was an 'un-threatening' topic.

'Spot,' he said flatly. 'Original, isn't it?'

Abbie met the snapping brown eyes and

decided they were much less aggressive than their owner tried to make out. 'See you again then, Spot,' she said, and met another pair of brown eyes that weren't really fierce at all.

'Huh!' retorted Spot's owner. 'Summer won't last for ever!' and he stumped off along the path without looking back.

But Abbie went back to the Travel Agency office smiling a little at the absurd encounter. At least it was a start – she had 'made contact' of a sort.

'What's so funny?' asked Sandra, busily chalking up 'special offers' on the blackboard that went outside the door in the street.

'I met this grumpy old man with his white dog,' she said. 'And his conversation was rather weird.'

'Oh, you must mean The Prof,' said Sandra. 'Yes, he is a bit weird.'

Abbie looked surprised. 'The Prof? Why do they call him that?'

'Because he's supposed to be very clever... Invents crosswords or something. For The Times – or it might be The Telegraph...' She was looking at Abbie with amusement. 'You mean he actually spoke to you?'

'Shouldn't he have?'

'Of course he should,' Sandra said testily. 'He's probably lonely as hell. It's just that he never does – that's all.' She almost glared at Abbie. 'You've had a break-through.'

'Have I?' A thought had been nagging at

Abbie for some time about Sandra, and now she put it into words. 'Sandra – when I was looking for a room, how come you knew exactly where to send me? Are you by any chance one of Tubby's – er – network?'

Sandra's bright, merry glance grew thoughtful. 'You know what it's like in here... We see all sorts... Just now and then, someone comes in on the spur of the moment...Maybe they're in trouble, or had a row with someone, or just plain desperate to get away from boredom...' She looked seriously at Abbie. 'Now and then they tell you about it – mostly they don't...' She shrugged. 'But if I can point them at Tubby's, I usually do.'

Abbie nodded. 'It's everywhere, isn't it?' she said sadly.

'Loneliness? Someone to talk to?' Sandra nodded. 'Universal ailment,' she said. And then looked rather searchingly at Abbie. 'By the way, Maurice was asking about you.'

'What about me?'

Sandra looked almost awkward. 'Well, he works in with a couple of tour operators who specialise in solos–'

'Don't tell me he's a Tubby fringe, too!'

Sandra began to giggle. 'What a prospect! A Tubby fringe!'

'Well, is he?'

'Y-es, sort of.'

Abbie was amazed. 'How on earth far does

Tubby stretch?'

'Two yards and more,' said Sandra, quoting Shakespeare's view of Falstaff, and they giggled even more.

Finally, Abbie grew serious enough to ask a question. 'What about these solo tours?'

'Usually they have their own couriers and tour guides,' Sandra explained, 'But sometimes they ask for someone from this end to accompany the party – especially on coach tours.' She looked at Abbie with faint enquiry.

'So?'

'Maurice wondered ... if you'd be interested in going?'

Abbie stared. 'Where to?'

'Oh, the usual. Not very far flung. Solos are usually a bit timid and – er – conventional.' She grinned. 'Say, Greece ... or the Costas ...or Cyprus... Simple places.'

Simple places! Thought Abbie, who had never been further than France or Germany, and that was on ski-ing trips with Tim and his family, (well chaperoned and well cosseted), and one long holiday in Spain when she was reading languages at college.

'What – what would one have to do? Have you done it?'

'Oh yes,' said Sandra airily. 'Often. But I've got commitments now. It's not so easy to swan off.' She grinned at Abbie. 'Whereas you–?'

Abbie sighed and then had the grace to smile back. 'Whereas I am footloose and fancy free – yes.'

'It's a doddle really,' said Sandra. 'See them on and off things, make sure no-one gets left behind. Usually, you're free during the day while they enjoy the sights or sit on the beach – or you may have to go with them on excursions. And then you meet them in the bar in the evenings and listen to grievances and sort out problems!'

'Sounds fascinating.' Abbie's voice was dry.

'No, really, it's not too bad. And you get a free holiday!' She tilted her head on one side and looked at Abbie, smiling. 'Interested?'

'I – er – I might be.'

'Good,' said Sandra. 'I'll tell him.' She saw the beginnings of panic in Abbie's face, and added: 'It might not be for a while yet, anyway.'

Abbie rubbed a hand over her eyes and said, a little wearily: 'I'm sorry to sound so unenthusiastic ... especially over such a good offer. It's just that ... I need to do things *slowly* at present.'

'I know,' said Sandra cheerfully. 'Not to worry. There's no hurry, is there?'

'No,' agreed Abbie. 'There's no hurry...'

And, indeed, she realised, there was no hurry – not about anything. She could take her time – feel her way – find out what she wanted to do – where she wanted to go...

And meanwhile, she had mysteriously acquired all these unexpectedly watchful good friends to keep an eye on her and tactfully steer her in the right direction. She decided, on thinking about it, that she did not mind their gentle interference at all. In fact, it was rather comforting.

'Nothing to worry about,' said Sandra, breezily stamping a few flight tickets. 'Isn't it nice?'

3. SOLOMON'S GLORY

Behind the Duchess's house on the corner, there was a row of small neighbourhood shops at the top of the parallel street. Abbie was coming back from buying some milk, when she suddenly came across Pauline's boy, Bobby, lying prone on the pavement, with one hand reaching down frantically through the narrow bars of a storm drain, trying to grasp something just out of reach of his desperate fingers.

'Bobby?' Abbie said, stopping to have a look. 'What on earth are you doing?'

The child lifted a grubby, tear-streaked face and regarded Abbie furiously. 'I can't reach it,' he said. 'The blurry thing's gone right down!'

'What's gone down, Bobby?'

'Me money.' Bobby's voice wobbled between rage and tears. 'Me goldfish money.'

'Your *goldfish* money?'

'I got just enough for a tub of fishflakes – and now it's gone and Charlie'll starve! What am I going to do?'

Abbie crouched down beside Bobby and peered through the mud-encrusted bars of the grating. There was nothing visible but an oily sludge of water and some floating leaves. It was clear that the coins – whatever they were – had sunk to the bottom and were gone forever.

'How much was it, Bobby?'

'One pound fifty. I had it in me hand, but someone barged into me and I fell over...' He did not exactly wail, but he was very near it.

'Was it your pocket money?'

Bobby kicked angrily at the drain with one furious foot. 'No. It was what Tubby give me for "waiting".' He looked at Abbie anxiously, as if he thought an explanation was necessary. 'Mum can't run to much pocket money, see – not while my Dad's inside.'

'Inside where?' asked Abbie, who was really very green about Bobby's kind of life. And then she understood, and hastened to make amends for her lack of tact. 'I see – well, how about coming into the pet shop with me, and we'll buy some fish food together.'

Bobby stared at her in disbelief. 'Straight up?'

'Straight up,' said Abbie. 'I can raise one pound fifty.'

They went in together, and Bobby went straight over to the shelf where the fish food was kept. Abbie was slower, and stood looking round her in the gloom. It was a small, shabby pet shop, dark and dusty, with a strong smell of stale food, damp sawdust and caged animals. There was a row of cramped little cages along one wall, containing guinea-pigs, gerbils, hamsters, and some rather lethargic-looking rabbits. Above these were a few wire cages with budgerigars and small finches flitting about rather unenthusiastically in their confined quarters. The whole place somehow smelt of decay and sloppy management, and it made Abbie shiver.

She was just going to join Bobby at the counter, when she saw the bird. It was in a small cage (much too small for its long, slender body and broad tail), hidden away in a narrow, lightless corner, and looking out of its dark prison in an attitude of helpless despair. It stared at Abbie out of its strange, dark eyes, and something about its anguished glance seemed to pierce her. *'Help!'* it seemed to say to her. *'Please, help…! Get me out of here!'*

She went a bit closer to have a look. The gently curving back and sturdy tail seemed to be a greenish-black colour, with a half-hidden sheen of blue within it which only became apparent when it moved. Its head was crowned with a thick, long-shaped crest of very fine, dense feathers, almost like close-cut hair, of a brilliant red. At least, Abbie thought, it was *meant* to be brilliant, but it was somehow dimmed and travel-stained with dust and grime. The face-feathers began with a pale soft grey surrounding a curious ring of orange round the eyes, and shaded towards gold and then to reddish brown on the rounded breast. The folded wings reflected the same iridescent blue-green sheen as the tail, but Abbie thought there was a glimpse of scarlet flight feathers folded neatly away underneath. It was a beautiful bird – beautiful and caged, and desperately sad.

'What kind of bird is that?' asked Abbie, looking across the dim room at the pet shop owner. He was a smallish, baldish man, with a surly mouth and quick, nervous eyes.

'I – uh – it's African,' he said, and stopped there, as if he had said enough.

'Yes?' Abbie was still only mildly enquiring. 'Where from in Africa? Hasn't it got a name?'

The man looked sulkier than ever. 'The – client who brought it in said it was a kind of turkey... He called it a Turkey-Crow.'

Abbie looked unimpressed. 'It doesn't look anything like a turkey. Are you sure it isn't an endangered species? I've never seen one like it before.'

'No, it's not,' snapped the man crossly. 'It's a Turkey-Crow. He told me.'

Abbie shook her head. 'I've never heard of it... And the cage is *much* too small for it. Can't you find a better one?'

The pet shop owner moved grumpily over to his till behind the counter and glared down at Bobby. 'And what do *you* want?'

'A tub of goldfish flakes,' said Bobby promptly, offering the round carton of fish food for his inspection. 'The–' he looked round for Abbie anxiously, 'the lady says she'll pay... My money rolled down the drain.'

'Oh yes?' said the shopkeeper, disbelief in every pore.

'It did. Honest,' protested Bobby, and turned beseeching eyes on Abbie.

'It's true,' she said, smiling, and handed over the money to the suspicious trader. 'And what about that cage?'

The man took the money ungraciously, and turned away to his till, snarling over his shoulder: 'If you're so bothered about the bird, why don't you buy it?'

Abbie sighed. 'I would if I could. But a small flatlet wouldn't be much better than this – and anyway, I don't think pets are allowed.'

'Pity,' said the man. 'So, if you can't take it off my hands, suppose you stop telling me what to do?'

There was no answer to that, Abbie knew, and she made no attempt to reply. But she went back to have one more look at the sad, lonely bird before she left the shop. The dark, gold-rimmed eyes were still regarding her with desperate appeal. She felt the shock of their terrible sadness hit her like a physical blow – and she stooped nearer to meet that accusing stare with a sorrowful one of her own.

'I'm sorry, bird,' she whispered. 'I'll try to do what I can...' She looked back at the petshop keeper and said warningly: 'I think the R.S.P.C.A. ought to know about this.'

The man scowled in response, shrugged his shoulders, and turned away. And Abbie, almost reluctantly, turned her back on the bird in his dark corner, and followed Bobby out of the shop.

But all the way back up to her room, the bird's dark, despairing gaze stayed with her, and would not be dismissed.

In the morning when she got to work, Abbie rang the R.S.P.C.A. about the bird, and asked them to take whatever action they could – and at least insist on a bigger cage. They promised to go and have a look, and if they found that it was an endangered species, or needed special expert attention, they'd contact their colleagues at the R.S.P.B.

It was the best Abbie could do for the moment, and she gave a small sigh of relief as she put down the phone. But at the back of her mind she still felt the tug of despairing sadness that the bird had somehow laid on her heart, and she knew she had not done enough.

'Cheer up,' said Sandra. 'You've done what you could. It's out of your hands now.'

But somehow it wasn't out of her hands, and she knew it. That soundless cry for help still rang in her ears – or in her heart.

She had almost reached home that evening when a breathless, even more tear-streaked Bobby ran up to her, spilling out bad news.

'Oh, Abbie – I bin waiting for you – I done somethink awful!' He clutched desperately at her arm.

Abbie looked down at the tearful, freckled face, and saw that the small boy was really upset about something. 'What have you done, Bobby?'

'It's the bird, Miss – the poor bird.' In his distress he was confusing Abbie with the teacher he was always trying to explain things to, and always getting it wrong.

'The bird?' said Abbie sharply. 'What bird?'

'You know the one, Miss – the one you was worried about... I thought it would be all right, see – I thought it would know what to do – but it didn't.'

'*Bobby!* What have you done?'

'It was the man in the shop,' Bobby began again, half-crying with fright and hiccupping at every other word. 'He said he was going to wring its neck – it was only trouble, he said, and he put it out in the shed at the back so's the inspector wouldn't see it – stuck it in a sack, cage and all – I *saw* 'im!'

Abbie only just refrained from shaking him. 'Go on, Bobby. What did you do?'

'I waited till he'd gone inside,' said Bobby, between gasps, 'and then I went into his shed and undid the cage and – and sort of *let him go.*' He looked at Abbie with wide, shocked eyes, aware of the enormity of his crime, and suddenly began to weep in earnest. 'But he wouldn't go,' he wailed. 'He just stood there – as if he didn't know what to do – as if his wings wouldn't work... So I – I sort of gave him a shoo and a little push...' He turned to Abbie piteously. 'I thought he'd fly off and be h-happy-ever-after – but he only got as far as the tree.'

'Which tree, Bobby? Where did he go?'

'Up there!' said the child, pointing upwards at the old city plane tree on the corner. 'He's up there – sort of stuck – and the other birds are setting on him!'

And indeed, as Bobby pointed and Abbie peered upwards, confused clapping of wings and squawking of raucous birds' voices broke out overhead.

'What shall we do?' cried Bobby. 'How can

we get him down?'

'I don't know,' Abbie said, 'but we'll <u>have</u> to. He'll die out there in the cold. He's not used to English nights.'

Bobby let out a louder wail. 'I didn't want him to die!'

'No, of course you didn't,' said Abbie crossly, wondering whether she ought to send for the fire brigade with a ladder. The fine old tree was much too tall to climb.

But as she peered upwards again, trying to spot the bird among the leafy branches, a renewed uproar of scolding birds' voices broke out, and a long, blue-black shadow with a flash of crimson flight feathers launched itself out of the tree in a downward glide, pursued by a trailing mob of angry pigeons and magpies, all flapping and shouting together.

'He's going on to the roof!' yelled Bobby. 'Look! He's landed up there!'

'Come on,' ordered Abbie, and grabbed him by the hand. 'Upstairs – quick! They'll kill him if we don't stop them!'

Together they pounded up the stairs and into Abbie's front room, and across to the window that looked out on to the flat roof. Sure enough, there was a crumpled heap of a bird crouched down near the far edge of the little lead-roofed extension, and what seemed like a whole flock of angry pigeons and screaming magpies dive-bombing the stunned bird as it lay there.

'I'll get him!' said Bobby, starting to climb out of the window.

'No, you won't, Bobby – you stay there!' commanded Abbie. 'It's much too dangerous. I'll go carefully. See if you can find something to wrap him in when I get him back.'

She left the frightened small boy casting round the room for a bit of blanket, while she cautiously climbed out of the window onto the small lead roof.

I hope it'll bear my weight, she thought. I'd hate to fall through on to the César Franck girls...! The thought made her smile a little, and somehow steadied her nerves. She decided it was safer to crawl forward on hands and knees rather than try to stand up, and she did so, with painful slowness, torn between a desire to rescue the bird with all possible speed and an equally urgent certainty that she must not frighten it still further, in case it took off again.

The squawking overhead diminished a little as the other birds saw her coming, but the flurry of wings persisted all round her, and made her feel dizzy and insecure. At last, she reached the pitiful mound of feathers, fending off a couple of more audacious pigeons with an uplifted arm as she came near enough to grasp the helpless bird.

Carefully, she put out a hand and touched

the silken curve of its back, and finding that it made no resistance, gathered it close against her, cradled in one arm, while she turned round with painful slowness and began to crawl back towards the window.

'It's all right, bird,' she said aloud. 'You're safe now... I'll take care of you... Bobby didn't mean any harm...'

She went on talking to it softly as she edged her way back to safety, and finally reached the window, leaving the furious wing-beats of the pigeons behind her. The bird did not stir against her arm, but lay there, limp and silent, with its beautiful crested head lying helpless and uncaring against her shoulder.

'Careful!' said Bobby. 'Give him to me.'

But Abbie just shook her head and somehow climbed in through the open window without dropping the bird on the floor.

'A cardboard box,' she said, looking round at her all-too-tidy room. 'That's what we need...' Then she remembered the geraniums that little Miss Ashridge had given her... They had been in a fairly strong box. 'Over there!' she directed. 'Behind the bookcase. Bring it over, will you?'

The box was still full of crumpled newspaper, and, under Abbie's instruction, Bobby laid the piece of blanket on top of them.

'That will have to do for now,' said Abbie. 'What the poor thing needs most is rest and quiet...'

Gently, and with infinite caution, she laid the exhausted bird down in its makeshift bed. An extraordinary feeling of latent power had assailed her as she held the bird in her arms – seeming to flow from the beautiful, frightened creature to her in a stream of strange warmth and recognition, almost as if they had known and loved each other from the first moment of their meeting – or even long before – and now Abbie stood looking down at it anxiously, in a mixture of fear and admiration. Was it injured by its precarious flight, she wondered? Or so badly frightened that it would die of shock? Or had the other birds damaged it with their vicious beaks?

The delicate, crested head lay passively still, the curved back and folded wings glimmering with their special blue-green iridescence, the long, broad tail spread out behind it – but though it did not move, Abbie thought it was not in pain, just very tired.

'Let's cover it up and let it go to sleep,' she said to Bobby. 'I think it would rather be left alone,' and she laid her own silk scarf over it, and tiptoed away.

'Will it be all right?' asked Bobby, large-eyed and subdued after his own fright.

'I hope so,' Abbie answered. *'Oh, I hope so!* If it seems worse, I might have to take it to the vet in the morning...'

'I'm sorry, Abbie,' said the small, contrite

boy. 'I only wanted to help.'

'I know,' Abbie told him soothingly. 'I know you did... But what were you doing there in the first place?'

'I only went to have another look,' he said, ''cos I knew you was worried about the bird...'

Abbie nodded. She understood well enough the compulsion that the strange bird seemed to put on them. What she didn't know, though, was what on earth she was going to do with it now she had got it in her care. Still, she would deal with that when she had time to think. The best thing now was to let the bird rest – and wait to see whether it would recover before making any more plans.

'I think you'd better go home now, Bobby,' she said. 'Your Mum will be wondering where you are.'

He agreed quite readily now that the crisis was over. 'But you will tell me how he is, won't you?' he asked, his eyes still anxiously fixed on her face.

'Of course I will. Now go on home and stop worrying...! I'll come into Tubby's tomorrow, and tell you all the news. Will that do?'

'Brill,' said Bobby, his naturally cheerful disposition beginning to re-surface. 'See you tomorrow,' and he skipped happily away down the stairs.

But Abbie turned back and sat down by the bird, prepared for a long, anxious vigil.

All that evening and late into the night, the bird did not stir. Abbie, sitting patiently beside it, wondered once or twice if it had died of shock and fright, but when she leant close and laid a hand on its smooth feathers, its body felt warm under her fingers, and she could feel its brave heart beating. She had been afraid it would be cold during the long, dark night, so she had filled a hot bottle and wrapped it in an old jersey – tucking it down under the blanket so that its warmth would rise up and comfort the stricken creature.

She remembered that she had reared a baby blackbird once – against everyone's warnings and predictions. It had fallen out of its nest, and lay there, cold and half-naked on the spring grass. Abbie had used a hot bottle to keep it warm, and settled it in a kitchen colander lined with hay. She had fed it on bread and milk, and tiny drops of brandy, she remembered, and contrary to everyone's expectations, it had thrived... It used to go to sleep in her hair, she recollected, convinced that it was safely enfolded in the comforting protection of a mother's wing...

But she couldn't do that with this strange, exotic creature. It was too big, for one thing, and much too frightened... And what did it eat? Not bread and milk, probably. But with that beak – a softbill, didn't they call it? – it wouldn't be seeds or nuts – and the bird seemed too large for an insect eater. Then it must be fruit, she thought – and tried frantically to remember what she had got in her cupboard... Raisins, she thought, sultanas? But they ought to be soaked first... Grapes, certainly – there were some on the table, and apples...? It would have to do for a start... And it would want water, wouldn't it, as soon as it recovered? If it recovered.

She sat on through the night, dozing in her chair, and towards morning, when the light was beginning to grow in the sky, she heard a faint rustling, and the bird began to move. The covering silk scarf slid off, and beneath it the beautiful crested head lifted, the dark, golden-ringed eyes opened and began to take in this new prison.

At least there aren't any bars – yet, thought Abbie. But she knew she couldn't let the bird go free. It would have to be caged somehow.

Now, she told herself sternly, now is the time to look at its injuries and find out what must be done... She had often helped her mother to examine one or other of the hens who had flown into some wire, or been attacked by a cat. She knew what to do for them... Would this bird be so different?

Gently, she laid both hands round its wings, holding them close, and lifted it out on to her knee. The bird's crested head came round to look at her, the body went a little stiff with alarm, but it did not struggle.

'It's all right, bird,' she said, crooning at it softly as she worked to check each leg and each toe... Nothing wrong there, but she noticed with interest that the bird had one reverse toe on each foot, to make it easier to grasp the small branches of the trees it ought to be living in.

'That's a clue, bird,' she told it. 'I shall soon be able to tell you who you are. But you know that already, don't you? It's only the stupid human beings who are ignorant...'

Carefully, she drew out each perfectly-shaped wing to its full length, marvelling at the brilliant red of its primary leathers beneath the glossy sheen of close blue-green plumage where it joined the sturdy back... No problem here either, she thought, with a sigh of relief. For a broken wing would have been painful and difficult to mend, she knew, and very often led to infection and even to death.

She turned the bird over in her hands to look at the golden-brown breast – and here there were a few torn feathers and one or two pecks from angry beaks that had drawn blood. Nothing was bleeding now, though, and she thought a gentle wash with mild disinfectant might be enough for the moment.

'You've been lucky, bird,' she said, smiling a little, and dared to lay one caressing finger on the crested head. 'But what you really need is a bath... A nice tropical rainstorm would do – but since I can't provide that, maybe a flower spray would help...'

She went on holding the bird between her hands for a few more moments, and then, satisfied that she could find no more injuries, she laid it gently back in its box. The sculptured scarlet head turned again to look at her, the eyes dark and unblinking but somehow – she fancied – no longer afraid, no longer assailing her with their desperate despair...

'Maybe you'll get used to me,' she told it softly. 'Maybe you'll find I'm not so bad... If only I can find a way to make you more comfortable, and give you more room to spread your beautiful wings – even if I can't set you free.'

It occurred to her then that the bird might be ready to drink, so she went over to her little sink and filled a small sugar bowl with water and placed it close to the bird inside the cardboard box. She also brought over a few grapes, and waited to see what would happen.

I must get help for it soon, she thought. As soon as everyone wakes up. Should I take it to the vet, I wonder? Or won't that frighten it even more...? And oughtn't I to tell the petshop owner...? (Even if he did mean to wring its neck!)... And how can I get the bird a big enough cage?

Mackintosh! She thought suddenly. He knows about pigeons, he told me so... And he probably wakes up early to stoke the boiler... He'll know what to do. I'd better go and see if he's up yet.

She took one more look at the bird, and saw that two of the grapes had already gone. 'That's good, bird,' she said. 'At least I've found out what you like to eat...' and she fetched one or two more grapes from the bowl on the table. 'I won't be long,' she told it. 'Don't be afraid... You're all right here.' And she covered it up again with the silk scarf, hoping it would settle down. Then she hurried downstairs to look for Mackintosh.

She found the old man stooping over his old-fashioned boiler and stirring the embers with a long-handled poker. Breathlessly, she explained about the bird, and the difficulty she was in, and what she had tried to do for it so far.

Mackintosh listened to her patiently, and then he laid down his poker, shut the boiler door, and said: 'I'd better come and see.' Then he led her back to his own rooms for a moment, pausing to mutter something to Mrs Mac, who was cheerfully banging about in the kitchen and singing 'Over the rainbow' in a cracked, optimistic voice.

'Used to keep birds,' he said to Abbie, coming out with a bottle of hydrogen peroxide and a wad of cotton wool in his hand. 'See what we can do.'

Together, they washed the bird's cuts and scratches, teasing out the tangled feathers, and Mackintosh produced a small pair of tweezers from his pocket to pluck out any broken ones, for – he explained – they were better removed before they caused any infection. 'Ought to give it a dusting of penicillin powder,' he added. 'Got some downstairs... But we'd better finish cleaning it up first.'

'I wondered if we could use my flower spray...?' asked Abbie.

'Good idea. Gentle. Not enough to startle it – or make it cold.'

They worked cautiously and slowly, and were both astonished at the amount of dirt and dust that came off its feathers on to the cotton wool.

'The poor creature,' said Mackintosh. 'Almost choked to death with London grime. Didn't that man know anything?'

Abbie shook her head sadly. 'Not much, I think.'

'What did he call it? A *turkey?*'

'Turkey-Crow, he said.'

'There's no such thing,' stated Mackintosh. He looked at the bird again, more attentively. It was looking much better, the iridescence on its tail and back shone in the light, and all the blues and greens and fiery reds of its plumage glowed with a new, luminous brightness.

'You're a mystery, bird,' she told it. 'But we'll find out...'

'I've got a book,' said Mackintosh. 'I'll look it up.' He pondered for a moment, and then added quietly: 'But first I think we'd better tell the Duchess.'

'Will she be up yet?'

Mackintosh laughed. 'You don't know the Duchess. She goes jogging in the park every morning – before breakfast.'

Abbie was astonished. 'Amazing!'

'It's her training,' explained Mackintosh. 'Stage people like to keep in trim.' He grinned at Abbie kindly. 'I'll go and fetch her – she won't bite!' He put out a gentle hand and touched the bird. 'You'll do now... Abbie'll look after you.'

Then he went downstairs to look for his employer.

The Duchess, when she came, was wearing a shocking pink tracksuit, purple trainers, and a purple turban to match. She did not seem in the least out of breath – either from her jogging or from climbing three flights of stairs. She stood for a while contemplating the bird in silence, and then said with humorous compassion: 'My poor bird. All that finery – all that splendour – and no one to see it. I know the feeling!'

Abbie looked at her and smiled. Her landlady was an ally after all.

'Mackintosh,' said the Duchess. 'You could rig up a cage, couldn't you?'

'I daresay I could,' agreed Mackintosh, carefully not sounding too eager.

'Free-standing. With a floor,' added the Duchess.

Mackintosh nodded. 'Temporary. No mess.'

Abbie hardly dared to breathe. 'You mean – I can keep it?'

'If you know how,' countered the Duchess. 'For the time being,' she added. 'Unless you want to take it to the zoo?'

'I don't want to,' admitted Abbie. 'But – but maybe I ought to?'

The Duchess and Mackintosh looked from the bird to Abbie, and then at each other, exchanging silent messages.

'It seems all right with you,' admitted Mackintosh, who understood birds. 'Another move so soon might kill it.'

The Duchess nodded briskly. 'That's settled then.' She turned to Abbie, smiling. 'What are you going to call it?'

Abbie hesitated. 'I – I hadn't really thought... I don't even know if it's male or female!'

'What do you think, Mackintosh?'

'I'm not very good at sexing birds,' said

Mackintosh cautiously. 'But I'd say it was male.'

The Duchess nodded. 'Those bright colours!'

'But in some breeds the female is as bright as the male,' admitted Mackintosh, showing off what knowledge he had.

'Bobby called it a "he",' murmured Abbie.

'Kids' instincts are often right,' stated Mackintosh weightily. 'Well then, Abbie–?' prompted the Duchess. 'What's it to be?'

'It would have to be Solomon,' said Abbie slowly. 'Not because he's all that wise (though he may be), but–'

'*Solomon in all his glory was not arrayed like one of these!*' quoted the Duchess, in her most musical and compelling stage voice. 'And if he turns out to be a girl, you can call him Lily!'

They grinned at one another. And if Mackintosh failed to understand the allusion to lilies, he did not say so. 'Well, we did wash him first,' he said, smiling, 'so I suppose he's been christened.'

'Splendid!' The Duchess beamed and turned to the bird with ceremony. 'Welcome aboard, Solomon.' She struck a fine theatrical pose and lifted up her strong stage contralto in instant song. 'Consider yourself at home. Consider yourself one of the family!'

The bird turned its scarlet-crested head from side to side as if listening to her voice, and then it uttered a low, soft-toned murmur – something between a dove's gentle coo and a blackbird's fluting whistle. It was the first sound it had made during all its traumatic ordeal, and the Duchess was delighted. Abbie was, too, and took it as a good omen.

'I think he approves,' she said. 'Don't you, Solomon?' Then the Duchess went downstairs to have her breakfast, and Mackintosh hurried after her in search of chicken wire and a hammer.

It was still quite early in the morning when Mackintosh came back to start on the cage, but Abbie was already beginning to worry about going to work and leaving the bird alone. I'll have to ring Sandra, she thought, and arrange to do an extra day instead later in the week. The Travel Agency worked on a system of rotas so that it was open six days a week – thereby not losing the Saturday trade, and Abbie took her weekend turn with Sandra and Maurice, and got given a weekday off in lieu. It was a flexible arrangement, and one that gave everyone a chance to fulfil the other commitments of their lives. Abbie thought Sandra would not mind a change of plan, just this once...

'You are a commitment, Solomon, do you know that?' she said to the bird, and smiled when the beautiful head lifted at the sound of her voice.

Mackintosh, unrolling chicken wire, began to laugh. 'That tree you've got,' he said, gesturing at the tall, thin weeping fig tree in a terracotta pot that Abbie had put in one corner of her living-room, 'we could put it inside the cage – and add an extra tough branch or two to perch on – the bird would like that.'

'Good idea,' agreed Abbie. 'He must be a forest bird, I think, if he is a fruit eater.'

The old man put down his hammer for a moment. 'I brought the book,' he said, producing it from his pocket. 'I can't see anything like him among the ordinary Cage Birds. But there's something here, at the end, among the Rare Exotic Birds...It's not the right colour – but could he be a *Turaco?*'

Abbie stared. 'That would account for the name *Turkey-Crow*...The man obviously got it wrong.'

'See here,' said Mackintosh, pointing with a stubby finger, 'there's a White-cheeked Turaco – it's not that, and a Hartlaub Turaco with a *blue* crest. They both come from Africa – and there's a Great Blue Turaco... There's more than likely other varieties, too... It's sort of the right shape, though the colours are too pale and green...What do you think?'

'I think you're probably right,' said Abbie. 'But which variety is Solomon?' Mackintosh shook his head. 'You need an expert there.'

'Well, at least we've established *something*,' approved Abbie. 'And they are fruit eaters. It says so.'

'And they're not endangered,' added Mackintosh, 'at least, not yet... Though it says: *"Rare Breeders. Imports getting scarce."*'

'That reminds me,' Abbie said, knowing she could expect the practical old man to give her a sensible answer, 'what ought I to do about the petshop owner?'

Mackintosh gave a vicious twist to a corner of wire. 'Leave him to me. I know that bloke. He's been in trouble before for neglecting his animals... I'll see what he has to say, and report back to you, shall I?'

'That would be fine,' said Abbie. 'I ought to pay him something. The bird is probably very valuable.'

Mackintosh snorted. 'I'm not so sure about that. We'll see. He'll probably be glad to have you take it off his hands – at the price he paid for it, and no questions asked!' He went on quietly working at the cage, and presently went off to look for a couple of extra branches to use as perches. 'Got some in the boilerhouse,' also promising to bring up the penicillin powder on his way back, 'used it on my budgies when they had a fight.'

The bird had remained very quiet all through these preliminaries, and showed no inclination to move out of its cardboard box yet, though Abbie fancied the set of its

160

elegant head grew more alert and aware of its surroundings as time went by. And when Mackintosh returned with the penicillin powder, it allowed Abbie to lift it up and hold it firmly in her hands while the protective antibiotic powder was dusted on to all the small punctures and scratches.

'I've been thinking,' said Mackintosh, 'we could rig up a bit of an aviary with a flight path outside along the flat roof – if we could back the cage up against the window, so that it could get in and out...'

'Wouldn't it be too cold for it?'

'Not yet awhile. It's pretty near summer temperatures still. But it would have to come in at night.'

'How would I catch it?'

'You wouldn't have to. It'd come in of its own accord. Birds are sensible creatures.' He paused, considering the matter. 'But you'd have to keep it inside in the winter.'

He went over to have a look at the window. It had two opening panes, each with its own old-fashioned fastening. Either of them would give the bird enough room to go in and out, if the two wire cages were lined up so that the openings could be made to coincide.

'It would spoil your view a bit,' said Mackintosh. 'All that wire mesh...'

'I wouldn't mind that,' Abbie told him, 'if it made the bird happy.'

'...And we'd have to ask the Duchess.'

'Of course.'

They grinned at one another. 'I'll see to it,' said Mackintosh. 'Won't be for a day or two. Give him time to get used to this one first.'

He went on fixing the cage, its wooden framework and its plywood floor, the sturdy, branched perches, and Abbie's tree placed firmly in one corner. And at last came the moment when he said triumphantly:

'There. How does that suit?'

'It looks absolutely splendid,' said Abbie. 'He won't know himself with all that space!'

'Shall we try him in it?'

'D'you think he's ready?'

Mackintosh inspected the bird with an experienced eye. 'Seems all right to me.'

'Well then,' said Abbie, 'why not?' And she lifted the bird out of the box, held him for a moment in her hands so that the firm, warm body could feel safe and protected, and then set him down carefully on the floor of the new cage.

'Put some water in,' counselled Mackintosh. 'And some fruit. Make him feel at home.'

Abbie did as she was told, and then stood back to see what would happen next. Mackintosh softly closed the door of the cage, and also stood back to watch.

For a few moments, the beautiful bird did nothing at all. Then it took a few hesitant

162

steps towards the fruit on the floor, picked up one grape in its beak, and flew up to the nearest perch under the leaves of Abbie's fig tree.

'Perfect!' murmured Abbie.

'He'll be all right now,' agreed Mackintosh.

And Solomon, looking out at them from the safety of his concealing leaves, uttered another small crow of quiet approval.

Perry hated London. After the green, remote fastnesses of the Angolan forest – the tall trees – the rich river banks – the bejewelled forest clearings full of flowers – and no sound except the calling of birds and chattering of monkeys among the branches – this great, teeming city seemed to him full of noise and choking fumes and ceaselessly hurrying people. He never stayed there longer than he could help, but now, he knew, he had got to go round on the money-raising circuit and fulfil his promise to Duncan.

Duncan. The anxiety that had lain at the back of his mind all the way home surfaced again, and he determined to try to get through to the hospital in Luanda as soon as was reasonably practicable. Communications were apt to be difficult, he knew, but he had to try.

He went first to his club. It was an old-fashioned place, and most of its furniture and its members were far too old, but it suited Perry. It was neutral, it was central, and no one bothered him much – or even recognised him, except the porter, Stevens, who had been there for years.

'Good evening, Dr. Farquhar. It's good to see you back.'

Perry smiled. 'Hallo, Stevens. Same old place, same old people?'

'Much the same, sir,' Stevens grinned back. 'New carpets in the bar.'

'Progress!' said Perry. 'This I must see!'

But he didn't. He went up to his room and put a long-distance call through to Luanda. They said (as usual) that there might be some delay. He was used to that out in the field, with the rest of the team, the only means of communication was by radio. It didn't always work, and there wasn't always anyone listening, but they survived on the whole, and usually succeeded in raising someone on the air-waves if they persisted long enough... There was no way he could reach them from here, though. If the news about Duncan was bad, he couldn't tell them. They would have to find out for themselves.

The phone rang, while he was still worrying uselessly about the exchange of news, and after a bit of argument, he succeeded in getting hold of Eduardo da Silva in person.

'He's holding his own,' said the doctor's

cautious voice. 'That's all I can say... We had to operate to mend that lung when it collapsed. I have to admit it was dicey, with the condition he's in, and the heart did play up a bit... But he's resting now, and he seems a little stronger today.'

'Good,' said Perry, not missing the lack of optimism in the quiet voice.

'Is he conscious? Tell him I called.'

'Of course,' agreed da Silva, and then, as if compelled to utter a warning to that anxious caller on the line: 'Perry–'

'Yes?'

'Don't hope too much.'

'No,' said Perry heavily. 'No, Eduardo. I know the score... Just – give him my love.'

'Will do.'

'I – I'll call again in a day or two, shall I?'

'Yes. Do that. And leave your number with us, will you?'

The bleak exchanges covered a multitude of emotions: on Perry's side, fear and dread, and the sorrowful knowledge that a lifetime's friendship might be at an end; on da Silva's side, the perennial sadness of a good doctor who knows he cannot work miracles.

'Bless you, Eduardo, I know you're doing your best,' said Perry, suddenly choked with unwanted tears, and rang off before he made more of a fool of himself.

A drink, he said, swallowing hard. Better go down and inspect the bar. There's nothing more I can do tonight.

He went down to a new carpet that was rather too red and too thick, and ordered himself a Scotch.

'Perry,' said a voice. 'Back from the wilds? Where've you been this time?'

'Angola,' said Perry, turning round to see who it was who remembered him. Not many did these days, he came home so seldom.

'Panky!' he said, recognition suddenly dawning. 'Monty Pankhurst!'

'In the flesh. Very,' agreed Panky, grinning.

In fact, it was true. Monty Pankhurst – known among his more facetious friends as 'Hanky Panky' – was a big, fleshy man, more than a little overweight and more than a little slow moving in consequence. But his mind wasn't slow moving at all. He was reputed to have a phenomenal grasp of high finance and many interests 'in the city,' but in spite of these preoccupations with wealth and high-powered transactions; he was a curiously unpretentious and kindly man.

'You're just the man I need,' said Perry. 'I have to raise a lot of money rather fast.'

'Don't we all!' said Panky, swirling his gin-and-tonic round in his glass. And then, with a gleam of mischief in his small observant eyes, he added:

'Tell me more.'

So Perry told him about the Research Project – Duncan's dream of cataloguing all the flora and fauna in those fast-disappearing fragments of forest before it was too late, and the faithful team who were struggling to fulfil his hopes but were fast running out of money ... and the catastrophic attack by the unknown night marauders who had done so much damage.

'And Duncan was hurt? Badly?'

'Yes, I'm afraid so.'

Panky looked at him hard. 'Prognosis not good?'

Perry sighed. 'He has always been a fighter ... but–'

'But?'

'It's all the more imperative that I get the cash-flow problem sorted out. He put me in charge.'

Panky nodded. 'I see.' He thought for a moment. 'How have you been funded up to now?'

'Duncan had a research grant from his own university. And he got a small one from the Angolan authorities – only they haven't really any money to spare, not since the civil war. But they are quite keen to set up another wildlife sanctuary and a captive breeding programme, if Duncan can arrange to train enough people locally... They know very well the forests are disappearing, but they can't stop the timber trade, or the clearance of land...' He shook his head sadly. 'Funds are strictly limited – there is so much re-building to do, and it is too early to expect them to think of a tourist trade bringing in money from wildlife projects. People must come first... And the oil revenue is mortgaged!'

Panky's glance was shrewd. 'Any help from other sources?'

'Oh yes. The Portuguese have an interest – especially as they are helping with the land revival project... And one of the timber companies actually contributed something. They wanted to improve their image!'

Panky laughed. 'Will they renew?'

'I think so – if pushed.' He rubbed a tired hand over his hair. 'And there's a pharmaceutical company that helped. They are interested in Judy's research into medicinal plants. I think they will come up with a bit more. But all the amounts are small.'

'Where did the rest come from?'

'Mostly out of Duncan's own pocket ... and certain friends of his at home.'

'Will they stump up again?'

'I don't know...' Perry sounded doubtful. 'I think some of them are dead!'

Panky's sharp little laugh broke out again. 'How did Duncan get mixed up with Angola anyway? It's not the easiest of countries to get into, is it?'

'You can say that again!' admitted Perry. 'As a matter of fact, it was Judy – our botanist – who began it. She went out with an Aid team to advise on crop management during the famine... Self-help, really, in a land so ravaged by civil war that nothing was growing anywhere. Whole communities had fled, leaving the land untilled, and so on... Judy was good at sustainable crops, and also got interested in the natural resources of the forest areas... Paul was good on pest control. Jonty advised on the most hardy and productive livestock and so on...'

'And you?'

Perry shrugged. 'Reliable strains of poultry,' he said, grinning. 'They'd lost almost all their stock. Those that didn't get eaten died of starvation anyway.' He gave Panky another fleeting grin. 'They weren't very interested in their rare wild birds – unless they were eatable!'

Panky nodded. 'So ... how did the research programme manage to change to conservation?'

'Oh, by slow stages. We still do our main work for the food chain. We wouldn't be allowed to stay otherwise. But then Duncan sort of ... branched out.'

Panky laughed. 'I can imagine.'

'The authorities trusted him by then – even admired his work – though rather grudgingly, and the U.N. peace-keeping force kept a fatherly eye on the project.

After all, it may be a source of wealth to them one day, and Duncan is – er – very persuasive...'

'I'll bet.'

'Besides,' added Perry soberly, 'it's a threatened environment. Duncan loves a challenge.'

Panky agreed. He knew Duncan of old. 'How much longer do you need out there?'

Perry shrugged. 'As long as it takes... No, I should think another six months might do it. That would take us through two years' seasons. Though of course we would like longer... And if we are to set up the wildlife reserve and the breeding programme, that would really need continuous funding... It would mean a lot of lobbying and nego-tiation – even if the precarious peace holds.'

Panky nodded again.

'And, more than anything, we need to per-suade the local native people to co-operate, and to train some of them to take over. That takes time.'

'The ones who attacked you don't sound very co-operative.'

Perry grinned rather ruefully. 'It's tribal, you see. Nearly all the trouble is tribal. This group and that group – jealousies – super-stitions – rivalries. What the war was all about, really. Hard to eradicate ... but our own locals are very friendly and helpful. One of them – Nguni Xavier, our chief assistant, is absolutely indispensable. He was trained by Duncan, who sent him to college at his own expense.'

'Did he, indeed?' Panky was somehow enormously impressed by Perry's calm and rational assessment of their needs and priorities. Duncan had chosen a good successor, he thought, if the worst happened, which Perry seemed to think likely.

And for some reason which he could not quite analyse in his own mind, Panky liked the idea of money – the tiresome stuff – being put to such far-reaching good use... Better than city mergers and shady deals and fat directors' salaries... The painstaking recording of threatened life in a disappearing green world seemed infinitely more rewarding. He decided there and then to do what he could to help. And Panky's help was considerable.

'What you need is Lucinda Hope-Covington,' he said.

'Who the hell is she?'

Panky's grin was purely malicious. 'The most successful social fund-raiser I know and I *mean* successful. She's a great organiser. Charity balls, receptions, launch parties, garden parties, celebrity recitals – you name it, she runs them all... Anything that seems to her a good cause, particularly if it includes a personable man among its assets.'

'I'm not *personable!*' Perry exploded. 'For God's sake, leave me out of it.'

'But I can't, Perry. You know that, don't you?'

Perry groaned. 'Yes, I suppose I do. I have to see my publisher tomorrow. I have the second part of a book to deliver. And he believes in lecture tours and launches and–'

'Lionising?'

'Don't talk to me of *lions!*' growled Perry.

'Well, but you must know what to expect?'

'Yes, I do,' admitted Perry. 'And the thought appals me.'

'But if it means money for Duncan?'

'Of course,' said Perry wearily. 'What else can I do?'

Panky nodded with quiet satisfaction. 'Leave it to me,' he said, smiling in real sympathy at Perry's reluctance. 'I'll be in touch...' and he sauntered off, and left Perry staring at his empty glass.

After a moment's thought, Perry ordered another.

In the morning it was wet, and London became immersed in grey sludge. Perry went to see his publishers in Covent Garden with depression already setting in. Willoughby Press was an old-established and scholarly house that liked erudite books by experts which did not make them a lot of money but which brought them a certain prestige. Consequently they paid badly, but tried to make up for it by going in for lecture tours and 'educational promotion' in a big way. Bernard Swift – Perry's editor –

was a pleasant if somewhat solemn man, who greeted Perry and his manuscript with cautious optimism.

'We've timed the publication of Volume One to coincide with your visit,' he said with slow deliberation, 'so that we can boost interest in Volume Two at the same time as launching number one. You can add a bit of tantalising new information in your lectures, can't you?' He gave Perry a pale, hopeful smile.

But Perry that morning was seized with an enormous impatience and a fierce desire to stop all the unnecessary chat and get on with things at breakneck speed. His mind was making rings round the ponderous Bernard's promotional plans, and he was only just able to prevent himself jumping up and shouting: 'For God's sake get on with it!' But he clamped down his absurd and irrational rage, and tried to listen dutifully while Bernard laid out his itinerary. *Money for Duncan!* he kept telling himself. Stop carping, and do as you're told!

But Bernard was not entirely a fool, and he could see very well that his favourite author was not really listening to a word he said. So he shot a surprisingly shrewd glance in his direction and said suddenly:

'This Duncan business – is it serious?'

'Yes,' said Perry. 'Very. Duncan is dying – and all we can do is sit here talking about launches and lecture tours.'

And at this point his patience suddenly ran out and he got to his feet rather too swiftly. 'I'm sorry, Bernard. Can we talk some other time...? I have to get over to the Portuguese Embassy now... I – I'll be in touch–' and he rushed out of the room, leaving Bernard Swift looking after him open-mouthed.

He did in fact go to the Portuguese Embassy, where a pleasant official talked guardedly of 'revitalising' Angola's economy with outside aid, and spoke warmly of the valuable work Duncan MacNab and his team were doing, and how he hoped to 'renew their support', though he was careful not to say when or by how much. Perry did his best to sound persuasive – especially over the long-term project of the wildlife reserve and captive-breeding programme, which might at least ensure that some of the endangered species did not die out altogether. And he did detect a spark of sympathetic enthusiasm in the courteous official's dark brown eyes – which he hoped was a good sign.

Then, feeling that he had done all he could for the moment, he went for a walk in the park. To Perry – used to long and arduous treks in both forest and savannah, London distances seemed absurdly small and tame – his legs longed for wide spaces and rough terrain to stretch themselves among. So St

James's Park passed in a flash of impatience – even though he stopped to admire the iridescent heads of the mallards on the lake, and he soon found himself crossing the traffic at Hyde Park Corner and going on into the (slightly) wider reaches of Hyde Park and Kensington Gardens and the Serpentine.

It was raining still, and the few people who were about were hurrying, heads down, shoulders hunched against the persistent drizzle. But Perry didn't mind the rain – he was used to it. During the rainy season in Angola it sometimes went on for days on end... And the forest and dried-up savannah rejoiced, bright birds and swinging monkeys flashed among the wet leaves, strange, brilliant flowers suddenly sprang into being, and you could almost hear the trees drinking – and everything smelled green and fresh and bursting with new growth...

Here, the trodden grass was brown with summer, and the only birds in sight were a few bedraggled pigeons and some optimistic London sparrows looking for crumbs – and some more mallards with shining heads, swimming in the lake. (At least *they* were rejoicing in the rain.)

Perry paused for a moment in his headlong flight from his own anxious thoughts, and stood looking round him, watching a couple of children chasing a ball through the sodden grass. There was an old man sitting on a bench in the rain, with a dog lead in his hand. He sat quite still, staring at nothing, and did not seem to notice the fine sheen of moisture settling on his shoulders. What was he doing there, Perry wondered, sitting so still, with a dog lead in his hand, and no dog to go with it?

He almost wanted to go up to the old man and ask if he was all right, and where his dog was – but Perry was too shy for that. He could talk happily to his colleagues out in the wild rainforest, or to the local villagers who came out to help with their work – and he often talked to the elusive birds he was trying to capture on film or in his notebooks as they slipped unobtrusively in and out of the shadows and hid behind the leaves... But in London – teeming London that was full of hurrying, uncaring people – he was curiously tongue-tied. He didn't know how to reach them – or even if he wanted to ... except that this particular old man looked so quenched and bewildered, with his fixed, unseeing gaze and his drooping arms in their shabby, too-long sleeves...

No, said Perry to himself. He'd probably resent me interfering. If he wants to sit in the rain and brood, who am I to say he shouldn't? He probably likes his solitude just as much as I do...

So he walked on, and did not stop to ask the old man about his dog. But he felt a bit ashamed of being so absurdly diffident.

Eventually, he turned out of the park towards Paddington, still unable to walk the restlessness out of his legs. There was a café on the corner that looked inviting, and he almost hesitated, feeling a strange compulsion to go in out of the rain. It was called Tubby's, and it looked the kind of unpretentious, no-frills place he liked... Warm and comforting, in a city where no-one knew or cared how he felt... But he remembered suddenly that he had promised to meet Monty Pankhurst and the 'awful' Lucinda Hope-Covington in the Ritz bar at six. Why the Ritz? he asked himself. That jumped-up, gilt-and-gingerbread pile of bogus glamour? But he supposed, from what Panky had told him, that it was the Hope-Covington's natural habitat.

'Darling Panky,' said Lucinda, as she watched Perry approaching them across the bar, 'you didn't tell me he was so good-looking!'

Panky laughed. 'He wouldn't thank you for saying so.'

Lucinda raised one beautifully curved eyebrow. 'Not susceptible to flattery?'

'Not susceptible to anything,' stated Panky, for once offering a serious warning.

'Except money for Duncan MacNab?'

'Precisely,' agreed Panky. 'But even there,

he doesn't like–'

'Fawning on sponsors?' Lucinda smiled rather thoughtfully. 'Then I'll have to do it for him, won't I?'

'*Will you?*' asked Panky, and it was a straight, urgent appeal.

Lucinda's gaze was still resting on Perry's thin brown face, not missing the warring emotions of anxiety, grief and determined friendliness in his diffident expression. 'D'you know, I rather think I will,' she said softly, and waited for Perry to come up to them and speak first.

Perry, for his part, saw a nonchalantly poised, elegant woman in an extremely well-cut black velvet suit, golden hair (genuine or not, he couldn't tell) shining under the lights in a stylish chignon, blue, intelligent eyes assessing him shrewdly, but not seeming as formidable as he had expected.

'Am I late?' he said. 'I got carried away by your wet and empty park...' He turned courteously to Lucinda, summoning all his charm (which was considerable) for this important meeting. He knew it mattered a lot to Duncan and his team. 'It's awfully good of you to see me. Has Panky filled you in?'

'He has,' Lucinda said, smiling straight into those worried, candid grey eyes. 'And I'm so sorry to hear about the attack on Duncan MacNab... Have you had any more news?'

'No,' said Perry, surprised at the real sympathy in her voice, 'but he's holding on...' A strange expression of extraordinary tenderness crossed his face for a moment. 'He doesn't know the word "defeat"!'

Lucinda nodded gracefully. 'So I imagined...' She turned her smooth, sculptured head to include Panky in the three-sided conference. 'Then we must mount a successful campaign, mustn't we?'

Perry stared. It seemed that this calm, unexpectedly beautiful woman was won over already. He couldn't think why. 'I–' he glanced at Panky with a wild appeal. 'I'm not very good at this sort of thing– But I'm sure you and Panky know the ropes.'

'Yes,' agreed Lucinda, and looked from one man to the other with sudden, sparkling mischief, 'we know the ropes, Panky and I!'

There was a moment's silence, while Panky wondered what indiscretions Lucinda was about to reveal, and Perry wondered why he got an impression of hidden pain behind the mischievous smile.

'You'd better introduce me to your publisher,' said Lucinda, getting down to business at once. 'If you're going to do a few lectures, I'd better orchestrate them a bit.' She grinned at his look of alarm. 'You'd be surprised who will come to a lecture if there's a champagne reception thrown in!'

Perry blenched. 'I can't afford–'

'Oh, don't worry about *that*,' she said, waving a dismissive hand, 'I know how to get free catering – I do it all the time! Advertising is all...' She grinned encouragingly at Perry's bewildered face. 'The thing is to make the occasion as glittering as possible, and then all the richest people come!'

Panky saw Perry's appalled expression, and intervened mildly. 'Lucinda – break him in gently. He's not used to the lure of riches!'

They all laughed, relieved to have got the preliminaries over, and Panky signalled to a hovering waiter for more drinks all round.

Perry sighed. He knew he had to go through with this – but he had a sudden, dreadful longing for the dappled green shade of a jungle clearing, and the clear, distant calling of birds...

'It won't be so bad,' said Lucinda, who seemed to understand him better than he had thought. 'You can go on being your austere, scholarly self – while I make a fool of myself batting my eyelids at susceptible tycoons.'

Perry laughed. 'Don't you mind?'

She shrugged fluid shoulders. 'Why should I? It's all in a good cause, isn't it?' There was a curious, flat acceptance in her voice that made Perry suddenly ashamed. Who was he to show reluctance in accepting her methods? She was a skilled and clever organiser, but, he realised now, not particularly self-seeking. She just enjoyed getting the right people together at the right time – and hoping that the resulting contacts would please everyone... Wasn't that what he wanted, too...? And wasn't it exactly what Duncan would do, if he was here?

'I'm sorry,' he said to Lucinda humbly. 'I'm afraid I'm very green.'

She smiled at him. 'Jungles are green, I'm told,' she said.

The bird liked Abbie's green tree. It perched, half-hidden in the leaves, and looked out at her with its strange, gold-ringed eyes in a gaze that was no longer despairing but merely inquisitive, and now and then uttering a quiet, almost sotto voce call, like someone thinking aloud.

'I do believe you're getting used to me,' said Abbie, offering the bird a piece of apple, which he accepted politely. 'I know it's not the same as flying free in the jungle... Is it the jungle where you live? A forest, anyway. But this is the best I can do for the moment.'

The bird looked at her enquiringly, head on one side to listen to her voice.

'And Mackintosh is making you an aviary outside,' she told him. 'You'll be able to fly about... As long as it's not too cold for you... You'll like that, won't you?'

The bird seemed to consider the matter.

Then it said something noncommittal that might have been yes or no.

Abbie smiled at the alert red head, and went to answer yet another knock on the door. Since the bird's coming, she had received a continuous procession of visitors. First of all, it had been cheerful Mrs. Mac with a plateful of chopped-up fruit, and the helpful news that her friend, Al, the greengrocer on the corner, would be happy to let Abbie have his leftovers and damaged fruit at the end of each day. Then it had been little Miss Ashridge, delicately offering the bird grapes and one small green fig, and gazing wide-eyed at his brilliant crested head and smooth, iridescent body.

'Isn't he *beautiful*,' she breathed. And after her, came the two music students, Nicky and Sammy, blue jeans, straight hair and earnest faces, and, for some reason, Abbie could not quite fathom, full of apologies.

'We're sorry about the noise,' said Nicky, who was small and dark and rather pretty.

'The noise?' Abbie repeated. 'Oh, you mean the César Franck?'

'That's it,' nodded Sammy, who was taller and fairer but just as pretty, and just as intense. 'Student concert, you see. Big chance – agents coming – you know how it is.'

Abbie didn't, but she nodded sympathetically nonetheless. 'Not to worry,' she told them, smiling. 'Anyway, I think Solomon likes music.'

'Does he?' The girls regarded the bird seriously. 'Maybe it reminds him of other birds singing?' suggested Nicky.

'Some birds,' scoffed Sammy. 'A squeaky violin and a thumping piano?'

Abbie laughed. The bird put its head on one side and listened. It seemed to like the sound of laughter. 'How did you get a piano in there?' she asked, intrigued by the vagaries of this extraordinary household.

'Oh, it belongs to the Duchess,' explained Nicky airily. 'She's got two, you see. An upright for practice, and a grand for showing off. We've got the upright... And Mackintosh got it up there. He's a wizard at fixing things.'

'I know,' agreed Abbie fervently. 'He fixed up Solomon's cage.'

'Did he? I wondered how you managed to get hold of such a big one.' Sammy looked at the bird again, with thoughtful eyes. 'Is he happy, do you think?'

'I don't know,' Abbie said. 'But at least he's better off than he was... The only alternative would be some sort of tropical bird house ... but the vet seemed to think he needed peace and quiet first.'

Nicky looked interested. 'You had the vet – *up here?*'

Abbie nodded. 'And the RSPCA man – I thought I should, and I didn't want to frighten Solomon even more by trying to take him somewhere else...'

Sammy looked impressed. 'I hope you're grateful, bird,' she said, offering him one of Abbie's grapes.

'V.I.P. treatment,' approved Vicky. 'And that reminds me, would you like a free ticket to our concert?'

'Why free?' asked Abbie, smiling.

'Compensation – perpetual repeats of tricky passages – noise nuisance!'

'Oh, I don't know,' protested Abbie. 'It was better than that!'

'But will you come?'

'I'd love to,' Abbie told them. 'I'm sorry I can't bring Solomon, too.'

They grinned, and jointly decided to clatter down the stairs again. 'It'll be Beethoven next term,' they warned, and went away laughing.

Synco came next, with a mango and a passion fruit that 'one of the boys' had brought back from a gig. He was as laid back as ever, and viewed the bird with a sardonic eye. 'Another refugee?' he said. 'Hi, Solomon. Odd-bird-out, are you...? I know the feeling.' He looked at the bird's beautiful, listening head and began to sing softly: *Here we sit like birds in the wilderness,*

Birds in the wilderness...'

Then he grinned at Abbie, and added: 'Can he sing? Maybe I could synchronise him.'

'Don't you dare,' laughed Abbie. 'He's only just beginning to be himself as it is.'

'Individual talent?' Synco's eyebrows shot up. 'Separates you from the herd.' He looked at the cocked, intelligent head with sympathy. 'Are you lonely, bird?' he asked softly.

Solomon moved a little further in among his leaves, and made no comment. But Abbie did. 'Synco, *don't!*' she protested. 'I feel bad enough about his captivity as it is...'

'Don't see why,' said Synco. 'Not your fault. I'd say you'd done him proud, you and Mackintosh between you.' He pushed a rather shrivelled-looking passion fruit through the wire of the cage.

Solomon eyed it with interest, and after a moment's hesitation, came down to investigate.

Synco sighed. 'You can get round most people with food,' he said bitterly.

Abbie just looked at him. 'What's the matter, Synco?'

He gave her a fleeting grin. 'He's too beautiful,' he said. 'I'm jealous!'

Abbie laughed.

'And he's got you to look after him,' Synco added slyly, looking as if he expected Abbie to throw a pillow at him any minute.

But at this point, Solomon suddenly uttered a small, muted crow, and it seemed to them so apt that they both began to giggle.

'Better go,' said Synco, starting to slope

185

off. 'Before he makes any more personal remarks!' But he paused by the door and added: 'The boys often bring back funny fruit from places they go to – on gigs and so on... Bring some more up sometime?'

'Yes,' agreed Abbie. 'He'd like that.'

This time Solomon did not crow, but he did not look disapproving either.

Because of the bird's coming, Abbie had not been to the park for some time. She had spent the first few lunch hours rushing back home to see how he was getting on, and the weekend seemed to be taken up with more bird-watching, or with filling in extra time at the office to make up the hours she had lost. So it was quite a while before she found herself sitting on her usual bench, and realised that she was looking across at the old man with the white dog. Only the white dog wasn't there – only the old man, silent and alone, with the dog's lead in his hand.

What can have happened? she wondered. Did the dog get run over or something? And why does he sit so still like that, staring at nothing, with a useless dog lead in his hand...? I'll have to ask him in a minute, he looks so lost.

She tried a tentative smile in his direction – after all, they had exchanged a few words, and a sandwich, before – but the old man made no response. Then she got out her sandwiches, and carefully offered him one. Still no response. At last she plucked up enough courage to ask the dreaded question, knowing she was probably being extremely tactless, but also knowing she had to break that stony silence somehow. 'What happened to Spot?'

The seamed, blank face contorted into what might have been a grin or a scowl, the snapping brown eyes were almost black with anger. 'He went and died on me, didn't he?' he said flatly. 'Dogs do, you know.' His glare was fiercer than ever. 'Like people,' he added in a kind of abrupt snarl that was rather like his departed dog's voice.

'I'm sorry,' said Abbie gently, not knowing how to offer comfort.

'Being sorry won't bring him back,' he growled.

I can be sorry for you, though, can't I? thought Abbie. But she did not dare to say it. He would have been angrier than ever. So instead, she moved to sit on the seat beside him, and once again offered him a sandwich.

This time, he took one in his hand, but seemed uncertain what to do with it.

'I've got a bird,' said Abbie, biting into her ham-and-tomato.

'A what?'

'A bird. A strange, very beautiful tropical bird. He escaped from a pet shop.' She glanced at the old man to see whether he was listening. 'Shall I tell you about him?'

The hunched figure shrugged weary shoulders. 'Suit yourself.' But he didn't say 'No!' and he did absentmindedly take a nibble at his sandwich.

'Well, it was like this,' said Abbie, and began to tell the whole story. She did not know if the old man was really listening or not, but he didn't interrupt, and he didn't move away – and when she held out another sandwich, he took it automatically, and presently began to eat it in the same absentminded fashion as before.

'So I called him Solomon...' she finished, and looked round to see if there was any response.

But the man also knew his bible, and managed a faint, creaky smile. 'The glory bird...?' he murmured.

'Would you like to come and see him?' Abbie suggested, greatly daring.

The angry brown eyes looked at her in astonishment. 'You don't know anything about me.'

'Yes, I do,' said Abbie. 'People call you the Prof because you are very clever and make up crosswords or something. And you like fresh air and dogs.'

'Not all dogs,' growled the Prof, but he was nearly smiling again.

'It's not far,' said Abbie, noting the half-smile. 'Won't take you long.'

The Prof shook his head at her with fierce reproof. 'See here, young lady, you can't go inviting strange grumpy old men up to your room to see a bird!'

'You mean – it sounds like *"to see my etchings"*?' She grinned at his disapproving face, suddenly bubbling with mischief.

The Prof glared even more furiously, and then all at once began to laugh. 'Oh well, why not?' he said. 'What have I got to lose?'

'Not your virtue, certainly,' said Abbie, joining in his laughter.

The Prof shot her a very sharp glance. 'I don't know about that,' he said. 'I told you before you were *threatening!*' But he got to his feet quite readily, and began to walk along by her side. 'All the same,' he added warningly. 'I might have a knife. Or be a psychopath.'

'I suppose you might,' said Abbie, not believing a word of it.

'You are *much* too trusting, young woman.'

'Sorry,' she said, and then added with only a small amount of bitterness:

'I always was.'

The Prof made no comment on this. But at the fruit shop on the corner, he stopped suddenly. 'What did you say the bird ate? Fruit?'

'Yes,' agreed Abbie. 'Almost any kind, I think – and berries, probably.'

The old man fished in his pocket for

change, and looked suspiciously at the rows of displayed fruit outside the shop. Then he carefully selected the best bunch of grapes he could find, regardless of cost, and handed them to Abbie. 'Bribery,' he said. 'Corruption comes next!' and gave a thin cackle of malicious laughter.

But Abbie only grinned back, and led him into the Duchess's house and up the stairs to see the bird.

He stood in front of the wire cage for a long time admiring the elegant crested head and the gleaming curve of its back. And the bird looked back at him out of its orange-rimmed clever black eyes, and seemed to accept his presence without fear. He was silent so long that Abbie began to wonder if he had gone into some sort of daydream and fallen asleep on his feet, but at last he said in a strange, choked voice: 'I miss him, you know...'

'Of course,' agreed Abbie. 'Of course you do.'

'We didn't see eye to eye,' he admitted painfully, 'but we rubbed along together all right...' He was still looking hard at the bird's bright colours, and would not turn round. 'It's so quiet,' he added, with a faint attempt at self-mockery, 'with no-one to swear at.' He leant forward and tentatively offered the bird a grape.

Solomon viewed it with caution, and then

uttered a gentle low-pitched whistle of acknowledgement.

The old man was delighted. 'Communication,' he said. 'In a benighted world... Solomon, I salute you.'

For answer, Solomon came down from his tree and delicately accepted the grape.

'Would you like a cup of tea?' asked Abbie, seeing that the barriers were down.

'I don't mind if I do,' accepted the Prof, with as good a grace as he could muster, and carefully laid the dog lead down on a chair.

The most unexpected visitor that came to see the bird was Henry Grey, the quiet civil servant 'away at weekends – no trouble at all.' But he didn't come alone, he brought Olive Ashridge, smiling and quite rosy with pleasure at being asked to make the introduction. The trouble was, Henry Grey was shy – so shy that he found it quite impossible to approach Abbie unasked, even when he had something quite useful to offer.

He stood there, impeccable in his charcoal grey suit, wispy hair brushed tidily sideways, anxious mouth almost trembling below that too-long, fastidious nose, and his pale blue eyes fixed on Abbie's face in almost childlike appeal. 'I hope you don't mind–' he began, 'but Olive – Miss Ashridge – was sure you wouldn't object–'

'Come in,' said Abbie, smiling. 'I expect you've come to see Solomon, haven't you? There he is.'

Both Olive Ashridge and Henry Grey went over to stand in front of the cage, admiring the bird with approving, observant eyes.

'I think he's more beautiful than ever,' breathed Olive. 'His colours seem brighter.'

'And you don't know *exactly* what he is?' asked Henry in his precise, somewhat pedantic manner.

'Well, no–' Abbie told him. 'We think he is a Turaco – but we aren't sure which variety. I believe there are several different ones that come from different parts of Africa...'

'The thing is,' said Henry awkwardly, arriving at the reason for his visit, 'I've had this invitation. I thought of offering it to Olive first – I know she does go to lectures sometimes – but she suggested it would be more use to you...' He paused for breath, and looked rather beseechingly at Olive Ashridge to help him out. But she was still gazing at the bird, and Abbie was standing there, waiting for an explanation, so he had to go on. 'It's at a rather smart place – too smart for me, really. These things do come into our office, you see, because we are concerned with exhibitions and overseas contacts...' He stopped, aware that he was floundering helplessly.

'Why don't you give it to her, Henry?' said

little Miss Ashridge, smiling at his discomfiture, 'then she'll understand.'

Henry looked at her gratefully, and brought out a large white card with gilt edges, and handed it to Abbie. It said:

'*THE LAST RESORT*
A lecture by Dr. Peregrine Farquhar on the threatened wildlife of the dwindling rainforests of West Africa.'

'He's an expert on birds,' Henry explained. 'Very knowledgeable. He's been working out there with Duncan MacNab – the famous naturalist. I thought – Olive thought...' He turned once more to Olive in mute appeal.

'We thought if you went to it, you might be able to ask him,' said Olive breathlessly. 'He'd be sure to know.'

Abbie gazed from one to the other, and then down at the card in her hand, hardly knowing what to say. 'But – don't you want to go?' Henry shook his head, relieved that he could answer that. 'It's at the weekend.' He gave Abbie a shy, apologetic smile. 'You see, Abbie – it is Abbie, isn't it? – my mother lives alone now – since my father died some years ago... So I go home most weekends... She looks forward to my visits, and I – I hate to disappoint her.'

Abbie nodded, understanding both his reasoning and his embarrassment at having to explain it. But that still left Olive Ashridge. She turned to her smiling, bright-eyed friend, holding out the card. 'But you–?'

'Oh no,' said Olive. 'Too grand for me. And, contrary to what Henry thought, I don't really go out much in the evenings.' She grinned at Abbie. 'By the time the library closes, I've had enough.'

Abbie still looked doubtful. 'Are you sure?'

They both nodded at her with enthusiasm. 'Yes,' they said. 'Besides, you owe it to Solomon,' pointed out Olive. 'He deserves to know who he is.'

Abbie smiled. 'In that case, how can I refuse?'

And Solomon, hearing Abbie's voice close to him, uttered a quiet, resonant note of approval.

It was, as Henry Grey said, a rather smart affair. Abbie was a little overwhelmed by the number of elegant, flawlessly dressed women and their well-suited escorts in the audience. The lecture took place in the conference room of a fashionable hotel, with a reception to be held afterwards in the adjoining 'Chandelier Room' – which was, in fact, the old ballroom. Abbie already knew the hotel because – at the other end of her job at the Travel Agency – she was often sent to meet groups of visiting tourists, particularly Americans and Germans, who liked somewhere central and fairly sumptuous for their base. She had visited it several times on official business, and found it stuffy and overpriced, with far too much chintz and gilt for her taste. But the roof garden was pleasant enough, and one of their most valuable assets.

Abbie was greeted by a stunningly well turned-out blonde woman who said: 'Darling, how lovely of you to come,' and then turned away and said it all over again to someone else.

I hope the lecture won't be full of name-dropping and social chitchat, thought Abbie, viewing the well-heeled audience with a rather sceptical eye.

'Who was that?' she whispered to her neighbour in the next chair, and then wondered whether she ought to have admitted her ignorance or advertised her uninvited presence quite so obviously.

But the woman next to her smiled and answered: 'That's Lucinda Hope-Covington. Superb organiser – knows everyone.' She leaned towards Abbie confidingly. 'It's a fund-raising bash. She'll get the moneybags rolling.'

'Oh,' said Abbie, not sure how to answer this.

And then Lucinda came on to the platform, followed by a tall, lean man with a gentle smile and compelling, visionary eyes.

'Welcome, everyone,' said Lucinda, in a surprisingly warm and persuasive voice. 'I expect you all know of the famous Duncan MacNab and his team of dedicated naturalists, and their conservation work in the African rainforest. Well, here is one of his team, home on leave for a short time, on a rather urgent mission ... and also to promote the first volume of his book *"The Last Resort"* which describes the work of the team and the survey of wildlife they are engaged in... I will leave him to tell you all about it. Ladies and gentlemen – Dr. Peregrine Farquhar.'

Perry stood up. He had already given three of these lectures – dutifully keeping to his publisher's schedule – and he knew very well what he wanted to say, but he also knew that this one was different, this audience was less discerning and less interested in his subject than the earnest conservationists and bird lovers who came to his humbler venues, but it was also more important. And he was nervous. This was where the money was, and he had to reach them somehow. But then a vision of Duncan's grizzled, fighting head came into his mind, and that weary voice giving his last order to Perry: *'Get your priorities right!'* and he knew how to begin.

He told them about the dwindling patches of fragile rainforest – islands of emerald and jade, leaf and liana, and the tall beauty of the mahogany trees crashing down at the ruthless hands of the loggers wielding their chainsaws. He told them of the bright birds flashing their rainbow colours through the dappled shade – some of them known and catalogued and already being given a chance of safe breeding in the national parks – and some so rare and spectacular than even Perry himself was not sure of their species or their origin, and could only try to capture their unique and glorious plumage on film and enter their details painstakingly in his log of rare or endangered species.

He showed them some slides of these, and was not surprised when his audience murmured and exclaimed in admiration. Abbie did, too – but none of these beautiful exotic birds resembled Solomon, hiding in his small fig tree in a London attic.

Then Perry went on to tell them of the flowers, the unknown herbs and plants of healing, that grew on the forest floor, and the bromeliads halfway up in the trees, and the equally brilliant butterflies that hovered over them. And that made him show yet more slides to dazzle them.

From there it was only a small way on to talk of his colleagues – Judy, and her endless search for the scarce, the threatened and the unknown in the forest plant life, her delicate fingers testing, collecting seed, labelling, listing, pursuing small but vital experiments and lab tests that might discover a plant's medicinal qualities, and the growing of precious seedlings that might save them from extinction... And 'Sticks' the Insect Man, equally tireless and conscientious. And velvet-voiced Jonty, who could almost charm the monkeys off the trees, and had already logged everything on four legs that he could find, from the gorillas of Maiombe to the Angolan giraffe.

The question of 'logging everything' led him on to the raid on the research hut, the damage inflicted, both on their equipment and on Duncan himself when he went out to intervene. And that led him, accompanied by more murmurs of shock and sympathy, to talk about Duncan himself, and his dream of getting all this cataloguing done before it was too late, of setting up another small wildlife sanctuary where they could at least hope to undertake captive breeding, and of persuading the authorities and the local native people to co-operate in saving what was left of their forest and the creatures that lived in them. For, he told them, they were all endangered now, as their precious habitat got eaten away by the bulldozers creeping acre by acre across the forest floor.

'Duncan MacNab,' he said, by way of conclusion, 'is a man of vision – a man with a dream. And it is up to us to make that dream come true.'

It was a passionate appeal, spoken by a man who was fired with the same fierce desire to save and to protect as his old friend and mentor, Duncan, and it enthralled his audience, Abbie among them. When he had finished talking and put the slides away, and the applause had died down, he was surrounded by well-wishers and questioners and celebrity-grabbers to such an extent that Abbie knew she could never get near him, and anyway felt suddenly so overcome by shyness that she wouldn't have had the nerve to speak to him even if he was standing beside her.

She followed the general flow of people into the Chandelier Room where someone thrust a glass of champagne into her hand and someone else offered her a canapé. The noise of chatter was increasing steadily and the crush was considerable, making Abbie want to cut and run, but she kept her eye on Peregrine Farquhar's distinguished head, and hoped there might come a moment when there would be space enough to approach him. So it was that she saw a hotel porter come up behind him, murmur something in his ear, and gesture towards the telephone in the lobby behind the reception room. Peregrine turned sharply, put down his drink, and strode off across the room.

And Abbie, not knowing quite why, also put down her glass and followed him. She stood a little way off, watching him through the glass of the phone booth, and wondered why she was so certain that it was the right thing for her to do.

He spoke rather briefly on the phone, listened intently, sighed, and spoke again, rather softly and sadly. Then he laid down the phone and stood still. He stood there so long that Abbie began to be worried, and she thought as she watched him, that his face was growing steadily paler under the artificially rosy glow of the hotel lights.

At last he put a hand up to his eyes, as if he could not see very well, and made an uncertain, lurching turn away from the phone booth, the hovering porter, and the noisy reception crowd behind him. He seemed bewildered, and not in the least sure where he wanted to go.

Abbie decided she could not bear it, and went quietly up to him and laid a detaining hand on his arm. 'Can I do anything?'

He looked at her rather wildly, but in some strange way not as if she was a stranger. 'Get me out of here.'

'Permanently?'

'N-no,' he said, with a swift breath of remembered duty. 'A breather...'

'There's a roof garden.' She glanced at his beleaguered face. 'You could see the sky...?'

'Lead me to it,' he said, still sounding driven and confused. But he allowed himself to be steered towards the lift, and up the next four floors to the door that led to the hotel roof garden.

It was still light outside – the lecture had ended early enough for the reception to take up most of the evening – but the hotel flood-lights were on, making pools of brightness on trees and shrubs, and casting strange shadows in between. There was a stone para-pet all round the carefully planted garden, and above it all was a clear, evening sky.

Perry lifted his head to look up, and took a deep, controlling breath. 'I'm sorry–' he began.

But Abbie didn't let him go on. 'I'll fetch you a real drink,' she said. 'Whiskey?'

He nodded. 'Thanks...' and then seemed unable to say any more.

Abbie left him alone, and hurried down in the lift to the hotel bar where she bought a double whiskey and carefully carried it back in the lift. She did not stop to speak to anyone or to explain where their guest of honour had gone. No one seemed to have missed him, anyway. They were all chatter-ing away as noisily as ever.

Up in the roof garden it was quiet and empty – the sound of traffic below muted by distance. Perry was standing at the farthest corner of the paved terrace, looking out over the city at the summer sky.

Silently, Abbie handed him his drink, and

turned to go away and leave him in peace. But he said suddenly: 'Don't go.'

She paused, hesitating between shyness and a desire to be some help. Could she really be any use to this shocked, bewildered man?

'I'll have to tell them,' he said.

Abbie waited, and when he said nothing more, she asked gently: 'Tell them what?'

'It's Duncan.' It seemed to him that actually putting it into words made it worse. More final, somehow. *Duncan is dead.* 'Duncan MacNab died this morning. They rang through from Luanda to my club...' His voice wavered a little, and then he said again, in a driven voice: 'I'll have to tell them.'

Abbie was silent, thinking it out. She could see how awful it would be to have to announce such a thing to that gossiping, champagne-happy gathering.

'Must you do it tonight?'

He paused, trying to consider it rationally. 'Yes, I think so... It'll be on the news tomorrow – if not tonight ... and in the papers... I can't let them go home thinking all is well... There's money involved. They'll think I was covering up disaster.'

'Is it disaster?'

He looked at Abbie strangely. *Is it disaster?* 'It is for me,' he said simply.

'Yes, I know,' Abbie answered – as if she really did know what it meant to Perry, 'but you said ... Duncan MacNab was a man of

vision – a man with a dream.' She deliberately quoted his own words to him. *And it
is up to us to make that dream come true.*

He stared at her, arrested by the certainty
in her voice. 'Did I say that?'

'So it *needn't* be a disaster,' she said reasonably. 'You can make sure of that... You've
only got to tell them so.'

He was silent, and Abbie wondered if she
had said too much and upset him more than
ever. It didn't seem to occur to either of
them that they were talking like old and
trusted friends, not like strangers at all.

At last he said in an odd, half-laughing
voice: 'You make it sound so simple!'

'It is, really,' Abbie pointed out. 'To a man
like you. You're all right when you're doing
something.' She looked at him, smiling a
little in the deepening twilight. 'And now
you'll have plenty to do.'

That was true, and he knew it. There was
the research group to contact. And Duncan's family. Did he have any family left...?
And what about funeral arrangements and
all the terrible tidy planning and parapher-
nalia of death...? But he need not think of
all that now. There was nothing he could do
about any of that tonight. All he had to do
now was somehow manage to tell that rich
and privileged gathering down below that
the head of his research team – their leader
and their inspiration – was dead. Plenty to

do. And this was the worst task of all. Or was it...? What did it matter what all those people thought...? Burying Duncan would be much worse. And carrying on his work without him would be worst of all...

'Don't worry about all that now,' said Abbie, as if he had voiced all his anxieties aloud. 'Just tell me what to do about tonight.'

He turned back from his churning thoughts and really looked at the girl beside him – a quiet girl with very beautiful grey eyes and a gentle voice, and dressed in something plain and blue-grey like the evening sky...

'I don't even know your name...' he said.

'Abbie.' She smiled at him reassuringly. 'Here to take orders.'

He managed a difficult smile back. 'Well then, Abbie – could you find Lucinda...? Lucinda Hope-Covington – the woman running this show...?'

'Yes,' said Abbie.

'Tell her what's happened, and ask her what I ought to do... She'll know. Just – give me a little while longer on my own up here, and come back and tell me – I'll be ready then.'

'Yes,' said Abbie again. 'Have your drink.' And she went away and left him alone in the shadows.

Lucinda, when Abbie found her, listened without fuss, detaching herself from several talkative friends and drawing Abbie away into a corner. She seemed to accept, also without fuss, that Abbie was somehow in Perry's entourage, and said at once: 'Tell him to come down when he's ready. I'll get everyone silent to hear the news.' She looked at Abbie shrewdly and added: 'And tell him not to worry about spoiling the party... It won't do them any harm to come up against reality – and it may actually do his cause good.' Then she grinned at Abbie and added another afterthought: 'No. Better not tell him that. It'll sound too callous. But it's probably true.'

Abbie nodded. 'I expect you're right,' she agreed sadly. But she found that she rather liked Lucinda Hope-Covington, in spite of her designer clothes and matching voice.

'I'm glad you're here to look after him–?' said Lucinda, casting about for a name.

'Abbie.'

'Oh yes, Abbie, of course. Well, take care of him, Abbie, and bring him down all in one piece if you can. I've got my hands full here.'

'Yes,' assented Abbie. 'Of course.'

She found Perry where she had left him, but the whiskey glass was empty. 'I've brought you another,' she said. 'Will it help?'

'Probably,' he admitted, and gulped it all down in one reckless swallow. Then he followed Abbie down to face his captive, heedlessly cheerful audience.

'Abbie,' he said, as they went into the crowded room. 'Can you get me out rather fast afterwards?'

'Yes,' said Abbie, and gave his arm a reassuring squeeze as she led him up to the impromptu platform that Lucinda had hastily arranged in the middle of the floor.

Perry stood on it, facing the garrulous throng, and waited for silence. When it came, with one or two half-whispered inquisitive questions enquiring what it was all about, he held up his hand and spoke.

'Ladies and gentlemen, I am sorry to spoil your fun. But I have just had some very sad news from Luanda. Duncan MacNab died in his sleep this morning.'

He waited for the shocked murmurs to die down, and then went on. 'But I have been reminded by one member of the audience of the words I used about him earlier.' His gaze rested for a moment on Abbie's upturned face before he quoted the whole passage again. Then he continued: 'I just want to emphasise that I am pledged to do just that – make Duncan's dream come true, and I would like you all to charge your glasses and drink a toast to Duncan MacNab and all the great work he has done.'

He looked round rather wildly then, for he had forgotten to grab a glass of champagne before he spoke, but Abbie was quick to notice, and passed a full glass up to him just in time.

'To Duncan MacNab!' he said.

And Lucinda led the assembled company in a strong and relieved rejoinder. Everyone was glad to have something positive to do in this difficult moment. And drinking a toast was easy. It was clever of Perry, Lucinda thought, to find a way out for them – and it would do the party no harm to be turned into a kind of cheerful wake.

But Perry turned to Abbie urgently then and said: 'Now! Please–' and together they edged rather swiftly out of the crowd and through the hotel foyer towards the street. They had almost got to the door when Lucinda came after them. Abbie's heart sank. She didn't think Perry could stand much more at the moment.

But Lucinda merely clasped him in a fond embrace, and said: 'That was perfect, Perry. Now don't worry about a thing. I'll be in touch tomorrow, and you can tell me then what you want done.' She drew back from him a little and looked into his face with easy kindness. 'Go home and get some sleep. That's the first priority.'

She did not know it, but that phrase 'the first priority' brought Duncan's tired, insistent voice so vividly close in his mind that he felt the tears rise behind his eyes, and stumbled away from her into the street before he disgraced himself altogether.

Lucinda looked at Abbie and said: 'Look after him, Abbie. The hotel will get you a taxi. He's had about enough, I think.'

Abbie nodded, and followed Perry out into the summer evening, wondering why everyone seemed to assume that she was responsible for his welfare. But a fleeting thought came to her that she didn't really mind. She had half expected to find that he had fled down the street and gone off by himself, but she found him waiting for her, as if he did not quite know what to do next.

'A taxi?' she suggested.

He shook his head. 'I'd rather walk.'

'Where to?'

'Anywhere,' he said. And then, realising that he was being unreasonable in expecting her to accompany him, he added awkwardly:

'But you–?'

She looked at him straight. 'Don't you want to be on your own?'

'No,' he said. And his eyes, looking bleakly into hers, were filled with an unspoken appeal.

'All right,' said Abbie. 'Let's walk through the park. It's still quite light...'

She turned him round to face the right way, for he still seemed confused and disoriented, and began to walk in companionable silence by his side.

They walked in unspoken accord for quite a long time, while the golden afterglow of sunset faded into evening blueness and dusk ran between the trees and the glimmering lake... But at last Perry said abruptly: 'Was it really all right – that toast business? It must have seemed awfully callous!'

'No,' said Abbie roundly. 'It wasn't callous at all. You gave him a good send-off.'

'A kind of wake?'

'Exactly.' She glanced at him and added in a carefully neutral voice:

'I did the same kind of thing myself once.'

'What?'

'Turned an awkward situation into a wake.'

'After a death?'

'Well ... yes, I suppose it was a kind of death,' she said, her voice becoming a little distant with remembered hurt. But then she turned to him resolutely and said: 'Tell me about Duncan – how you met and how long you've been working with him?' for she felt that Perry needed to talk, to bring his old friend near again, before the silence became too fraught and full of anguish to bear.

So Perry talked, and told her the whole of his long history of friendship and mutual obsession with conservation, from his undergraduate days till this last research project in the vanishing rainforests of Africa. He talked until he was tired, and Abbie listened and said very little until she saw him give a sudden convulsive shiver that almost rocked him on his feet.

'What is it?' she said. 'Are you cold...? Is it shock?'

He shivered again, and shook his head. 'No... At least, I suppose shock might trigger it off...' The rigours were getting fiercer, and he stopped for a moment to hold on to the railings.

'Trigger what off?' asked Abbie, for it was clear that something was wrong, and she had better know exactly what it was and how to deal with it.

'It's all right,' he told her between chattering teeth. 'Only malaria... It does this sometimes... I've got–' he tried to steady his breathing, 'I've got some pills somewhere...' He was struggling to get a small bottle out of his pocket. Then he looked round rather helplessly at the empty street, wondering where he could get a drink.

Abbie was wondering that, too – and working out that it would be too late for Tubby's to be open – for they had long since exhausted the small miles of the two parks and were now on the edge of Paddington – not far from Tubby's, and not far from the Duchess's house, either.

'I live not far away,' she said, taking a swift decision. 'You'd better come up to my rooms. At least I can give you a hot drink.'

He looked at her with half-humorous despair. 'I don't know – I walk you off your feet, and then I collapse on your doorstep... In fact, I've used you unmercifully all the evening...'

Abbie smiled at him in the deepening dusk. 'Don't worry. I've decided I rather like it.'

He laughed, and managed to control another chill that threatened to overwhelm him. 'I haven't asked you what you were doing at that overdressed party...! Not really your scene, I'd have thought?'

'You mean I wasn't dripping with diamonds and wild silk?' she said, taking his arm and steering him firmly down the road towards her door.

He tried another laugh, but it wasn't a success and ended in a worse rigour than ever. His teeth were actually chattering.

'Well, of course, I came to hear you speak,' she told him, holding tight to his arm as his feet seemed to be uncertain which way they were going.

'Really?'

'And to ask you something.' The bird, she thought. Solomon and I have the great ornithologist on my doorstep. But how can I bother him with it now?

But he heard the sudden diffidence in her voice and turned to look at her. 'Ask me something? What about?'

'About a bird,' said Abbie. 'But never mind that now. Let's get you safely inside where you can shiver in comfort.'

He allowed himself to be propelled in the right direction, but he was persistent nonetheless. 'What bird? Where?'

'Right here,' said Abbie. 'You'll see him in a minute... I'll tell you all about it when you're feeling better. This way... Mind the steps...'

She got him inside the door, and up the stairs, and somehow managed to get him into the flat, and led him over to the long sofa-bed in the corner of the living-room. But he was shaking so much by then that his legs wouldn't hold him up any longer, and he more or less fell on to the sofa and lay there, exhausted and defeated, while Abbie hurried over to find blankets and hot bottles and put the kettle on.

Before Abbie came in, the room had been in semi-darkness, with the fading twilight diminishing moment by moment outside the windows, and Solomon had decided it was bedtime and had retired quietly to his fig-tree and hidden his bright head behind the leaves. But now, with the lights switched on, and movement, and conversation outside his cage, he woke up again, and came out to have a look, knowing very well by now that when Abbie returned extra titbits of fruit were usually forthcoming.

Abbie saw the bird come out, the vivid scarlet head cocked in enquiry, the clever, gold-ringed eyes watchful and alert, but she was busy with Perry's hot drink, and did not immediately go over to offer Solomon his evening snack.

'Hot toddy,' she said to Perry, handing him a steaming glass. 'Infallible for colds. I daresay it's good for malaria, too?'

'Standard cure!' he agreed, smiling.

But the sound of Abbie's voice clearly meant something to the solitary bird, and he let out a low, musical call in response.

Perry sat up in astonishment and looked round. 'Good God!' he exclaimed. 'What's *that?*'

'That is Solomon,' said Abbie. 'And if you'll lie back and let those pills have a chance to work, I'll tell you his story – as far as I know it.'

Perry, wondering if he had drifted into some kind of time lapse and was back in the forests of Africa, lay back in stupefaction and just listened.

'...so you see,' finished Abbie, 'we did the best we could for him, Mackintosh and I – but we don't know exactly what he is...'

'You are right. He *is* a Turaco,' said Perry. 'A Red-crested Turaco from the West African forest...' He stared at Abbie, and then looked across at the bird again, in pity and wonder. 'They are endemic only to Angola. How in the world did he get so far from home?'

'I wish I knew,' said Abbie. 'It might tell us a bit more about how to look after him...' She remembered then that she hadn't yet given the bird his expected treat, and went

213

over to put some extra chopped-up fruit through the wire of his cage.

Solomon eyed it with interest, hopped down to floor level in order to investigate, and uttered another gentle crow of satisfaction.

'Why, he's *talking* to you!' exclaimed Perry, awestruck.

Abbie looked surprised. 'Shouldn't he be?'

Perry shook his head in disbelief. 'A wild Turaco?'

'You mean Turkey-Crow,' said Abbie, and was relieved to see him laugh. 'But couldn't he have been bred in captivity?'

Perry thought not. 'It's very unlikely. They don't breed easily in captivity – and they are pretty rare in any case. Exporting them is probably illegal – though of course people always get round it somehow.'

Abbie nodded. 'But he seems so tame.'

'My guess is, he was captured very young – probably as a nestling – and reared for the exotic bird trade. That way, he would have got used to being handled by human beings, poor creature. God knows what he may have been through – those traders and dealers in the wild bird markets are totally unscrupulous.'

Abbie sighed. 'But you think he's all right now?'

He smiled then, and actually got shakily to his feet and went to have a long look at the bright bird in his large, makeshift cage. 'I think he's a lot better off than he ever dared to hope...What did you call him? Solomon?'

'Yes.'

He nodded, still smiling a little. 'Do you know what kind of flowers the lilies of the field were supposed to be?'

'No?' Abbie was delighted that he understood her.

'The Martagon lily, or the poppy-anemone Coronaria.'

'Oh,' breathed Abbie. 'Both brilliant scarlet!'

'Exactly,' said Perry, and they both looked at Solomon's beautiful scarlet-crested head and smiled at one another.

By the time Perry had finished another hot drink, and they had discussed the bird in a bit more detail, it was getting very late, and though the rigours and chills had died down, Abbie could see that he was still tired and shocked, and tending now – perhaps because of the pills (or the whiskey?) – towards drowsiness. But she was also thankfully aware that the bird had played its part in distracting him from present grief and all its attendant worries. For the past hour, at least, he had not thought about his own problems – only those of a lonely exile with a shimmering scarlet head... And maybe, if she kept him warm and quiet (like the bird) he might drift off to sleep and forget the sorrows of the day for a while.

But Perry was still wide awake enough to realise, too, that it was getting late and he ought not to be here at all. So he sat up, rather groggily, and made vague noises about going home.

'What would you do about it out there?' asked Abbie, smiling a little at his swaying figure.

'About what?'

'An attack of malaria.'

'Oh.' He grinned weakly. 'Just what you've been doing. Whiskey, quinine and pills – and lots of blankets if we had any.'

'And then?'

'Fall into my little truckle bed and sleep it off.'

'Exactly,' said Abbie. 'So you can do it now.'

'What?'

'Sleep it off,' she said patiently. 'You're already in the next best thing to a truckle bed. Why try to move?'

Perry looked at her in frowning bewilderment, but he knew he was fast losing control of the situation as the tide of drowsiness lapped over his swimming senses. 'I ought to go home–'

'No, you shouldn't. You're not fit to go wandering about the streets of London. And anyway, I promised your Lucinda to take care of you.'

'She's not my Lucinda,' he protested. 'God forbid!'

'I'm glad to hear it,' said Abbie, grinning. 'She is a bit high-powered! But she's certainly very concerned about your welfare. So lie down and be sensible.'

'But–'

'You'll be much better able to cope with everything tomorrow after some sleep,' Abbie insisted. 'It's only common sense.'

Perry had to admit that she was right, and a chilly journey to a chilly bed at his club was the last thing he wanted at the moment – if he could get there at all. 'Not fair on you–' he muttered, rather thickly.

'Nonsense!' retorted Abbie. 'Besides, you can keep an eye on the bird!'

He grinned at that, and lay back again among Abbie's blankets, but far from keeping an eye on Solomon, he shut his own eyes in weary submission and promptly fell fast asleep.

Abbie tiptoed about, switching off lights and renewing the hot bottle at Perry's feet, and laying an extra blanket over him, but he did not stir. He was far out by now in the dreamless dark where no hint of remembered sorrow could reach him.

She paused for a moment to look down at him in unspoken sympathy, and saw that his gentle, quirky mouth was smiling a little as if caught in happy recollection of times past... Then, satisfied that he would sleep in peace, she turned away and went to put the cover over the bright bird's cage.

'Thank you, Solomon,' she whispered. 'You've done your bit tonight... And now you've got a protector – and a very grand one, too... Aren't you the lucky one?'

Solomon looked at her out of his strange, wild eyes, and decided that he liked the sound of her voice so close to his cage. He made a small, quiet murmur of approval and retired for the night behind his leaves.

'Sleep tight!' whispered Abbie, to both of them. 'A fine night, and all's well.'

And she went away and left them in the enfolding dark.

In the morning, Abbie had to go to work, and she wondered whether she ought to creep out of the flat and leave Perry still asleep, but she had to feed the bird and take the cover off his cage so that he had some daylight hours, so she opened the living-room door cautiously, meaning to move about silently and not wake her fever-ridden visitor. But she found Perry awake and up – talking quietly to Solomon, with the cage cover already off in his hand.

'Are you fit to be up?' she asked, grasping at essentials first.

'Yes. I'm all right now.'

'You don't look it,' she told him flatly.

He laughed. 'Thanks for the vote of confidence.'

'Could you eat breakfast?'

'No, but Solomon could.'

She grinned, and went to collect the bird's morning ration of fruit, which she cut up for him carefully on the table before taking it over to the cage.

'Well, coffee, then?' she suggested. 'Or tea?'

'Tea would be wonderful,' said Perry.

'Is that what you would have at the Research Station?'

'Probably – if we hadn't run out of gas cylinders and it wasn't raining too hard for a fire.'

Abbie laughed, and got busy with the kettle. 'What's your programme for today, then?'

He sighed, rubbing a hand over his face and visibly pulling himself together to face the problems that were waiting for him.

'First, I must get back to the Club and do some telephoning.' He paused, trying to think clearly, but his head still seemed to be swimmy with fading fever, and he found it hard to concentrate. *Duncan.* The funeral... The Research Team... The fund-raising programme over here... Which was the most important? *Get your priorities right.*

'And then...?' asked Abbie, trying to find out if he was planning an impossible round of duties in his present precarious state.

'I don't know...' he said doubtfully. 'I think I have another lecture – somewhere – or it may be tomorrow... And I suppose Lucinda will be after me for some function or other... But it depends on the – the situation in Luanda. I may have to fly out there–' His hand rubbed helplessly at his eyes again, as if trying to make him see more clearly.

Abbie looked at him anxiously, and put a cup of tea down beside him, together with a round of toast that he hadn't asked for. But he took a piece without thinking, and began to chew it absent-mindedly.

'I don't think you ought to take on too much of a schedule in your present state,' she said severely. 'You don't want to collapse again.'

He smiled at her with sudden mischief. 'You sound like a reproving school mistress.'

Abbie blushed. 'I didn't mean to – order you about!'

But he was still smiling, and – Abbie noted with satisfaction – was quietly demolishing the toast as he talked. 'I think you've earned the right to do just that!' he said, and they looked at each other and both began to laugh.

Somehow, they both managed to get through a modest breakfast, and then it was time for Abbie to leave for work, and Perry, without making any comment, prepared to follow her down the stairs.

'Goodbye, Solomon,' he said, as he turned to go. 'I hope I can come and see you again soon...' and he looked at Abbie with a half-smiling question in his eyes.

'Of course you can,' said Abbie, answering the eyes. 'We'll look forward to it.'

It was as simple as that. No fuss. No plans laid. But he was coming back. And Abbie secretly rejoiced, though she was almost ashamed to admit it.

They went downstairs together, and at the bottom they met the Duchess, resplendent in her pink and purple tracksuit, fresh from her run in the park.

Oh my God, thought Abbie, what will she say about me having A MAN in my rooms overnight? But she did a swift U-turn in her mind, and decided the best thing was to be direct. 'Oh, Duchess – this is Dr. Peregrine Farquhar, the ornithologist. He has been advising me about Solomon...'

The Duchess looked Perry up and down with her finest and loftiest stage regard, and then grinned. 'Bird Fancier?' she said, eyebrows tilted in a quizzical upward curve.

Perry laughed. 'Very much so.'

'Good,' said the Duchess. 'We could do with one of those round here. Couldn't we, Abbie?'

Abbie looked at her, speechless, but the Duchess only laughed and patted Perry's arm in a proprietorial way. 'Come again soon,' she commanded, and went off, still chuckling, into her own rooms and shut the door.

'Wow!' said Perry as they went down the steps together. 'That's some lady! Is she really a Duchess?'

'No, of course not.' Abbie was smiling now in relief that he had not taken offence. 'But you can see why we all call her that.'

'I can indeed,' agreed Perry, laughing, and they walked on together to the corner of the road, and stood looking at one another while the morning traffic roared past. 'I could take the underground,' he said.

Abbie shook her head firmly. 'A taxi. No battling with rush-hour crowds.' Then a thought struck her. 'Have you any money on you?'

He looked surprised, and searched his pockets, finally unearthing a battered leather wallet. 'Yes. Enough to get back to the Club.'

Abbie grinned at his vagueness about practicalities, and put out a hand to a passing taxi. To her surprise it stopped in midstream and came round in a sweeping turn to their side of the road.

Perry got in, and leaned out again to smile at Abbie. 'I can't begin to thank you – but I'll be in touch soon.'

'Take care,' said Abbie.

And that was that. She watched the taxi ease its way back into the traffic, and then resolutely turned the other way and went to work.

4. BIRDS IN THE WILDERNESS

The first thing that Perry did when he got to his room in the Club was to ring the hospital in Luanda and ask to speak to the Senior Registrar. But when he did finally get through to Eduardo da Silva, he was in for several surprises.

'It's all right, Perry,' said his old friend, 'everything has been arranged.'

'H-has it?' Perry was not certain what was meant by this.

'Duncan left strict instructions,' explained da Silva, his kind voice sounding warm and unexpectedly close over the phone. 'He wanted to be cremated at once, and his ashes to be kept here at the hospital till you return to collect them.'

'Is – that feasible?'

'Oh yes. We have a small chapel of rest here, you know.' He paused, and then went on with Duncan's carefully thought out instructions. 'And then he wanted you to take them back to the research camp and

223

scatter them in the forest.'

'I see.' Perry was almost too overcome by this far-sighted planning to speak at all.

'It makes sense, Perry,' Eduardo said gently. 'Doesn't it?'

'Yes...' He hesitated, and then said more certainly: 'Yes, I suppose it does. He loved the forest.'

'Exactly. And it's typical of Duncan. No fuss. Simplest way out possible. Everyone satisfied.'

Everyone satisfied? Perry sighed. 'You're right, of course. It's what he would want...' He was silent for a moment and then asked urgently: 'What about the rest of the team? Do they know?'

'Yes. I managed to contact them on their radio. They understand what's happening... And Jonty said he'd take the jeep down to the nearest village and try to reach you by phone.'

'Ought I come out right away?'

His friend the doctor considered the matter. 'Isn't what you are doing over there important? To the team, I mean?'

'Yes, it is rather. But it could wait.'

'Well, I suggest *you* wait,' said da Silva. 'At least until Jonty gets through to you. There really is no hurry here.'

No hurry here. Not now. It was too late to help Duncan any more.

'Duncan was most insistent that you

should go home, wasn't he?' said the compassionate voice on the line, with just a hint of laughter in it now as he added: 'And we're all obeying his commands, as usual.'

Perry gave a small, shaken laugh in reply. 'Yes, I suppose we are... All right, I'll wait to hear from Jonty.'

'Good.'

'And Eduardo–'

'Yes?'

'Thanks for all you've done.'

'Thank Duncan,' said the doctor firmly. 'He knew exactly what he wanted. There's nothing to worry about now.'

'No,' said Perry, and rang off before he choked.

Nothing to worry about now.

But even so, he fretted about the rest of the team and the continuing work of the research project, and whether he ought to be lionising himself around London when he would so much rather be out there with them on the job.

Later that morning, Lucinda came round to see him, with a new project in her mind that successfully stopped him worrying about his research colleagues for the moment.

'Perry – I think we should have a memorial service for Duncan. After all, he was a great man, and very well-known in his field, wasn't he?'

'Yes,' agreed Perry bleakly. 'He was.'

'He must have had a lot of friends?'

'Oh yes. Everywhere he went.'

'Could you get a list of them?'

'I – yes, I think so...'

Lucinda looked at him out of those very blue, very clever eyes and said with surprising diffidence: 'Would you let me arrange it?'

'I – er – yes, I'd be glad to,' said Perry. 'Only, when it comes to the actual ceremony–?'

'Of course you must plan that yourself,' she agreed at once. 'And maybe your publisher could help?'

Perry nodded. Bernard Swift would be sure to know all the right people to ask, and the right things to say, and the right things to do... But his heart shrank from the prospect, knowing that Duncan would hate it all.

'If we're out to raise funds for the project,' said Lucinda gently, 'we need to do things in style.'

'I know,' Perry agreed sadly.

'From all I've heard about him,' Lucinda remarked, 'I don't think Duncan MacNab would object to that!'

Perry looked at Lucinda's smile and decided that it was entirely without malice – so much so that he found himself smiling back. 'Nor he would,' he admitted. 'In fact, I think he'd enjoy it!'

Lucinda leant back in her chair and breathed a sigh of relief. She had got through a tricky situation rather well, she thought. 'It can be the Duncan Memorial Fund now,' she added, and was even more relieved to see Perry's quick nod of approval.

And presently, Panky came into the Club lounge and sat down with Lucinda to talk about ways and means and 'serious sponsorship' – but Perry, who was beginning to feel shivery again, excused himself on the pretext of going upstairs to take some more pills.

'Is he all right?' asked Panky, sounding quite anxious.

'I don't think so, no,' said Lucinda. 'He's very strung up.'

'A touch of malaria, he said.'

'It's not only that, though, is it...? Grief takes people different ways.' Lucinda sounded curiously wise and sad for someone who was usually so flippant and lighthearted, and Panky glanced at her in surprise.

'Is he speaking tonight?'

'No. Tomorrow. They've given him a day in between.'

'Just as well,' said Panky. 'He looks fit to drop.'

Lucinda didn't look too worried. 'He'll keep on his feet. He's the enduring type.'

Panky was not so sure. 'I'll – look in on him later. See if he wants anything.'

Lucinda nodded. 'You do that, Panky. He'd rather have you than me fussing over him!'

Panky laughed. 'I daresay you're right!'

But when he went upstairs and knocked at the door, he found Perry pacing the floor in helpless frustration, looking flushed and feverish and rather angry.

'I can't get through to them!' he explained. 'I have to wait for them to reach me – and it's driving me crazy.'

Panky looked at him critically. 'Did you take those pills? You don't look all that good to me.'

Perry snorted impatiently. 'I'm all right. I'm used to these bouts. They don't last long.'

'Don't you get jabs for malaria these days?'

'Oh yes. Of course. But I've been in so many out-of-the-way places – and once it's in your system, you get these – recurrences.'

Panky nodded. 'Bit of a nuisance.'

'Oh well – quinine and whiskey – the same old remedies!' He grinned apologetically at Panky. 'I'm sorry I'm so tetchy. I'm a bit worried about the team out there without me–'

'Naturally.'

'And, Panky–' he looked at him a little desperately, 'I don't much like the idea of having this memorial service or whatever without them. The whole team should be there.'

'Well, why not? They could fly home, couldn't they?'

'What with?' said Perry simply. And then added in a flat, realistic tone: 'They'd never

228

agree to wasting all that money on fares. They'd say it could be spent on something more useful.'

Panky was just about to make a sharp comment on that when the phone on the bedside table shrilled loudly.

'Yes?' said Perry, springing across the room in one stride.

'Long distance,' said the hotel telephonist, 'hold the line...' There was a series of clicks and then Jonty's voice came on, loud and clear, and sounding comfortingly close.

'Perry...? Oh good, I've caught you first time. How are you?'

'I'm OK,' said Perry, untruthfully. 'What about you – and the others?'

'We're managing,' said Jonty, his velvet voice deep and reassuring. 'Pretty sad, of course. Like you. But we're keeping on keeping on. I'm writing you a report.'

'Jonty! You don't have to do that.'

'Yes, I do. You can use it for ammunition. Lists of needs and so on... Make 'em realise how short we are... How are you doing in the persuasion stakes?'

Perry sighed. 'I don't know yet – but I've got some good allies, including Monty Pankhurst. D'you remember him?'

'Oh yes. Panky. If *he's* in on it, you'll do all right.'

Perry laughed a little bleakly. 'Jonty – they could probably carry on for a bit here without me – d'you want me to come out?'

'What, now?'

'Yes. Now.' He waited, half-expecting Jonty to take a very long time considering the matter. But he didn't.

'No, Perry, of course not. You go on and do all the things you're supposed to do over there – and we'll carry on quite well till you come back... Judy's got plenty to do replacing the stuff they smashed, and Sticks is up to his eyes in some new strain of beetle he's found... And I – well, you'll see when the report arrives. We're all quite busy.'

'Any reaction from the authorities?'

'Yes. They've promised to make good all of our breakages – if I send a list to Luanda.'

'That's something, anyway.'

'Well, I think they feel responsible – though no-one can really be responsible for mindless thugs like that. But they realise that Duncan was well known everywhere – an international figure – and if that marauding gang was ever caught – which it won't be – its members would be up for manslaughter at least, if not for murder.'

'I know,' said Perry heavily. 'But they won't ever find them.' *And finding them won't bring Duncan back* ... but he did not say it. Why state the obvious?

'All the same, they will be pretty embarrassed,' said Jonty, 'especially if it's on the international news. Is it?'

'I – er – haven't heard the news today,' said Perry, trying to avoid admitting that he had been too ill to hear anything. He glanced wildly at Panky, who had made a vague move to go when the phone call came through, but had been restrained by an imperious wave of Perry's hand. 'But Panky's here. I'll ask him– Is it on the news?'

'Yes,' confirmed Panky. 'Quite a eulogy. Now he's dead, they all begin to admit he existed!' He sounded curiously bitter, and Perry glanced at him again in surprise. 'But it all helps,' added Panky, suddenly smiling at Perry. 'Tell Jonty it'll help to get his funds.'

Perry stared at him for a moment, not sure whether to be pleased or revolted, and then repeated Panky's remark.

'Yes,' agreed Jonty grimly. 'And I can hear the distaste in your fastidious voice, Perry, my upright friend, but Panky is right. *Capital* is what we have to make out of it – for Duncan's sake.'

Perry knew Jonty was making good sense, and he knew, also, that there was just as much grief behind that gentle, beguiling voice as there was behind his own. He stood rebuked. *For Duncan's sake.* Of course. It was all for Duncan's sake... But there was another question in his mind that had to be answered.

'Jonty – did we do the right thing in taking him to Luanda?'

'Yes,' said Jonty firmly. 'You know we did.

There was a chance he might make it if we got him to hospital... There was no chance here.'

'But ... he would rather have died out there in the bush.'

'Maybe.' Jonty still sounded firm and certain. 'But we would have spent the rest of our lives wondering if he would have survived if we'd got him to hospital.' He paused for a moment, and when Perry did not reply, added quietly: 'Let be, Perry. It's as he wished – and by all accounts he's still ordering us around now, as usual!'

Perry smiled rather perilously into the phone. 'There's talk here of a memorial service,' he said slowly. 'What do you think?'

'Good idea. Rally a few old friends together.'

'Yes, but – you all ought to be here, too.'

'No,' said Jonty. 'All that way? All those fares...? No. The work comes first.'

'I don't know,' worried Perry. 'I'm not sure that it <u>does</u> – in this case?'

There was a small silence while Jonty thought about it, realising from Perry's voice that he was much more upset than he cared to admit. 'No, Perry,' he said at last. 'You go ahead with all the recognition he can get over there – it's important... We'll have our own quiet little ceremony here when you get back. Did Eduardo tell you about the urn?'

'The urn...? Oh yes – yes, of course.'

'We'll find his favourite tree, Perry. I know the one – and we'll scatter him far and wide. He'll be part of the whole thing then. That's what he'd like.'

'Yes,' agreed Perry. 'That's what he'd like...'

'Must go,' Jonty told him, judging that Perry had reached the end of his tether somehow. 'You all right? The Mal come back?'

Perry's eyes went wide. 'How–?'

'Always does when you're stressed,' said Jonty. 'Dose yourself up. Need to stay on your feet. Our ambassador. We depend on you.'

'Oh Lord,' groaned Perry. 'Don't expect too much.'

'Only the best – from you!' Jonty said, laughing at the other end of the line. 'We'll await developments. Eduardo can get me on the bush radio again if need be – otherwise, we'll expect you when we see you. All right? Everyone sends their love. God bless.'

He rang off then, before Perry could answer, and left him standing, bereft, with the phone in his hand... It had been Duncan's favourite salutation – to all of them, whenever he left them, wherever he went... and the last words he had ever said to Perry... *God bless, Duncan, wherever you are!*

'What you need is a drink,' said Panky, pushing Perry into a chair. 'Got any up here?'

'Yes.' Perry waved a vague hand. 'Over there–'

'And then, I think, a doctor,' Panky went on, pouring out a stiff whiskey from the bottle on the table.

'Not necessary,' Perry protested. 'I know what to do.'

'I daresay.' Panky was not to be put off. 'We need you alive and kicking tomorrow. Stay there. I'll see to it.'

Perry stayed there. It was less trouble than trying to go anywhere else. And presently a brisk and friendly doctor arrived, with Panky just behind him. He listened quietly to Perry's rather dim explanations, and then got him on to the bed to be examined. But when Perry took off his shirt and stretched out on the coverlet, the kindly doctor's face expressed surprise, and his clever fingers came out and touched the livid bruising on Perry's right side.

'Where did you get this?'

'What...? Oh, I'd forgotten.'

'Forgotten?'

'It was when Duncan MacNab was attacked,' Perry explained. 'Everyone was hitting out in all directions... I think I whacked someone with a stick–'

'You mean, someone whacked *you* with a stick?'

'I suppose so – yes.'

The doctor's sensitive fingers probed a

little, and Perry winced. 'Yes. A couple of cracked ribs there, I suspect. Better get them X-rayed tomorrow.'

'Oh no,' groaned Perry. 'I need to be on my feet. Not lying down!'

Panky spoke crisply then – as crisply as the doctor. 'Better do what he says, Perry. No point in taking more risks than necessary.'

Duncan took more risks than necessary, Perry thought. Why should I be different? But he was suddenly too tired to say so. 'All right, tomorrow–' he murmured. 'But I'm speaking in Oxford at eight.'

'We'll get you there,' said Panky. 'Only, for God's sake rest up today, and give yourself a chance.'

'Quite so,' agreed the doctor, smiling, and preceded to give Perry a useful injection for malaria and several quiet words of advice and instruction before he went away.

Panky went away then, too, and left Perry blessedly alone, dozing fitfully on the bed where they had left him.

But after a while, his tired mind suddenly remembered the bird – Solomon – with his brilliant crested head tilted enquiringly towards him ... and the bird's gentle owner with the lovely, compassionate eyes... How Duncan would like you – both of you – he thought, and smiling, fell asleep.

It was a day or two later when Abbie

235

remembered the Prof and decided to go and look for him in the park. He would probably like to know Perry's verdict on the bird's identity. By this time she had managed to tell both Mackintosh and little Olive Ashridge about it, and even young Bobby, who still took a proprietorial interest in the bird, and often turned up after school 'to have a look.' It was surprising how many people now came up the stairs to her flat with offerings of fruit, and though the bird was still shy, it did not seem to mind their attentions... All the same, she thought, I do wonder if I am doing the right thing – or whether he would be better off in some tropical birdhouse or others... I must ask Perry when he comes. It didn't seem in the least odd to her that she was already relying on his judgment – and on his return. Perry would come soon – and he would know what to do.

In the meantime, she had better make sure the old Prof was all right, for he was somehow a bit on her conscience. She found him sitting on his usual bench, looking pinched and cold in spite of the warm day, and still clutching the empty doglead in his hand. Cautiously, she sat down beside him and got out her sandwiches.

'Good morning, Prof,' she said, and offered him a ham-and-cheese.

'Is it?' he growled. But he accepted her offering, though rather ungraciously.

Abbie was undeterred. 'Well, I think it's a good morning,' she told him, biting into her sandwich. 'The sun's shining, I've got the day off, and I've had some news about my bird.'

The old man grunted crossly, but then couldn't hide his curiosity. 'What news was that, then?'

'He had a visitor – the great ornithologist, Dr. Peregrine Farquhar came to see him.' (She didn't think Perry would much like being called 'great,' but it sounded good. And, judging by his skill as a lecturer, and his description of his work in the field, he probably was.)

'Huh!' snorted the Prof. 'Move in high circles, don't we?'

Abbie laughed. 'Not really. It was – er – a chance encounter...' (But was it chance? She had gone to that lecture on purpose, meaning to buttonhole Perry... And hadn't she, instead, taken what chance she could of making herself useful and getting to know him...? She felt a bit guilty when she thought about it – though she had acted purely out of sympathy for a man in trouble.)

'Well?' barked the old man in his gravelly voice. 'What's the verdict, then?'

'Oh...' Abbie pulled herself together. 'Well, he is a Turaco – a Red-crested Turaco. And he's endemic only in Angola ... so Perry thinks there probably aren't any others like him over here.'

'Endangered species?'

'N-no – Perry says not, except that nearly all the rare birds are endangered there, because of the forest being cut down so fast. There's hardly any left.'

'Loss of habitat.' The old man nodded his head wisely.

Abbie was surprised. 'You seem to know a lot about it.'

'Not a lot,' contradicted the Prof. '*Some*. I do read, you know!'

Abbie grinned at him apologetically. 'Sorry! Not many people do these days!'

'You can say that again,' he growled.

There was silence for a moment while Abbie offered him another sandwich, and he transferred the empty doglead to his knee.

'Well?' Abbie said, not put off by the silence. 'Are you coming to see him or not?'

The Prof looked at her peevishly. 'I thought you'd never ask!'

And they both began to laugh. So they finished the sandwiches together, and strolled on through the park towards Abbie's attic flat in the Duchess's cheerful house.

But as they went, Abbie began to notice that the old man walked slower than he used to, and seemed at times to be almost tottery on his feet, though he said nothing about it. It worried her rather, and in the end she decided to let her concern show.

'Can I ask you a rude question?'

'I daresay.'

'Have you been eating anything lately?'

He glanced at her sideways, and something about the fierce flash of independence in his eyes made Abbie wonder if she had asked too much. But he answered non-committally, and without his usual bad temper. 'Now and then.' And when she made no comment on that, he added: 'Why?'

'You don't seem quite as spry and lively as you used to be–?'

'When I had Spot?' he finished for her, in a light, dry voice.

'Yes, perhaps so...' She was deliberately leading him on to talk of the dog – if he would. Maybe even remembering their perennial battleground of walks would help to thaw the old man's angry, knotted-up distress.

'Well, I suppose yanking him from one lamp-post to the next, and arguing the toss about which side of which tree he wanted to cock his leg on was a kind of exercise!'

Abbie laughed – but it was a gentle sound. 'Not so much fun, walking on your own?'

'No fun at all,' he grumbled, but he understood why Abbie was troubled, and added, by way of grudging reassurance: 'I do it, though.'

'Good,' said Abbie, daring to smile at his mutinous face. 'And eat sometimes, I trust...?

We can't have you fading away altogether, can we?'

'*Why not?*' rasped the old man, in his most uncompromising voice. And then, seeing Abbie's shocked look, he relented a little and said:

'Take no notice... I'm a crotchety old devil. I told you so before... Let's buy some fruit for the bird.'

They climbed the stairs together, and both went over to look at the bird before Abbie put the kettle on. 'Hallo, Solomon,' she said. 'I've brought you a visitor. And he's brought you a present...'

She always talked to the bird when she came in, and the beautiful, crested head always tilted to listen to the sound of her voice, and sometimes there came a soft, answering chirrup, as if he was making some kind of response, half under his breath.

This time, Solomon came out from his leaves and made a small, decisive crow of welcome, and then climbed down to the floor of his cage to investigate the latest offering.

Once again, the old man spent a long time just looking at him in silence, his shoulders hunched, as if warding off hurt. 'He looks well,' he said at last. 'Brighter, somehow.'

'Yes,' agreed Abbie, busy with the tea. 'Mackintosh – that's the caretaker here who built the cage – got me some vitamins to give him to supplement his diet...' She wished silently that she could give some vitamins to the old man as well – for it was all too clear that his diet needed supplementing. He was beginning to look very frail. But she knew she couldn't say any more... Maybe she could introduce him to Tubby's.

She was just pouring out the tea, and surreptitiously providing a few extra biscuits, when there was a knock at the door.

'Company?' growled the old man, looking as if he wanted to get up and run.

'Probably some more admirers for the bird,' said Abbie, smiling. 'Stay there and drink your tea. It's not important.'

But it was. Perry was at the door. He stood there, looking almost as awkward as the old man, and smiled back at Abbie in diffident appeal.

'I hope I'm not intruding–? I've brought a peace-offering for Solomon.'

'Come in,' said Abbie, her smile suddenly becoming radiant. 'This is the Prof. He brought a peace-offering, too.'

'Spoilt bird,' said Perry, and went to have a look. 'He *does* look well!'

'That's what the Prof said.'

'Kinda *brighter*,' confirmed the Prof. 'Vitamins, she says.'

Perry grinned in relief that he was accepted without fuss, and gave Solomon a piece of kiwi-fruit which he had chosen and cut up specially. The bird looked at it doubtfully, and then decided that it was just what he needed.

'Sit down and have some tea,' invited Abbie. 'And tell us how things are going. Are you better?'

'Yes.' Perry dismissed it airily. 'The doc gave me an extra jab. I'm fine now.' He didn't mention the cracked ribs which still hurt, especially when he laughed. But he wasn't likely to be doing much laughing in the near future, he reflected grimly. Then he saw Abbie looking at him, and decided that there probably were things to laugh at after all.

The tea party progressed quietly, with Perry explaining about the memorial service, and touching on his contact with the other members of his team, and the newly-christened Duncan MacNab Memorial Fund; and the old Prof listened politely and showed a surprising grasp of the situation in his dry, sardonic way.

'Stir 'em up!' he said, grinning balefully at Perry. 'People are like puddings. Need stirring.'

Perry nodded, understanding him very well.

'Then they might *rise* to the occasion,' added the Prof, with a cackle of wicked laughter. Then, as if stirred by his own voice giving him the exact cue he was looking for, he rose to his feet and said brusquely: 'Must be going now.'

'Oh,' protested Abbie, disappointed because she had been planning other things for the Prof, 'but I was going to take you down to Tubby's.'

'Who?' He looked at her suspiciously.

'Tubby's... It's a little café I go to ... not far from here.' She cast a hopeful glance in his direction. 'Small and cosy ... lovely food ... and Tubby, the man who runs it, is lovely, too!'

'Not today, Abbie,' said the Prof firmly, and then added with surprising politeness: 'Thanks all the same.'

'Another time, then?' Abbie insisted, determined to get a meal into him somehow, sometime.

But the old man was not to be cajoled. 'Maybe,' he allowed cautiously. And that was as far as he would go.

He went over and said goodbye to Solomon, exchanging looks of doubtful recognition, and said softly: 'Keep smiling, bird!' Then he turned to Abbie and Perry, as if they were already a pair engaged in warding off each other's darknesses, and added knowingly: 'And you two, as well.' Then he stumped off down the stairs, leaving them smiling after him in some astonishment.

'I thought he was the one in need of consolation,' said Abbie, laughing. 'But he seems to think we are, too!'

Perry laughed as well. (There, he said, I

knew I'd be laughing soon.) 'A very astute old man.' Then he looked at Abbie more seriously. 'Consolation? For what...? And who is this Tubby who is "lovely, too"?'

So Abbie told him about the old man and his dog – and about Tubby and his curious network, and the warmth of his friendly little café that was already the nearest thing to home and home comforts that she had met so far in London. She did not tell him why she was living alone in the big city, so far away from the countryside she loved, or why she was painfully endeavouring to follow Tubby's advice and lay her own ghosts in whatever way she could... But Perry was no fool, and in the end, because he somehow needed to know what moved this girl of glancing laughter and hidden sadness, he said abruptly: 'Why, Abbie?'

She looked at him and sighed, unsurprised at his question. 'Oh, you know how it is. Women with broken hearts go in for good works... And men go off and shoot tigers. Do you shoot tigers?'

'Only on film,' said Perry, laughing (again!)

But somehow they both felt that positions had been stated, a stage had been reached – and various barriers of pride and grief had been quietly demolished.

'I really came to ask you out to a meal,' he said at last.

'Shall we go down to Tubby's?'

He shook his head. 'Not tonight. This is a special occasion.'

'Is it? Why?' But she knew the answer, really.

'Let's say, in honour of the Rescue Service,' said Perry, and led her away down the stairs and out into the summer evening, where even the greyest streets were gilded with rose and amber light from the setting sun.

Perry took her to a place that seemed to be all muted grey silk with carpeting to match, and was so quiet and discreet that Abbie guessed it must be wildly expensive. It was both restful and curiously reassuring to be on the receiving end of such perfect service – and such perfect food – but, even so, Abbie's fiercely puritan upbringing compelled her to protest.

'Perry, this is all very wonderful and enormously flattering, but ought you to be spending all this money on me?'

'Yes, I ought,' Perry said, and grinned at her with a lightening of mischief in his sombre expression. 'Don't you like it?'

'Of course I like it,' Abbie admitted, unable to resist that grin. 'But you're meant to be raising funds, not making extravagant gestures!'

Perry actually laughed. 'I've just launched a book, remember? And almost all the royalties are going to the Fund. I think I'm allowed a few small luxuries.' He screwed up his eyes at her. 'What a puritan you are!'

Abbie sighed. 'It's my father's fault. He always set me impossible standards!' Her smile was rueful now, and oddly tender. 'That's the penalty of living with a saint!'

Perry was interested. He leant forward to fill up her glass and said seriously: 'Tell me about it.'

So Abbie described life at the Vicarage – her vague, other-worldly father and her practical, all-loving, all-enduring mother – the beautiful, rambling old house that was so cold in winter that the water froze in her tooth mug overnight – the sprawling, overgrown garden, rich with tumbling roses and laden, ancient fruit trees – and beyond the garden, the green meadows knee-deep in clover and moon-daisies, and the blue-grey rolling hills beyond...

And, of course, however hard she tried to skirt round it, the spectre of Tim and his betrayal could not be entirely ignored, it somehow coloured her description of that beloved, lost landscape and all it had meant to her, and even got into the carefully neutral timbre of her voice... So much so, that Perry, who was bent on discovering the cause of her hidden sadness, said suddenly and gently: 'What happened, Abbie?'

She hesitated for a moment, and then said in quiet understatement: 'Just a boy-and-girl idyll that came apart... It was part of my childhood, really – all mixed up with flowery meadows and absurd, impossible promises...' She looked into his face with honest, half-humorous self-appraisal. 'It was time I grew up!'

Perry's smile was almost as tender as hers when she had been thinking of her father. 'Would you say you were grown up now?'

'Oh no,' Abbie laughed. 'I've got a long way to go yet! But I'm trying.'

'What makes you think you haven't arrived there yet?' There was a serious intent behind his smile.

'Well,' said Abbie judicially, fingering her glass and wondering if the wine was making her too talkative, 'for one thing, I'm still such a hopeless optimist. I keep on expecting things!'

Perry let out a muted shout of laughter. 'Oh, Abbie! In that case, none of us ever grow up at all!'

'No,' agreed Abbie, smiling. 'I hope not.'

And they looked at one another in sudden recognition, as if they had crossed another threshold.

'Tubby's Place' might have been a good deal less luxurious and impressive than the restaurant Perry had taken her to, but it was as warm and welcoming as ever when Abbie went back to it an evening or two later – and she had a momentary pang of conscience for having deserted it for those more elegant surroundings. But Tubby himself didn't seem to have noticed her defection, and greeted her as cheerfully as usual – though he seemed slightly more rushed and harassed than was his wont.

'Hi, Abbie. Glad to see you. Busy tonight. Sorry!' And he rushed by, juggling with two plates of egg-and-chips and two sets of cutlery wrapped in red paper napkins.

'Where's Pauline?' asked Abbie, looking round at the crowded little café and the various patient or impatient customers waiting for service.

'Not shown up,' said Tubby, making a neat U-turn round two tables and dashing back to the counter for two more orders.

Abbie assessed the situation rapidly, and came to the conclusion that Tubby simply couldn't fulfil all those orders in the kitchen, and wait on the tables as well. 'Can I help?' she volunteered. 'At least I could carry things.'

Tubby glanced at her with a wild and desperate hope. 'Oh, Abbie – would you...? I expect she'll be along in a minute... But until then–? I'm frightfully pushed.'

'So I see,' grinned Abbie. 'Come on then – tell me what to do.'

It was the beginning of a fairly frantic couple of hours, and towards the end of it, when the customers had been satisfied and the rush had died down, Abbie leant on Tubby's counter and rested her aching arms and said: 'To think Pauline does this every night.'

'It's not always this bad,' Tubby told her, smiling. 'Tonight was just one of those evenings.' He glanced sideways at Abbie, and added kindly: 'You can sit down and take a weight off your feet now, if you like. It's easing off!'

But there was just one more customer signalling for more coffee, and while Abbie was bringing it over to him, Perry Farquhar walked in through the door. He looked at Abbie wide-eyed for a moment, but did not seem unduly surprised by the situation. He merely waited till she had delivered the coffee and then followed her over to the counter before he said quietly: 'Am I in the way? I didn't realise you worked here.'

'She doesn't,' said Tubby, who had somehow mysteriously found the time to come out of the kitchen and size Perry up with a very hard, shrewd glance. 'She's just helping me out in an emergency.' He grinned at Abbie, back once more to his old, cheerful, unharassed self. 'And I've just been telling her to sit down and rest her feet! They must be about ready to drop off by now.' He pushed Abbie firmly into a chair at the small, unobtrusive table that he kept for his staff at the side of the counter, ignoring her protests, and bustled off to get them two coffees 'on the house'. When he returned, he said smilingly to Abbie: 'Is this the famous Bird Fancier?' (He must have been talking to the Duchess.)

Abbie laughed. 'It is. Dr. Peregrine Farquhar in person.'

'Perry to his friends,' added the B.F, grinning, and held out his hand. He liked the look of Tubby.

And Tubby rather liked the look of him. He stayed for a moment talking to them, and then, perceiving that they would be very happy to be left alone, he went back to his counter and another customer. But while he was waiting for the hissing espresso machine to disgorge its next lot of coffee, a wild-eyed, dishevelled Pauline rushed in through the door.

'Oh Tubby,' she panted, lurching over to him as if she had been running in the marathon, *they've got Bobby!*'

Tubby looked at her sharply. 'What d'you mean, they've got Bobby? Who has? Where?' Then, seeing that Pauline was near collapse, he put an arm round her and led her over to Abbie's table, where she sank down on to the spare chair, half-hidden by the counter, and sat there gasping and trying to get her breath back.

'Do you mind?' said Tubby to Abbie. 'Keep

an eye for a second. I'll get the brandy.'

Abbie and Perry looked at each other and then at the distraught woman beside them, and both spoke at once.

'Take it easy,' said Perry.

'Take your time,' said Abbie.

And even as Pauline nodded, still making desperate attempts to control her breathing, Tubby returned with a bottle of brandy and a glass into which he had already poured a sizeable tot of spirits. 'Now,' he said, 'drink that. And tell us what's happened.'

Perry, with exquisite tact, began to get to his feet, but Tubby stopped him with an imperious wave of his hand. 'No, don't go. We may need some cool, calm judgment here,' he murmured, and nodded approval as Perry sank back into his chair.

Pauline swallowed the brandy in one gulp, choked, and then began to talk. 'He didn't come home from school – he usually comes on his own. It's quite safe – or I thought it was. I mean, he gets off the school bus at the end of our road... I waited and waited, and when he didn't come, I went down to the school to have a look... It was all shut up by then, of course, but I met one of his mates – Jimmy Bates – on the way back, and he said he saw Bobby getting into a van with two men and he looked as if he didn't want to, Jimmy said, only one man had hold of his arm.' She took a shaky breath and looked up at Tubby piteously, her face grey with fear. 'And then – when I got back home – I had this phone call...'

'What phone call?' Tubby's tone was crisp.

'They didn't say who they was...' Pauline was struggling again to stay calm enough to get the words out. 'They only said *"tell Len to keep quiet..."* But I knew who they was, really, and when I said "what have you done with Bobby?" they just said it again: *"Tell Len to keep quiet. Then no-one will get hurt."*' She began to shake then, and added in a voice of nightmare: 'But I don't trust them, Tubby... They'll stop at nothing, that lot... And they've got my Bobby! What am I going to do?'

Tubby laid a hand on her arm and gave it a reassuring squeeze. 'Give us a few more details, Pauline. Then we might be able to help.' He poured out another stiff drink and handed it to her.

'I shall be drunk–' she said, gulping it down, and sounding on the edge of tears.

'Never mind that,' said Tubby. 'How does Len come into all this?' He glanced at Abbie, and added by way of quick explanation: 'Len's her husband...'

'The one who's "inside"?' asked Abbie, not mincing matters, since the crisis seemed too serious for anything but plain speaking.

'Exactly,' said Tubby grimly. 'On remand. Awaiting trial. Come on, Pauline, what's it all about?'

She took another shaky breath and tried to explain. 'It's the trial, see? The police want Len to testify... He might get a lighter sentence if he does...' She looked rather wildly from Tubby to the other two quiet listeners. 'Len was just the driver, see – didn't have nothing to do with the robbery... He was just paid to drive... But when the police closed in – there'd been a tip-off, see? – the others all got away, and left Len to get done for the lot.'

'Typical,' grunted Tubby.

Pauline sighed agreement. 'Always a loser, Len was...' Then she took another perilous breath and went on: 'But now they've got one of 'em – the one that paid Len to drive – and they need to pin it on him, d'you see? Identify him like?'

'Yes,' growled Tubby. 'I do see.'

'But they've got Bobby!' Pauline wailed, terror rising in her voice. 'And I don't know what to do!'

'You must tell the police,' said Perry. *'Now.'*

They all looked at him in surprise. But he was unperturbed. 'Maybe I ought not to interfere,' he said. 'I know I'm a stranger, and it's none of my business. But I've actually had dealings with a kidnapping before – and, believe me, the only way to get results is to let the police handle it...' He looked at Pauline, willing her to understand him. 'They are used to dealing with these sort of people,' he explained gently. 'They know how they react ... and probably, if they consult your husband, Len, they'll be able to find out where these people hang out – or at least what kind of places to look in...'

'But–' Pauline began, still dreadfully afraid, 'that lot – won't they–?'

'No,' said Perry firmly. 'They won't hurt Bobby. It's not in their interest to do him any harm. He's their *safeguard*, isn't he...? Or that's what they think.' Pauline saw the sense of that, and nodded doubtfully. 'Then – you think–?'

'I think Len will probably lead the police right to them,' said Perry, sounding calm and confident. 'But you must tell them now – and ask them to let you see Len at once. They'll be able to fix that.'

She looked helplessly from one to the other of them. 'I – I don't know if they'll listen to me...?'

Tubby shot a rather anxious glance at Abbie, and then at the few remaining customers in his café. 'I can't leave the place yet–' he muttered.

Perry also glanced at Abbie, signalling unknown messages of reassurance, and then got to his feet. 'I'll go with you,' he said to Pauline. 'I know how to talk to them.' A faint smile glimmered between him and

Abbie as he added: 'We'll leave you to take care of the café – you and Tubby – till we come back. All right?'

'All right,' agreed Abbie, trusting him without question. 'Good luck.'

'Yes,' affirmed Tubby. 'Good luck.'

And he and Abbie watched Perry lead the bewildered Pauline out into the street, where he hailed a passing taxi and drove her swiftly away.

It had been after eight o'clock when Perry and Pauline left, and it was nearly ten before Perry returned – alone.

Abbie and Tubby had spent an anxious couple of hours wondering how Pauline was getting on with the police, and now they both rushed over to Perry for news.

'Well?' Tubby demanded. 'Did you see them?'

'Where is Pauline?' asked Abbie, almost in the same breath.

'Give me a chance,' said Perry, with a faint but reassuring smile. 'Yes, we saw them. And, yes, they took the thing seriously. Pauline has stayed on to try to speak to Len tonight. And they'll see her safely home, and tap her phone so that they can trace the calls... They are sending someone round to interview the small boy – Jimmy, was it? – who saw the van and the two men bundling Bobby into it... They might get a lead from that – but they were hoping they'd get a great deal more out of Len, now that he knew his son was in danger.'

'I hope they're right,' muttered Tubby, not sounding too sure.

'What about Pauline? Ought she to be alone tonight?' asked Abbie, picturing the frantic mother walking up and down all night, waiting for news.

'They're sending a policewoman to be with her,' said Perry. 'I asked her if she'd rather come here – or to Abbie–' he glanced from one to the other of them apologetically. 'Took a liberty, I know – but she said she had to be at home in case they rang her again...' He paused, and then added, speaking directly to Tubby: 'And she said to tell you she wouldn't be able to come until Bobby was found – just in case they tried to contact her again.'

Tubby nodded. 'Understood.' He was frowning, but more in anxiety about Pauline and Bobby than about the fate of his café and its customers. 'Poor girl,' he sighed. 'She must be nearly out of her mind.'

'Yes,' agreed Perry. 'But the police seemed very confident that these people would not harm Bobby – he was too valuable to them; and they were fairly optimistic about finding him soon. I think they convinced Pauline a bit... It really all depends on how much Len can tell them.'

'Or *will* tell them?' suggested Tubby.

'But surely – now?' protested Abbie. 'With Bobby in danger?'

'I don't know,' Tubby said slowly. 'He's been too frightened to speak up till now. He might take them seriously and be even more afraid to say anything...' He glanced at Perry. 'It was touch and go whether we could even persuade Pauline to go to the police, remember – only you rushed her into it before she had time to think.'

Perry looked only mildly contrite. 'I know I was rather highhanded.'

'You were absolutely right,' said Tubby, and gave him a fleeting grin of approval. 'Let's hope Len has the sense to see it, too.' Then he looked at Abbie's tired, worried face and said very kindly: 'Go on home now, Abbie. You've been a tower of strength tonight... You're nearly asleep on your feet!'

Abbie smiled at him, and said rather jerkily: 'I'll feel better when there's some news of Bobby.'

'So will we all,' agreed Tubby.

'I think there will be quite soon,' said Perry, sounding curiously certain about it. Then he laid a gentle hand on Abbie's arm. 'Come on. I'll take you home.'

She admitted then, suddenly, that she was rather tired, and it was unexpectedly comforting to be taken under Perry's wing... Like a bird, she thought vaguely. Like my bird,

Solomon – safe and well-looked-after... But she remembered then that Tubby was going to be left in the lurch tomorrow, and he had been a good friend to her.

'I could come and give you a hand tomorrow evening?' she said over her shoulder, as Perry propelled her to the door. 'Just for the evening rush?'

'Oh, Abbie, bless you!' agreed Tubby. 'But get a good night's sleep first.' He followed them to the door of the café, preparing to lock up after them, and then said seriously to Perry: 'Thanks. You've been a tower of strength, too!'

Outside in the street, the two of them stood looking at one another, almost shyly.

'We could go and have a quiet drink somewhere?' Perry suggested.

'Or you could come back and see the bird?' Abbie retorted, and they both began to laugh. Then, by mutual consent, they began to stroll down the street towards the Duchess's house.

'I never asked you how you came to turn up at Tubby's?' Abbie enquired.

'I went to the house – and I met a strange, long thin boy who said you were probably at Tubby's.'

'Oh, that must have been Synco.'

'Who?'

'Synco. He merges music, or something! Synchronises. Though he says it probably ought to be <u>synthesises</u>, but "the boys" called him that and it stuck.' She laughed at his bemused expression. 'And he whistles to Solomon.'

'Does he get any response?' Perry's trained mind was immediately interested.

'Sometimes... He asked Solomon if he was lonely–' She grew grave suddenly.

'And I – I still wonder sometimes–'

'Wonder what?'

'If he would be happier in some tropical birdhouse?'

Perry considered the matter. 'He would probably be on his own there, too. More so than he is with you... They couldn't put him with other species very well – and they'd be unlikely to have another like him...'

Abbie sighed. 'What would you like to do with him? Could he go back to the wild?'

'No,' said Perry. 'Not without being re-acclimatised and taught how to survive... But if we could really set up our wild-life sanctuary and get the captive breeding programme going – he might be very happy there, especially if we found him a mate...' He turned to her, smiling in the half-dark of the late summer evening. 'Pipe dreams, I'm afraid...'

'But they *may* come true.'

'Yes,' he agreed, a little sadly. 'They may...'

'Come on up and have some tea,' said Abbie. 'I know you like tea best... And you can tell me how your plans are going... Who knows? Solomon may be part of them yet!'

They climbed the stairs together and went to have a look at Solomon. His cage got the last rays of the setting sun, and even the afterglow seemed to linger round it, so he was still awake, and looked at them out of bright, inquisitive eyes.

'I'm sorry to be so late with your supper,' said Abbie, and went to cut up the fresh fruit for him, though she thought it was probably too late in the evening for him to feel like eating. 'I only meant to stay at Tubby's for an hour,' she said, not sure if she was apologising to Solomon or to Perry. 'But couldn't leave Tubby in the lurch.'

'Of course you couldn't.'

'And – as it turned out – I'm glad I stayed ... though I didn't do much for Pauline.' She looked at Perry. 'But *you* did... And she was a total stranger to you!'

'Not total,' said Perry judiciously. 'After all, she's Bobby's mother – it was Bobby who rescued Solomon in the first place! So naturally I'm concerned!'

Abbie laughed, though still a little anxiously. 'That's very curious logic! But it was wonderful of you to take so much trouble...' She paused, and then added: 'I know you were being deliberately optimistic for Pauline's sake – but do you really think Bobby will be all right?'

'Yes,' said Perry slowly. 'I do. They'll keep

him very safe, but they won't harm him...
He's a valuable asset... But he may be rather
frightened, if they lock him up somewhere.'

Abbie sighed. 'I'm afraid he may be ...
though I somehow think Bobby isn't easily
frightened...' She looked at Perry with sudden appeal. 'Isn't there *anything* we can do?'

Perry hesitated, and then said rather
unhappily: 'There's something <u>you</u> could
do... But – I don't like having to do this,
Abbie – I can't be any use to you tomorrow.
I have to be in Cambridge...' He shook his
head crossly at his own commitments. 'I
can't get out of it ... but I'll be back late
tomorrow night – and if there's anything for
us to do, I could help after that.'

Abbie nodded, accepting his planned
schedule without question. She knew it was
too important to shelve. Too much depended
on it. 'You said I could do something?'

'Yes. That small boy – Jimmy something –
I think you should try to see him... I have a
feeling he might tell you a bit more about
what he saw than he would to the police...'
He grinned at Abbie somewhat wryly. 'I
suspect the kids don't get on too well with
their local constabulary round here!'

Abbie grinned back. 'You could be right...
I'll find out about him from Pauline...
thought I'd go round to see how she was,
anyway, on the way to work.'

Perry leaned back in his chair, looking at

her with a surprisingly affectionate glance. 'You're a glutton for punishment, aren't you?'

Abbie laughed. 'So are you, come to that. What else have you got planned?'

'Well, I think there are only two lectures left, after Cambridge. And a couple of meetings with sponsors – Lucinda is arranging those, with help from my devious friend, Monty Pankhurst. Did you meet him at that awful reception?'

'No,' said Abbie. 'But then I didn't meet anyone much–'

'Except me!' he said, smiling. 'And I monopolised you the whole evening!'

'I'm not complaining.' Abbie was smiling, too. 'But who is this Monty Pankhurst? Is he important?'

'For the fund-raising business, yes, he is. Very.' There was faint distaste in his voice, and Abbie did not miss it.

'You don't much like all that side of it, do you?'

'No,' admitted Perry. 'But I know it's necessary. Only, I'm not much good at sucking up to wealthy tycoons! I'd much rather be out in Africa, photographing birds!'

Abbie nodded, still smiling a little at the thought of Perry 'sucking up' to anyone at all. 'You will be going back there soon,' she said soothingly, and realised with a pang that there was regret in her mind even as she said it.

'There's the memorial service to get through first,' he said.

'Will it be an ordeal for you?'

He stopped to consider before answering. 'I suppose it may be... A lot of Duncan's old friends – all wanting to take part and say something nice about him...' His glance met Abbie's with rueful honesty. 'My first thought was that Duncan himself would have hated every minute of it...! But Lucinda pointed out that it would actually help his cause, and he – knowing that – would probably laugh!'

'I can see that he might!' agreed Abbie, meeting his ironic glance with a hint of mischief in her own.

'And that reminds me,' added Perry, as if it followed on from some other secret thoughts, 'I should like you to be there.'

Abbie was startled. 'But – I didn't even know him.'

'I'm not so sure about that,' murmured Perry obscurely. 'You seem to think alike... And anyway, you've rescued a bird. That puts you on the side of the angels.'

'Does it...? Even if he ought to be at home in Africa?'

Perry looked at her with the same strange mixture of recognition and affection he had shown before. 'But – as you say – he may be part of the pipe-dream yet!'

He is already, thought Abbie. For this is all

a pipedream, really. And whether the rest of it comes true or not, I don't want this bit to end.

But Perry was watching her – almost tenderly, as if he knew her thoughts and perhaps even shared them. 'I must go home now,' he said softly, 'and leave you to dream in peace.' Then he added, as if to reassure her: 'But I'll be back – to offer what help I can.'

Abbie began to protest then. 'Perry, you don't have to–'

'Oh yes, I do,' he said, smiling down at her. 'We're all part of the same dream now.'

When Abbie got to Pauline's flat in the morning, she found her – as she had expected – pacing the floor, chain-smoking, and looking grey with worry. And there was no sign of the young policewoman who was supposed to be looking after her.

'No news yet?' asked Abbie, though the answer was fairly obvious. 'And why are you alone?'

Pauline shook her head. 'She's only gone out to make her report. She'll be back...' She looked at Abbie grimly. 'I keep waiting for the phone to ring – but I dread it ringing just the same.'

Abbie nodded, understanding very well. 'Have you had a cup of tea yet this morning? Shall I put the kettle on?'

'I – yes, if you like,' Pauline shrugged, not

really interested.

'Did you talk to Len? Was he any use?'

Pauline stopped her pacing for a moment and sighed. 'Yes and no... He did his best...' She made a sad little gesture with her hand, as if making helpless allowances for someone who ought to have been a source of help and comfort but was hopelessly inadequate. 'He said he never knew where they hung out. He only met one of them in a pub. He told us the name of it – the Betel and Chisel, down south of the river somewhere... The police are going to follow it up, but the gang won't be there now. Len says they only used it as a meeting place to fix up drivers. He never saw the others till the raid, and they wore masks.'

Abbie sighed too, and brought Pauline a cup of tea and persuaded her to sit down and drink it. 'The little boy – Jimmy – where does he live, d'you know?'

'Yes, I do. Why?' Pauline looked at her suspiciously.

'It's only that I thought – Perry thought – he might be slightly less scared of talking to us than to the police.'

'Yes, he might.' Pauline's expression was still grim.

'And he might remember something more about that van,' went on Abbie, hoping Pauline would co-operate.

Bobby's mother gave her a pale, pain-washed grin. 'I suppose it's worth a try... He lives two doors down from here – number twenty-four. You might just catch him before he goes to school.' She clasped her hands round her cup, as if she was cold. 'Abbie – he will be all right, won't he...? Your friend Perry said he would, and I – I sort of believed him, somehow.... But was he right?'

'Yes,' said Abbie firmly. 'I'm sure he was right. Didn't the police say so, too?'

'Yes,' admitted Pauline. 'But I – I think I'd sooner believe your friend Perry than them!'

Abbie smiled. 'Perry was quite certain they wouldn't harm Bobby. He's too valuable to them.' She laid an arm round Pauline's hunched shoulders and gave them an encouraging squeeze. 'Just keep on believing it, Pauline. It will be all right.'

Pauline looked up at her piteously. 'Oh God, I hope so!'

And at that point they heard the young policewoman coming back up the stairs, and Abbie turned to go. There wasn't much time left to talk to young Jimmy before she had to be at work and he had to be at school.

'I'll look in this evening on my way back,' she said. 'If there's anything else I can do, tell me! Here's my work number.'

She passed the policewoman, Terry, in the hallway of the flat and said: 'I hope there's some news soon. She's feeling pretty desperate.'

'I know,' Terry said. 'We're doing our best.'
She smiled hopefully at Abbie, who hurried
off, not waiting for any more.

Young Jimmy Bates, when she found him,
was sleepily shovelling down cornflakes in
his mother's kitchen, and not feeling very
forthcoming. But, to Abbie's surprise, the
boy's mother spoke up sharply, turning
round from the sink to glare at him. 'Now,
think, Jimmy! It's important. Your friend
Bobby's in real danger! Anything you can
remember might help.' She aimed a tired
smile in Abbie's direction. 'That poor
woman! She must be nearly out of her
mind!'

'Yes,' agreed Abbie. 'She is.' She turned
back to the small, freckled boy, intent on his
breakfast. 'Well, Jimmy?'

'It was just a van,' he said, shrugging
indifferently.

'What colour? Did you notice?'

'Yeah.' He sounded quite casual about it.
'Grey, wiv blue lines – kinda smart.' He gave
Abbie a brief, gap-toothed grin. 'I told the
police that,' he added virtuously.

Abbie nodded approval. 'Did you get the
number?'

'Only a bit.'

'What d'you mean, only a bit?'

'Well, I seed the letters, see? An' I 'mem-
bered some of 'em... There was a C and a
T... Like Cat. I can spell cat.'

'C.A.T.?'

He looked doubtful. 'Didn't see the A...'

'Did you tell the police that, too?'

'Yeah.' He spooned up a few more cornflakes. 'But they said it wasn't no good wivout the numbers.'

'Oh, I don't know,' said Abbie, sounding encouraging. 'I think it might help quite a lot.'

Jimmy looked at her sideways, seeming vaguely pleased. 'There was a bird on it,' he said suddenly.

'A *bird?* Where?'

'On the side. Kinda painted on. Wiv the name...'

'Name? What name?' Abbie almost pounced on him.

'Couldn't read it,' he told her. 'Funny letters... Kinda curly and loopy.'

'Weren't *any* of them readable?' Abbie persisted. 'Think, Jimmy!' Jimmy thought. It was clearly a process he didn't much like. 'Nope,' he said, sounding far too disinterested. Abbie wanted to shake him, 'Mighta bin a zed,' he added, as an afterthought.

'Zed?'

'You know ... sort of zig-zaggy and curly ... all wound up in the bird.'

'What kind of a bird, Jimmy?' (Maybe, she thought wildly, it could be a good omen? But of course it's only a coincidence.)

'Just a bird,' he said, shrugging again, and

pouring himself out some more milk. 'Wiv wings...'

Abbie sighed. 'A bird with wings, and a zed?'

'Might've bin two,' he added grudgingly. 'Like Buzz ... or Fuzz?' But at that word, he looked at his mother with a wary, knowing smile and slid down off his chair. 'Gotta go now. Be late for school.'

'Jimmy!' scolded his mother. 'You just wait here till the lady's done with you!'

Jimmy paused, one foot already sliding out of the door. 'Gotta go. Honest!'

Abbie smiled at him. 'You've been a great help, Jimmy. Did you tell the policeman about the bird and the buzz-word?'

'Nope,' said Jimmy. 'Forgot. Sorry.' And he disappeared out of the door like a small streak of lightning.

'Kids!' said Jimmy's mother. 'They do what they like these days!' Then she smiled at Abbie with sudden warmth, changing the harsh, weary lines of her face into something much softer and younger. 'I hope it helps... I'll get some more out of him later on, if I can.'

Abbie nodded her thanks. 'Every little bit helps. You never know what may be important.'

'I hope to God they get Bobby back soon,' said the woman fervently.

'So do I,' agreed Abbie, and rushed off to

work, feeling that she had done very little so far to make that prayer come true.

But on second thoughts, she decided to risk being late for work, and went back to Pauline's flat and recounted Jimmy's latest bits of information to Terry, the young policewoman.

'Could you phone it through to whoever is in charge?' insisted Abbie. 'I suppose it might be useful?'

'Yes, it might,' agreed Terry, though she didn't sound very helpful. 'What I don't understand is,' said Abbie, pondering the matter, 'why use such a conspicuous van? Birds and curly letters? And blue lines?' Terry sighed. 'It's a regular pattern with those people... They use what looks like a respectable trade van with a fairly obvious professional trade name – like electrician – or plumber – or laundry service, that's a regular one... Then they can park it where they like in the street, near wherever the raid is going on, without exciting any comment. They sometimes even wear a uniform... And afterwards, they just drive off on their next "business call", and no-one is any the wiser.'

Abbie stared. 'But it would be known afterwards – if someone observant like Jimmy happened to be watching.'

The policewoman nodded. 'But by then they've either ditched it, or sprayed it.'

'I see,' said Abbie sadly. 'Then – it's not

much help?'

'I wouldn't say that,' Terry answered carefully. 'As you say, someone else like Jimmy may have seen it... Anyway, I'll certainly pass it on.'

Abbie nodded, and looked round the living room for Pauline. 'Have you persuaded her to lie down?'

'Yes. Her doctor came and gave her a sedative.'

'I'm glad,' said Abbie. 'She was in an awful state.'

Terry agreed. 'And it won't help Bobby if she collapses.'

'Let's hope it won't be much longer,' sighed Abbie, and made a second attempt to rush off to work.

On the way back from the Travel Agency that evening, Abbie called in on Pauline again, and found her up and pacing about like a caged lion, as usual.

'Any developments?' asked Abbie, regarding the startling pallor of Pauline's face with some misgiving.

'Another phone-call,' said Pauline, sounding almost sulky with frustration.

'What did they say?'

'The same as before – *"Have you told Len to keep quiet? I hope so, for your sake!"*' She looked at Abbie out of dark, haunted eyes. 'And when I asked about Bobby, they just laughed and said: *"No-one's got hurt – so far–"'* She shuddered. 'Oh Abbie – I daren't think about what they meant by that.'

'It's only bluff,' said Abbie stoutly. 'They just want to scare you into doing what they want – warn off Len.' She turned to the young policewoman, Terry, in quick appeal. 'That's all, isn't it?'

'Yes. That's all. Just bluff,' Terry agreed, and smiled encouragingly at Pauline.

(But all the same, thought Abbie, the police have sent Pauline a 'minder.' They must think she might be the next one to get 'leaned on'.)

'We traced the call,' said Terry, trying to sound cheerful.

'Any good?'

'Not much – a telephone box, of course.'

'Where?'

'South London – somewhere between Elephant and Castle and Lewisham...' She sighed. 'But of course they could be using any phone at random...'

Pauline burst out suddenly: 'It's all so useless! Why can't you people stop pussy-footing around and <u>do</u> something!'

'We are doing something, believe me,' said Terry patiently. 'But it takes time to pin them down.' She looked at Pauline with as much firmness and conviction as she could muster. 'We'll get there in the end.'

'So long as it's not too late for Bobby,'

whispered Pauline, half-choking, and turned away from them both to resume her restless pacing to and fro in front of the window.

Abbie couldn't think of much more to say that would be any comfort, so she merely went across and hugged Pauline's stiff, angry body and said: 'I'll try to come back later...' and went off to do her promised stint at Tubby's.

It was a busy couple of hours, and she did not have much time to talk to Tubby, but before she left to go home, she told him everything that had happened so far that day, and ended by saying: 'I just hope the police *do* know what they're doing. It's having a terrible effect on Pauline.'

'It's the waiting,' agreed Tubby. 'Nothing's worse than waiting... Let's hope they get a breakthrough soon.' Then he packed Abbie off home, saying she looked 'tired to death' and was just as bad as Pauline for worrying. But, he told her, he had a gut feeling it was going to be all right.

'Oh God, I hope so,' said Abbie, and hurried home to feed the bird.

I'd almost forgotten him in all the excitement, she thought, feeling contrite – and stopped on the way to buy him some extra fruit.

She was just going up the steps to her front door when Synco came out, carrying a guitar.

'Hi,' he said, stopping to aim a tentative smile in her direction. 'Any news of Bobby?'

Abbie stared at him. 'Not yet. How did you know about it?'

He shrugged leathery shoulders. 'Everyone knows round here. The Duchess told them... Asked us all to keep our eyes peeled and our ears to the ground!' He grinned, rolled his eyes, and bent down to lean one ear against the nearest stone step. Abbie laughed. 'You are a fool, Synco.'

'Not so,' he contradicted gravely. 'I like young Bobby – cheeky young tyke, but still... And he found the Bird!' He looked at Abbie quite soberly. 'And I do get about a bit, you know... Might come up with something.'

Abbie nodded. 'Anything might help.'

'How much do we know so far?' he asked, and Abbie could see that he was seriously offering to help.

'Well–' she began, and for some reason she could not quite explain, found herself telling him in great detail all that young Jimmy had told her about the van, and what Terry, the policewoman, had been able to add.

'A bird with wings and a zed....?' Synco muttered, sounding curiously absent.

'Two zeds, it might've been,' corrected Abbie. 'Like buzz or fuzz...'

There was along silence while Synco seemed to sink even further inside himself, searching for some memory or some glimpse of something which eluded him. Then he said suddenly: '<u>Buzzard Aerials!</u>'

'What?'

'Knew it reminded me of something... I've seen that van before ... round our street – where the warehouses are – by our studio...'

Abbie was startled into real excitement. '*Where*, Synco? Whereabouts in London?'

'Off the Old Kent Road,' he said. 'Beyond the Elephant...'

Abbie stared in disbelief. 'But that's where–'

'Yes,' he nodded. 'Where the phone-call came from...It must be. They've got a bit of one of the old warehouses and a lock-up garage. I've often seen them going in and out with stores and such...'

'Stores?' said Abbie.

Synco's bright, knowing eyes were full of sardonic understanding. 'Wait a bit. They've got an office, and a name on the door... Lemme think... United Enterprises!' He grinned at Abbie. 'Covers a lot, doesn't it...? I wonder if–?' He shifted his guitar into his other hand and prepared to leap down the steps and get into his battered old Volvo that was parked by the door. 'I'm going there now,' he began. 'I'll see what–'

'Oh no, you're not,' said Abbie, grabbing him firmly by the arm. 'You're coming back inside to phone the police. If what you think is true, they'll have to handle it.'

'*With* back-up,' agreed Synco, seeing the logic of it. 'OK. Let's phone them first.'

The police, when Synco finally got through to the right department and Inspector Travis 'who was handling the case himself', sounded almost pleased by the information. They agreed that it was 'very useful', and took down clear instructions from Synco about how to get there. They also told Synco, very sternly, not to try to do anything without them, but to go to his studio as usual, and behave as normally as possible. 'No amateur muscling in, please!'

In return, Synco – sounding cool and collected and totally unlike his usual vague, laid-back self – retorted: 'May I make a suggestion?'

'Yes?' The crisp voice sounded alert and interested.

'If you are coming in a car – or more than one – use a plain one, and put a sticker on the windscreen about pop-music or recording agents or something. We have quite a few recording artists and bands visiting the studio... That way they won't suspect anything.' He paused, and added drily: 'Pity to find the bird flown.' He glanced at Abbie over that word 'bird' and smiled.

Inspector Travis agreed and seemed about to hang up, but Abbie signalled wildly to Synco, who said swiftly into the phone: 'Hang on a minute. Yes?'

'Ask him if we ought to tell Pauline?' she said.

Synco repeated the question.

'No,' said Travis. 'Not yet. Don't want to raise false hopes...'

'But – oughtn't she to be there?' asked Abbie, grabbing the phone from Synco.

'No,' said Travis again, apparently unconcerned by the different voice. 'It's kind of you to think of it, but I'm afraid it's often true that the mother is the last person who ought to be there. Emotions can get out of hand and ruin the whole plan of campaign.'

'Yes,' agreed Abbie reluctantly. 'I see. But you'll be able to get through to her at once and tell her if – if you are successful?'

'Of course,' said Travis. 'At once.' And this time he did ring off, deciding that there was no time to lose.

'Now,' said Synco, beginning to enjoy himself, 'I'll be off.'

'Not without me,' said Abbie, following swiftly.

'Synco!' said the deep stage voice of the Duchess close behind them 'What are you up to?'

'Gotta lead, Duchess,' Synco called back from the car... 'Near the studio. Can't stop. Sorry.'

'Sorry!' echoed Abbie, climbing in beside him, and the old Volvo shot off into the evening traffic at the end of the road.

Perry liked Cambridge – it was familiar ground to him – but this time he did not enjoy his visit. He felt restless and unsettled, and somewhat irrationally convinced that Abbie or Pauline – or both – would do something reckless and dangerous about Bobby before he got back.

He gave his lecture – fairly erudite and technical this time – and went for the ceremonial drinks that preceded the equally ceremonial dinner in hall. But in the middle of a conversation with a rather gushing lady whom he did not know, he suddenly decided to cut the dinner and go back to London forthwith.

'But you *can't!*' said Lucinda, who, of course, was there as usual to organise everything.

'I'm sorry,' said Perry firmly. 'I'm afraid I must.'

Lucinda looked at him out of those very demanding blue eyes of hers and realised that long-lashed appeals would be useless. Perry, when he made up his mind, was immovable.

'I can make your apologies to the Dean,' she said in a resigned tone, 'but there's someone here you must meet first.'

'Can't it wait?'

'No, it can't, Perry. In matters of sponsorship and funding, you can't *afford* to wait.'

'Oh very well,' said Perry, sounding only a shade too impatient. 'Lead me to him. Or is it a her?'

'It's a him,' Lucinda told him. 'And be polite! I think what he has to offer will interest you.'

She led him across to a squarish, quietly impressive man with a seamed, brown face, a small pointed beard, and very shrewd black eyes.

'Perry – this is Anatole Raspin. He has something to ask you.'

Perry shook hands, looking at the stranger with polite enquiry.

'When is the Memorial Service?' asked Anatole, in a quiet, oddly accented, rather musical voice.

'Er – next week,' said Perry, glancing at Lucinda for confirmation. 'Next Friday.'

'I knew Duncan MacNab very well,' he said, still in the same quiet, gentle voice. 'Long ago... In Mauritius. In fact, I think he actually saved my life on one rather hairy occasion!'

Perry smiled. 'But, of course – you must be the great Dr. Raspin from Senegal? Duncan told me about your work together... You will be at the Memorial Service, won't you? Lucinda, you are in charge of the invitations.'

'Thank you,' said Anatole politely. 'But that is not what I wanted to ask you.'

'No?' Perry stood still and waited.

'Your colleagues from the Angolan Research Unit will not be coming?'

Perry shook his head sadly. 'I'm afraid not. It's really not practical. They decided themselves that the work was more important.'

'But you would like them to be there? *Duncan* would like them to be there?'

'Of course,' said Perry, wondering where this was leading. 'It's just a matter of–'

'Finance?' The seamed brown face seemed to be smiling. 'Forgive me for being so inquisitive, Dr. Farquhar. You see, I happen to own an airline.'

Perry stared.

'And it occurred to me that one donation I could make, that no-one else could, was free passage for your team to come to London, and free passage back with you in charge, once this was over.' The bright, intelligent eyes were fixed on Perry's face with smiling deference. 'But, of course, only if you thought it's a good idea?'

Then Perry's defences suddenly broke. 'I think it's a *wonderful* idea,' he said, with tears not far from his voice. 'I was hating the idea of having to go through it without them. It seemed all wrong, somehow.'

Anatole Raspin nodded understanding. 'That's settled then. Will there be time to reach them?'

'Oh yes.' Perry was smiling too, now – a

great weight of guilt lifting from him, enormous relief flooding in. He had truly hated the idea of that grand, prestigious service without his colleagues – Duncan's true friends – being there. 'We can get word to them through the hospital radio at Luanda. And there's a very efficient small plane network that would bring them into the main airport.'

'Good,' said Anatole. 'Just give me the details...' He looked at Perry's stunned expression and laughed. 'Don't look like that, my friend...! This is something I would really like to do. As I said, Duncan was an old and trusted friend. It is only right that his present team should be with him on this occasion.'

Perry gulped, and nodded again, feeling too overcome to speak. But Lucinda covered for him very skilfully by bringing him another drink and saying: 'There. I told you Anatole had something interesting to offer!' and they all dissolved into saving laughter. 'The Dean is grieved, but not affronted,' she reported cheerfully. 'So when you and Anatole have made your plans, you can go.'

Perry turned to her gratefully. 'You think of everything!' Then he went off with Anatole Raspin into a quiet corner where they exchanged various addresses and phone numbers.

'I will see you again,' said Anatole, smiling. 'I am sorry you have to go now. I think we have things to say to one another – you and I.'

'Yes,' agreed Perry, curiously warmed by this simple approach. 'It's just that I – I have a feeling a friend of mine may be running into danger...' It was a strange thing to say, and he was almost scared of putting his vague premonitions into words.

But Anatole took him seriously. 'In that case, of course you must go,' he said. 'I have learnt never to ignore such warnings.' He gave Perry's arm an approving tap. 'In fact, you should go now. Without delay. But we shall meet again.'

Perry met his smile with an unexpectedly vivid one of his own. 'I hope so!' he said, and went rather swiftly from the room.

When they arrived outside Synco's studio, Abbie stood looking around her for a moment while Synco made a great point of unloading his guitar and some extra gear before going in through the unpainted door and climbing the stairs.

The half-derelict warehouses were ranged on two sides of a square, with the tall, shabby one housing the studio standing at right angles to the other, equally shabby one which Synco pointed out as the home of 'Universal Enterprises'.

It was getting dark now – the summer evenings were beginning to close in as autumn approached – and one or two lights gleamed in Synco's building, and only one high up on the top floor of the other.

'Couple of other offices in my lot,' explained Synco. 'Cheap rent – it's falling down, really. But it suits me. Plenty of space, and no neighbours to grumble at the noise.'

Abbie was still looking at that far, high-up lighted window. 'Do you make a lot of noise?'

'Only on run-throughs and such – we have a sound-proof recording studio behind. The synthesiser and the keyboards are in there. We only have a practice keyboard out here.'

She nodded. 'Have they–' she gestured vaguely towards the other building, 'have they ever complained?'

'Not they! Too busy with their own affairs.' He took Abbie's hand and thrust the guitar case into it. 'Better look legit,' he said, grinning, and picked up the rest of his gear and led her upstairs.

There were a couple of closed doors on the first floor, and one open with light coming from it on the second. And here a voice called out: 'That you, Synco?'

'Me,' agreed Synco. 'And friend.'

'Pass, friend,' said the voice, and a tousled, red-bearded head came round the door.

'May be visitors later,' said Synco. 'Don't panic.'

The bearded face grinned and withdrew. 'So long as I know.'

'That's Wilf,' Synco explained. 'Photographer. Own dark room. Keeps an eye on the place.'

'Useful,' observed Abbie.

They went on up to the top flight and into the studio. The outer room was biggish and plain, painted white, and someone had made the two windows into one wide one, looking out over the warehouse square they had just left.

Abbie went across and stood looking out of it, trying to locate that high, lighted window... It would be about level with this one, she thought; and then, by leaning a little sideways, she saw it.

Could it be where a small boy was kept hidden? But why would one window so high up and so obvious be kept lighted when the rest of the building was in darkness...? Unless someone was *with* the small boy, as a minder...? And if there were others of them downstairs, why weren't their lights on?

'No sign of Buzzard Aerials,' said Synco. 'But, come to think of it, vans have gone into that lock-up one day, and different ones appeared the next day.'

'*Different* ones?'

'Different *coloured* ones,' said Synco drily. He leant forward a little, watching the street below, and nudged Abbie. 'Look! Told you so... Food going in. I know that take-away bag. Use 'em myself.'

They looked at one another hopefully, but Synco was quick to add: 'May be nothing – just hungry Enterprisers?'

But it *might* be something, thought Abbie. Small boys get hungry, too... And at that point, dim lights did come on in one of the downstairs rooms, while the small light at the top of the warehouse burned as bright as ever.

Synco took out his guitar and strummed it idly. 'Better sound willing,' he said, grinning.

But a thought struck Abbie then. 'Synco – could they hear us over there?'

'Could who hear us?'

'Say, someone up there?' she said, pointing sideways towards that little lighted window. 'But they wouldn't advertise it, would they...?' she added, half to herself.

Synco looked at it too, judicially. 'Probably wouldn't think anyone would be looking,' he said. 'Or listening,' he added, with a faint grin at Abbie.

'But – *could* he hear?' (She dared to use the word 'he,' not knowing whether she was building up false hopes or not.)

'Might,' said Synco, still observing that tiny window. 'If we opened our windows... It's a warm evening.'

They exchanged doubtful glances.

'A bird...' murmured Abbie. 'A song about a bird?'

They considered the matter.

285

'*Hark, hark, the lark,*' – no, that's too fancy,' said Synco, who seemed to know a lot more about classical music than he let on.

'And *"The Cuckoo is a pretty bird!"* is all wrong,' put in Abbie. 'Isn't there a pop song about a bird?'

'Not that kind of bird,' said Synco, grinning. He picked up his guitar again and strummed a chord. '"*Here we sit like birds in the wilderness...*"' he sang suddenly, and looked at Abbie with enquiry.

'Yes!' she said. 'He might know that.'

'He would know it,' said Synco. 'I sang it to him the day after you rescued the bird ... while he was still a bit – er – browned off with himself.'

Abbie looked at him in surprise. This was a different side of Synco. 'Did you? Did it cheer him up?'

Synco shrugged. 'Not much...! But he might remember it.'

Abbie went over and opened the wide window. 'Come on, then, Synco, sing!'

And together they stood by the open window and bawled out the silly words of the song while Synco strummed like mad on his guitar, and even managed to beat out a rhythm on the pedal-drum that was lying beside the rest of the drum-kit on the floor.

The noise was terrific up there, but Abbie wondered how far it would carry across the empty space between the two buildings.

286

'Could I go down and fetch something from your car?' she suggested. 'I want to hear how it sounds.'

Synco paused in his wild strumming. 'Nothing much left to bring... Here, take this–' and he handed her a small pair of soft-headed drumsticks. Then he gave her the car keys and said 'Mind how you go!' and began to play and sing louder than ever.

Abbie went out, laughing, but she knew it was not really funny – trying to beat out a message of hope to a prisoner was no joke at all...

'What the hell is Synco playing at up there?' asked Wilf, as she passed his door.

'Experimenting,' said Abbie. 'Sorry – do you mind?'

'No,' admitted Wilf, in an easy, good-natured voice. 'I can always wear ear-plugs.'

Abbie went on down the stairs and went out into the street. The noise followed her. She stood there, looking up, and the sound of Synco's clear young voice came clearly to her – so did the guitar – so did the drum-beat...

She glanced at the doorway of the other warehouse, but no one came out to complain. There was no sign of life at all – except for that one dim light somewhere out at the back, and that one small, brighter one upstairs.

Sighing, Abbie unlocked the car, ostentatiously picked up the drumsticks she had carefully carried downstairs inside her jacket, relocked the car, and went back upstairs. It seemed silly to take such elaborate precautions, but maybe someone was watching – was already too much on their guard...?

'It's OK,' she yelled at Synco. 'Loud and clear!'

She went across to him and began to join in the song again, and presently, as they went on singing and watching that window, they both thought they saw something move within the room.

They both stopped singing and looked at one another, though Synco's clever hands went on strumming out the same old tune on his guitar.

'Was it – someone?' asked Abbie.

'Think so... Smallish ... pale face?'

They stared hard at the window, and once again something moved and seemed to come close to the window, and a faint, white fluttering disturbed the image of fading sunset on the flat glass...

'Looked like a thumbs-up sign,' said Synco. 'Didn't it?'

'I don't know–' said Abbie slowly. 'I hope so... Synco, I think we'd better come away from the window for a bit.'

'Yes,' he agreed. 'Too obvious.'

But before he could say any more, his 'visitors' began to arrive. Two quiet, unobtrusive cars drew up outside Synco's warehouse door. A group of cheerful-sounding people emerged from the cars, and after a brief but fairly searching look round at the general scene, went up the steps and rang the intercom bell on Synco's door.

Synco pressed the button that opened the door, and made no comment. But after a moment, one set of footsteps ascended the stairs. The rest seemed to have dispersed elsewhere.

'Can they get away at the back?' asked Abbie urgently.

Synco shook his head. 'Not without climbing a six-foot wall. No access for cars at the back – or lorries, either. But the police could get in the building from the back.'

Abbie nodded, and presently the footsteps came near, and a quiet, grey man in plain clothes came through the door.

'Any sign of life?' he asked Synco, without preamble.

'Someone went in with food,' said Synco. 'And–' he looked at Abbie, seeming uncertain what to say.

'And–?' The quiet man's very observant eyes looked from Synco to Abbie.

'We think the boy's up there.' said Synco, deciding to risk the Inspector's wrath. 'We – er – sang a song...'

'*Sang a song?*'

'One he knew,' put in Abbie. 'And – and

something came near the window... I think he waved...'

'Made a thumbs-up sign,' added Synco.

'No,' contradicted Abbie, thinking it out. 'Not that...'

'Not that?' The Inspector was still very crisp.

'I think he was trying to point at the roof,' she said.

The clever eyes sharpened. 'The *roof*...? Could he get up there?'

'I don't know,' said Abbie doubtfully. 'Could he, Synco?'

'If it's like this dump – yes, he could,' said Synco. 'But it's not very safe... I've been up on mine... Flat roof, caving in here and there ... where people have stripped the lead off... And the fire-escape's only half there... Very dicey.'

He nodded. 'We'll go in quietly. No need for the boy to panic.'

'He's afraid of the police,' said Abbie. 'But he knows I'm here with Synco, and he trusts us. He won't panic unless he sees a lot of men running after him. But his minders might.' There was warning in her glance.

Inspector Travis looked at her with respect. 'Then we must move swiftly – and silently,' he said, 'before they have time to think. And you'd better stay put,' he added severely. 'You've done quite enough!'

Synco and Abbie looked at each other,

wondering how the silent police raid would go, and what else they dared do to help.

But suddenly, all hell broke loose across the square. The 'Universal Enterprises' door opened violently from within, and various startled people spilled out into the street. And from the opposite side of the square, various other shadowy figures rose to their feet and came forward to meet the ones trying to escape the net.

A brief fight ensued and several bodies landed on the concrete floor of the warehouse yard, and were promptly sat on by their assailants. There were no shots fired, Abbie noted thankfully.

'All over, bar the shouting,' said Synco.

But it wasn't.

Someone in the yard below began shouting and pointing upwards at the top of the building, and when Abbie and Synco looked up, they saw a tiny figure outlined against the sky, and another, burlier figure that was somehow immensely menacing, trying to cross the roof to reach the small one running away.

'He's making for the fire-escape,' said Synco, in a voice of horror – for he knew how dangerously unsafe that perilous escape route was.

'Can we get from one roof to the other?' asked Abbie, beginning to run.

Synco ran with her, his long legs rapidly

overtaking her. 'Yes. But it's tricky...' He pushed open a narrow, sloping trapdoor at the end of the passage, and held it wide enough for Abbie to slip through. 'Careful!' he said.

Abbie was careful. She remembered rescuing the bird on her own little flat roof, and how fearlessly young Bobby had offered to climb out and fetch Solomon – and how frightened she had been, even on that small, safe expanse of sun-warmed lead...And this was much worse.

'I'll see if I can head that madman off,' said Synco. 'What's he trying to do, any-way...? He can't get away with Bobby now, with the police all over the place...' But he didn't wait for an answer. He sprinted lightly across his own expanse of flat roof, and crossed over on to the other side of the L-shaped cluster of warehouse buildings, coming up behind the wildly angry man who seemed to be chasing Bobby across the precarious stretch of ancient patched-up roof with its missing lead and rotting planks.

As he came closer to the furious figure, he saw with relief that one of the policemen from downstairs was also closing in on him from the other side. At least we can hold him off Bobby, thought Synco, but even as he thought it, the man's foot went through a gap in the decaying roof, there was a splin-tering crash of broken timbers, and the whole piece of roof the three men were standing on began to tilt slowly inwards towards the gaping hole that led to the floor below. In slow motion, it seemed, the terrified villain of the piece fell through the hole, and after him – even more slowly and painfully – slid the policeman, and after him, Synco, with the broken roofing planks falling in on top of them with a yet more ominous rumble of splintering wood and slithering lead.

Abbie was still behind them on Synco's side of the roof, and she stood there, horrified, as the sound of the crash reverberated round the warehouse square, and the dust settled over the hole... They can't be dead, she thought. It wasn't a very steep fall ... not very far... The others will get them out... They'll be all right.

But Bobby was still on the roof – on the other side of the hole – and he wasn't all right at all. He knows my voice, she thought. He'll listen to me.

'I'm coming, Bobby,' she called, ashamed that her voice sounded so weak and wavering. 'Stay there. Don't try to move. It's all right.'

And Bobby, who had looked for a moment as if he was going to jump right off the roof to get away, looked back over his shoulder at Abbie, and did as he was told.

I've got to get round to him somehow, she

thought, without setting off another roof-fall... I hope I'm light enough. Bobby certainly is... But what would be the best way to get him back...? I won't think of that yet. Concentrate on getting across to him... Just make him feel safe...We can sort out the rest later.

Vaguely, she heard shouts and men running down below, but up here she was alone, and there was a vast expanse of unsafe roof to cross... 'I'm coming,' she called again. 'Keep talking to me, Bobby. Did you hear us singing? It was Synco playing the guitar... Isn't he clever?' (Oh God, I hope Synco is all right.)

But Bobby could not answer her. Now that his ordeal was nearly over and he saw Abbie coming towards him, he suddenly became a frightened small boy and began to cry.

'Don't cry, Bobby,' said Abbie, more to keep up her own spirits than his. 'I'm nearly there. Keep still, won't you? Don't try to come towards me... It's safer to stay still...' She kept on talking, and moving inch by inch past the gaping hole, expecting every minute to feel the roof give underneath her. But it held, and she crept past the danger spot and crossed the last bit of empty roof to Bobby's side.

'There!' she said. 'I've done it! I told you I was coming.' She put her arms round the small boy and held on tight while he sobbed out his fright and relief against her shoulder.

'I – I would've waited for you,' he said, between gulps. 'When I heard the song, I knew you'd come... But he said he was going to move me somewhere else where no-one would ever find me, so I had to get out quick.'

'How did you get up here, anyway?' she asked, wondering if it might be a way of getting back.

'I c-climbed on some boxes ... on the bed...'

'Yes?'

'An' I could just reach the skylight... But I fell off, and I had to build all the boxes up again...' He clutched at Abbie's hand. 'I was just getting out when he came in...' He shivered a little. 'An' then he came after me...'

'Well, he can't come after you now, Bobby,' she told him. 'But we've got to get off the roof somehow... Where did the skylight come out, d'you know?'

But Bobby couldn't tell her, and the night was fast descending and making it too dark to see. She decided to take a few steps with Bobby away from the edge, so that at least they couldn't fall off in an unguarded moment. Then, she thought, I believe we'll have to wait till someone finds us. They know where we are. They won't be long.

She inched a little further inwards, holding Bobby close as she moved, but there was a sudden ominous crack ahead of her, and a bit more of the rotting roof timbers seemed to collapse inwards towards the hole... Better stay still, she thought. I daren't risk any more. I'll just have to keep Bobby safe and warm until they come... Safe and warm ... like I did the bird ... and he came to no harm.

But even as she wrapped her arms round Bobby again and tried to settle him more comfortably against her, a voice spoke from the darkness beyond the hole – a voice that she knew...

'Keep still, Abbie. Don't try to go any further. Help is on the way.'

'Perry?' she whispered. *'Perry?* Is it you?'

'Me, in person,' said Perry, and she could hear the smile in his voice. 'Is the boy all right?'

'Yes,' said Abbie, wondering if she was delirious or something. 'Bobby's all right. Aren't you, Bobby?'

'Yes,' admitted Bobby, who had stopped crying by now, but rather liked being comforted by Abbie.

'That's all right then,' said Perry's voice calmly and clearly. 'You're going to be rescued by the fire brigade. Aren't you lucky?!'

Bobby thought about that, and brightened up a lot. It might be rather fun to be swung down in one of those crane things.

'Is – how is Synco?' asked Abbie, hoping the news was good enough to tell her.

'He'll live,' said Perry, almost laughing.

'And the policeman?'

'He'll live, too... It was the poor fellow they fell on top of who came off worst.'

'He's not *poor*,' said Bobby indignantly. 'He locked me in! And he chased me!'

'Well, he won't do much chasing in the near future,' said Perry, and Abbie could almost feel his cheerful reassurance as a tangible force in the dark.

It was then that the roof decided to give another lurch inwards, and there were more splintering noises and clouds of dust. There was also the sound of voices talking upwards to Perry, and then a powerful torch beam shone across to where Abbie and Bobby crouched in the dark.

'Abbie,' said Perry very quietly, 'we think the bit of roof you are on is not very safe. Can you move back a little to the right...? Very slowly... Keep Bobby beside you... That's it – only a little at a time... Follow the beam of my torch... Just a little more ... that's the way... I'd come over to you, but I'm afraid to make things worse... A tiny bit further... Yes, that's right... That's enough, now. You're on a safer bit now... You can relax.'

Bit by bit his gentle voice coaxed her on, out of the danger zone on to a solider bit of roof, and all the time his torch beam kept just in front of her, lighting her way. And Abbie, though she was scared of every move, went on blindly and trustingly where he directed, and did not hesitate.

'There,' said Perry's voice, warm and consoling in the dark. 'Now you can rest a bit. You're safe enough there... Well done, Bobby. You've been very brave.'

Then they heard the fire engine coming, and soon there were floodlights and ladders, and efficient, friendly voices giving orders. And as soon as the first ladder was in place and another laid across the dangerous flat roof, Perry came treading softly out of the shadows, and crossed swiftly to Abbie's side and folded both her and Bobby in his arms.

'Thank God!' he said. 'All safe and sound! We can start rejoicing now.'

They took Bobby down first to where a tearful Pauline was waiting, having been brought to the scene in a swift police car. Then they came back for Abbie.

But by that time, Abbie didn't mind whether she was rescued or not. Perry had got there first.

5. WHILE THE TALL TREES STAND

When Abbie got back from work next day – having insisted that she was perfectly all right, thank you, and hadn't been injured at all, only frightened – she found Bobby waiting for her outside her front door.

'The Duchess let me come up,' he explained, 'and she give me a whole £1! She said I was lucky to be alive!'

Abbie laughed and let him come into the flat behind her. 'What's on your mind, Bobby?'

'I wanted to see the bird,' he said. 'And I was to tell you Tubby's having a party, and will you bring Synco, if he's better... And Mum says can I wait and come with you?' He looked at Abbie rather mutinously. 'She even brought me here on her way to work! She won't let me go anywhere on me own!'

'Give her time, Bobby. She's had a bad fright, you know...' She grinned at his protesting face. 'Things will get back to normal soon enough.'

'Cor, I hope so,' said Bobby, and went over to see Solomon in his cage in the corner. 'I got put in a cage like you,' he told the bird, offering it a nice bit of banana. 'What d'you think, Solomon? I landed on the roof, just like you did – and Abbie rescued me, just like she did you!' He offered another bit of banana, and Solomon cocked his beautiful crested head on one side and considered the matter. 'An' they sang me a song, Synco and Abbie did, all about you – so's I'd know they were there. Shall I sing it for you?'

Solomon regarded him intently out of those strange, golden-ringed eyes, and made no comment either way.

But Bobby was too bubbling over with new-found freedom to take no for an answer, and began to sing in a cheerful, almost-in-tune uninhibited treble:

'Here we sit like birds in the wilderness,
Birds in the wilderness,
Birds in the wilderness!'

He finished the verse, and turned to Abbie seriously. 'Is the wilderness where Solomon really lives?'

'Well, yes – sort of,' said Abbie. 'The wild forest, anyway – and perhaps the savannah, Perry says.'

'There you are then,' Bobby told the bird kindly. 'It's a song about your home. D'you like it?'

And this time Solomon answered with a low, gentle whistle of his own.

Abbie smiled at Bobby's delighted expression, and came over to give Solomon his evening ration of fruit and vitamins (as recommended by both Perry and Mackintosh). 'It's a funny thing,' she said, talking both to Bobby and the bird, 'when I was up there on that roof, I kept thinking – I was safe enough on our own little roof rescuing you, so it must be all right, up here on the big roof, too... In a way, Solomon, you stopped me panicking!'

'Me, too,' said Bobby seriously. He looked from the bird to Abbie, with large, devoted eyes. 'I thought – Abbie got you back safe – so she will me!'

They were just grinning at one another like happy conspirators, when there was a light tap at the door that Abbie had left slightly open, and Perry walked in.

'Am I interrupting? Tubby says hurry up, you are guest of honour, and the party's waiting.'

Abbie turned to him joyfully. (It didn't seem possible to hide anything today). 'We were just thanking Solomon.'

'Ah yes,' said Perry, smiling. 'The symbol of safe rescue!' He came over to the cage and bowed ceremoniously. 'Thank you, Solomon. You are an inspiration to us all!'

Abbie giggled, and Bobby didn't quite know what he was laughing at but joined in happily, too.

'Come on,' said Perry, linking an arm through Abbie's on one side and Bobby's on the other. 'I am acting as escort and chief bodyguard this evening – on Pauline's orders.'

Bobby groaned. 'Honest, she's a terror, my Mum!' But he decided he rather liked being escorted by Perry – in fact there was a bit of hero-worship going on there – and Abbie obviously liked it too, so he wasn't grumbling.

'What about Synco?' asked Abbie, as they went down the stairs.

'He's there already. They discharged him from hospital this afternoon. Only bruises and a dislocated shoulder. Pauline went to fetch him herself.'

He grinned at Abbie. 'And the Duchess is there, too. You'll be surprised. There's quite a gathering.'

'And balloons,' added Bobby, skipping along the pavement with irrepressible glee. 'And streamers. And sausage rolls. Mum made them.'

Abbie couldn't think of anything she could say to add to this cheerful catalogue, so she walked on beside them in happy silence.

And when they got to Tubby's she was reduced to yet more silence, for the uproar all round her was enormous. Synco had brought a pop group with him who called themselves The Bungees – perhaps for no better reason than that they jumped up and down a lot – and they were perched up on a makeshift platform, playing full blast. There were – as Bobby had predicted – balloons and streamers everywhere, and when Abbie arrived with Perry and Bobby, a general cheer went up that even drowned the pop group.

Then Pauline came over and hugged Abbie, and Abbie hugged Synco and asked him if he was all right, and the Duchess hugged everyone, including Tubby, and announced in her grandest theatrical voice that she wished to lead the company in singing 'For she's a jolly good fellow!'

But Abbie, greatly daring, begged her to make it 'they' not 'she' – because everyone had been involved in the rescue – Synco and the policeman, and Perry, and Inspector Travis, and the Duchess herself, for she had directed a frantic Perry to Synco's studio and the final showdown on the roof. Even red-bearded Wilf had helped – producing that powerful torch and showing Perry how to get up on to that fatal rooftop.

So, in fact, everyone sang the praises of everyone else, which made everyone happy, including Bobby, who simply couldn't stop grinning from ear to ear.

When Abbie had time to look round, she saw that Inspector Travis was actually there, grinning almost as widely as Bobby, and she went across to enquire about the policeman who had fallen through the roof with Synco.

'He's fine – only a few bruises, like your friend Synco. He'll be in presently to say hello to Bobby.'

Abbie smiled at him. 'That's good news. Did you find what you wanted – or *who* you wanted at that warehouse?'

'We did, indeed. All five of 'em – and a fine haul of stolen goods.'

'And they even found Buzzard Aerials,'

said Synco, coming up to them with a cheerful grin. 'In that lock-up garage.' He winked at Abbie. 'No time for a respray!'

While they were laughing, Bobby came bouncing up to them. 'Guess what, Abbie, it was on the news! We're famous!'

'Oh no!' groaned Abbie. 'They won't come looking for us, will they?'

But they did.

Before they had really taken in what Bobby was saying, a predatory man with a foxy face and a camera slung over his shoulder, pushed through Tubby's door, and an equally predatory-looking girl with a blonde fringe, a cigarette dangling from a rather red mouth, and very sharp, snapping brown eyes, came in beside him.

'How did you feel up there on the roof all by yourself, Bobby?' asked the girl, beckoning the man to focus his camera on Bobby's freckled face.

'Small,' said Bobby accurately, and after that, closed his mouth tight and wouldn't say another word.

The girl looked a trifle put out, and turned to Abbie. 'How about you? You're the one who rescued him, aren't you? Abbie, isn't it? How did you feel?'

'There wasn't time to feel,' said Abbie. 'And anyway, I was only one of the rescuers.'

The interviewer seemed a bit nonplussed by this, and looked round for a more co-operative victim. Her glance lighted on Synco, with his bruised face and his arm in a sling. This looked much more hopeful.

'You were the one that fell through the roof, weren't you? What was your reaction?'

Synco looked at her with innocent gravity. 'I had a sinking feeling,' he said.

There was a general ripple of relieved laughter at this, and then Inspector Travis strolled across and intervened. 'There are police proceedings pending,' he said. 'And as these people may be material witnesses, I'm afraid I must ask you to refrain from questioning them further.' His tone was mild, but his glance was decidedly steely.

'And this is a private party,' added Tubby, staunchly defending his friends. 'So I'm afraid I must ask you to leave.'

The girl looked at the implacable faces round her, and then at her cameraman, and shrugged. 'OK,' she said. 'It's your funeral. I thought you'd like the publicity.'

But the ring of faces was still ranged against her and made no response, so she gave an angry toss of her blonde head and started to move away towards the door.

'This way,' said Perry pleasantly, holding the door open for the two of them, and when they finally left, realising there was nothing more they could do, he shut the door carefully behind them, and grinned at Tubby. 'All clear,' he said. 'Now we can let our hair down in peace!'

And they did. The party from then on got very merry indeed, and in the midst of all the general good cheer, Pauline succeeded in taking Abbie aside to add her private heartfelt thanks.

'It'll be much better for Len now,' she whispered in Abbie's ear. 'No pressures either way. The Inspector thinks he may get off fairly lightly.' She sighed, and added in a slightly dazed voice: 'I can't believe it's all turned out so well.'

Abbie gave her arm a reassuring squeeze. 'It's about time things started going right for you!'

Pauline's eyes were on Bobby as he moved purposefully about the room, handing everyone drinks and sausage rolls on Tubby's instruction.

'He's taken quite a shine to that Synco. And to your Perry,' she said, smiling. 'He misses his Dad, you know – though of course Len's no hero.'

And Synco is, thought Abbie. And Perry probably is as well, but he's certainly not 'mine'... But as she thought that, she found Perry looking at her as if he knew her thoughts, and soon he had managed to edge his way past the pop group and come across the room to her side.

'I know we can't go yet,' he murmured. 'But there'll be time later on...'

Time for what? wondered Abbie, hardly daring to think about it. But she smiled and nodded, and went on enjoying the party, trying not to remember that Perry's life was already ordered and committed, and he would be going back to Africa soon.

The party ended, as all good parties should, with everyone going home aglow with good food and drink and happy camaraderie, calling goodnight to each other in the darkening street, and walking off together in cheerful, chattering groups. Inspector Travis slipped away to his unobtrusive plain car, and took with him Constable Willis (who had turned up, bruises and all, to present Bobby with a Mars bar and a friendly 'Glad you're alive and kicking!'). The Duchess strolled off with Synco and little Miss Ashridge (who had arrived at the last moment from the library, breathless but delighted). The Bungees climbed into a purple and yellow striped car with a sunshine roof and a rainbow painted on the back door. Pauline and Bobby went home, and Tubby stayed behind to lock up.

And Abbie and Perry were left to wander on through the quiet streets alone. 'You never told me what you were doing there,' said Abbie. 'On the roof, I mean. I thought you were supposed to be in Cambridge?'

'I was,' agreed Perry. 'But I decided to come back.'

'Why?' she asked, not daring to take anything for granted.

'You know why,' Perry said. Then he went on in a soft, half-dreaming voice: 'I met a strange man in Cambridge – Anatole Raspin – and he said you should never ignore warnings of danger... In fact, he said I should go *now* – so I did.'

Abbie was silent for a moment, accepting the implications without comment. But at last she said quietly: 'Well, whatever the reasons, I'm glad you came.'

He grinned and hugged her arm close against his side. 'So am I... Abbie, I give the last talk tomorrow, and then I'm free for a day or so before the last arrangements for the Memorial Service... When could you escape?'

Abbie looked at him doubtfully. 'What had you in mind?'

'A day in the country...? I know you miss it. Have you ever been to Frant?'

She looked surprised. 'In Sussex, isn't it? Near Tunbridge Wells...? No, why?'

'Because it's very beautiful in the autumn. Bracken and silver birches – and deer in the park. And,' he grinned, 'I have to see a man about a bird... Could you come?'

She hesitated, feeling somehow that she was walking open-eyed into a strange and frightening country. 'I – yes, I've got Monday off. I'm working on Saturday.'

'Then Monday it is,' said Perry cheerfully, as if he had solved all the world's problems in one swift decision.

'Perry–' she began, trying to warn herself rather than him.

'It's all right.' Perry interrupted gently. 'Nothing to worry about... We do need to talk, that's all.'

'Yes,' she agreed, suddenly capitulating, unable to deny the sense of unquestioning trust that Perry seemed to instil in her. 'Perhaps we do.' Though she was still a bit afraid of what words might do. She thought she preferred this undemanding silence between them, when no words were needed at all.

'A day out of time,' said Perry softly. 'Is that too much to ask?'

And Abbie could not answer.

A day out of time it was. The sun shone, the sky was a flawless blue, the golden bracken crunched under their feet, and the silver birches tossed coins of bright gold over their heads.

Perry took her first to a small house near the church in the village, where a smiling woman called Hannah gave them coffee while Perry and a white-haired, thinnish man with penetrating eyes under bushy eyebrows talked about birds.

It did not take long, and Perry soon rose

to his feet, saying cheerfully: 'We will see you on Friday, Lewis, won't we?'

The older man nodded gravely. 'I'll be there.'

Perry laid a gentle hand on Abbie's arm as she got up to join him. 'Abbie is a rescuer of birds, too,' he said, smiling.

'Indeed?' said Lewis, intrigued. 'How come?'

So Abbie told him about Bobby and the strange, beautiful bird, and how it came to be rescued.

'A Red-crested Turaco?' exclaimed Lewis, amazed. 'How on earth did it come to be in a small London pet shop?'

'We don't know,' said Abbie, looking at Perry doubtfully.

'The cage-bird trade is still fairly unstoppable,' said Perry sadly, 'however hard the conservationists try. And officially it's not an endangered species – yet.'

Lewis sighed. 'But endemic only to the Angolan heights?'

Perry hesitated. 'Yes – and the last remaining bits of forest near the coast...' He also sighed, thinking of many things to do with Duncan MacNab's struggle to preserve what was left of a disappearing world, and then he looked across at Abbie with affectionate relief, as if she dispersed his anxieties just by being there. 'But at least Solomon is safe and well-looked-after now.'

'What are you going to do with him?' asked Lewis, turning to Abbie. Once again Abbie looked at Perry, as if unsure how to speak of the future.

'Keep him for the moment,' she said. 'While the winter weather is here. At least he is warm and fed, and has room to breathe... But in the spring–?'

She hesitated, and did not know how to go on.

'If we got the captive breeding programme set up out there,' said Perry slowly, 'we might be able to take him back to his own natural habitat. But I doubt if we could let him go...'

'Is that likely to happen?' Lewis sounded curiously insistent.

Perry looked from him to Abbie and smiled. 'You sound almost as anxious about him as Abbie. But yes – with the new funding Lucinda and Panky have managed to find, it really might.'

Lewis nodded his satisfaction. 'That's good to hear.' He glanced at Perry, almost shyly, and added: 'Don't forget – if you need a fairly knowledgeable volunteer ... I wouldn't mind making myself useful.'

Perry stared at him in surprise. 'Really...? I'll bear that in mind!' He smiled at his friend with sudden gratitude. 'Willing volunteers are not all that easy to find, believe me!'

'I believe you,' Lewis laughed. 'But then

I'm an aficionado.'

They grinned at one another, and then Lewis said to Abbie: 'Why d'you call him Solomon?'

'Because of the colours,' said Abbie obscurely. 'Though perhaps it should have been Joseph?'

But Lewis was not slow off the mark. 'Not arrayed like one of these?' he murmured. 'But those were the lilies of the field, weren't they?'

'They were,' agreed Perry, smiling at Abbie. 'But aren't the birds of the air just as gloriously arrayed?'

'They are, indeed,' admitted Lewis, thoroughly approving the idea, and he, too, smiled at Abbie. 'I must come and meet this Solomon one day – and discover if his scarlet crest is really as bright as a poppy anemone.'

They all stood looking at one another, suddenly united in a common cause, and then Perry said softly: 'Fellow conspirators... Come on, Abbie, we have the whole of the rest of the day before us.' He led her out into the sunlight and took her away to the burnished bracken-covered hills.

All day they walked, sometimes briskly, sometimes slowly idling to look at the shape of a tree, the filigree pattern of silver-birch branches against a blue, unclouded sky, the perfect shape of a fallen leaf, and the birds – the free-flying wild birds that flirted with sun and shadow, and made Abbie's heart ache a little for Solomon, still trapped in his wire cage, however wide and tall and tree-filled they had managed to make it.

'Look, there's a goldcrest!' said Perry, and they watched the brilliant yellow flash of its wings, and its small red head that again reminded Abbie of Solomon.

There were yellow wagtails by one of the small streams they crossed, and an even brighter yellowhammer flew out of a nearby hedge. Even the fieldfares and redwings, coming across the fields for a late scrounging of fallen apples in someone's untidy orchard, seemed to reflect a golden sheen of sunlight on their more sober feathers.

'Everything seems to be dipped in gold,' murmured Abbie, stooping to touch a yellow thistlehead. 'Even the blades of grass...'

'And even the deer,' added Perry softly, and pointed to where a group of golden-coated does stood patiently beside their magnificent lord and master, who was poised stock still on the hillside, his splendid antlers glinting with light against the sky.

They wandered on, and presently came to the edge of a vivid wedge of beech trees, their turning leaves ablaze with fiery light.

'It's part of a very ancient forest, I believe,' Perry said, waving a hand at the deeper woodland behind him.

'It reminds me of home,' said Abbie, and

313

her voice was dreaming rather than sad.

Perry looked at her quietly. 'It still means a lot to you, doesn't it?'

'Oh yes,' she admitted. But she realised that for the first time she could think of those beloved hills and beechwoods without regret... Somehow, in this place of golden peace with Perry beside her, all that anguish of loss seemed remote and had no longer any power to hurt her.

It was at this point that Perry decided to talk. He sat down on a convenient moss-encrusted log, and drew Abbie down beside him.

'The rest of the team are coming home for the Memorial Service.'

Abbie looked at him with a glowing face. 'That's wonderful news – especially for you, isn't it?'

'Yes. Especially for me.' He glanced at Abbie a little shyly, and then added: 'The whole thing makes more sense with them all being there.'

'Of course. How did you manage it?'

'That man at Cambridge I told you about – Anatole Raspin – runs an airline, and he offered to fly them home and fly us all back afterwards... It was too good an offer to refuse.'

Abbie nodded, knowing that must be true. 'How long will they stay?'

She had not dared to ask herself, let alone

Perry, how long he was likely to be here, or how much his absence would mean to her, but now it had to be asked.

'Oh, about a week,' said Perry. 'Not longer. We can't really leave the research station for too long unattended – though Nguni Xavier, our chief assistant, is there to keep an eye on things, and he's very reliable.'

Abbie nodded again. 'You're lucky to have him, aren't you? Was he there when the raid happened?'

'No, but he arrived soon after, to give what help he could.' He sighed, and then went on, almost apologetically: 'It's a difficult country, Abbie – so many warring tribes and factions, so much superstition and prejudice. And all sorts of masterless men with grudges and grievances left over from the civil war... You never know what to expect or who to trust... The so-called peace is still very precarious. And we are only there on sufferance. They could refuse us permits to stay on at any time.' He looked at Abbie, still in that odd, apologetic way. 'That's why I have to go back. I can't leave them to manage on their own.'

'No,' agreed Abbie. 'Of course you can't.' She was smiling a little at his troubled face, as if trying to undo the knots of anxiety behind it. There was silence between them for a moment, and then she asked quietly: 'How much more work is there to do?' She meant: 'How long will you be away?' But she didn't say it.

Perry understood her very well. 'About half a season's – from the research point of view. But if at the same time we are to set up this wildlife sanctuary and captive-breeding programme, it may take longer. We have to get the local people to help run it – and that means training.' He sighed again. 'I don't know how long that might take, or who would want to do it, besides Nguni – they all have enough problems out there simply trying to stay alive! And I don't know how long the authorities would let us stay... It's full of imponderables.'

Abbie met his rueful smile bravely. 'And then what–?'

He looked startled for a moment by her blunt question, and then answered it with characteristic honesty. 'When this project is finished, you mean? And the new set-up is working properly?'

'Yes. What then?'

He sighed, and gave a small, doubtful shrug. 'I suppose there will be other projects... And there may be a couple of years back at university.' He glanced at Abbie almost shyly. 'They rather want me to come back and – er – teach a few young enthusiasts how to be useful in the field.'

'Could you teach me?' Abbie asked, knowing that her question asked much more than the simple words suggested. Her voice seemed to drop into the silence like a stone into a pool, and the rings of meaning seemed to spread wider and wider as she spoke.

But Perry was not really surprised by her question. It was what he had at the back of his mind anyway. He looked at her with a mixture of tenderness and loving amusement. 'I'm sure I could. You'd be a model pupil!'

'I'd like to be useful,' she murmured, and it was clear to both of them that there was a whole future pattern of serious purpose behind her words.

'To the birds, I mean,' she added hastily, in case she sounded too pushing.

It was really the cue Perry wanted, and he was not slow to take of it. 'Abbie – am I right in thinking you need quite a bit of time to get over certain past hassles before you start thinking of the future?'

'Yes,' said Abbie steadily. 'You are.'

'But–' his glance was suddenly diffident, 'you know what I am trying to say, don't you?'

'Yes, Perry,' she said, still quietly and steadily.

'I'm coming back, you see,' he told her, still sounding shy and uncertain. 'I know I have no right to expect anything, or to hope for anything – and my life is always going to be a bit roving and unsettled ... but–' He drew a deep breath, and his eyes and his voice suddenly took on a deep and tender certainty. 'I don't know how it's happened – but there is already so much between us that is precious and important ... isn't there?'

'Yes,' admitted Abbie, in a small, strange voice, but her eyes met his with equal certainty.

'You are still very vulnerable...' he murmured, as if trying to ward off all the terrors of the world from her defenceless head.

'I'm tougher than I look,' protested Abbie staunchly, half-laughing at his protective tone.

'I know that,' Perry agreed, joining in the laughter. 'I saw you on that roof!'

'But I was petrified!' admitted Abbie honestly.

'I know that, too.' Perry's voice was full of laughing approval. 'But you ignored it!'

They looked at one another, laughter still flowing between them, but as their eyes met and locked, a sudden shock of awareness seemed to assail them.

'There is so much to learn...' murmured Perry obscurely. 'So much to do...' *Together*, he wanted to say. But he did not dare to say it yet. She was still very young, still very hurt, and still unarmed against the battles of the weary world... She needed space still, and time...

'There will be time,' said Abbie softly.

'Won't there...? We can wait?'

'Yes,' agreed Perry sadly. 'We can wait.'

But then he confounded all their careful reasoning by not waiting at all, and kissed her long and soundly under the fiery beech trees in the westering sun.

Perry met the rest of his team at Heathrow, and took them all back to the quiet, neutral surroundings of his club. It seemed to him the best place to stay, especially since they had recently opened their doors to women members too, and Judy could still be with them. And it was a place where they could meet Panky and Lucinda in comparative privacy to discuss all the final details of the Memorial Service.

He settled them all comfortably in the lounge for a drink and looked at them all with friendly concern. Judy, her straight brown fringe still in place after the long, exhausting flight, looked tired but stoically cheerful as ever. Paul (Sticks!) looked even drier and more like his nickname than ever, but he, too, was smiling with relief that the team were all together again – even in the alien surroundings of a busy capital city. Jonty, his velvet-brown eyes still as gentle as his voice, seemed unperturbed by the journey, and was regarding Perry with undisguised warmth as he said quietly: 'It's good to see you, Perry – and here is your report!'

And he drew a folder of papers out of his inner pocket.

Perry was almost shocked. 'Jonty– You don't have to do this the minute you arrive!'

'Oh yes, I do,' retorted Jonty, smiling. 'Duncan would have insisted…! *"Can't have you getting lax, can we?"'* And they all laughed.

Then Perry briefed them on how the proceedings of the Memorial Service would go and what they would be expected to do. 'I thought you could each do a bit of a reading…?' he suggested. 'I've chosen some bits that might be relevant – but if you've got better ideas, tell me… We can do what we like, really.'

They nodded, but they were obviously a bit too jet-lagged to think of anything much at present.

'Give us the pieces to have a look at,' said Jonty. 'And when we've slept on them–' he grinned at Perry, 'fig. not lit., I mean – we'll let you know. OK?'

'Yes,' Perry grinned back. 'And there's one small extra piece … about the lilies of the field… Judy, that's really your preserve. Could you add that to your contribution?'

Judy looked at him and, with uncanny perception, said: 'Isn't there anyone else you'd like to read it?'

Perry hesitated, and his team noted with astonishment that he nearly blushed. 'Er –

yes, but she might be too shy to read aloud, especially in that august company.'

'Well, ask her,' said Judy, and there was something about the affectionate glances of his colleagues that made Perry feel he was far too transparent.

'I'll see,' he said, and changed the subject abruptly. 'Anyway, I have to tell you the news about the fundraising is very good. We've got far more sponsorship than we dared to hope, and the Memorial Fund is already quite substantial ... Lucinda and Panky are coming in tomorrow to tell you the details.' He smiled at their slightly stunned faces. 'I thought you could do with a night's sleep before facing those two – good news or not!'

They all laughed their relief, and then Jonty gave his piece of good news.

'I have to tell you that the authorities have agreed to the wild life sanctuary project, providing it doesn't cost them more than allocating a piece of land, and we can find the funding elsewhere...They really haven't any money to spare, Perry, as you know very well, and inflation is running absolutely riot over there at the moment. But at least they've agreed in principle and are making hopeful noises about "a future tourist attraction". And Nguni has already found several willing trainees among the villagers. We are allowed to stay on until the project is up and running, they will renew our permits that far, but they will only let one foreigner stay on permanently – as a resident "crop and food economy" adviser.'

Perry looked at him in amazement. 'You've done half my work for me!'

'I know,' said Jonty smugly. 'But I thought I should pursue it while they are still feeling a bit guilty about Duncan's death. It could have become a major political incident, you know – so they were being extra - er – co-operative.'

Paul said, with sudden bitterness: 'It takes a murder to make these people see reason!'

Perry nodded sadly. 'At least some good has come of it.'

'Yes,' Judy agreed, with sturdy good sense. 'And how Duncan would laugh at the thought!'

It was the kind of salutary remark they needed to stop them from getting any sadder and Perry took his cue from Judy's challenging glance. He got to his feet and said: 'It's time you people had a rest. I'll take you up to your rooms, and we can meet later on for a meal.'

They looked at him gratefully. They really were rather tired, and though they would never admit it, the responsibility of running the research station without Perry had been quite a strain.

Jonty laid a hand on Perry's arm as they

paused outside his room, and said: 'Are you dreading this affair? Is it too big?'

'It is rather,' admitted Perry. 'But it is all part of the fundraising game, I suppose... At least for once he will get the recognition he deserves.'

'I'm sure he'd approve,' said Jonty gently. 'And we can have our own little thing out there later on... It'll be all right.'

'Yes,' sighed Perry. 'So we can... He'll be more likely to rest in peace in the forest where he belongs.'

'Don't you believe it!' said Jonty, smiling. 'Duncan will never rest in peace. As long as the work goes on, he'll always be there – egging us on!'

And Perry, chastened by Jonty's clear-eyed view, bowed his head and said 'Of course you are right. *He'll always be there!*'

It was a day or two after the trip to Frant that Abbie, feeling almost guilty for being so happy, went to look for the Prof again. There had been one or two chilly days, and a couple of wet ones in between, since Abbie had seen him last, and she was a bit concerned about the old man continuing to sit out there on his bench, wet or fine, and with no regard for the consequences.

She found him there as usual, but looking somehow smaller and more pinched and frail than before. But he glanced up and offered her a thin little smile as she sat down beside him.

'How have you been, Prof?' she asked, getting out her sandwiches.

'So-so,' he grunted, accepting an egg-and-cress. 'What've you been up to, then? Gallivanting?'

'Er – yes, a bit,' admitted Abbie, grinning. 'In Frant Park – among all the deer...It was lovely.'

The old man grunted again. 'Didn't mean that– Saw you on the box.'

'Oh, *that*,' said Abbie airily. 'Young Bobby got into a spot of bother. All over now.'

'Huh!' said the Prof. 'Risking your neck!' He wagged an admonitory finger. 'Keep your feet on the ground, my girl! It's safer.'

'Yes, Prof,' said Abbie meekly. 'I intend to.'

The Prof eyed her suspiciously. 'Doesn't look like it!' he said, and went off into a sly cackle of laughter that ended in a fierce bout of coughing.

'What do you mean?' asked Abbie innocently, deciding to play along with his teasing, though she was worried by that cough.

'Romping in the hay!' he grumbled. 'Waltzing in here, looking all lit up with lights! Anyone would think it was Christmas!'

'It will be soon,' pointed out Abbie. 'And it was bracken, actually,' she added demurely, but her smile was still too incandescent to be true.

'Mind you,' said the old man judiciously, 'he looked a bit of all right – that young man of yours.'

Abbie was just about to protest: 'He's not–' when she remembered with a sudden upsurge of joy that he *was*. Or at least, in so far as they had dared to commit themselves to anything – and she knew that the bond between them was now so strong it would be traitorous to deny it. So she said nothing, sternly repressing the bubble of happiness inside her, and decided to concentrate on the Prof and his racking cough.

'You know,' she said, 'it's all very well to lecture me – I think *you've* been gallivanting too much. That cough sounds awful.'

'Worse than my bite,' he said, glaring at her. 'Someone's got to do the barking,' and he waved the ownerless dog lead at her in sardonic explanation.

But Abbie was not going to be put off. 'Prof, you said you might come round to Tubby's some other time–'

'No, I didn't!'

'Well, you said *maybe*.' She glared back at him. 'So will you come tonight?' He began to refuse, but she cut him short: 'And don't say no, or even maybe, Prof, just say "yes".' The two pairs of eyes glared defiance, but Abbie clinched it by adding: 'You don't want me worrying about you all night, do you?'

The Prof snorted with rage. 'That's below the belt, that is!'

'Sorry,' said Abbie, unrepentant. 'That's the way it is.'

'Oh, *all right*,' snarled the Prof, in as ungracious a manner as he could muster – and that was saying quite a lot. 'Shan't stay long, mind,' he added, sourly.

'I'll see you there after work,' said Abbie, ignoring the grumps. 'About six. All right?'

'Suppose so,' he shrugged, but the cough still caught him when he moved his shoulders.

'Mind you turn up,' said Abbie. 'I'm counting on you!' And she went back to the Travel Bureau, hoping the old man would do as she asked.

Tubby's was as warm and welcoming as ever. Abbie arrived there a little early, and went to talk to Tubby about the Prof.

'I don't know what we can do if he's really ill,' she said doubtfully. 'I don't even know where he lives.'

'We'll deal with that when it happens,' said Tubby with reassuring calmness. 'I can put out a few feelers, in the meantime...'

Abbie smiled. 'The network again?'

Tubby grinned back cheerfully. 'We do what we can!' he murmured, and went to dish up another portion of his special steak-and-kidney pie.

At this point the old Prof pushed open the door, and stood looking round with suspicious caution.

'Over here, Prof,' called Abbie, hastily sitting down at the nearest table. 'Glad you could make it.'

The old man shuffled over to her, looking more like his old dog, Spot, with its hackles up than ever. 'Can't stop long,' he said.

'Well, you can stop long enough to have a bowl of soup,' said Abbie firmly. 'I'm having some. Tubby makes good soup.' And almost before she had finished speaking, Bobby had sprung out of nowhere and planked down two steaming bowls of soup and two large hunks of bread on the table between them.

The Prof looked at the boy with sharp, observant eyes, and Bobby looked back and grinned, all his freckles aglow.

'Hello, Prof,' he said. 'Abbie told me about you.'

'Did she, indeed!' growled the Prof, sounding more truculent than ever. Then he suddenly matched Bobby's infectious grin and enquired politely:

'Been falling off any more roofs lately?'

Bobby giggled. 'Not blurry likely! Once was enough. Wasn't it, Abbie?'

'*Quite* enough,' said Abbie fervently, and watched with hidden relief while the old man drank his soup.

'Tubby's Special is on the house tonight,' said the cook himself, strolling over to their table. 'Since we're talking of roofs – or is it rooves?'

The Prof looked even more prickly. 'How's that?' he rasped his voice full of suspicion.

'Saved our number one waiter, didn't she?' said Tubby, winking at Bobby. 'Ought to be on the house for ever after that!'

Abbie merely grinned, and ignored the Prof's mutinous expression. 'You'd soon go bust at that rate,' she retorted.

'Yes, but not *yet*,' Tubby countered, and brought over two plates of 'special' before anyone could make any further protest.

The Prof glared at them all, but, looking into their faces, he suddenly thought that they would be really hurt if he refused. It was a thought he hadn't considered much up till now, and it rather shook him. So, in a surprisingly chastened voice he said mildly: 'I don't mind if I do.'

It was a little later in the evening that Tubby had his brainwave. He came over to their table with a chessboard and a set of pieces in his hands. 'Could you give me a game, Prof?' he asked.

The old man's eyes lit up – but if he was pleased, he wasn't going to show it. 'How d'you know I can play?'

'Stands to reason,' said Tubby. 'You make up crosswords, don't you? Patterns. Same kind of brain.' He gave an exaggerated sigh. 'Not enough of 'em round here.' Then he set out the pieces and sat down opposite the Professor, without more ado.

Abbie was just wondering whether she could slide gracefully out and leave them to it, when Perry came in through the door, with three other people behind him.

'Thought I might find you here,' he said. 'I wanted you to meet the team – and they want to meet you and the bird.'

Abbie looked at them all shyly. They were just as Perry had described them – Jonty, the dark-bearded one, with velvet voice and matching eyes, Judy, sturdy and practical but curiously attractive in her no-frills style, and Paul, called 'Sticks', and she could see why, with his long, thin frame and dry, brittle manner. And all of them, she could see (and this warmed her to them more than all the rest) devoted to Perry, and determined to pursue whatever course he chose in furthering the work of Duncan MacNab.

'Hallo,' she said at last, holding out her hand. 'Perry has described you all so minutely, I feel I know you already!' She glanced rather uncertainly at Tubby, who was absorbed in his game and ignored her completely. 'Would – would you like to come and see Solomon now? Or do you want to stop here for coffee – or a meal, first?'

The team looked at Perry, who spoke for

them. 'Let's go there now. We can come back later to eat.'

Abbie nodded, and began to lead them out of the café. But then she hesitated, wondering whether she ought to just leave the Professor high and dry.

'Go on,' he said suddenly, not looking up from his game. 'Make hay – I mean, bracken,' and he let out a dry cackle, and moved another pawn.

Blushing wildly, she led them away to the Duchess's house, and soon they were all standing round Solomon's cage, admiring the immaculate sheen of his plumage and his brilliant scarlet crest.

'Solomon,' said Abbie, 'I've brought you some visitors – and they really are on your side... They're even trying to find a way to take you back to your own home country. You'd like that, wouldn't you?'

She was carefully putting bits of his evening ration of fruit inside his cage as she spoke, but Solomon did not immediately go down to investigate. He sat half-hidden in the leaves of his figtree, head cocked sideways to listen to her voice. He rather liked the sound of Abbie's voice, and when she had finished talking and he had considered the matter, he let out a cautious remark rather like a *sotto voce* crow.

'Amazing!' purred Jonty in his deep, warm voice.

'So *elegant!*' added Judy, smiling from the bird to Abbie.

'Remarkable,' agreed Sticks, sounding as dry as ever – but even he was smiling.

'Am I – do you think I am doing the right thing?' asked Abbie, anxiously looking from one to the other of them. 'Is he at all happy, do you suppose?'

'A lot happier than he was when you found him, by all accounts,' said Jonty, and glanced at Perry for confirmation.

'Certainly,' agreed Perry, also smiling at Abbie's worried expression. 'No-one really knows, of course, what a bird feels... But he's warm and well-fed, and he has a reasonable amount of space to move about in – and he likes the sound of Abbie's voice. He even responds!' His smile was full of gentle teasing. 'I think we can assume that he is as happy as any caged bird can expect to be.'

Abbie sighed. 'But he's still a captive, though,' she said.

'Well, as you say, we may be able to put that right – at least in part,' said Jonty. 'Perhaps Perry hasn't had time to tell you yet – we've got permission for the wildlife sanctuary, and that will include our captive breeding programme.'

'That's wonderful news,' Abbie exclaimed, turning a glowing face to Perry. 'So everything Duncan MacNab wanted may come true, after all?'

'It may,' agreed Perry slowly, not really daring to admit it even to himself. 'But it will take time...'

Abbie knew that to be true, and she heeded the warning in his voice. But even that did not stop her from being glad. It was Perry's dream as well as Duncan's – and its fulfilment made up the purpose of his days.

'That reminds me,' Perry said, trying to set aside the knowledge of parting and separation to come, 'we have a request to you. We are all reading various bits about Duncan's work – but we wondered if you'd like to read "Consider the Lilies..."?'

Abbie stared at him, and then turned to Judy. 'But that's *your* province, isn't it?'

Judy smiled. 'Yes, but I've got plenty to read. Perry's made sure of that. And, after all, you did christen the bird Solomon.'

Abbie still looked very doubtful. 'But ... all those grand people... And I didn't even know Duncan.'

'You saved one of his creatures,' said Perry softly. 'And – maybe you should represent ... the ordinary, uninitiated people who <u>could</u> help with conservation but mostly don't... The ones he was always trying to reach?'

The others nodded solemnly at this, and Abbie felt more confused than ever. 'I – I don't know...' she said uncertainly.

'It's only a few words,' pointed out Perry, wondering whether she was actually scared of reading aloud in such august company, 'but they are important ones.'

'Yes, I know,' admitted Abbie, looking at Perry and his team with a kind of desperate candour. 'That's what's bothering me!'

'What do you think, Solomon?' said Jonty, laughter behind his deep, dark voice. 'Isn't she one of us already?'

'Quark,' observed Solomon.

'Carried unanimously,' agreed Sticks, and Judy just laughed.

'Oh well, in that case...' Abbie began.

But before she could say any more, Perry cut her short with swift approval. 'Good. That's settled then.' He grinned at Abbie, knowing she had been rather steam-rollered into it, but he thought she was not really sorry to agree. But he didn't know how much Jonty's remark had meant to her. If the team could really think of her as 'one of us' then maybe the future course of her life might not be so bleak and lonely as she had thought...

'I – I could give you all coffee–?' she suggested, wildly trying to remember if there was enough milk.

'No,' said Perry. 'We've paid our respects to Solomon. Let's go and eat at Tubby's. It's the friendliest place in town!'

So they all trooped downstairs again, past César Franck, past Henry Gray and Olive Ashridge, and past Synco, who, Abbie supposed, was out doing a bit more 'merging' in his studio. But in the hall, they all met the Duchess, resplendent this time in ruby velvet and silver fox fur (out of date and disapproved of today, but you couldn't really throw it away, could you?).

'Ah!' she boomed. 'More bird fanciers?'

'*Fanciers*, anyway,' agreed Abbie, risking a grin all round.

'Judy, the flower lady,' said Perry, presenting her to the Duchess with due ceremony. 'Jonty, the animal man–'

'Ooh, goodie!' said the Duchess, regally taking his hand.

'Sticks, the butterfly man–'

'Fly-by-night?' queried the Duchess, who was clearly enjoying the situation.

'That's moths,' said Sticks, meticulous as ever, but he held out his hand and smiled nevertheless.

'Delighted,' intoned the Duchess, in her grandest manner. 'Abbie, what fascinating company you keep. I should like to ask them to one of my Evenings...' She turned graciously to Perry, aware that he was the leader. 'Will you come?'

'Alas!' said Perry, playing up to her like mad. 'We are flying back to Africa at the end of the week... But we are honoured to be asked!'

The end of the week, thought Abbie, and resolutely thrust the thought from her.

But Perry knew her thoughts, and took her

hand firmly in his. 'Come on, Abbie... Time is precious.'

He turned with smiling deference to the Duchess as he left. 'Forgive me, Duchess, but I have to keep my team well fed and well watered – like Abbie's bird!'

'Of course,' agreed the Duchess, airily waving a dismissive hand. 'Good hunting! The night is young.'

And she watched them go, laughing, into the street, before she turned away to her too-quiet, empty room and her game of solitaire.

But outside, the team went cheerfully on to eat at 'the friendliest place in town,' and Abbie and Perry strolled slowly after them, hand in hand, and did not say a word.

So then it was time for the Memorial Service. And it was much less daunting, much less grey and stiflingly formal and polite than Perry had expected. Lucinda had been clever. She had found a church that had some particularly beautiful stained glass, and the sun had decided to shine on this special day, streaming through the windows in a blaze of light and laying bright patterns of purple and Madonna-blue and green and crimson on the pale stone of the pillars and the polished stone tiles of the floor. The whole building seemed to be swimming in colour and light, so that even before the august company was assembled, or the choir was in place, somehow the heart lifted to all that shimmering radiance and accepted the mystery and magic of that ancient place of worship without any word being said.

But of course the words needed to be said, and one by one the famous friends of Duncan MacNab got up and spoke of him and his work with affection and pride. The team read their chosen pieces – each representing their own particular field – the flowers – the birds – the mammals – the insects – and each found an anecdote or one of Duncan's famous jokes to lighten the proceedings and make his friends smile. And Abbie followed Judy, and lifted up her shy young voice and added her chosen words:–

'"Consider the lilies of the field.
They toil not, neither do they spin,
Yet Solomon in all his glory
Was not arrayed like one of these."'

And she thought of the bird, alone in his cage, dreaming of the wild forest where he could fly free ... and she thought of Duncan MacNab, whom she had not known, but who had fought all his life to save the creatures of the forest and leave them in their happy freedom – and then she thought of Perry, whom Duncan had taught to follow after him, and the team who were at this moment so loyally supporting him, and she knew with sorrowful but absolute certainty that she could not – *must* not – ever try to deflect him from his promised purpose...

But then it was time for the choir to sing their praises, too. And here again Lucinda (consulting carefully with Perry) had been clever. For they were a skilled choir, full of warmth and pure young voices, and they had chosen the Benedicite – the perfect canticle to sing for Duncan MacNab.

"'O all ye works of the Lord, bless ye the Lord,'" they sang, the boys' flute-like trebles soaring up into the sun-gilded arches, and then they began the long, marvellous catalogue of all creation – all living things on earth.

"'O ye Sun and Moon, O ye Stars of Heaven,
O ye Showers and Dew, O ye Winds of God,
O ye Fire and Heat, O ye Winter and Summer,
O ye Dews and Frosts, O ye Ice and Snows
O ye Nights and Days, O ye Light and
Darkness,
O ye Lightnings and Clouds, O let the Earth
bless the Lord
O ye Mountains and Hills, O all ye Green
Things upon the Earth,
O ye Wells, O ye Seas and Floods,
O ye Whales and all that move in the Waters,
O all ye Fowls of the Air, O all ye Beasts of the
Field,

O ye Children of Men, O ye holy and humble men of heart–"'

And here Abbie suddenly thought of her father, and Perry thought of his old friend, Duncan, who had never sought glory, but only the welfare of the creatures he loved.

"'Bless ye the Lord!"' finished the choir, *"'Praise Him and magnify Him for ever!"'*

And Perry – and his team, and a good few other dedicated conservationists in the crowded church – thought of the long procession of living things that filled the green earth, and were each and every one in their own miraculous form a vindication and an act of praise for their Creator, whoever he might be. *"'Praise Him and magnify Him for ever!"'* they echoed in their hearts, and somehow Duncan MacNab was part of the singing, part of the praise.

He is with them now, thought Perry. He can run with the leopard and sing with the free-flying birds, and walk in the tall grasses with his face lifted to the sun like the flowers of the field, and dance for one day of glory like the dragon-fly... He will never be tied to the anguish of men again...

Beside him, Abbie put her hand in his and did not speak. And Jonty, leaning close, murmured: 'He's safe enough now...'

The crowd began pouring out of the church, and the organ played valedictory music for all to hear, but Perry stood still and watched the sunlight turning the dust to flecks of gold and laying more jewel colours on stone and wood, and even on to Abbie's upturned face. And suddenly, as he stood there, an extraordinary sense of rightness and fitness seemed to grow within him. Somewhere, somehow, Duncan had set his seal of approval on the whole occasion. He understood its purpose – and he understood his friends' need for the ceremonies of departure... And, Perry fancied almost guiltily, his old friend understood little Abbie and her place in the scheme of things... But that was another story, and another departure, and maybe another fulfilment in another time... But meanwhile, he was sure, even as they sang Duncan's praises for all that had gone before, they had his blessing for all that was to come. *And the work would go on.*

'Time to go,' he said, smiling at his friends, smiling at Abbie. 'Everything is all right now.'

Abbie had not intended to go to Heathrow to see them off. She felt that she and Perry had said all they could say to each other now – their 'day out of time' had been perfect and complete – and it would only embarrass him to have to say goodbye to her in front of all his friends.

But she hadn't reckoned with Lucinda,

who was in her most managing mood and simply swept Abbie along with everyone else, including Panky, to give Perry and his team a rousing send-off. For the media had got hold of the story of Duncan's Memorial Fund and his gallant team, led by the well-known author and conservationist, Peregrine Farquhar, who were going back to the wilds to finish Duncan's work for him.

Perry was a bit fed up with all the fuss, but Lucinda pointed out to him, loud and clear, that this was still all part of the fund-raising enterprise, and the more people knew about it the better.

'She's right,' said Panky, looking at Perry's mutinous face. 'Keeps the shekels rolling in. Don't look so disapproving. It'll soon be over, and then you can shake the dust of Sodom and Gomorrah off your fastidious feet!'

Perry laughed, feeling a bit shame-faced. 'Am I really such a prig?'

'No,' said Panky judiciously. 'You are just a little unused to man's wicked ways – out there in the jungle.'

Perry sighed. 'This seems a much more impenetrable jungle to me!'

'You can say that again!' agreed Jonty, at his elbow, and everyone round them laughed.

'It's time we were boarding,' said Sticks, who liked to be precise about time-tables.

A few camera bulbs flashed, someone tried

to ask Judy a silly question and was shooed off by Jonty, and a camera-man started walking backwards, trying to film the party as it moved on towards the boarding gate.

Perry stopped Abbie for a moment, and looked into her face with sudden, searching gravity. 'I'm sorry to make you come. I asked Lucinda to insist...! I'm afraid I'm as sentimental as the departing troops over the white cliffs of Dover...! I wanted to look back and see your face at the last...'

Abbie grinned. 'Have I got a face like a white cliff?'

Perry's serious gaze danced with sudden tenderness, and his voice deepened as he answered. 'No, little Abbie.' Smiling, he laid his hands round her face and held it still. 'You have a face like a hopeful angel! A face to be loved and cherished, and never to be forgotten.'

Then he stooped and kissed her in front of all the assembled company, and went away with the others down the long corridor to the waiting plane.

'You'll miss him,' said Lucinda kindly to Abbie's stricken face. 'But he'll be back.' She tucked her arm through Abbie's companionably, and Panky fell in beside them. They seemed to have arrived at a mutual decision that Abbie needed taking care of just then.

'Let's go up to the flight deck,' Lucinda suggested. 'We can watch them take off.'

So they stood looking out of the wide windows at the runways far below. And presently, Perry and his party appeared on the tarmac, looking very small and far away, before they all climbed into the airport bus that took them out to the plane. Perry looked up once, as if he really could see her among the sea of watching faces, and lifted his hand in a last, loving salute. Then he was gone. And presently the great silver bird that was taking him away from her purred into life, taxied down the runway, turned with ponderous slowness, and then began to rush down the flight path, lifted into the air and pointed its nose to the east.

Well, he's gone, she thought. And I may never see him again. How has it happened in so short a time that I should care so much?

'Come on,' said Lucinda, steadying her as she stumbled a little. 'What we all need is a drink. Mind how you go.'

Mind how you go, thought Abbie. And though her feet obediently followed Lucinda, the rest of her followed that throbbing silver bird into the distant eastern sky.

'We are having one of my Evenings,' announced the Duchess, using the royal 'we'. 'On Sunday – so that everyone can come, even Tubby.' She fixed Abbie with her most commanding regard, privately noting that the child seemed rather too pale and sad again. 'You will come?'

'I'd love to,' said Abbie, smiling. And then a thought struck her. 'Could I bring the Prof?'

'Who?'

Abbie explained about the old man grieving helplessly for his departed dog. 'I don't know where he lives,' she said. 'But if I can find him in the park, shall I ask him?'

'Do!' boomed the Duchess. 'It'll do him good. Can he sing?'

Abbie looked startled. 'I shouldn't think so. He's all growls and grumps. But I think he's an old softie underneath – and Tubby likes him.'

'Oh well, then,' agreed the Duchess, as if that settled the matter. 'Bring him along. Synco's coming. And the César Franck girls... And Olive Ashridge.'

'What about Henry Grey?'

The Duchess made a face. 'If he gets back in time from Mother! I shall make him sing, too!'

Abbie looked alarmed. 'Have we all got to do something?'

'Oh yes! A Soirée.' The Duchess beamed with enthusiasm. 'In Victorian times, you know, everyone did their party piece! All part of the fun.'

Abbie wasn't at all sure it would be fun, but she couldn't back out of it now.

'Wear something *bright*,' ordered the Duchess suddenly. 'Festive spirit, and all that. English winters are much too grey. Eight o'clock sharp. Don't forget!'

'I'll be there,' said Abbie.

It was an amazing evening. Synco had brought his friends, The Bungees, who, as the Duchess put it, 'let out several sharp bursts of tribal song'. Synco himself played his guitar, and sang a funny, sad song about a field of daisies, which seemed to be a cross between Irish folk song and English pop ('merged' by Synco). And then, seeing that Bobby was at the party, he launched into *'Here we sit like birds in the wilderness'* just to remind him of the day of the rescue. Bobby joined in happily, and so did Abbie, meeting Pauline's eye in a private moment of rejoicing.

Then an old-fashioned stand-up comic called Stan Merrilegs (it *can't* be his real name! thought Abbie) did a lively patter song that ended in a tap dance on the best bit of the Duchess's polished floor. He was followed by a long, sad man called Clarence, who was a conjuror and who persuaded the Duchess to come on and have coloured scarves pulled out of her silver turban, and finally a live rabbit, which he gave to Bobby to look after.

After this, a strangulated tenor came and stood by the piano, where, to Abbie's surprise, Olive Ashridge was presiding, and launched into a very good parody (at least

Abbie hoped it was a parody) of a Victorian ballad, beginning: *'Take thou this rose...'* in which the Duchess – right on cue – snatched the proffered rose out of his hand before he could utter another screech of song. After which, amid the laughter, he bowed politely to the Duchess and invited her to join in a duet. *'If you were the only girl in the world,'* he squawked.

'And you were the only boy...' blared the Duchess in her fruitiest contralto. (And Abbie could not help reflecting that they would make a funny couple if they were.)

And when they had finished, the Duchess went on to sing a much more up-to-date number from one of the current musicals, just to prove that she wasn't past it yet.

After her, came a fluffy soprano in lots of pink tulle, who joined the strangulated tenor in yet another duet, and then unexpectedly burst into a florid operatic aria, accompanied by a rather panic-stricken Olive Ashridge at the piano.

But then the César Franck girls came and took over the piano 'to add tone to the proceedings' and gave a really spirited account of the last movement of their much-practised Sonata. And when that was over, they surprised everyone by plunging into a cheerful medley from 'Fiddler on the Roof', which made Abbie and Synco look at one another, and then at Bobby, feeling that the theme was a little too apt.

When Nicky and Sammy had received some deserved applause, a small man riding a one-wheel bicycle and rotating a plate on top of a stick balanced on the end of his nose, came teetering into the room and wobbled precariously round it before falling off almost into the Duchess's lap.

And meanwhile, Mackintosh went round filling up everyone's glasses, and Mrs Mac went round offering sausages on sticks and vol-au-vents and mince pies.

At this point, to Abbie's surprise, the old Prof (whom she had persuaded rather grudgingly to come) suddenly answered the Duchess's imperious challenge to 'do something' by bursting into The Jolly Blacksmith in a thin, rasping but unexpectedly tuneful tenor. The clever, snapping eyes sparked with malicious humour as he reached the familiar refrain:

'I care for nobody, no, not I,
And nobody cares for me!'

'Bravo!' said Olive Ashridge, who had swiftly sprung to his assistance at the piano, and who was determined to miss the point of his sardonic choice.

'My sentiments exactly,' murmured Synco.

'And mine,' agreed the Duchess, untruthfully, giving the Professor a rather overpowering pat of approval.

Abbie had begun to think she had got away with not doing a party piece, but now she found herself being propelled towards the piano by a firm, irresistible force.

'D'you want to sing or play?' demanded the Duchess, smiling wickedly.

'Er – play, I think,' said Abbie, wildly trying to remember some of the voluntaries she used to play on the organ in her father's church. And after a moment's hesitation she settled down to a piece from Bach's Christmas Oratorio, and her thoughts turned to the winter fields of home, and the little church crowded with her father's parishioners at the Midnight Service... I must go home for Christmas, she thought. I can't run away from it any longer. I owe it to them at home... My mother will want me there... *But what shall I do about the Bird?*

'Sing something, Abbie,' commanded the Duchess, breaking into her nostalgic thoughts of home, and Abbie pulled herself back to the present, trying to think of a suitable song. But she couldn't think of anything lighthearted enough for the occasion. I wonder if I dare try 'Silent Noon'? she thought... And if I dare, will it throw me completely...? It speaks so much of Perry and me – of that special day out of time that was so full of marvels... And can I remember the accompaniment? I used to know it by heart...

'Come on, Abbie,' insisted the Duchess, beaming with the kind of implacable bonhomie that could not be denied. 'You must have got a favourite song?'

'Yes, I have,' she admitted reluctantly, 'but–' Then she thought suddenly of Perry kissing her goodbye in front of all those people, and a reckless desire to match his bravado came over her. 'All right then,' she said, 'here goes–' and her hands began the long, sonorous slow chords of the introduction. Quietly, gently, Vaughan Williams set out his magical evocation of Dante Gabriel Rossetti's famous sonnet.

'"*Your hands lie open in the long fresh grass...*"' sang Abbie, in her young, true voice that was almost like a choirboy's. But here the memory of those long slow days of summer, the lost idyll of her unshadowed childhood, caught up with her, and for a moment it was hard to go on. But then Perry's face, Perry's voice, came back to her and cancelled the shadowy past with a new, more potent magic. '"*Your eyes speak peace...*"' she went on softly, and then in a hushed voice of spellbound recollection: '"*'Tis visible silence, still as the hourglass...*"' Her hand automatically moved on to the high, sweet chords that seemed to conjure up the breathless transience of those enchanted moments.

"'Deep in the sun-search'd growths, the dragonfly
Hangs like a blue thread from the sky...'"

Her voice almost trembled then, but she steadied it, remembering Perry's plea for that 'one day out of time', and knew that she had to go on to the end, for the song spoke with Perry's voice... '*"So this winged hour is dropped to us from above*",' she sang, and drew herself together for the final, rapturous affirmation:

"'O clasp we to our hearts for deathless dower
This close-companioned, inarticulate hour,
When two-fold silence was the song –
The song of love...'"

Well, I've done it now, she thought, waiting for the kind ripple of applause that would allow her to escape. Let the cat out of the bag with a vengeance. Laid myself open to all sorts of teasing, too.

But the applause, when it came, was prefaced with a little sigh all round, as if everyone of them there was conjuring up past moments of silent magic – and no-one seemed inclined to tease her at all.

'Well done, Abbie,' declared the Duchess, toasting her with yet another full glass. (She was getting distinctly merry by now.) 'And now that you've made us all shed a nostalgic tear or two, how about another drink?'

Abbie turned to find the old Professor standing at her elbow, looking at her with bright, knowing eyes – and decided to echo his usual words of grudging acceptance.

'Thanks,' she said, grabbing a nearby glass from Mackintosh, 'I don't mind if I do!'

They stood together in the clearing, Perry and his team, looking up at the tall shapes of the mahogany trees thrusting their heads above the forest canopy. It was a narrow strip of forest now – and always diminishing as the loggers did their blind, destructive work – but it was still beautiful, remote, and full of strange wonders. Sunlight filtered greenly through the tangled overgrowth of leaves and lianas, and down below on the forest floor, they were standing in a green shade, full of shadows, fleeting shapes and echoing bird-calls.

'Here?' said Jonty, spreading his arms wide. 'Under this tree...? It was his favourite– The oldest in the forest.'

Perry nodded, and Judy, uninvited, stepped forward and put her arms round the gnarled and knotted trunk of the ancient tree – that is, she embraced it as far as her arms would go, but that was only about a quarter of the way round its solid girth. Paul too, looking more Sticklike than ever, moved forward and laid a long spider hand on the rough bark, as if saluting an old friend.

What should we do? wondered Perry. Sing a hymn? Say a prayer...? He didn't somehow feel that Duncan would want those kind of trimmings out here. They had done all that in London.

'My people have made him a song,' said Nguni's soft, warm voice close behind him.

'His people' were the small tribal village community in the valley below, who had mostly managed to survive intact in spite of the war, though some of their men had been killed in the fighting. Duncan MacNab had done much to protect them and get their fragile village economy working again, advising on crops so that at least they were not starving, setting up the school again, and a small health clinic to deal with simple emergencies, and helping them to rebuild a primitive sort of stockade so that inside it they were reasonably safe from roving marauders. The village people loved him for it. In fact he had become something of a legend to them over the years.

'They go to his school now,' explained Nguni carefully, 'and many of them go on to the city for more learning, but when anything seems important to them, the old ways still stand.'

Perry nodded, understanding what Nguni was trying to say. 'It is natural. The old songs are still a comfort.'

Nguni smiled. 'Yes,' he said softly. 'But this is a new one. They have made it specially for him.' He looked at Perry shyly. 'Would you permit them to sing it for him?'

Perry turned to the quiet brown face beside him. There was so much concern and sympathy in the watchful eyes that he was unexpectedly reassured. 'I think Duncan would like that.'

Nguni's smile was curiously gentle. 'He was close to my people, the Seeing-eye Wiseman – close to the forest and the things that grow.'

Perry stared at him. 'What did you call him?'

'The Seeing-eye Wiseman. Everyone called him that.'

Yes, thought Perry. The Seeing-eye Wiseman. He was that to me, too.

'Tell your people to go ahead,' he said, surrendering suddenly to the ancient lore of these ancient people who understood the forest and its ways as no ordinary English research worker ever would. 'And we will release the ashes when you tell us the time is right.'

Nguni's anxious face relaxed into warm-hearted approval. 'I will tell them,' he said.

He disappeared then through the shadowy trees, as he and his people were wont to do, and the four English research workers were left looking doubtfully at one another.

But presently the singing began. It was far off at first, a mere throbbing of drums and a whisper of chant, but gradually it grew nearer, and the half-seen shadowy shapes among the trees slowly came into focus and became a long line of sinuous bodies, weaving and chanting through the dappled shade until they formed a ring of singing homage round the ancient tree in the centre of the clearing.

'He brought help and knowledge to our forest,
The Seeing-eye Wiseman in his seeking and
* understanding.*
He knew the gorilla and the swinging monkey,
He saw the singing cricket and the leaping
* leopard,*
He protected the young of the antelope,
And the flying fruit-bats in the caves of our
* ancestors,*
The Seeing-Eye Wiseman in his seeking and
* understanding*
Let our friend the Seeing-Eye Wiseman go
* free!'*

The singing rose up like a warm veil of sound round the tree, and Perry realised they were singing in their old Kimbundu language, not in the modern Portuguese of their everyday common speech. He and his team, ordered by Duncan, had been careful to learn as much of this old tribal language as they could, for it helped in their dealings with the older villagers as they attempted to identify the species and specimens in their painstaking work of cataloguing. Many of the old names were still useful, and much of the old village lore was of immense value. Now, he found himself carefully translating the words of the chant in his own mind as the singing grew all round him.

'He knew the bright wings of the sun bird,
And the bees that made wild honey in the tall
    white tola tree,
The Seeing-eye Wiseman in his seeking and
    understanding
He knew as friends the flowers of the forest,
And the rainbow butterflies that fed among
    them,
He knew the fruits of the trees and the riches at
    their roots,
He searched like the shaman for the plants that
    heal
And blessed them with the names of his
    learning,
The Seeing-eye Wiseman in his seeking and
    understanding.'

And here the chanting ceased for a moment while the ring of dark dancers grew closer to the huge bole of the ancient tree, and lifted their hands up to its massive strength in a kind of wordless salutation. And Perry, still translating the Kimbundu words in his mind, was amazed at how alike they were to his own thoughts at the end of the Benedicite in the Memorial Service in far-off London. And at this, of course, his thoughts turned fleetingly to Abbie – and the feel of her hand clasping his in silent sympathy was so strong that he almost turned round to look for her.

Then the chanting began again, but this time more slowly, as if the final words they sang were the most important of all. And as they sang, another ring of women and children circled the tree, and each of them was carrying a small, lighted rush lamp, the wick swimming in palm oil, which they held high to make an airy nimbus of light round the dark trunk of the tree.

'Let our friend the Seeing-eye Wiseman go free,
Let his spirit rise up like the morning mist
And join the great spirits of the forest.
Let him sing with the singing birds among the
   branches,
Let him grow sweet and tall with the rain
And ripen with the seeds in the sun,
Let him be one with the forest,
The Seeing-eye Wiseman in his seeking and
   understanding.
Let him live for ever while the tall trees stand!'

Oh God, thought Perry, *while the tall trees stand?* How long will that be, I wonder? But the chanting had stopped again, and he became aware suddenly that the whole company of dark faces was looking at him, the women and children as well, holding their small glowing lights high in the forest shade.

'Now?' he murmured to Nguni, who had been singing with the rest had come forward to stand beside him.

'Now,' agreed the tall black man, and gave Perry a small, private smile of reassurance.

Perry looked at his friends, waiting for their nod of assent, and when it came, lifted the small copper urn high in his hands.

'Let our friend the Seeing-eye Wiseman go free!' he said, in English, though he knew his colleagues also understood most of the Kimbundu chant.

And they, understanding him, repeated it first in English and then in Kimbundu, so that all the company could say it too.

'Let him live for ever while the tall trees stand' came the answer, in a deep, powerful growl of affirmation.

The small lights were lifted high as the words were repeated, and then Perry opened the lid of the little copper urn and scattered the soft grey dust of its contents upon the still forest air... And as he moved his hand, a small, sweet-scented wind came out of nowhere and took the fine motes of dust and sent them drifting out into the green secret spaces of the forest until they were lost to view.

And the singing began again, quieter now, and the long column of chanting villagers wound away through the trees, and drifted and faded, like the dust, till nothing was left but silence under the cool green shade of the trees.

Then Perry and his friends each lifted a hand in farewell, and walked away through the quiet dusk and said no further word to break the receiving silence.

6. PAPER BOATS

It was getting near to Christmas, and Abbie was thinking of ringing her mother to discuss plans, when Mary Somerford telephoned first.

'Abbie – I don't know how things are with you, but, if you can, I think you should come home for Christmas.'

Abbie's heart gave a small lurch of fear. 'I was thinking of coming anyway. Is anything wrong?'

Her mother seemed to hesitate a little, but when she spoke her voice was calm enough. 'No – not wrong, exactly. But there are changes underfoot.' She paused, and then went on reassuringly, as if she could almost hear Abbie's unspoken anxiety on the line, 'I'll tell you all about it when you come... How long can you stay?'

'Not very long. I've only got one day off besides Boxing Day. It's the peak of the winter holiday season... And I've got this Bird...'

'What bird?'

'I'll tell you all about him when I come,' said Abbie, laughing. 'I'll be there on Christmas Eve...' Then she grew more serious. 'Is Dad all right?'

Her mother sighed. 'Yes, Abbie... More or less... We'll talk when you come,' and she prepared to ring off.

So it is my father, thought Abbie. I wonder what's wrong...? But aloud she only said softly: 'Give him my love – and save some for yourself!' and waited to hear her mother put down the receiver.

I must talk to Mackintosh about Solomon, she thought. And I must try to find out what is happening to the old Prof over Christmas. Somehow, I don't like the thought of him being all alone...

She went first to the basement flat to look for Mackintosh.

'He's out in the yard,' said Mrs Mac. 'Chopping wood. The Duchess likes a log fire at Christmas.'

'Don't we all?' smiled Abbie, thinking of the roaring fire in the Vicarage hall when the carol singers came on Christmas Eve.

'Tell 'im to come in,' Mrs Mac called after her. 'I've got mince pies in the oven.'

Abbie found Mackintosh up to his eyes in wood chips and small logs, looking a bit red in the face with exertion. 'I've come about the Bird,' she said. 'My mother wants me home for Christmas, and I don't know what to do about him.'

'Leave him where he is,' Mackintosh said, splitting one more log for good measure. 'Travelling about in a small cage in the cold wouldn't do him much good.'

'That's what I thought,' admitted Abbie doubtfully, 'but–'

'I can see to his food,' Mackintosh volunteered in a matter-of-fact tone. 'I know what he likes by now.'

'Won't he be lonely?'

The caretaker grinned cheerfully. 'I'll pop in when I can ... and you can leave the radio on... He likes music, doesn't he?'

'He seems to,' agreed Abbie.

'And you'd better leave that small heater on, in case it gets cold.'

'Will it be safe?'

He nodded. 'It's up on the wall, isn't it? Can't fall over... Anyway, I'll be keeping an eye.'

Abbie looked at him gratefully. 'I wouldn't want to upset the Duchess!'

'Or burn the house down!' Mackintosh

countered, chuckling. 'Don't worry. I'll see to it.'

It was Mackintosh's set phrase: *I'll see to it.* And Abbie knew he would do just that.

'Solomon likes you,' she said, still feeling a little guilty about leaving him.

'He likes anyone that feeds him,' the caretaker said, smiling.

But Abbie knew that was not entirely true.

'And anyway,' he added, seeing her sceptical look, 'I'm used to birds.'

That seemed to clinch the matter, and Abbie suddenly remembered Mrs Mac's promise of mince pies. They went in together, amicably discussing Solomon's diet, and presently they were all drinking coffee and eating mince pies in Mrs Mac's warm kitchen.

Then she had to find the Prof but here she was unlucky. He was not in the park on either of the days when she went to look for him, and when she asked one or two of the other 'regulars' whom she had come to know in the lunch-hour park community, they hadn't seen him either.

Eventually, she went back to Tubby's to explain the problem. 'Has he been in for a game of chess or anything?' she asked.

Tubby shook his head. 'He came back once – last week. To tell you the truth, I was surprised he even got that far... But he hasn't been back since.'

Abbie looked worried. 'Did you have any luck finding out where he lived?'

'Not so far ... but we're still trying.'

She smiled at Tubby's round, sympathetic face. 'Thanks, Tubby ... I know the network's still working!'

He patted her arm. 'Go on home and enjoy your Christmas. We'll find him, I'm sure – and see that he gets a Christmas dinner!'

Abbie laughed, touched by Tubby's genuine concern, but there was still a small, nagging doubt in her mind. Had she really done enough...? But it was too late to do anything more now. Her train to the west country was waiting and she had to go. She said an unexpectedly affectionate farewell to Tubby, hugging him hard, and then went to collect her suitcase from her flat and say goodbye to Solomon.

'I'll be back in four days,' she told him, offering an extra titbit of chopped-up apple. 'And Mackintosh is going to look after you. I hope you won't be too lonely.'

The beautiful head tilted, the shimmering red crest glinting in the winter sunlight. He seemed to be listening attentively to Abbie's soft voice, and after a considered pause, uttered a low, gentle call.

'That's it. Happy Christmas, Solomon,' she said. 'I'll be back soon...' and she fled down the stairs, wondering how a mere bird should have managed to wind himself round her heartstrings so soon.

It's like Perry, she thought helplessly. I didn't mean to get involved, to feel anything ever again... But here I am, loving a bird and loving a man. Who can explain the absurd longings of the human heart?

She emerged into the street and found a cruising taxi. But all the way to Paddington station she was arguing with herself about the extraordinary pull on her emotions that one red-crested bird and one far-away ornithologist could have... I am lost, she said. Why deny it? Who can escape the power of love?

The old Vicarage was as beautiful as ever – golden stone lit by pale winter sunshine, mossy tiles weathered to a gentle russet-grey. But to Abbie's eyes, seeing it suddenly after long absence, the lovely house had a slight air of genteel decay, like a society beauty who had seen better days and was now gently sliding into dim old age.

But before she could even acknowledge her vague sense of regret and unease, her mother came out of the house, arms out-stretched, with Rusty, the old cocker spaniel wagging exuberantly beside her in his own special welcome.

'Abbie – how lovely. Come in by the fire. Tea's ready.'

Abbie hugged her mother, feeling a sudden

rush of affection sweep over her as she put her arms round those familiar shoulders.

'You're thinner,' said Mary Somerford, looking at her reproachfully. 'So are you,' countered Abbie. 'What's been happening to you...? Where is Dad?'

'Blessing the Crib. Children's Service. He'll be in presently.'

'And then out again for Midnight Mass, I suppose?'

Mary smiled and sighed both at once. 'It's a busy time for him... He'll be able to relax on Boxing Day.' She led Abbie inside to the glowing log fire in the drawing room. 'Sit down while I get the tea – I won't be long,' she said, and left Abbie staring at the flames and wondering when her mother would tell her what was wrong.

She didn't have to wait long. Mary brought the tea tray in and sat down beside her, an expression of serious determination on her resolute face.

'We'd better talk now, Abbie, before he comes in. I think you may be – a bit shocked by his appearance.'

'Why? What's wrong? Is he ill?'

Mary Somerford hesitated, and then went steadily on. 'Not specifically – but he is deteriorating.'

Abbie's heart seemed to clench with alarm. 'In what way?'

'He is getting vaguer and more forgetful ...

more withdrawn, somehow. Half the time he doesn't really seem to be here at all... And once or twice he's wandered off and been missing for almost a whole day...'

'What do the doctors say? Do they know what's wrong?'

Once again there was a fractional hesitation before her mother answered, and when she did, her voice was low and curiously shaken. 'Well – they haven't officially diagnosed it yet, but they have a good idea...'

Abbie looked at her in mute enquiry.

'They could be wrong, Abbie. It might be nothing but tiredness. They've suggested a long rest, to see if he pulls out of it, but–'

'But?'

'They think it could be Alzheimer's.'

Abbie stared at her, appalled. 'Oh God. Could it be?'

'I'm afraid it could... But we won't jump to conclusions yet.' She gave Abbie a small, rueful smile, and got very busy for a few moments with pouring out tea.

'So ... what will all this mean to you...? To father's way of life, I mean?' Abbie was beginning to see the implications.

'It will mean,' said Mary steadily, 'resigning this living. Retiring early.'

'Can you afford to?'

'We've *got* to, Abbie. He can't cope with the work any more... I've already been to see the bishop to explain the situation.'

'What did he say? He's quite fond of Dad, isn't he?'

'Yes, he is. And he came up with a compromise solution. The Diocese wants to amalgamate several parishes anyway, ours among them. The Vicarage will be sold to boost falling church funds, and there will be one priest-in-charge for all four parishes. But the Bishop would like your father to help out with occasional services, and go on with his ordinary social work in the village as long as he can... That way, he will fill in the gaps that an over-stretched priest-in-charge cannot meet, and also he won't feel entirely useless.'

'Does he agree?'

Mary sighed and looked at Abbie with reluctant honesty. 'I haven't told him, Abbie. I thought – I thought we'd get over Christmas first ... and then he'll have to go and see the Bishop himself. Officially, I don't know anything about it yet.' Her eyes were pleading. 'Let him have a happy Christmas, Abbie – that's why I particularly wanted you to come home. It will be the last time in this house ... the last time he is in charge of his own parish...'

Abbie could hear the unshed tears behind her mother's voice, and she felt rather like crying herself.

'Will he – do you think he will mind a lot?'

'I don't know...' Mary sounded helpless

and uncertain. 'It's difficult to tell these days what he really feels...' She gave Abbie another brief, sad smile. 'But he'll be so glad to see you. At least we can count on that.'

Abbie nodded slowly, hoping she was right. 'Where will you live?' she asked suddenly.

For a moment her mother looked a little awkward, and then she said quietly: 'I thought ... we might take over your cottage.'

Abbie looked astonished. 'Aren't Tim and Linda there?'

'Oh no,' said her mother. 'They've gone.'

'Gone?' echoed Abbie. 'Gone where?'

Mary shrugged. 'Somewhere up north, I believe.' She was looking at Abbie now with half-smiling affection. 'You won't have heard, of course – but things have been happening here since you left.'

Abbie was mystified. 'What things?'

Her mother's expression had a faintly sardonic tinge to it now. 'The parishioners are a loyal lot, you know... They didn't approve of what happened – and they made it abundantly clear.'

'How?' Abbie was still puzzled.

'In all sorts of ways. The shops wouldn't serve them. The builders refused to come. No one would speak to them. It became very painful – people cut them dead in the village street... And then there was the mysterious business of the double bed.'

'What mysterious business?'

'It caught fire.'

Abbie stared at her mother in disbelief. *'Caught fire?* How could a bed catch fire?'

Mary was openly smiling now. 'Don't ask me...! A fault in the electric blanket, they said.'

'In *midsummer?*'

Mary's smile grew. 'No-one seems certain how it happened. And Simmonds, the village bobby, didn't seem to want to make very searching enquiries!'

'Was there much damage?'

'Oh no. Only the one room. Someone alerted the fire brigade... It was day time, you see – while Tim and Linda were both at work... It was only a small fire. They put it out quite quickly.'

The two pairs of eyes met in dancing amusement. 'Very curious,' said Abbie.

'Yes, well, that more-or-less finished them, really. And then Tim lost his job, so they decided to cut their losses and go elsewhere.' Mary's mouth had a momentary curl of distaste. 'I can't say I'm sorry, really.'

Abbie sighed. 'It must have been difficult for Tim's parents.' After all, she reminded herself, she had been quite fond of them – her future in-laws – and their friendship went back a long way.

'I don't think they were sorry either,' said Mary, with a faint grin. 'For the time being...'

And then they heard Abbie's father come

into the hall and call out: 'Mary? Has Abbie arrived?'

Her mother smiled encouragingly at Abbie. 'At least he hasn't forgotten you were coming!' she murmured, and added more loudly:

'In here, James. Yes, she's come!'

James Somerford came into the room quite briskly, but Abbie was shocked to see him looking so stooped and grey. He seemed to have aged ten years since she saw him last. For a moment his eyes, looking into hers, seemed to be filled with a kind of bewildered appeal, as if he was asking her to explain to him what was happening to his clouded mind, but then his expression changed and became full of loving recognition. His only daughter had come home in time for Christmas, and his day was complete.

'Abbie, my dear!' he said, and folded her in his arms. 'How good to see you!'

'I would have come before–' Abbie began, feeling instantly guilty when she heard the pleasure in his husky voice.

'No,' her father said, smiling down at her. 'Trying your wings. Can't come back until you can fly!'

'That reminds me,' said her mother, busy pouring out more tea all round, 'what was all that about a Bird, Abbie?'

'Oh, Solomon,' said Abbie, relieved to find that her mother had so skilfully turned the conversation into easy channels. 'Well, it was like this...' and she told them all about him, wondering as she did so, with a small pang of anxiety, whether the Bird was all right and not missing her too much.

Her parents were both fascinated, and her father was particularly pleased about the biblical name – and of course then Abbie had to tell them about the Memorial Service for Duncan MacNab, and Perry, and how he had insisted on her reading the small passage about the lilies-of-the-field... And however calmly and rationally she recounted the story, there was a curious softness abut her voice when she spoke of Perry, and a radiance about her smile that she could not quite disguise.

Her mother made no comment, but her affectionate glance moved from her daughter's face to her husband's for a fractional moment, and for once James returned her look with a smiling one of his own. Mary rejoiced secretly. It wasn't often, these days, that communication with James was so instant and so clear.

'A red-crested turaco?' said James, sounding on the spot and interested. 'That's rare, isn't it?'

'Well–' Abbie hesitated. 'It's endemic only to Angola... And Perry says the habitat is going – they are cutting down what remains of the forest far too fast... So, although it is not officially listed as a threatened species, it soon will be.'

Her father nodded. 'What will you do with him?'

Abbie's eyes seemed to grow distant and strange as she answered. 'If Perry's plans go well and he can set up the captive breeding programme, he might be able to take Solomon back to his own bit of forest... That is, if he can get the permits and things.' She sighed.

'And if not–?' asked Mary.

If not? thought Abbie. If Perry's plans *don't* go well? Will he come back at all? It won't only be Solomon who will be left high and dry... But aloud she answered her mother's question in a calm and steady voice. 'Then he'll have to go to some tropical bird sanctuary or other over here... He will need more space to fly about when the summer comes.' She did not admit, even to herself, how much the prospect filled her with dismay.

'There are different kinds of freedom,' murmured her father, and his eyes seemed to take on an even greater distance than Abbie's.

The two women looked at each other, but before they could make any reply – if there was any kind of reply possible – there was a ring at the front door and the sound of faint singing outside.

'It's the carol singers,' said Mary, getting to her feet.

'Do we still give them mince pies and

mulled wine?' asked Abbie, also getting up to help her mother.

'Coffee, nowadays,' corrected Mary, smiling. 'They got so merry going round the village that they kept falling asleep in the midnight service, and the choir ground to a halt!'

Abbie laughed, and Mary went to open the front door and let the carol-singers in. And James, knowing he was going to see most of his parishioners and his choir later on, slipped quietly away to his study and forgot about them altogether.

They sang all the old favourites – with the current angel-choirboy producing a pure, clear treble for *'Silent Night'* and the Page in *'Good King Wenceslas'*, with the best village bass who was also chief bell ringer as the King. Everyone managed to reach the high notes in *'Hark the Herald Angels Sing'* and only one stray tenor forgot to stop singing when it was the boys' turn in *'O Come All Ye Faithful.'*

Mary and Abbie listened dutifully and passed round the mince pies and coffee afterwards – and all the members of the choir beamed happily at Abbie and told her how glad they were to see her back. Eventually they left in a cheerful group, and went singing down the street, storm lanterns swinging, on their customary round of the village houses, in a tradition that had been established many generations ago.

Abbie and her mother returned to the comfortable fireside in the drawing-room, and settled down with a glass of sherry each.

'What else is there to do?' asked Abbie, remembering past Christmases when her mother seemed to be up to her eyes in kitchen preparations.

'Nothing much,' said Mary. 'We're having chicken, not turkey.'

'Not one of ours, I hope?' protested Abbie. 'Not Bessie or Matilda?'

'Certainly not!' said Mary. 'It would choke me! Besides, they're too old for anything except boiling!'

'I'm glad to hear it,' Abbie grinned. Then she grew serious. 'Is Dad all right in there?' She waved a hand at the closed study door.

Mary smiled. 'Oh yes. He's all right with his books... We'll get him out for supper presently... And we may have to remind him about the midnight service.'

Abbie looked at her mother. 'Do you often have to do that?'

'Do what?'

'Remind him to take the services?'

'Oh ... yes, sometimes.' She met Abbie's accusing gaze serenely. 'He's all right when he gets going, you know... The old routine takes over.'

Abbie nodded, secretly appalled at how much covering up her mother must have been doing over the past months.

'Mum,' she said abruptly, 'do you want me to come home?'

'<u>No</u>,' said Mary forcibly. 'That's the last thing I want.'

'But–'

'No, Abbie. You've got away – you're building a new life now. Keep it that way... I told you before that I was worried about the Tim business long ago. It didn't really give you a chance to escape and be yourself, did it?' She gave her daughter a rather perilous smile. 'As a matter of fact, Abbie, I was terrified you'd get caught up in all this and feel obliged to stay – *and I don't want you to.*'

Abbie looked at that perilous smile and sighed. 'Did you know – even then – that something was wrong?'

'With your father...? Well, yes. You can't be married to someone for over forty years and not know when something is not quite right.' She shook her head slowly. 'It was nothing specific ... just a feeling.'

Abbie was still looking at her sorrowfully. 'But – it's a lot to face on your own.'

Mary shook her head again, this time more firmly. 'No. Not really. I married him, Abbie... In sickness and in health, and all the rest of it... And,' she smiled at her daughter with no dissembling, 'I love him, you know ... even after all these years. It doesn't change. That makes everything all right.'

Abbie felt the tears rise behind her eyes at this simple statement. It was so typical of her mother. Straight to the heart of the matter – no frills or evasions. Not in the least afraid of the truth... But even so, Abbie felt she had to persist a little further, with the uncertain future in mind.

'Yes, but if things got really difficult–? You would send for me then, wouldn't you?'

Mary looked at her and did not answer.

'*Please*,' said Abbie, using all her powers of persuasion. 'Don't you see? I would *need* to be with you then.'

And at that fierce appeal, Mary capitulated. 'Well, yes, then – if it came to that ... but things are all right at the moment. I can manage quite well... You know your father, Abbie, he's the gentlest soul alive. He's no trouble ... and he trusts me. We understand each other pretty well...' Her smile was both tender and firm at once. 'And what we both want most is that you should have a life of your own and be happy. Understand?'

'Yes,' agreed Abbie reluctantly. But she felt ashamed to be getting off so lightly. '*He's no trouble, and he trusts me*,' said her mother's voice in her mind. But what if things got worse, and he was some trouble, and he *didn't* trust her?

'That's enough now,' said her mother briskly. 'It's Christmas Eve, remember? Come and help me get the supper. And then we'll call your father.' And she turned a smiling face to Abbie, and led her away to the kitchen.

It continued to be a traditional Christmas. James Somerford came docilely to supper, looking a bit vague, though he smiled at Abbie over the potato dish and said warmly: 'It's good to see you sitting there!'

But later, when they were dawdling over coffee in the drawing-room, he sat staring into the flames in silence for a long time and then shook his head, almost plaintively, and murmured: 'Too much in my head tonight... Maybe I should go to bed early.'

Mary glanced at him swiftly, hiding her anxiety. 'You have to get through the midnight service first, remember.'

'Have I...? Why?'

'It's Christmas Eve, dear. That's why Abbie's home.'

'Oh yes, so it is,' he said, and offered Abbie a shy, apologetic smile. 'And I'm so glad you've come home...' He sighed, and rubbed a bewildered hand over his eyes. 'I'm afraid I'm getting very forgetful...! If it wasn't for Mary, I think I'd forget who I was altogether!'

'Well, I know who you are, James dear,' said Mary robustly. 'You're the much-respected vicar of St. Michael's – and the villagers would be most disconcerted if you failed to turn up! I think they love this service more than all the others – so we mustn't disappoint them!'

'Of course not,' agreed James in a chastened voice. 'Well, in that case, I think I'll have a little rest in the study first... You'd better call me when it's time to go over.'

Mary nodded tranquilly. 'Good idea. Abbie can come and fetch you.'

She and Abbie exchanged cautious glances and watched the stooping figure turn rather wearily and uncertainly away to the sanctuary of his book-strewn bolthole.

But when Abbie finally went to collect him, he lifted his head sharply and looked at her for a moment as if she was a stranger.

'Yes?' he said, sounding curiously beleaguered and angry. *What do you want?*'

And Abbie, staring back, felt a sudden lurch of fear as her father's face seemed to become alien and hostile – the face of someone she did not know.

'It's time to go over for the service, father,' she said, trying to sound as normal as possible.

The tension in James Somerford's body relaxed suddenly, and his eyes became alert and clear, with no trace of the bewildered anger that had assailed him before. It was almost as if the strange, frightened creature that had looked out of his eyes had gone, and left the old, loving countenance that Abbie had known so long. 'Oh, yes, the service,' he said, and smiled. 'I'm afraid I'm a trial to your mother,' he added sadly. 'She's very patient.'

'Nonsense,' said Abbie roundly. 'She loves looking after you. It's her chief role in life.'

Her father's expression softened, but his glance was once more full of that urgent, unspoken appeal she had seen in them when she first arrived. 'We are celebrating Christmas,' he murmured. 'Women always accept the most difficult roles...' He sighed and shut his eyes for a moment, almost as if offering up a silent, private prayer of his own. 'I just hope...' he went on, speaking almost to himself, 'I just hope the sword doesn't pierce her heart also...'

He did not explain – he did not really need to – but he reached out and took Abbie's hand in a convulsive grip as he got slowly to his feet. 'Come, then. Let us go over together,' he said.

They sang all the favourite hymns and carols all over again in the lovely candle-lit church, and the local handbell-ringers played several extra carols and several traditional sweet-sounding chimes. The best choirboy sang his best solo, and the oldest tenor sang his last before he retired, and the organist excelled himself in the voluntary. And most of James Somerford's parishioners shuffled humbly forward to the altar rail to greet the Newborn on Christmas morning... And afterwards, everyone in the village seemed to want to shake Abbie's hand and tell her how glad they were to see her back. They stood in little knots, gossiping in the frosty air, and then moved off to their own firesides and their stocking-filling and last minute turkey-stuffing, calling 'goodnight' and 'happy Christmas' over their shoulders as they went.

'Soup in the kitchen,' said Mary. 'To warm us up. And then bed, I think... It'll be a long day tomorrow.'

They sat companionably round the kitchen table, not talking much. And Abbie felt, strangely, as if she had never been away... There had been so many Christmas Eves like this in her golden childhood... Only, she knew now that there was a shadow over this one which seemed to make its comforting warmth and happiness more precious than ever.

Oh Perry, she thought, where are you tonight? Are you celebrating Christmas out there in the threatened remnants of the fragile rainforest?

And is your chosen world really more threatened and more fragile than mine?

Hodie, said her father obscurely. 'This Day... We may as well rejoice in it while we can...' And he got up then, and uncharacteristically kissed Abbie before he went up to bed. Then, as if in an afterthought, he turned back and laid a gentle hand on his wife's shoulder. 'What a blessing you are,' he said to the room at large, and wandered off into the hall and began to climb the stairs.

Abbie and her mother looked after him fondly, and did not say another word.

Christmas Day itself was full of services and meals, and people coming and going with extra small gifts and messages of goodwill. Abbie and her mother seemed to be busy all day long providing drinks and cups of tea, and making sure that James went over to the church when he should, and came back safely to a re-vitalising hot meal before the next stint.

For the most part, he seemed to manage pretty well, but after the last service of the day when he really could look forward to a nice restful evening, he failed to come home at all.

Mary Somerford waited a while, growing increasingly worried, and then sent Abbie over to the church to look for him. The main door in the west porch was locked up for the night, but there was still a light on in the vestry, and Abbie went round there to try the little side door. It was still open, and she went quietly inside. Maybe her father was still talking to someone, or counting the offertory money, or something?

But he wasn't. There was no one in the little vestry, though its light still shone out over her father's Christmas vestments, laid out neatly on the old oak chest in the corner. But where was her father?

She crossed the small space, and went back into the church through the inner door, and stood looking round the empty building in the dark. She could not see anything at all, except the small glow from the hanging sanctuary light, and went back into the vestry again to fetch a candle and some matches. She lit the long wax candle and held it aloft as she walked back into the church and stood looking uncertainly down the shadowy aisles. The small, flickering flame cast strange shadows on the stone walls and pillars, making even deeper recesses of darkness beneath the arches...

But there was no one there... She walked steadily down the central aisle, turned into the side aisle that held the Lady chapel, and stooped to go in through the little open archway. It was a tiny chapel, fitted out with blue hangings and kneelers, and a Children's Corner at one end, where a serious, gentle-faced Madonna presided over a collection of children's toys donated for the local hospital. There was no other furniture in the narrow space except one rather beautiful old prie-dieu placed strategically in front of the blue-robed Madonna.

And there, stooped forward so that his head rested tiredly on the slope of the carved oak prayer desk, was her father. Abbie hesitated for a moment, wondering if she was interrupting some deep contemplation or other. But then the steadiness of his breathing made her realise that he had simply fallen asleep... Only, she wondered, still hesitating to disturb him, what extreme of anguish had driven him into this little side chapel and its secret prayers in the first place?

But she knew, really, what was troubling her father, and why he had fled in here at the end of what was probably his last full Christmas Day as vicar of this parish... James Somerford knew, she was sure, without being told, what the future had in store for him.

'Father?' she said gently, taking a cautious step forward. 'It's time to go home now.'

The heavy head lifted slowly, and James turned a dazzled face towards Abbie and her candle. 'Is it?' he said. And then, more certainly, 'Yes – I suppose it is.'

'Mum's got supper waiting,' Abbie said, trying to keep to simple, everyday things. 'She wondered where you were.'

James got to his feet rather shakily, and held on to the prie-dieu for a moment to get his balance. 'Did she...? Have I been long?'

Abbie smiled at him. 'Just a little longer than usual... Haven't you said enough prayers for one day?'

'No,' sighed James, but he smiled back with returning awareness. 'It's never enough, Abbie... Never. That's the trouble!' And he turned, quite readily, to follow Abbie through the silent church. 'You look like Florence Nightingale!' he said, as they came back into the vestry, and Abbie put down the lighted candle.

'Nothing like so useful!' said Abbie, and stooped to blow out the perilous flame. 'But at least I found *you!*'

And she linked her arm through his and led her father home.

On Boxing Day, having found out that her mother was paying a round of 'duty visits' and her father was resting in the study, Abbie went for a long walk in the frosty fields, accompanied by her old friend, Rusty. It was not exactly a white Christmas this year, but frost sparkled on every leaf and twig, and there was a shimmer of silver on all the hills. It was the kind of crisp and sunny day that was made for walking, and she went a good deal further than she meant to, admiring each frost-furred leaf and frond of bracken on the way.

She had set off with the intention of trying to walk off her anxiety about her father – or at least come to terms with it; and also to face up to something else she hardly dared to admit – the strange, aching gap in her life that Perry's departure had left... But somehow, walking these familiar hills, she found herself calmed and reassured by their wide, undemanding spaces. They were there – these hills she had known since childhood – unchanging from time immemorial, and they would still be there long after her father, and she and Perry, too, were gone... The fears and griefs that were assailing her now were no more important to these ancient hills than the fall of a frosted leaf.

It will be all right, she told herself. My mother has already accepted whatever the future may bring. She is facing it with her usual unshakeable calm. And I think my father knows a lot more about it than he lets on. Who am I to panic in the face of such black courage?

And as for Perry? Maybe he will come back as he promised, or maybe he won't. But we had our golden day – and what I feel for him now will not change. Even if he doesn't return, my life is already enriched beyond measure. Who am I to complain?

So she walked on, gradually relaxing into a mood of quiet acceptance as she watched the sun slope down behind the pure, dark outlines of the hills. 'Rusty,' she said, 'it's nearly sunset. Time to go home.'

And the old dog wagged an enthusiastic tail and turned his head towards supper and firelight and the familiar homeward paths he knew.

But on the way home, a thought struck Abbie, and she turned aside from the Vicarage garden and went on through the village to another house at the far end of the street. She stood for a moment looking up at it, as if trying to make up her mind about something, and then went forward slowly and rang the bell.

After a few moments the door opened, and the woman who stood there gazed at Abbie in a kind of incredulous gladness. 'Abbie... How – how *lovely* to see you... Will you come in?'

Abbie smiled up at her. 'I've got Rusty with me.'

'Oh, never mind that. Come inside out of the cold... Reg will be so pleased to see you.'

So Abbie followed Ruth Wilson, the woman who would have been her mother-in-law, into the house. After all, they were good to me in the old days, she told herself. It's not their fault that things went wrong. They weren't to blame for Tim's betrayal... It's high time I made my peace with them.

'I just felt I couldn't come home and not come to see you,' she said.

Tim's mother gave a small gulp of surprise. 'Oh, *Abbie!*' she said, and looked about to cry.

But then Reg came in, equally surprised

and pleased, and hastily offered Abbie a Boxing Day drink. 'How long are you down for?' he asked, making slightly awkward conversation.

'Only till tomorrow. The office is busy over the holiday period.'

'Do you like living in London?' asked Ruth, clearly finding it difficult to imagine such a thing.

Abbie smiled. 'It's different. But I've made a lot of friends – and I've got this Bird to look after.'

So she told them all about Solomon, reflecting, as she did so, how many times her beautiful rescued bird had helped conversation and made her friends relax – and even made her new friends all along the way. And as she talked, she watched these two nervous, over-anxious people begin to thaw and become the familiar, easy-going friends she used to know: Ruth Wilson, plump and warm-hearted, her fair hair much more silvered than Abbie remembered, her blue eyes still a bit apologetic and shiny with un-shed tears; and Reg, big and fair like his son, and – also like his son – unable to handle complicated emotions.

In a way, Abbie thought, I'm quite sorry for them. They didn't ask for any of this to happen. But I can see now that I must make this short. They don't really know what to do.

'I must get back,' she said, smiling.

'They'll be wondering where I've got to.' She rose to her feet, and Rusty followed her, wagging hopefully, anxious to get home.

'How – how are they?' asked Ruth, and Abbie could hear the shyness and regret in the tentative voice.

'Pretty good,' lied Abbie, and then amended it slightly. 'Though my father is getting a bit frail.' She looked at Ruth with deliberate kindness. 'I think Mum would love to see you.'

'Really?' The blue eyes filled with tears. 'I thought–'

'I know.' Abbie cut her short. 'But that's all over now. How are they, anyway, the two of them?'

Ruth glanced wildly at Reg and then back to Abbie's untroubled face.

'All right ... as far as we know... They don't – get in touch very often.' Abbie nodded. 'New start – like me. It takes time!' She grinned at Ruth and Reg, who both seemed bereft of words.

But Ruth started forward as Abbie and Rusty went to the door. 'Abbie – Tim told me about how much you did to help ... when Linda ran off ... I can't begin to–'

'Past history now,' said Abbie firmly. 'We had to salvage something, didn't we?' Somehow, including Ruth and Reg in the conspiracy seemed to put everything on an easier footing, and she could see the relief in both their faces. 'Come on, Rusty,' she said, 'time for your supper,' and she escaped rather swiftly from the house, smiling over her shoulder at the two embarrassed people who stood uncertainly behind her on the step. 'Don't forget to come and see Mum,' she added, and strode off down the street with Rusty at her heels. Phew! she said to herself. I'm glad that's over. It won't be so difficult next time!

'You've had a long walk,' said her mother, busy with more soup on the Aga.

'I stopped off to see Tim's parents,' said Abbie, helping herself to a scone that was lying conveniently to hand.

Mary looked at her approvingly. 'That was good of you.'

Abbie shook her head. 'No, Mum. It wasn't their fault. They were – pathetically glad to see me...' She sighed, and added with a hint of mischief: 'I told Ruth to come and see you.'

'Did you, indeed!' said her mother. But the two pairs of eyes met in smiling accord.

Her father came in then, seeming alert and cheerful at that moment. 'Did you do what?' he asked, also grabbing a convenient scone.

'Told Ruth Wilson to come and see Mum,' said Abbie. After all, they had to mention the awful past sometime.

'Quite right,' said her father, buttering his scone. His far-seeing gaze rested on Abbie's face with open affection. 'D'you remember sailing paper boats in the stream?'

Abbie stared at him in surprise. But then she realised what her father was saying. 'Water under the bridge?'

'Exactly.'

'It's funny – a complete stranger said that to me in London one day.'

Her father smiled. '"*Sweet Thames run softly...?*"' He fished in his pocket and brought out a rather crumpled piece of folded paper. 'Anyway, I made this for you today. I thought you could launch it before you go?'

Abbie's eyes, looking into his, were rather too shiny. 'What a lovely idea. Shall we do it together?'

'Why not?' said James, and looked across at Mary, who was watching both of them with affectionate understanding. 'Coming?' he said.

'What, now?' Mary protested. 'But it's getting dark.'

'Yes,' said James. 'Darkness is coming. But there are still some glimmers of light.' His glance was curiously insistent. 'And the street-lamp shines on the water,' he added reasonably.

So Mary, aware that her husband was intent on a special ceremony of his own, took the soup off the hot-plate and followed the two of them out into the village street and down to the little stone bridge that spanned the stream. The clear water gleamed darkly under the streetlamp, as James had said, and the pebbles at the bottom were lit with sudden jewel colours.

'This side?' asked Abbie, leaning over the parapet to look down at the swift-flowing stream.

'Yes.' James grinned at her like a mischievous small boy. 'And then you must *run* to the other side to see it come through!'

Abbie laughed and held the little paper boat in her hand, leaning far out over the parapet to reach the deepest channel of the brook.

'Let her go!' said her father. 'And give her your blessing! We've all of us got some letting go to do.'

Mary Somerford and Abbie looked at each other, but James did not say any more. He stood looking down at the dark water, waiting for the little boat to come through the arch.

So Abbie let it go, and the tiny paper boat fell headfirst into the stream, but, miraculously, it righted itself, and sailed bravely under the arch and came out on the other side, careening wildly in the swift current.

'There she goes!' said James, leaning out to watch the little white triangle sail by.

'There she goes!' repeated Abbie and Mary softly.

Together, the three of them watched the moving water till the fleck of white had disappeared into the shadows.

'*Ave, atque vale*,' murmured James. 'Clear water, now.'

Abbie returned to London fairly convinced that her father knew very well what was happening to him, and was prepared to face the future with his usual serene trust in the decrees of Divine Providence. But her heart ached for her mother, who was going to have to cope with an increasingly difficult situation as time went by. She had made one more attempt to persuade Mary to send for her at once if things got difficult, but had only succeeded in getting the reluctant reply: 'We'll face that when we come to it.'

So she had left them both smiling gallantly on the doorstep of the old Vicarage – probably the last time Abbie would ever see them standing there – and gone to catch her train, resolving to herself that she would come down to see them more often. That would be the only way to be sure what was happening to them and what help they needed. Therefore, beset by these anxious thoughts, she was a little sad already when she got back and stopped off on the way home at Tubby's to enquire about the Prof.

'No-one's seen him,' Tubby told her. 'But someone said the old man used to sit in the small private gardens in Maybury Square sometimes with his dog when he didn't want to go so far as the park – so maybe he lives round there.' He glanced at Abbie's worried face, and added: 'I've got someone over there looking out for him.'

Abbie smiled at him gratefully. 'Thanks, Tubby. Maybe I'll go and have a look round there myself at the weekend.'

'I might have news for you by then,' said Tubby. 'Call in, won't you?' He was looking at her rather anxiously, reflecting that she certainly had got a little pale and thin again since that nice fellow Perry Farquhar had gone back to Africa, and noting now that something about her Christmas visit home had added to that faint air of hidden sadness.

'Of course I will,' Abbie said, smiling at his troubled face. 'I can't miss my Tubby Special, can I...? But I won't stay now,' she added. 'I'm on my way home to see the Bird. I hope he's been all right without me.'

'Mackintosh is very reliable,' said Tubby. 'He understands birds.'

'I know,' Abbie agreed, but that did not deter her from hurrying away – almost running, with her suitcase banging up and down beside her – in her haste to make sure Solomon was safe and well.

She went first to see Mackintosh, who was

sitting in his kitchen, fixing an electric stove that had gone wrong.

'The Bird is fine,' he said, looking up at Abbie with calm certainty. 'He's eaten all his food, and come down to see me every time I came in, but I think he missed you.'

'How do you know?' asked Abbie, instinctively trusting Mackintosh and his knowledge of bird psychology.

'Well, he always looked beyond me, in case someone else was coming into the room too – and when no-one else came, he looked kind of disappointed.'

Abbie laughed. 'Aren't you imputing rather a lot?'

Mackintosh shook his head. 'No. He was looking for you. And when you go up there, I bet he crows!'

She smiled at his vehemence. 'You're very persuasive, Mackintosh! I'll go and find out how he feels right away...! And thanks for looking after him.'

'It's a pleasure,' said Mackintosh honestly. 'He's a nice Bird.'

And he smiled after Abbie as she fled upstairs to see whether his prediction was right.

'I'm back, Solomon,' she said, as she came into the room. 'I hope you haven't been too lonely? Are you all right? Are you glad to see me?'

And Solomon crowed.

At the weekend, true to her word, Abbie went to Maybury Square to look for the Prof, and discovered the small private gardens – a little oasis of green in the middle of the busy square. There was a padlock on the gate, but she found that the chain simply lifted over the gatepost, so that anyone could go in and make use of the wooden benches in the quiet, leafy space.

And there, on the farthest bench among a tangle of weedy rhododendrons, sat the old Prof, apparently dozing in the pale winter sunshine.

'Oh, there you are, Prof,' she said, advancing towards him in hopeful welcome. 'How are you getting on?'

But to her horror, instead of answering her, the old man seemed to stare straight through her for a long, slow moment, and then toppled slowly sideways off the narrow wooden bench to fall in a crumpled heap on the ground.

'Prof!' she cried, running to him. 'What is it? What's the matter?'

But he could not hear her. He was far out in the bitter no-man's-land of bodily collapse. The world around him was not there any more. Abbie turned him over, took one look at his grey, uncaring face, and ran for help.

There followed the usual nightmare of phone-calls, ambulances and paramedics, and hospital emergency. Abbie found herself being treated as that mysterious entity 'next-of-kin,' though she was nothing of the kind, and did not even know the Prof's real name. But at least she was able to explain the situation to a sympathetic nurse, and then found herself offering to go back to his address (found in a shabby wallet in his pocket) and see if she could find anyone who knew him or belonged in his life.

'I'll come back and report,' she said, looking anxiously into the kindly nurse's face. 'How – how is he, do you know?'

'They are still looking,' said the nurse. 'But it's certainly hypothermia, and possibly pneumonia... These old people out on the streets in all weathers – they don't have a chance!'

'I know,' said Abbie miserably. 'I did try to persuade him ... at least to get a hot meal. We had a sort of scheme to help ... but he wouldn't listen.'

The nurse nodded. 'They get obstinate when they are old,' she said sadly – and there was a world of knowledge in her compassionate voice.

'I – I'll see what I can find out,' said Abbie. 'Please – look after him!' and her luminous smile was so full of entreaty that the friendly nurse actually blinked.

Abbie hurried off to a long, thin street full of tall, thin houses, and walked down its length till she found Number Twenty-three. To her surprise, it was not a particularly shabby house, and the street itself was not down-at-heel or poverty-stricken either. The atmosphere seemed to be one of quiet, anonymous respectability more than anything, and she went up the steps of Number Twenty-three wondering what to expect.

'Oh, you mean Professor Anderson?' said the ground floor flat tenant, coming into the hall in answer to Abbie's knock.

'You mean – he actually is a professor?' said Abbie, amazed.

The ground floor tenant – a youngish, cool-looking blonde – nodded, smiling. 'Oh yes. *Was.* Cambridge or something. Very erudite! Why? What's happened to him?'

'He's in hospital,' said Abbie. And went on to explain the situation. 'I volunteered to come round and find out if he had any family – relations near at hand...? And to pick up a few things for him from his flat, if I could?'

The blonde looked at her critically. 'Do you have any identification?'

'Yes. And a note from the hospital, if that helps?' She fished out her own driving license, together with a piece of paper with a printed hospital address at the top. 'Maybe – er – you could come in with me?'

'Not me,' said the blonde. 'You want Marty. She's in charge here, really. I'll see if she's in,' and she went across the hall and banged on the other closed door.

Marty, when she appeared, was older than the blonde, and friendlier, but just as shrewd. She listened carefully to Abbie's story, and then agreed to take her up to the Professor's flat.

It was only two rooms, but it was scrupulously neat and clean. Almost too neat and clean. It scarcely looked lived in, and the small kitchenette at the end of the living room showed no sign of cooking or a recent meal. There were a lot of books on the shelves, and a desk full of orderly papers, including the skeleton plan of an unfinished crossword puzzle. Here there were slight signs of recent work – a biro with its cap off, a couple of loose pages with scribbled notes on them, and an open book. But nothing was really untidy or too cluttered. The only out-of-place thing was an empty dog bowl on the floor by the desk, and an old brown leather collar lying beside the scribbled notes.

Abbie stood looking round her sadly, feeling her heart clench with pity as she understood how the lonely old man filled his time. It was all so neat and soulless – so cold and comfortless, and the dog's possessions – so carefully preserved – were the only things in the room that spoke of companionship and warmth.

'Did he – does he have any family, d'you know?' she asked Marty.

The woman beside her shrugged, though not unkindly. 'Not that I know of. No-one came to see him.'

'Didn't he have any letters?'

'Only the crossword payments. I know about those, because he used to pay me the rent the day after they came – as soon as he had been down to the bank. Regular as clockwork.'

Abbie sighed. 'There must be someone?'

'He has a solicitor,' said Marty suddenly. 'He asked me to witness his will or something the other day. I think it was Simmonds or Simpson. Wait a minute, he kept a note of it somewhere – told me to get in touch with them if anything happened to him.'

Abbie stared at her. 'Was he *expecting* anything to happen to him?'

Marty shrugged again, but this time her smile was rueful and not at all casual. 'D'you know, I rather think he was.'

She had gone over to the desk by this time, and was carefully turning over the papers, examining each one before she set it down. 'Here we are,' she said at last, triumphantly waving a small, neat card that had been placed very precisely under a round glass paperweight. 'Simmonds and Henderson – Grey's Inn Road... You'd better have this. Give it to the hospital.'

Abbie nodded and put it away in her handbag. 'Should I – should we find some pyjamas and things, do you think?'

Marty agreed, and together they collected a few necessary bits and pieces from the Professor's painfully sparse possessions in his bare bedroom.

'Thanks,' said Abbie at last, following Marty down into the hall. 'I'll – I'll let you know how he is...'

Marty's rather bleak expression softened a little. 'He's not a bad old boy, you know. No trouble – especially now he hasn't got Spot to swear at.'

'No,' said Abbie sadly. 'That's the trouble really, isn't it?'

'What?'

'No-one to swear at.'

Marty laughed, but her eyes were as sombre as Abbie's. She knew the score, too. 'Well, tell him to get well, from me,' she said, and smiled briefly at Abbie and went back inside her door.

When Abbie returned to the hospital, she handed in the bundle of pyjamas and spongebag, and gave the solicitor's card to the sister-in-charge. 'That's all I could find out,' she said helplessly. 'I'm sorry–'

The sister smiled. 'It'll help.'

'Could I see him, do you think? I'm not a relative.'

'But you are *Abbie?*'

'Yes. Why?'

'He's been asking for you.'

Abbie was astonished. 'But he was unconscious when I – when we brought him in.'

'Well, he's not unconscious now – at least, not all the time... Come with me – it may ease his mind to see you. But you'd better not stay long. He's very tired.'

'No, of course not,' said Abbie humbly, and followed the bustling sister to the long ward known as Men's Medical.

The Professor lay propped up on pillows, looking small and frail and rather flushed. His eyes were closed, and his breathing was harsh and hurried, with a strange, rasping catch in it. And one waxy old hand was still clutching a dog's lead in its bony fingers.

'He wouldn't let it go,' murmured the sister, half-severe and half-indulgent. 'Made a terrible fuss. We decided to let him hang on to it for the time being.'

Abbie looked at her gratefully. 'He lost his old dog recently ... I'm afraid he took it rather hard.'

The sister, who was really very kind-hearted as well as shrewd, nodded and said: 'I thought it was something like that... Well, I'll leave you. Just a few minutes, mind!'

Abbie sat down beside the Professor's bed and wondered what to do. Was he awake? Or even conscious? Would the sound of her voice upset him? Or would it reassure him...? She didn't know. But at last she laid her own hand across those bony fingers and murmured: 'Hallo, Prof.'

The deep set, shadowed eyelids opened slowly, and the Prof's familiar, belligerent glare shot out at her. 'Where've you been? Gallivanting?'

'I went home for Christmas.'

'No bracken?' He tried a feeble cackle, but it turned into a fearful bout of coughing.

Abbie managed to give him a sip of water, but it didn't really seem to help.

'Bird all right?' he asked, snatching at another laboured breath.

'He's fine,' said Abbie. 'I think he actually missed me.'

The Professor tried a snort. 'I missed you,' he said.

Abbie was amazed, but she hid her surprise and merely said: 'Well, I'm here now.'

'Hate it,' he said, and coughed again.

'The hospital?'

'No air...' He tried to lift himself a bit higher on his pillows. 'Can't breathe in here...' He shot her a sly, hopeful look. *'Get me out?'*

Abbie sighed. 'I can't Prof. You're not well enough to move yet.'

He tried another snort. 'Better in the Park!'

Abbie shook her head gently. 'Not in winter, Prof. That's the trouble, isn't it?'

His glare tried hard to be fierce. 'I was all right out there...' he said, and his voice took on a strange, dreaming quality. 'We used to look at the ducks...' he murmured. 'Spot and I ... and watch the little boats on the lake... Spot nearly caught one once...'

Abbie didn't know if he meant the ducks or the boats, but she did not interrupt his dreaming. There was even a reminiscent smile on his tired face. 'Go back there...' he drowsed. 'Later...?'

'Yes, Prof, later. When spring comes,' Abbie promised. 'The sun will be warmer then... Even the Bird can't go out in winter. He has to wait for the spring, too...' She talked on softly, watching the lines of weariness fade from the old Professor's transparent face. 'You both have to get well and strong,' she said. 'And on the first day of spring in the warm sunshine, Solomon will be able to fly out in his little aviary and look at the sky, and you'll be able to go out in the Park... Won't that be lovely?'

But when she looked down for an answer, she saw that the Prof was asleep. Quietly, she withdrew her hand that he had been clutching in a fierce, desperate grip, and tiptoed silently away.

I'll come back tomorrow, she said to herself. And bring him some flowers to remind him of the Park. Perhaps he will be feeling stronger by then.

But when she got to the hospital the next evening, they told her that the Professor had died quietly in the night. There was nothing more to do, except to leave the flowers beside his empty bed.

Abbie went round to tell the others in Number Twenty-three, and inevitably found herself involved in the Professor's small, unpretentious funeral, in spite of her protests that she was not family and had no real right to be there.

'Of course you must be there,' snapped Marty, quite crossly. 'You're the only one who paid him any attention at all. This niece, whoever she is, has never taken the slightest notice of him.'

'What niece?' enquired Abbie.

It turned out that Mr. Simmonds, of Simmonds and Henderson, had unearthed a niece in California, who was flying over for the occasion.

'It will be only us few from here,' explained Marty, 'and her... And I think Simmonds will come.' She looked at Abbie hard. '*Please*, Abbie. The Prof would like you to be there.' And, of course, that clinched it for Abbie.

So the pitifully small party gathered together, chilled by the bleak, impersonal surroundings of the crematorium. Abbie could not help comparing it in her mind with the lights and music and distinguished company of Duncan MacNab's Memorial service. Never mind, Prof, she said. I'm re-membering you – and I daresay you couldn't care less by now, playing with Spot in those Elysian Fields or whatever... God speed, old friend...'

She came out with Marty and the blonde girl from the ground floor flat, to find a thin, grey-haired woman waiting to speak to her.

'Are you Abbie Somerford?'

'Yes?'

'I'm Molly Anderson. I gather you have been very kind to my uncle...'

She smiled at Abbie in a tentative, slightly nervous way. 'I live so far away, you see. I didn't know he was alone and ill...'

Abbie smiled back – less shyly. 'He was very independent... He wouldn't accept help from anyone anyway!'

Mollie's expression became less shy and more rueful. 'I think he was always like that – even when young – by all accounts!' She looked at Abbie more urgently. 'Anyway, I wanted to ask you – will you come back with us for a few moments?'

Abbie hesitated. 'Oh, I – I don't think so.'

'Please,' said Molly insistently. 'There is something Mr. Simmonds wants to say to you.'

'To me?' said Abbie, astonished. 'But I don't even know him.'

'Nevertheless,' persuaded the anxious woman firmly, 'he wants to see you.'

So Abbie rather reluctantly went back with Marty and the Professor's niece – the blonde girl had gone off on her own – and followed them into Marty's living room to drink a glass of sherry. And there, Mr. Simmonds – as grey and thin as Molly Anderson but much less nervous – asked them all to sit down for a moment, as the professor's will affected them all. He placed a few papers on the table in front of him and put on his glasses, and then looked over the top of them at the three women in front of him.

'There will have to be certain formalities before probate,' he began, 'but I thought you might care to know certain facts now. Especially as you, Miss Anderson, are flying back to the States almost immediately.'

'Yes?' said Molly, sounding a bit bewildered.

'The fact is,' Simmonds went on, 'the Professor was not, as most people supposed, very badly off. He had a good pension and some good shares. He simply didn't like spending money.'

They looked at him in mute astonishment, waiting for what he could divulge. Abbie and Marty glanced at one another with a hint of a smile, but Molly looked curiously unsurprised by the solicitor's remarks.

Mr. Simmonds cleared his throat and began his brief statement in a dry, unemphatic tone. 'He left the bulk of his money – some thirty thousand pounds – to the Battersea Dogs Home, because, in his words, 'they need it more than my relations.'

There was a glint of amusement in his dry voice, and in the glance he exchanged with Molly Anderson, who did not seem unduly disturbed or put out.

'But,' he went on smoothly, 'there are certain other bequests he wished to be settled first.' The glint of humour was still there as he glanced once again at his three listeners. 'To you, Miss Anderson, he left his books, including all his first editions which are in some cases quite valuable, because – I quote– "she is an academic, like me, and she will take care of them."' He cleared his throat again, a little pedantically, and added, as if in compensation for what might have been a disappointment, 'Together with the sum of five thousand pounds to assist with their transport.'

Molly Anderson gave a small nod of satisfaction, apparently well content with the dispensation. 'It's all I need,' she murmured to the company at large.

But Mr. Simpson had not finished yet. 'To his landlady, Marty Jackson, the rest of his possessions, which as you know were few, together with the sum of one thousand pounds, in recognition of many past kindnesses.' He looked up again, but since no one spoke, he went on to the end of his list. 'And to Abbie Somerford, also for past kindnesses, his stamp collection.'

There was a stunned silence at this, and then Abbie said in disbelief:

'Are – are you sure?'

'Oh yes,' answered the solicitor, smiling. 'Here it is. It has your name on it. And the instruction: *"For the Bird"* – if you know what that means?'

'Yes,' Abbie admitted, swallowing hard. 'I know what he means...'

'It is quite a valuable collection,' remarked Simmonds, observing Abbie's confusion with a faint air of mischief. 'It is probably worth a couple of thousand pounds. We had it valued, but you had better take more expert advice on that.'

'*Two thousand pounds?*' whispered Abbie. 'But – but I can't!' She looked rather wildly from Simmonds to Molly Anderson. But they were both smiling at her, and so was Marty, who was tactfully going round again with the sherry.

'He wanted you to have it,' said Mr. Simmonds reasonably. 'I don't see how you can refuse.'

'What did he mean about the Bird?' asked Molly Anderson curiously.

So Abbie told them all about Solomon, and how the old Professor had liked to come and see him and feed him special grapes, and stay and drink a cup of tea with Abbie as part of the ceremony. And as she recounted this, she found herself very near to tears, remembering how much the fierce old man had unbent when he was talking to Solomon, and how the Bird had tilted his beautiful, shimmering head sideways to listen to the sound of his voice.

'It – it sort of made up for Spot – his dog – you see,' she finished lamely. 'He just needed someone to talk to...'

The others all looked at her, acknowledging sadly, each to themselves, that she was right. The old Professor had only needed someone to talk to.

'Well, you had better take charge of it now,' said Simmonds, handing over three shabby-looking stamp albums. He smiled at Abbie with genuine friendliness. 'And I hope Solomon appreciates it!'

There was a general quiet murmur of laughter round the room, while Abbie looked down at the Professor's neat handwriting *'For the Bird'* with dilated eyes.

'There was one other curious remark of his,' added Simmonds into the small silence. 'He made me write it at the end of my instructions. It was this – also directed to Abbie. *"Don't you dare be sorry. Remember the blacksmith."'*

Abbie stared at him, the tears even nearer than before. She could not speak. But once again Molly asked her what the old man meant.

'I – he once sang a song for us, at the

Duchess's party...' she explained haltingly. 'It was called the Blacksmith... And it said – it said: *"I care for nobody, no, not I. And nobody cares for me...!"* But it wasn't true!' she added in a sudden upsurge of denial. 'It wasn't true at all!' And she burst into tears.

There was a long moment of silence, while the others looked at Abbie's bowed head in sympathy and some shame. For they hadn't cared about the old Professor at all, and they knew it. But then Abbie recollected that everyone was waiting for her to pull herself together and release them from embarrassment, and she remembered what Perry had done when he heard the news of Duncan's death.

'I think,' she said unsteadily, 'we ought to drink his health, at least – shouldn't we?'

So they did, in cheap sherry, though perhaps of all of them, only Abbie had a really clear picture of the old Professor, sitting in the sun on a Park bench, with his white dog, Spot, at his feet.

'Hail and farewell,' she murmured, remembering her father and the white paper boat sailing away into the dark.

7. FLYING FREE

It was a grey winter – at least, for Abbie. What with the worrying news about her father, and the old Prof's death, and – most of all – Perry's continuing absence, she found herself beset by a sadness which she couldn't shake off.

Her friends worried about her, especially Tubby, though she did not complain to them, but even young Bobby could not manage to make her smile a lot, however many antics he got up to.

She talked a lot to the Bird in the dark winter evenings, absurdly comforted when he cocked his head and seemed to be listening. She told him about her father, and her anxiety about his future and what it would do to her mother. She told him about the old Professor and his legacy of the absurdly valuable stamp collection, and her own sense of guilt because she hadn't been there over Christmas to keep an eye on the old man. And she told him about Perry – but even to Solomon she could not admit quite all she felt about that perilous, enchanted friendship.

'He says he's coming back to fetch you,'

she told the Bird, smiling at the listening, scarlet head. 'And one day you'll be able to fly free in a place that is always warm and leafy... You'll like that, won't you?'

Solomon looked at her with bright, intelligent eyes, but he made no comment. He just quietly demolished a grape, as if to say he was quite all right here, thank you, for the moment.

Abbie sighed. He is more patient than I am, she thought. He doesn't ask for more than I can give... Why should I? But her heart continued to ache for news of Perry, and she could not deny it.

However, her friends got tired of her pale, sad face, and took matters into their own hands. Lucinda Hope-Covington, who had promised to keep an eye on Abbie, decided to contact Anatole Raspin. And Sandra went to see her boss.

So one day when Abbie arrived for work, Sandra jerked a thumb at the inner office, and said: 'Maurice wants to see you.'

Abbie looked alarmed. What have I done?'

'Dunno,' shrugged Sandra. 'Better find out.'

Nervously, Abbie knocked on Maurice's door.

'Oh, there you are, Abbie. How many commitments have you got at home at the moment?'

Abbie stared. 'I – er – none.'

Maurice nodded his clever, dark head. 'That's what I thought. So how do you feel about going to Grasmere?'

Her stare got wider. 'Grasmere? The Lake District? Wh-when?'

'Next weekend.'

She sat down on the nearest chair. 'I – what would I have to do?'

'Take a Solo group up. You walk, don't you, being a country girl?'

Abbie was horrified. 'Yes – but I couldn't look after a whole lot of others.'

'Oh, you wouldn't have to do that. The walks are all well marked, and all optional to their own choice. And any planned expeditions or climbs always include a guide.'

'Oh.' Abbie still sounded very doubtful.

'You'd only have to shepherd them to and from the meeting points – and meet them in the bar in the evenings to listen to their complaints, if any!' He grinned at her. 'You're a good listener, I'm told.'

She still looked alarmed. 'I don't know if I'd be – competent enough?'

'Oh, come on, Abbie. You've got plenty of commonsense – and initiative, from all I hear.'

'Y-yes, but–'

Maurice laughed at her reluctant face. 'No more excuses. Coach goes next Saturday. Sandra will fill you in.'

The Bird, thought Abbie, clutching at

straws. What shall I do about Solomon? Can I ask Mackintosh to look after him for a whole week? Or is it a fortnight? She dared to voice that question aloud. 'How long for?'

'Ten days, including the coach trips.'

'Can I – could I let you know tomorrow?'

'No,' said Maurice. 'Let me know now. Yes or no?'

Abbie, looking into her boss's determined face, knew she had to say yes if she wanted to keep her job.

After that, things seemed to move very fast. Mackintosh told her not to be a fool, of course he would look after the Bird. Sandra waved tickets at her, and Tubby lent her his best pair of binoculars to look at the birds and the mountains. One of the César Franck girls lent her a brand-new cagoule she had only worn once. And, to her astonishment and not a little consternation, Olive Ashridge announced that she and Henry Grey had taken up the last two places on the tour and were coming with her. 'To – to walk?' asked Abbie, instantly appalled at the thought of falls on the rocks and broken ankles.

'Oh yes,' said Olive, all smiling and rosy. 'Henry loves walking, and so do I.' She looked at Abbie out of eyes that were somehow brimming over with reckless excitement. 'And Henry is very keen on Wordsworth! He's always wanted to go to the Lakes.' She saw Abbie's doubtful glance, and plunged on, blushing furiously. 'The hotel is in Grasmere, right by the lake. Henry found out all about it... And we thought, since you were going to be in charge, we'd feel safe and looked after!'

Abbie almost groaned. She was still privately horrified, but she tried to disguise it. 'Well, I hope you enjoy yourselves. But you can't walk all day!'

'Oh no,' explained Olive breathlessly. 'Henry's got it all worked out. We can walk a bit, and sit down a bit, you know! There are proper trails to follow... And the wild daffodils will be out, won't they?' Her voice sounded as eager and hopeful as a child's. 'And we can sit and drink coffee on the hotel terrace in the sun and look at the view!' She beamed at Abbie. 'There'll be plenty to do!'

Abbie sighed. 'Don't expect too much,' she warned gently. 'The sun doesn't always shine – especially in the Lakes!'

But Olive was not to be put off. She hesitated and then added shyly: 'You see, Abbie – it's Henry's only hope of a real holiday. His mother is going into a Rest Home for a whole fortnight... He felt – we felt we had to take the chance while we could.'

'I see,' said Abbie, smiling. And indeed she did see the whole sad little story of Henry's commitment to his ailing mother, and the fragile relationship with Olive Ashridge that could never really come to fruition... Of course they had to take their chance, she thought, and if I can make their holiday a happy one, I will!

So there she was, smiling encouragingly at a whole group of anxious travellers, trying to persuade them (and herself) that they were all going off on a happy, adventurous journey. Apart from Henry and Olive, they were youngish mid-thirties people, mostly shy and uncertain what to expect, as this was a tour arranged by the Solo operators. And once Abbie realised that they were shyer and less sure of themselves than she was, she found it much easier to be calm and reassuring for their benefit.

The coach trip was uneventful, and the journey along the winding road that led to the lakeside hotel went without a hitch. They arrived at dusk – too late to see the mountains, except as ghostly silhouettes pricked with faint lights on the lower slopes, but not too late to see the lake glimmering in the half-dark, and the pale, sloping lawns that led down to the water's edge. There was a long, thin jetty running out from the shore, with a tiny boathouse at the end, and Abbie looked at it with longing, thinking how good it would feel to be walking along it with the lake around you on all sides, away from everyone. But it was time to unload her passengers, and she saw no chance whatever of being away from everyone. Not now. By this time, she had sorted out their names and characters roughly in her mind, and thought they all seemed friendly and co-operative, and probably easy to manage. But how they loved to talk! Still, she reminded herself, they are all lonely people. This is their one chance of company. Why should I mind?

The hotel itself was a wide, gentle sort of place that had been a large country house for several generations before its conversion. It was welcoming and carefully not too smart, with deep armchairs and generous log fires to warm the guests' hearts (and feet) on chilly nights. The entrance hall had a wide mahogany staircase, and the bedrooms seemed to be mostly on one floor above. But while her party was busy sorting itself out, the hotel receptionist approached Abbie and asked whether she would like to have the boathouse bedroom which was away at the end of the jetty with the lake all round it. They thought she might like to be on her own, free of her charges at night? Or would she prefer to be in the hotel with them? Abbie considered the matter carefully, but she had seen that boathouse 'with the lake all round it' and she knew she couldn't refuse. There was so much space and silence out there, so many shimmers and reflections of light in the still, dark surface, so much peace beneath that far night sky...

'Oh – the Boathouse, *please!*' she said, and secretly rejoiced.

Perry was restless. In fact he was more than restless. He was downright edgy. He couldn't understand it. The work was going well, the authorities had suddenly become co-operative, and the wildlife sanctuary was well on the way to becoming a reality instead of a dream. So why was he feeling so unsettled and so depressed? There didn't seem to be any insuperable problems to be solved. The materials they wanted for the fencing and cages were available, they could just about afford them, and it seemed probable that they would be able to set up the captive-breeding programme very soon. So what was the trouble...? *The captive-breeding programme – and Abbie's Bird!* He would be able to go home and fetch them soon. *Them?* Would Abbie agree to come? And if she did – to see the Bird safely home – what then...? Would she agree to stay? And on what terms?

He knew then what it was. The reason for this feeling of caged indecision. He wanted Abbie. He wanted to go home and tell her that he simply couldn't go on without her. But would she listen? Would she want to come...? Wasn't it too soon to expect her to be ready to plunge into a till-death-do-us-part relationship? Because that was the kind of commitment he wanted. He knew it now.

But she had asked for time... She had obviously been deeply hurt by whatever it was in that 'childhood idyll' that went wrong... And she was still very young. Had he given her enough time...? Could she possibly feel as strongly as he did that the strange bond between them was rare and precious, and must not be denied...? Must be consummated?

He did not know. He did not know anything any more. His whole world seemed to have been turned upside down by emotions and longings he had not thought existed. Not in his ordered, disciplined life, where the research always came first. Always *had* come first. But not any more. Abbie came first. And he had to go home and tell her so.

When he went to Jonty and said rather awkwardly: 'Er – do we need that extra equipment for the lab urgently?' he was faintly surprised at Jonty's affectionate smile as he answered.

'Yes, we do. And it wouldn't do any harm to stir up the sponsors again – especially if the breeding cages are needed soon.' He patted Perry's arm. 'Don't look so guilty. Go on home and ask her.' He grinned at his astounded face. 'It'll be a relief to have things settled. You're like a cat on hot bricks these days.'

Perry had the grace to look contrite. In fact, he nearly blushed. So when Lucinda

Hope-Covington's message suddenly came through on the bush radio, it seemed almost heaven-sent. His friends at the Luanda Hospital had passed it on. And it simply said: *'Anatole Raspin wants to meet you in London re funding. Lucinda.'*

'There you are,' said Jonty. 'Perfect excuse. Go on home.'

So Perry went.

When Abbie awoke in the morning, the little boathouse bedroom seemed to be full of floating light. It shimmered on the walls and the ceiling, and even on the floor and on her bed. She sat up and looked round in amazement. For the whole little building was awash with light. It came flooding in from the windows at every angle, for the room was octagonal, and the early, far-off sunlight was somehow picked up by the surface of the lake and thrown back straight into Abbie's eyes. When she looked further, she saw that the high, distant mountains behind the great bulk of the fells were tinged with golden light from the sunrise, and behind their flawless outlines was a sky as deep and blue as the sea. And all round her was the unbroken silver surface of the lake, reflecting sky and cloud and the tawny flanks of the hills. Breathtaking! she thought. All that silver space and quietude... And it's going to be fine for my walkers, I do believe.

She found her party drinking coffee and eating hot croissants in the dining room, and greeted them cheerfully. Olive and Henry told her they had got their day all mapped out, and she need not worry about them. They were going to see Dove Cottage, and there were other things to look at in the little town, including several nice-looking cafés! And after that, Olive said, they would probably wander round to Rydal Water and Wordsworth's other house, Rydal Mount, and look for Dora's Field and the daffodils. She still sounded like an eager child out of school.

'There's no need to *look* for the daffodils,' protested Sue, the youngest member of the party, who was just as enthusiastic as Olive. 'They're everywhere. I've had a look already!'

The others agreed, and announced that they were going on one of the easiest walks this day, starting at Grasmere and going round the lake and the wooded hillside to Rydal, and it seemed sensible to Abbie to go with them and enjoy the views herself. And towards the end of the walk round Rydal Water, they climbed up to the woods on the hillside and found Dora's Field and the wild daffodils. They also found Olive and Henry, who had got there by a shorter route and were stooping over the pale golden heads of the flowers in rapt enchantment.

'So small – and so perfect!' said Olive,

lifting a glowing face to Abbie who was standing beside her.

'And so many!' added Henry, in a voice of awe. For indeed the whole hillside seemed awash with the pale gold of their windblown heads.

Olive looked at the glory all around her and sighed, turning away to stare down at the quiet waters of the lake below them. 'Isn't beauty *fragile?*' she murmured, and wandered away to join Henry who was now admiring a flock of lapwings, their wings flashing in the sun as they rose into the air and then settled on the fields below the hillside.

Yes, thought Abbie sadly, remembering Perry and their one golden day among the bracken fronds of Frant Park. Isn't beauty fragile? And then she remembered, too, that Perry was desperately trying to save the fragile beauty of the rain forest on the other side of the world... Fragile, she thought, looking again at the drifts of daffodils, but always there in my mind.

Eventually, they all wound their way back round the lake to the hotel, looking rosy with sun and fresh air, but clearly a bit tired.

'You've all done quite enough for the first day,' she told them, smiling. 'You'll be terribly stiff tomorrow.'

'I'm terribly stiff already!' laughed Sue, who shouldn't have been since she was the youngest and most agile of them all. 'I feel as if I've walked a hundred miles!' But her cheerful smile and curly blonde hair seemed as full of sparks as ever.

'I'm not stiff at all,' boasted Olive Ashridge, and shot a happy glance at Henry. 'We took it rather more easily than you!' She smiled at the others with transparent happiness. 'But I expect I will be *stiff* tomorrow!' she admitted, not wanting to sound too cocky.

'Hot baths all round,' said Abbie, grinning.

'And lots of mulled wine in the bar,' added one of the others, laughing.

It was fairly easy to please them, she thought, and tomorrow would be even easier. So Abbie's task began to seem much less daunting than she had feared.

During the next few days, a natural routine grew up around her little group, and she found that she had time to do a little exploring on her own. Sometimes she went with the group on their walks, and sometimes she wandered out alone and left them to their own devices. Olive and Henry, it was clear, were very happy to be on their own and she did not try to include them on any of her expeditions. But every new excursion in that wonderful Lakeland country produced new marvels and surprises for Abbie's enthusiastic group, and they were only too happy to recount them all to Abbie every evening in the bar.

Abbie, for her part, loved this wild hill country with its deep, silent lakes, but found it strangely disturbing. It was not like the warm, gentle country of her West Country hills of home – even though they had wild daffodils, too, among those woods and hills and tranquil fields. But this country was somehow fiercer and wilder, and more of a challenge. Her friends, she knew, had sent her here to help her escape from the haunting ghost of Perry. But somehow the high, bare shoulders of the fells and the dark woods above the silver lakes seemed only to bring Perry nearer, and the ache for his presence seemed to burn ever deeper as she gazed at all this unspoilt splendour alone and could not share it with him.

I'm a fool! she said. An ungrateful fool! I ought to be revelling in every minute of this, not clutching at shadows! But each evening as she walked out along the jetty to her room in the little boathouse, she would pause at the end and look out over the silent lake and think of that twofold silence they had shared when they had felt as one. And she would look up at the sky, trying to pierce the distances between Grasmere and far away Africa, and wonder if Perry remembered that silence, too.

In London, such was the urgency building up inside Perry that he went straight down to the Travel Agency to see Abbie, thinking she would be at work.

But when he enquired he was met by a cheerful Sandra, who said airily, 'Oh, she's in the Lakes.'

Perry was appalled. 'The Lakes? What on earth is she doing up there?'

Sandra shrugged casual shoulders. 'Part of the job. Shepherding a bunch of walkers.' Her smile was affectionate and somehow reminded him of Jonty's. 'She was feeling blue, Perry. Things were rather getting her down. The boss thought she needed a boost.'

He stood there, confused and shaken by his own disappointment. He had come home in a rush of hope, determined to plead his case, to sweep her off her feet with passionate declarations, to prove to her beyond all doubt that their two lives should be together, their future one. And she wasn't even there!

'How long will she be away?' he asked, his voice sounding bleak and flat in the empty office.

'Only ten days,' said Sandra sunnily. 'She'll be back.' Her grin was getting positively roguish. 'Can't it wait?'

'No, it can't!' snapped Perry, all too aware of time limits and the need to get back to the work with Jonty and the others. And, as he stood there, he felt a sudden strange compulsion within him telling him that it *couldn't wait...* It was the same faint prickling of imminent danger that he had felt that time in Cambridge when Abbie had got trapped on the roof... His thoughts drifted to the clever, observant face of his benefactor, Anatole Raspin who owned the airline, and his precise voice saying: *'I have learnt never to ignore such warnings...'*

'No,' Perry said again, more certainly than ever. 'It can't wait. Give me her address. *Now!'*

Meekly, and with a none-too-secret smile, Sandra obliged.

'Thanks!' growled Perry, and hurried off to see Anatole Raspin.

They had arranged to meet at Perry's club, and when Perry finally arrived, he found his unobtrusive guest sitting in one of the deep armchairs, peacefully sipping a drink.

'My friend,' said Anatole, smiling, 'I am glad to see you.'

And Perry realised with a sudden shock of recognition that he was unexpectedly glad to see Anatole, too. The small, neat man was as precise and formal as ever, the beard as pointed on the sharp chin, but there was somehow genuine warmth in the friendliness of those clever eyes.

'It's good to see you, too,' agreed Perry, holding out his hand.

Behind him, his favourite barman hovered.

'Welcome back, Dr. Farquhar. Your usual?'

Perry grinned. 'Afraid so, George. I'm incorrigible.' He sank into a chair beside Anatole, a drink in his hand, and they began to talk.

'I want to hear about your plans for the Captive Breeding Programme,' said Anatole. 'What exactly does it involve?'

So Perry told him, not leaving out the need for the new cages, the keepers to look after them, and the money to pay them and feed the animals.

'I think we can make a go of it,' he said. 'We've tried to foresee the contingencies that might arise, but of course there'll always be some we haven't thought of...'

'Of course,' murmured Anatole.

'And–' Perry gave him a rueful grin, 'it's hard to explain to the authorities that the programme needs *time*. You can't get animals to breed to order. They need to acclimatise and feel safe, and to bond with their new mates, and so on. You can't hurry them.'

Anatole nodded. 'That is exactly why I wanted to see you.'

Perry raised an enquiring eyebrow. 'Oh?'

The airline owner smiled and leant back in his chair. 'I have been doing some lobbying behind your back,' he said, smiling. 'I have – er – interests in Luanda ... and therefore, the authorities are anxious to cooperate...'

Perry was interested. 'So?'

'So I am offering to help you set up the Duncan MacNab Foundation, with sufficient funds to maintain your programme for five years, on condition that the authorities will let you stay on as Director and you are willing to do so.'

Perry looked at him, speechless.

'And after that,' went on Anatole, 'if the project is successful, the authorities will probably continue with extra funding to top up the Foundation income. It should be pretty well established by then.'

Perry was still staring, but now his gaze softened. 'Why are you doing this?'

Anatole's smile was as gentle as his voice. 'I told you before. Duncan was my friend. Isn't it what he would want?'

Perry's eyes were now distinctly misted. 'Yes,' he said. 'It is.'

'Well then, that's settled.' Anatole got briskly to his feet. 'We'll arrange details before you go back.' He stood looking at Perry with a distinct fleck of amusement in his shrewd gaze. 'So now you can go off with a clear conscience to find your Bird-girl.'

Perry looked even more astounded. 'How did you–'

'Oh, Lucinda is very – er – on the spot.' He grinned. 'She doesn't miss much.'

'So it seems,' growled Perry. But he wasn't really annoyed. How could he be, when all his problems seemed to be solved in one extraordinary meeting?

'Will she come with you, do you think?' asked Anatole, still sparking with mischief.

'Oh God, I hope so!' breathed Perry. 'But with all this to offer – how could she refuse?'

'That's what I hoped,' said Anatole smugly.

Perry laughed, but his voice grew serious as he added: 'Anatole – I can't begin to thank you.'

'Don't thank me. Thank Duncan,' said Anatole. 'He always was a persuasive man!'

Then he gave Perry a playful tap on the arm, and went neatly and purposefully from the room.

It was on one of their walks near the end of the week that disaster struck. Several small groups had gone off in different directions, arranging to meet at a pleasant cottage that served teas to wandering walkers. Abbie, slightly bothered by the party splitting up so much, had decided to join the last group which contained Henry and Olive, for once being sociable, and make sure that everyone arrived for tea as planned. She was walking quite slowly ahead of her group, looking anxiously at the weather that showed signs of turning misty, when she heard a small cry behind her, and the sound of slithering feet on rock. She turned sharply, and almost cannoned into Henry, hair flying and eyes

427

wild with fright, rushing towards her in terror.

'Oh Abbie, she's fallen...! Olive's fallen...! What shall we do?'

'*Where?*' said Abbie. 'Show me.' And she hurried back up the path to where a frightened little group of walkers stood huddled together, looking down.

'She saw a flower,' gasped Henry. 'She w-wanted to see what it was... She was reaching out, and her foot slipped...'

'*Where?*' said Abbie again, trying to contain Henry's hysteria.

'Down there – over the edge,' he whispered, pointing. 'Not far down ... sort of on a ledge. I looked over...' His voice wavered, and he looked at Abbie piteously. 'I'm afraid of heights, Abbie... I'm no good in an emergency... But I'll go down... I must go down. It's my Olive down there – and it's my fault. I should have stopped her!' He took a great gulp of air, and added helplessly. 'What ought I to do?'

Abbie did not answer at once. She flung herself down flat on the ground and looked over the edge of the stony path that wound round the flanks of the mountain. The sides of the slope were strewn with shale and boulders between outcrops of slippery rock, but not desperately steep, and there were small ledges here and there, protruding from the stones and scrubby undergrowth of the sides. On one of these lay Olive Ashridge, spread out and silent, with her eyes shut. It was not possible to tell at that distance whether she was badly hurt or not, but Abbie didn't like that ominous stillness.

'What you must do,' said Abbie, getting to her feet and looking round at the others, 'is this. You must all go on down to the tea place and alert the rescue services. Henry, you can organise that. And you must all stay there till I come – except Henry.' She turned to him, knowing that positive orders would calm him best. 'You can come back with the rescue people, Henry, and show them where we are. You will help Olive far more doing that than trying to get down there to her yourself. You might fall as well, and then where would we be?'

'I – I think I ought to stay...' began Henry.

'No,' said Abbie firmly. 'You must look after the others. I will stay.' She glared round at their anxious faces, willing them to co-operate. 'Just get yourselves down safely to that tea place, and STAY PUT. Don't go anywhere with this mist coming down. Wait for me. The rescue team will bring us down. They are used to this sort of thing. Then we can all go home together.'

'But what will you do?' asked one of the others, who seemed less terrified than Henry.

'I'm going to climb down to Olive. It's not

far, and it's not very steep. I'll be all right, and I can stay with her and keep her warm till the people come. Understand?'

'Yes,' said the practical one. 'But, if you don't mind, we'll wait and see that you get down there safely first.'

Abbie looked doubtful about this. It might take precious time. But she supposed it made sense. It wouldn't do to let them all run down the mountain in a panic, not knowing what was happening behind them.

'Here,' said another of her walkers. 'Take my chocolate to keep you going.'

'I've got a pocket torch,' said someone else.

'And a spare jersey...'

Gratefully, Abbie loaded her pockets with useful items, slung the spare jersey round her neck, and clambered over the edge of the path. Don't look down, she told herself. Take it step by step... It's not far to go... She didn't tell Henry that she was afraid of heights, too. But suddenly, vividly, she remembered Perry's voice, calm and clear and gentle, on that splintering rooftop in London. *That's it ... only a little at a time ... take it slowly... Just a little more... That's the way... It's all right now...*'

Automatically, her feet searched for ridges of solid rock, her fingers for hand-holds and shrubs to cling on to, and she inched her way slowly down the sloping rockface, with

Perry's voice always in her mind urging her gently on. And presently she did dare to look down, and saw that she was very close to Olive now, but a little too far to the right. Slowly, she edged her way over, starting a cascade of pebbles under her feet which made her breath catch with fright. But the small rivulet of stones petered out, and she found her feet on solid rock again.

If ever I get out of this alive, she thought, I must tell Perry how much he helped! And suddenly, clinging there, spread-eagled on the rock, she realised with blinding clarity what her own troubled heart had been crying to tell her for so long. She loved Perry – completely without reservation. And if he asked her to go to the ends of the earth, she would go without a backward glance.

But I'm not going to the ends of the earth, she told herself sternly. I'm on a mountain slope, and I'm going to take care of Olive Ashridge till help arrives. Get on down there and stop dithering!

So she went on climbing down, while her wayward heart sang a very different song. And at length she reached the ledge and put out a tentative hand to touch Olive's limp, uncaring body. But as she did so, Olive opened her eyes and smiled at her hazily.

'Oh, there you are,' she said. 'How good of you to come.'

Abbie almost laughed. But instead she

431

called up to the anxious row of faces looking down from the top: 'It's all right. Olive's going to be all right! Hurry on now. Get help as fast as you can!'

She waited to see the row of faces disappear, and then turned back to Olive, and from then on it was easy. She wrapped her in extra coats and jerseys, and tried to feel if anything was broken. But Olive said she was perfectly all right, thank you, just her head hurt a little and she felt a bit shaky.

'Silly of me, really... I shall have some fine bruises tomorrow.'

So they just sat there together and shared the chocolate (though Abbie was doubtful about letting her eat anything) and waited patiently for the rescue team to arrive.

'You know,' said Olive, her head close to Abbie, who had an arm round her shoulders, 'distance is a funny thing. I could have sworn my father was down here just now.'

'I know,' said Abbie. 'I had a visitor, too.'

In the end, everyone got home safely. Various useful taxis ferried everyone back to the hotel, and Olive was taken off to hospital, with Abbie and Henry in attendance, where the doctors announced that nothing was broken but she might have mild concussion and they would like to keep her in over night. And Henry stopped pacing the corridors and looking pale green with fright and self-reproach, and was allowed in

432

to hold Olive's hand. So finally a rather weary Abbie staggered off to her own room at the end of the jetty. But this time when she stood looking out at the black and silver lake, she did not waste time on sad regrets or longings, for something inside her rejoiced secretly and she could not deny the strange song of love that it sang.

It was dark when Perry got to Grasmere. Lights were winking along the shores of the lake, and the sharp bright points of stars were pricking the night sky above the dark bulk of the fells.

The taxi dropped him off at the entrance to the hotel, and he went up the steps of the lighted doorway to the gentle, welcoming warmth of the foyer, trying vainly to shut down the absurd mixture of terror and anticipation that was assailing him.

'I think she's down at the boathouse,' said the receptionist cheerfully. 'Her charges are all resting before dinner. They've had quite a day, what with the rescue and everything.'

'What rescue?' asked Perry sharply.

'One of the walkers fell off the path. Miss Somerford went down after her. Quite a heroine she is tonight.'

'Anyone hurt?' Perry's voice was still sharp.

'Nothing serious. Mild concussion, they say. They're keeping her in overnight.'

'And Abbie? Miss Somerford?'

'Oh, she's fine. Just a bit tired, that's all.'

'And she's down at the boathouse?' repeated Perry urgently. 'Where is that?'

'It's her one moment of respite, you see,' Her grin was conspiratorial. 'Away from the madding crowd and all that.'

'Yes,' agreed Perry, trying to be patient. 'How do I get there?'

The girl behind the discreet mahogany counter smiled and pointed. 'Down the steps. Along the path to the right. You'll find the jetty at the bottom of the slope. There's a light on the edge of the lake to stop you falling in!' She gave Perry a dazzling smile. 'The boathouse is at the end of the jetty. You can't miss it... Miss Somerford has it as an annexe bedroom. We thought she might like to be away from her tour group at night!' She glanced up at Perry again, with a faintly roguish grin. 'And we're pretty full at the moment, you see, because of the daffodils.'

'I see,' said Perry, who didn't see at all. Daffodils? What had they got to do with it? But it didn't matter. He had his directions. He knew the way. Abbie was there – just at the end of the jetty... But would she be glad to see him? He was suddenly so terrified that he actually paused and wondered whether to turn tail and run.

But he didn't. He went out of the hotel door and down the steps ... along the path

434

to the right ... sloping down ... the cool scent of water close to his feet, and a shimmering mirage of light and dark and wavering stars in the mirrored surface of the dreaming lake ahead... And ah! there was the light that saved him from walking over the edge, and there was the jetty stretching out across the lake in a pale, silvery path.

He walked along it slowly, feeling the water lapping against its ancient timbers from either side, and surrounded by the same shimmer of lamplight and starlight on dark water that he had met at the edge of the lake. It was all round him. He seemed to be walking in liquid light and dark into shadows filled with strange glints and sheens, as if reality had slipped away behind the shifting shapes of dreams... Nothing seemed real any more – except the certain knowledge that Abbie was somewhere there, inside that nimbus of light...

And then he saw her – that small, remembered profile lifted to the night sky, so that it reflected the faint glimmer of starshine. Her whole slender outline perfectly still as she gazed up at the far bright stars... And Perry, watching her, found himself so profoundly moved by her silent presence that he could not speak at all.

But Abbie, staring upwards at those distant galaxies, was remembering how close Perry had felt that day, and wondering if he

435

was looking up at strange bright alien stars in the velvet darkness of an African sky, and maybe thinking of home...? But no, he can't be, she told herself sternly. It's another world there, far away ... and work to do... No time to think of home, however close he has felt today...

And then she saw him. That loved, remembered face silhouetted against a luminous darkness shot with gleams of light – the deep, far-seeing eyes staring straight at her in a fixed gaze of curious intensity that seemed almost spiced with fear.

And as she saw him standing there, and realised that his shadowy figure was not a figment of her imagination, she was pierced with such an exquisite sense of joy that she almost cried out.

Instead, she took a small, tentative step forward and whispered: 'Perry? Is it you?'

He also took a shy step forward and answered: 'Abbie...? I came home because–'

But there was no need to say any more. No need to explain anything, to ask anything, to plead for a hearing... They both knew this instant, with absolute clarity that this was the moment of truth. Doubting was over. Caution was thrown to the winds. The little space between them was very small, and it was soon filled with two shadows merging into one. They stood together in enchanted silence, while the gentle waters of the lake lapped round them, and the far bright stars wheeled overhead on their ceaseless journey across the skies.

They came back slowly. That is, time seemed to have slowed down altogether, and they wandered through an enchanted, sun-drenched landscape of new green larch trees and pale gold daffodils, drifting hand-in-hand like children. But Abbie was adamant that she could not neglect her tour, especially after what had happened to Olive, so Perry just accompanied her on whatever walk she and her charges chose, and waited as patiently as he could till it was time to go home. This small, timeless interlude among the lakes and fells was God-given, they felt, so they took it thankfully, both of them aware that they needed time to adjust to this new-found happiness. You couldn't live on the high peaks for ever, they told themselves... But it was hard to come down, all the same. The rest of the tour indulged them, watching their rapt faces with affectionate, knowing smiles, but then none of them said anything to intrude on their private world of secret joy. Any more than they commented on Olive and Henry, who also seemed to have found a new source of personal contentment since the drastic events of the hillside rescue.

But in the end, perforce, Perry and Abbie did come down from the high country of dreams, and so did Olive and Henry. And they all went quietly home with the rest of the cheerful tour – Henry to see his mother and make some startling re-arrangement of his life, Olive to rest her still aching head and wait for news which she scarcely dared to contemplate, and Perry and Abbie to say some necessary farewells and fetch the Bird. Could they really fetch it, Abbie wondered? Would they be allowed to take it back all the way to its natural home? And would she, Abbie, be allowed, into Angola at all, whether as the Bird's keeper or as Perry's companion?

Perry assured her that he would get busy right away with the necessary permits and export licences and all the difficult flight arrangements involved in transporting live animals. He had done it before – he knew the ropes, he said. And since they were actually putting right a wrong, and return-ing Solomon to his rightful place, he thought the authorities would agree. And, he added, strangely enough the name of Duncan MacNab still opened doors in matters of conservation.

Abbie went to see her boss, Maurice, to explain about the changed course of her life. But she found that Sandra had briefed him well, and he knew all about it. He beamed cheerfully at her, told her he was glad she was alive and more or less in one piece, if not of sound mind, and he was sorry to lose one of his best assistants. Then he gave her a bonus with her wages (which Abbie was sure she didn't deserve), and added a hearty kiss, saying surprisingly; 'You deserve to be happy. Go for it!'

Then it was Tubby. But he simply embraced her fondly and said: 'Supper on the house tonight. Perry's coming!' And Abbie suddenly found herself surrounded by friends who had all come for a celebration meal (how Tubby ever made a profit, Abbie didn't know), and a chance to wish her well.

Bobby, eyes wide with admiration, said: 'I heard all about it. You rescued Olive, and the rescue team rescued you, and Perry came, and now you're going to Africa! Are you really taking Solomon home?'

'Yes, we are,' said Perry, coming into the café full of sparkling good humour. He turned to Abbie, smiling his good news. 'All set... No objections. You are officially Solomon's keeper, with a special permit... And we can make that more permanent in Luanda when we get there.' He glanced at her triumphantly. 'We can go!'

'When?' asked Abbie, suddenly thinking she ought to take Perry down to see her parents, but there wasn't time. The team out there were waiting for him. He was bringing out those precious pieces of laboratory equipment with him, and some extra things for Duncan's little health clinic in the village

– together with Anatole's wonderful five-year financial support to help the new venture to get established.

'On Friday,' said Perry, and then seeing her troubled expression, he added softly: 'It's not for ever, you know... There will be time for other things when we come home on leave...'

Abbie nodded, amazed, as always, that he followed her thoughts so well. But then Tubby opened a bottle of champagne with a cheerful plop, and the party began.

Everyone came – even the Duchess, who beamed hugely and said: 'Well, well. Hooked the bird fancier, have you? Have a good flight!'

Abbie wasn't quite sure what she meant, but Perry was, and clasped her hand tightly in his, saying: 'I won't clip her wings – or Solomon's, either!'

And Synco, sardonically regarding them all from behind his glass, began to sing *'Here we sit like birds in the wilderness'* again, and everyone dissolved in laughter.

But Bobby came up to Abbie and Perry then, with round, serious eyes, and asked; 'Is he really going home to the wilderness?'

'Yes,' smiled Perry. 'At least, as near to the wilderness as he can get! All among the tall trees and wide savannah grasses! And it will always be warm!'

'Cor!' said bobby wistfully. 'Isn't he lucky?'

I hope so, thought Abbie. Oh, I *hope* he

will be happy there ... but I wish we could let him go altogether... Maybe, in time, he will be able to fend for himself in the wild...? If it is possible, Perry will know.

And soon it was time to put Solomon into his travelling cage, and say goodbye to Mackintosh who had looked after him so faithfully while Abbie was away.

Abbie turned to Solomon, and spoke to him softly. 'You're going home, Solomon. What do you think of that...? You'll have to be patient for a little while in the dark... But soon you'll be back where you belong... Well, almost.... Happy ever after, like Bobby wanted you to be. Will you like that?'

Solomon regarded her seriously out of those strange, gold-rimmed eyes, and uttered a low coo of approval. He seemed to know it was time to go.

So they put him in his cage and covered him up and drove to the airport. He made no protest, and said no further word. Abbie and Perry looked at each other over the top of his cage, and breathed a sigh of relief. They were on their way.

The long flight ended at last, and another small plane took them on to the clearing in the forest near the research unit. But the new enclosure of the Wildlife Sanctuary was a little further on, so from there they had to go on in a Landrover, which was waiting for them with a smiling Nguni at the wheel.

They jerked and rattled along a bumpy track through the trees, and Nguni apologised for the rough ride. 'It's the mines, you see,' he explained to Abbie. 'Most of the roads are still very dangerous. No-one knows quite where the mines were laid in the first place... But out here, through the forest, there was not so much fighting.'

The forest, Perry explained, was dwindling fast as the loggers came through, and the settlers after them, clearing the land for crops... And after them, the refugees, still dispossessed of their lands, and still wandering about looking for some kind of subsistence level of existence. 'No-one knows quite what to do with them,' Perry said sadly. 'They set up camps, but the people wander off looking for somewhere they can call their own...' He sighed, and then went on to explain that the new Wildlife Sanctuary was being set up in a small pocket of unspoilt woodland, with the precarious blessing of the authorities, who might or might not be able to protect it for the foreseeable future.

Abbie looked up at the tall, beautiful trees, so long growing and so perfect in their maturity, and sighed. Will they still be here in fifty years time? she wondered. In ten years time? In five?

'They are too lovely to cut down,' she murmured.

Nguni shot her a look of warm approval. 'So Duncan MacNab believed,' he said. 'But of course, people always believe *they* must come first!'

Perry grinned at his trusted assistant. 'Quite a philosopher, you are, Nguni!'

But before anyone could say any more, they had arrived at the new enclosure, and saw that the rest of the team were waiting for them. There were Jonty, bearded and smiling, and Paul, looking thinner and more stick-like than ever, and Judy, neat and practical as usual, but full of suppressed excitement.

'It's our first customer, you see,' said Perry. 'They're all so pleased about it... And we've got Solomon a mate – that is, if he feels like getting to know her.'

'Where did she come from?' asked Abbie, wondering anxiously if Solomon was still all right in his cage during the bumpy ride.

'One of the villagers found her in the Bird Market,' said Nguni. He glanced at Perry. 'The boys often catch them young and sell them to the Market. It is an awful place, but they get good money...' He looked from Perry to Abbie as if apologising for something he could not help. 'That's why we need some ready cash,' added Perry, coming to the rescue. 'If we can offer as much – or a little more – we can save the birds, and some of the smaller animals, too, from a pretty ghastly trade.' He smiled at Abbie's worried face and said: 'Come on. Let's get Solomon out. He's been in that cage quite long enough.'

They lifted the cage down and carried it into the wire enclosure. It was a long expanse, and reached high into the encircling trees, so that the birds could have quite a lot of freedom.

'If they really acclimatise and learn to fend for themselves,' said Perry, 'we may be able to release them totally into the wild in the end... And if they breed meanwhile, so much the better...' He stood looking up at the trees for a moment in thoughtful silence.

Jonty and the others came up and stood beside them, also looking up. And Nguni joined them, standing close beside Jonty who was going to be left in charge of the Sanctuary with him when the others went home.

'Where is our new female?' asked Perry.

'She's up there somewhere,' replied Jonty. 'One of the trees is fruiting. She seems to think it's a banquet laid on specially for her.'

'What are you going to call her?' Perry said, still looking up.

'Why – Sheba, of course,' answered Jonty. 'What else, for Solomon's mate?'

Perry nodded, smiling, and then turned to Abbie. 'Well? Aren't you going to let him go?'

'Me?' said Abbie. 'I thought–'

'You found him, Abbie,' he said gently. 'You saved him and fed him... You must be the one to let him go.'

She looked from him to the others, and saw that they were all smiling – and all waiting. Even Nguni.

'All right, then,' she said. 'Solomon – it's time to go,' and she bent down and undid the cage door, so that the cramped, imprisoned bird could go free.

For a moment, Solomon did nothing at all, but stood staring at the open space where the wire door had been. Then he took a delicate, tentative step forward, and then another, until he stood clear of the cage on the open ground. The brilliant crested head lifted and looked upwards, the folded wings trembled with the memory of flight, and a thousand familiar scents assailed him from every side, but still he did not move away.

And then, from above his head, Sheba let out a small, shrill cry of welcome, and a fiery, crested head as bright as Solomon's own looked out from a wreath of leaves.

The bewildered bird on the ground tilted his head still further at the sound of the sudden call, and then the powerful wings suddenly spread, and with a flash of scarlet flight feathers, Solomon flew up to the topmost branch of the tree where Sheba was waiting. And swaying there beside her, hidden among the leaves, he sang a soft, quiet song of love to his beautiful new bride.

A song of love, thought Abbie, remembering the words she had sung in the Duchess's house when Perry first went away.

'When two-fold silence was the song, the song of love...'

She turned to Perry, and saw the same thought in his eyes. Then they looked up once more at Solomon and Sheba, and walked away together in perfect silence while the dusk came down among the trees.

The publishers hope that this book has given you enjoyable reading. Large Print Books are especially designed to be as easy to see and hold as possible. If you wish a complete list of our books please ask at your local library or write directly to:

Dales Large Print Books
Magna House, Long Preston,
Skipton, North Yorkshire.
BD23 4ND

This Large Print Book, for people
who cannot read normal print,
is published under the auspices of

THE ULVERSCROFT FOUNDATION

To renew or order library books visit
www.lincolnshire.gov.uk
You will require a Personal Identification Number.
Ask any member of staff for this

F   WEBSTER

The Wilderness Bird

£11.99

LARGE PRINT   L5/9